"You've been telling me you can see the future, is that right?" Mick asked in a low, tight voice.

"Yes."

He pulled the curtains closed at the carriage window, and Sophie's heart began to pound hard against her breast. *What is he doing?* she thought wildly.

He moved even closer. His hip touched hers, and she jumped. She started to move away, but his arm came up around her shoulders to prevent it. He leaned closer still, until his lips brushed her ear. "You still insist you can read people's thoughts?"

"Sometimes," she whispered. "I said sometimes."

He turned her toward him and tilted her head back. "Can you read my thoughts right now?" he murmured, his lips brushing against hers as he spoke.

"No."

"Thank God," he muttered, and kissed her.

PRAISE FOR LAURA LEE GUHRKE

THE CHARADE

"Guhrke's cast of engaging characters, the well-researched historical background, and a fast-paced plot provide a perfect context for the clever repartee and romantic tension between Katie and Ethan."

—*Publishers Weekly*

"Informative, thrilling, and spectacular."

—*Rendezvous*

"An outstanding Revolutionary-era romance. The real historical personages and the colorful narrative truly bring this tumultuous time to life and will garner Ms. Guhrke a satisfied readership."

—*Romantic Times*

"Fans of Revolutionary War romances will be left breathless by Laura Lee Guhrke's fabulous tale. The exhilarating story line provides an incredible glimpse at Boston on the eve of the fighting. . . . Ms. Guhrke scores big-time with a novel that deserves a large audience. . . ."

—*Affaire de Coeur*

"Exciting . . . Laura Lee Guhrke triumphantly makes 1775 Boston seem vividly bustling with life and energy."

—*Under the Covers*

BREATHLESS

"*Breathless* is one of those books that you will want to read more than once."

—CompuServe Romance Reviews

"*Breathless* is a captivating, wonderful read. . . . One of Laura Lee Guhrke's greatest strengths, aside from her excellent characterizations, is allowing the hero and heroine ample time for a true, deep love to develop. . . . The love scenes will also take your breath away. *Breathless* has 'keeper' written all over it!"

—*Bookbug*

"Readers who enjoy strongly written books about small towns will relish *Breathless*. The mystery adds an extra element of excitement."

—*All About Romance*

"This is a particularly well-plotted story. All the loose ends that might dangle in less-well-written books are tied. . . . The character development is excellent. The characters, main and secondary, are multidimensional and believable. The dialogue is sharp and engaging and frequently funny. . . . Readers will fall in love with [Daniel and Lily] as they fall for each other."

—*The Romance Reader*

Books by Laura Lee Guhrke

Breathless
The Charade
Not So Innocent

Published by POCKET BOOKS

LAURA LEE GUHRKE

Not So Innocent

SONNET BOOKS

New York London Toronto Sydney Singapore

This book is a work of fiction. Names, characters, places and incidents are products of the author's imagination or are used fictitiously. Any resemblance to actual events or locales or persons, living or dead, is entirely coincidental.

An *Original* Publication of POCKET BOOKS

 A Sonnet Book published by
POCKET BOOKS, a division of Simon & Schuster, Inc.
1230 Avenue of the Americas, New York, NY 10020

Copyright © 2002 by Laura Lee Guhrke

ISBN: 0-671-02369-1

First Sonnet Books printing December 2002

10 9 8 7 6 5 4 3 2 1

SONNET BOOKS and colophon are trademarks of
Simon & Schuster, Inc.

For information regarding special discounts for bulk purchases,
please contact Simon & Schuster Special Sales at 1-800-456-6798
or business@simonandschuster.com

Front cover illustration by Gregg Gulbronson

Printed in the U.S.A.

For Kristen,
who always asks me the
tough questions.

Acknowledgments

❧

I would like to say a very special thank you to two people who helped me with the research for this book: Paul Dew, Public Enquiries, New Scotland Yard, who answered all my questions, even the stupid ones; and Ray Seal of the Metropolitan Police Historic Store for the really cool photographs. My heartfelt gratitude to both of you.

Not So Innocent

One

❧

When he awoke on the morning of May 28, Mick Dunbar was not a happy man. Today was his birthday, his *thirty-sixth* birthday, and he had to face the bitter fact that he wasn't so young anymore.

On this particular morning, he even felt old. His shoulder ached from that bullet wound ten years back, he seemed to have more gray in his dark hair than he'd had the night before, and shaving off his mustache didn't make him look any younger. Mick knew it was going to be a long day.

The moment he arrived at Scotland Yard, he saw that the birthday jokes had already begun. His office was empty. His desk, his chairs, his case files were gone. Even the commendations he'd received in his career were no longer hanging on the wall.

"Thacker!" he shouted, watching as his sergeant

came running from the large room that served as the main office of the Criminal Investigation Department. "What happened here?"

The suspicious twitch of the sergeant's huge red mustache told Mick that Thacker was in on the joke. "Chief Inspector DeWitt decided today was the perfect day to repaint your office."

"I'll bet he did," Mick muttered. Even his own boss was not above a bit of chicanery. "So where'd he put me? The morgue?"

"No, sir. You're on the ground floor. I'll show you."

Mick followed his sergeant downstairs to the large main office of the constables. It was the worst place—other than the morgue—that the lads could have chosen. Anyone coming to report a crime was sent here first. It was noisy, crowded, and chaotic.

Thacker led him to the center of the room. Case files and reports were heaped on top of his desk and on the floor surrounding it. Mick, considered to be the most obsessively neat officer in the Metropolitan Police, looked at the mess and swore loud enough to be heard above the noise.

Laughter broke out all over the room, and he looked around to see the constables on duty grinning at him. But when he walked around the desk to sit down, he found the joke was not yet over. There was a cane hooked over the back of his chair.

Mick looked at the symbol of old age and scowled. Birthday pranks were common, and he was usually ready to laugh along with the others, even when he was the victim. Not this year.

He grabbed the cane from the back of his chair and handed it to Thacker. "Toss that in a dustbin."

"Happy birthday, sir." Thacker gave him a hearty slap on the back that sent a shot of pain through his aching shoulder. "You knew something like this would be on today."

"Aye, I knew."

"Cheer up, sir. I've had worse things done to me in Her Majesty's Navy." He grinned. "By the way, I could have told you it doesn't work."

"What?"

"Shaving off your mustache." Undeterred by Mick's deepening scowl, he continued, "How does it feel to be an old man?"

"Thirty-six is not old." Mick sat down, staring at the mountains of paperwork that completely hid the top of his desk from view. "Any new cases in this mess?"

Thacker pulled a pair of files from beneath one of the stacks. "Two new ones for you today, sir."

Mick removed one pile of paperwork from his desk and set it on the floor, clearing himself some space to work, then he took the files from the sergeant.

"A drowned body, female, found yesterday on the bank of the Thames just beyond Tower Bridge," Thacker explained, "and a viscountess claims her emeralds have been stolen."

The body sounded more intriguing than jewels. Mick opened that file first and read through the report of the drowning.

"The divisional surgeon believes it's a suicide," Thacker went on, "but he said you'll have to wait for the autopsy this afternoon before he'll swear to it."

"Of course it's suicide," Mick answered and shut the file. "The report says three witnesses watched the woman jump. Why did the River Police give this to the Yard?"

"Richard Munro said to tell you happy birthday."

"What a thoughtful fellow. Telephone his office and tell him he'd better meet me at the morgue about half past three. Cal will have finished the autopsy by then. Tell Richard if he doesn't meet me there, I'll tell his wife where I took him the night before his wedding."

Thacker laughed, and Mick set the first file aside. He picked up the second one. Glancing through it, he shook his head. "Some pampered viscountess losing her emeralds? No, thank you."

"She had worn the necklace to a ball, and she's certain she put it in her jewel case when she came home. She claims someone must have taken it between the night before last and this morning. She suspects the maid. It's probably an easy case."

Mick was not tempted by that. "Give it to one of the junior detectives. They need the experience."

Thacker took the file. "I'll have it assigned to—"

The sergeant was interrupted by a loud, indignant voice that boomed through the office of the constables like a powder blast. "I told you I want to see Inspector Michael Dunbar, young man, and he's not in his office. Where is he?"

Mick glanced up. When he saw the stout, red-faced woman standing by the front counter with a constable, he knew his day was headed straight down to hell.

It was Mrs. Tribble, his landlady, a woman with a raucous voice and an overbearing manner. When she glanced his way, Mick shielded his face from her view with the case file he was holding, but it didn't work.

Her boot heels thudded against the floorboards with her considerable weight as she marched toward his desk. "Mr. Dunbar, I have come to report a crime." She thumped his desk with her fist. "An infamous crime."

Mrs. Tribble was always coming to him with infamous crimes. A fortnight ago she'd misplaced a ring, insisting it had been stolen. The month before that, she'd claimed a man had made improper advances to her in the queue at the stop for the omnibus. Wishful thinking on her part, Mick suspected. "What is this crime?"

"My Nanki Poo has disappeared. He has been kidnaped."

Nanki Poo was a flat-faced, bad-tempered Pekingese. Some people thought Pekes were dogs, but it was Mick's opinion that as pets they left a lot to be desired and could be of far greater use to the world as dust mops. "When you receive the ransom note, bring it to me."

She stared at him. "That's all you're going to do?"

He heard Thacker smother a laugh, and he decided it was time to repay the sergeant for calling him an old man. "Not at all. Sergeant Thacker will begin the investigation." Mick stood up, smiling at the sergeant's look of dismay. "I have to be going, but you'll help Mrs. Tribble all you can, won't you, Thacker?"

Gesturing to the door with the hook of the cane in his hand, the sergeant said in a resigned voice, "Come this way, ma'am."

Mick left his landlady to Thacker and departed from the Yard, but he had barely stepped into Parliament Street when his day took another turn for the worse. He heard the sound of shattering glass, splintering timber, and frightened screams, and he glanced across the street to find that someone had driven a Benz motorcar up over the sidewalk and through the glass front doors of the Boar's Head Pub.

"Bloody hell." Mick made his way across the traffic of Parliament Street, hoping nobody was dead, because he'd end up being the one to visit the relatives and break the bad news. He hated that.

As it turned out, nobody was hurt by the incident except the driver of the Benz, who had a bleeding gash on his forehead and was too drunk to feel the pain. In his inebriated state, the idiot had decided it would be jolly good fun to smash in the front doors of the Boar's Head Pub.

Mick didn't agree. He arrested the fellow, not caring that he claimed to be Sir Roger Ellerton, and the son of an earl. Mick hauled Sir Roger into Cannon Row Police Station right beside the Yard, charging him with public drunkenness and property damage.

"You can't arresht me, you bashtard!" Sir Roger bellowed out a curse worthy of any longshoreman and slammed his fist into Mick's left cheek.

Mick was a big man, and though the impact of the other man's fist made him see stars for a second, it didn't knock him off his feet. He promptly returned the favor, and the dazed Sir Roger fell back into the arms of Anthony Frye, the day-watch sergeant. "Toss him in a cell," Mick ordered, "where he can sleep it off."

Anthony grinned at him over the top of Sir Roger's lolling head. "You're going to have a fine shiner there, old man."

"Thirty-six is not old," Mick said through clenched teeth.

"Happy birthday."

His reply to that was an obscene gesture that only made Anthony laugh. Mick filled out a report on Sir Roger, adding the assault of a police officer to the charges, and left the station. He caught an omnibus for Piccadilly Circus and spent the next six hours investigating one of his open cases.

It was after three o'clock when he started back for Scotland Yard. He stopped at a costermonger's cart on Cannon Row for a Cornish pasty, but the only ones left were mutton. Mick hated mutton, hated it with a depth of feeling akin to his hatred of Manchester United and newspaper journalists. Anyone with sense knew that Celtic, not United, was the only football team worth a damn, and newspaper journalists were the bane of every policeman's existence. Mutton wasn't fit for dogs. He decided to wait for dinner.

Back at the Yard, Mick went straight to the morgue, intending to confirm the suicide of the woman who'd jumped off Tower Bridge and close that case.

As far as dead bodies went, drowning victims had to be among the ugliest, Mick decided, staring down at the bruised and bloated remains of one Jane Anne Clapham, which lay on a table in the morgue. Slime and mud had dried to greenish-brown patches on the woman's skin, and algae from the Thames still clung to her blue-tinged lips.

He glanced at the two other men who stood around the table, Richard Munro and Calvin Becker. Cal, the divisional surgeon, was happily munching on sausage rolls from a paper bag in his hand as he gave Mick his report.

"Death is by drowning." He held out the bag to Mick and went on, "As to the bruising, it's all post-mortem, probably from the river currents banging the body about."

Mick pulled a sausage roll from the offered bag and popped it in his mouth, studying the dead woman as he ate. "Where did they find her?"

"Butler's Wharf. She floated down from Tower Bridge and got stuck under the pier. Couple of boys playing there found her."

"Suicide is clear, isn't it?" Richard asked. "Why climb up over the rail of Tower Bridge if you don't intend to jump?"

"When did she die?" Mick asked, looking at Cal.

"It's hard to say. A fortnight ago, at the very least."

It all seemed straightforward to Mick. "Anything else?"

"One odd thing," Richard said. "When we searched her flat in Bermondsey, we found a suicide note addressed to her son."

"What's odd about that?"

"Her son's been dead for fifteen years."

Mick wasn't intrigued enough by that to pursue it, and his caseload was heavy already. "She was an old woman, probably senile. Let's end this case, gentlemen."

Richard reached into his pocket and pulled out several folded sheets of paper. "In honor of your birthday, I thought you'd enjoy being the one to write the paperwork."

"Not a chance," Mick said, shaking his head. "The body was found in the Thames. You're the River Police. One of the advantages of my job is that I get to pick and choose my cases. You don't. This one's yours."

"Sure you don't want it? You know this woman."

Mick frowned, looking down again at the dead woman. "I do?"

"The Clapham case. We worked it together. We sent her husband, Henry Clapham, to Newgate. He died a few weeks later, killed by another prisoner. That was twelve years ago. We interviewed her, and she was at his trial when we testified."

Mick shook his head. "Lad, I've done so many cases, I'm lucky if I can remember the details of one I handled two years ago, much less twelve."

"Losing your memory? Getting old will do that to you."

Mick turned away. "I have real cases to work on. I'm going."

He left the morgue and returned to his temporary office. Back at his desk, he'd barely taken off his jacket before David Fletcher, one of the constables, was beside him.

"While you were out, you got a message from Bow Street Station," the young constable told him. "Billy Mackay telephoned to tell you it's the White Horse tonight, not the Boar's Head, to celebrate your birthday. And DeWitt wants to speak with you. He said he wanted you in his office the moment you returned."

Mick was pretty sure why his superintendent wanted to see him, and it wasn't about a birthday joke. Why did DeWitt have to get his knickers in a wad today of all days?

The first words out of the chief inspector's mouth confirmed Mick's guess. "Are you out of your mind?" he bellowed the moment Mick entered his office and shut the door behind him. "Do you know who Sir Roger Ellerton is?"

Mick shrugged. "He said he's the son of an earl."

"He's the son of the Earl of Chadwick!" DeWitt rubbed his hand across his nearly bald head, making the hairs he had left stand on end. His voice rose to a shout. "Chadwick is a cousin of the Home Secretary. The Home Secretary is the head of Scotland Yard, in case you've forgotten!"

Mick let out his breath in a slow sigh. His day was no longer headed to hell. It was already there.

DeWitt ordered that Sir Roger be released immediately, gave Mick a stern reprimand, and docked him a day's pay. He then reminded Mick that people like Sir Roger did not get arrested, and made it clear that if Mick did something like this again, he'd get a suspension. But as Mick was walking out the door, DeWitt spoke again, this time in a calmer tone of voice. "I have one more thing to say to you before you go."

Mick turned. "Sir?"

DeWitt grinned. "What do you think of your new office?"

"It's lovely," Mick answered with a grimace of a smile. "When can I go back to my old one?"

"In a few days. When the paint's dry."

Mick nodded, knowing full well his office hadn't needed any paint. "What color is it now—purple?"

DeWitt shook his head. "No, chartreuse."

"My favorite." Mick knew his superintendent was joking about the paint but not about Sir Roger or the suspension. He returned to his desk downstairs and tried to be philosophical about his reprimand, but he couldn't help feeling a bit of frustration.

Unlike Sir Roger, Mick had no titled relations to get him out of trouble. In fact, Mick had no family at all. Every trouble he'd had in his life, he'd paid for. Every success he'd earned the hard way. He'd done so well during his career that last year DeWitt had promoted him to a roving commission, one of only six such positions at Scotland Yard. The job meant a substantial raise in pay and allowed him to pick from among the most intriguing cases that came to the Yard.

Mick sat back in his chair. It seemed only yesterday he'd been a fresh-faced newcomer to the force, a cocky kid who knew more about how to break the law than enforce it.

Now things were different. After seventeen years in the Metropolitan Police, seventeen years of hard work, saving every shilling he could and living in a one-room flat, Mick could afford to have the one thing that had eluded him all his life. A home of his own.

He could envision it—something on a quiet street in a respectable neighborhood, with at least five bedrooms, indoor water closets, and a huge back garden shaded by ancient oak trees. It would be the perfect house for a man who had always dreamed of having a home and family.

But there was no point in purchasing such a house without a wife, and until he found the right woman and got married, he'd make do with a one-room flat, an obnoxious landlady, and a barking, ankle-biting dust mop.

Mick glanced at the clock on the wall. It was half past four, and he was supposed to meet Billy and Rob at the pub for his birthday in half an hour. He hadn't eaten all day, and his mouth watered at the thought of an underdone beefsteak, a plate of chips, and a pint of ale, but he couldn't tolerate the idea of leaving his desk in a mess. As he worked to put things back in order, a soft, West End, very feminine voice penetrated his consciousness.

". . . and I really feel that it is my public duty to report this. Being detectives, you'll know better than I how to resolve this situation. I have no experience with this sort of thing myself. Murder, I mean."

Mick lifted his head at the mention of murder and saw a young woman seated in front of Fletcher's desk, a woman who seemed ludicrously out of place in the offices of Scotland Yard. He saw the profile of a slender figure in a froth of pale yellow silk. Dozens of tiny, dark green bows trimmed her dress, many of them untied. Long, untidy tendrils of chestnut brown hair had come loose from beneath the unfashionable, wide-brimmed straw hat she wore.

"After all," she said to Fletcher, "I saw the poor man lying there, bloody and dead as dead can be. I'm certain you'll be able to do something."

Mick raised an eyebrow. Quite a startling statement from a woman who looked as soft as whipped butter. This might be a case worth investigating.

As if sensing his scrutiny, she turned her head in his direction. When she caught sight of him, her dark eyes widened with what appeared to be complete astonishment. Fletcher began asking her the questions customary to any police report, and she answered them without taking her gaze from Mick's. "Haversham. Miss Sophie Haversham. 18 Mill Street, Mayfair."

Fletcher wrote down that information, then asked the very question that was going through Mick's mind. "Now, what would a young lady such as yourself know about a murder, Miss Haversham?"

She didn't answer. Instead, she stood up and circled Fletcher's desk, leaving the bemused constable staring after her, his question still hanging in the air. She came straight to Mick.

"I think perhaps it would be best if I spoke with you about this, Mr. . . . umm—" She broke off and glanced at the brass nameplate on his desk. "—Inspector Dunbar," she amended. As she sat down, Mick caught the delicate fragrance of her perfume, something spicy and exotic, a scent he didn't recognize.

Though her clothes were expensive, her frayed cuffs told Mick the dress was not a new one. Genteel poverty, he guessed. There were dozens like her in the West End. She was nervous, twisting her gloved fingers together and apart as if gathering her courage. That was understandable if she'd found a dead body. Silent, she continued to stare at him with a sort of apprehensive fascination he couldn't fathom.

Mick was accustomed to the attentions of women. He was a big man, tall and dark, with blue eyes and a brawny body that many women found attractive. He didn't get too swell-headed over the attention, though, because most of the women he met were working-class girls who thought any unmarried man with straight teeth and a steady job was a good catch. But this woman wasn't that sort, and he found it odd that she was staring at him so intensely. It bordered on rudeness.

Not that he minded. He stared right back and enjoyed the view. She had thick-lashed brown eyes and the soft, pampered ivory skin typical of young ladies within her class. But when his gaze reached her mouth, Mick caught his breath. There was nothing ladylike about that mouth. It was a wide, generous cupid's bow with a plump, delicious bottom lip that would give any man, including Mick, lustful thoughts and wicked intentions. It took an effort for him to bring himself back to the business at hand.

He pushed aside a stack of files and reached for a pencil and notepaper. "You said you've come to report a murder?"

She continued to stare at him in silence for several seconds, then suddenly she shook her head as if coming out of a daze. "I'm sorry for staring, but I'm a bit rattled, you see," she said, her trembling voice validating the truth of her words. "Murder is rather disconcerting, isn't it?"

Without waiting for an answer, she rushed on, "Oh, I've dealt with a bit of crime here and there. Petty theft on the part of servants, and merchants who try to cheat you by putting too few herring in the barrel or short-weighting the flour, that sort of thing. And street urchins who look so innocent when they swarm around you and ask for money, then there you are without your reticule or a farthing in your pocket. But dealing with a murder, I'm afraid, is beyond my experience."

She paused for a quick breath of air, but not long enough for Mick to get a word in. "Of course, there was the time that Mrs. Archer hit Mr. Archer over the head with a frying pan. Cast iron. He died, but she never meant to *kill* him, I daresay, just cosh him on the head, and that's not the same thing as murder at all, is it?"

Mick stared at her, a bit stunned by the rapid stream of words. His carnal imaginings about her lovely mouth were forgotten as she continued rambling on about Mr. and Mrs. Frying Pan, and he wondered if she ever intended to come to the point.

"I didn't ever dream such a thing would happen," she went on, "and even if I had, I'm not certain I would have done anything to prevent it. Archer was a cruel man indeed, and even though he was her husband, I still say she was defending herself." Miss Haversham's nose wrinkled with distaste. "He drank, and men who drink can be unpleasant, even violent." She gestured toward Mick's face. "But then, you already know that."

Mick sat up straighter in his chair and felt a tingle along the back of his neck. It was a sensation with which he was very familiar, a sensation he usually got just before entering an opium den in Limehouse or turning down a dark alley in Whitechapel after midnight. A sense that he'd better watch his step and pay attention. "What do you mean?"

"Well, didn't a drunken man hit you?" she asked. "I'm getting quite a strong impression that's how you received that black eye." Before Mick could ask what had prompted her to such an impression, she spoke again, a tiny frown drawing her brows together. "Of course, I could be wrong. So many possibilities swirling around, and it's difficult to sort it all out. I get muddled sometimes."

Mick was not surprised. If there was an actual crime somewhere in all this, he wanted the facts as quickly as possible. "Tell me about this murder you saw."

"Well, I didn't actually see it with my eyes, but the impressions are so clear that I might just as well have witnessed it."

Mick didn't have the slightest clue what she was talking about. "So you have seen a murder?"

She lifted her head, looking at him with those pretty, chocolate brown eyes. "Of course. Isn't that what I've been telling you?"

There was no answer to that question. He tried again. "Where did this murder occur?"

"I'm not exactly certain." She closed her eyes and tilted her head to one side, causing a broken ostrich feather on her hat to fall forward across her face. "I've been trying to figure it out. I could clearly see greenery—trees, grass, and such. There was a border of rhododendrons and a bronze statue, though it had gone to verdigris, and those green statues are so hard to see amidst the shrubbery, aren't they?" She opened her eyes and pushed back the feather. "Of course! It was Robert Burns. So there you are."

Mick stared at her, feeling a bit dazed. He didn't

know what Robert Burns had to do with anything, especially since the fellow had been dead for nearly a century. "I don't understand."

"The statue I saw was of Robert Burns. So the murder must be in the Victoria Embankment Gardens."

"Must be? Don't you know where you were when you saw this murder?"

"Of course I know where *I* was," she answered. "I was in bed. I'm just not certain where the murder is, but now, because I remembered about Robert Burns, I am certain. Do you see?"

He didn't. How could she see a murder if she was in bed? His bewilderment must have shown in his face.

"It's difficult to explain," she said, "especially now that I've met you."

What did meeting him have to do with anything? A dull ache began between his eyebrows. He tried another question. "Did you see a body?"

"Oh, yes." She gave a shudder and recoiled slightly in her chair. "I'm so sorry to be the one to tell you about this."

Mick's patience was coming to an end. "Let me see if I understand you, miss," he said heavily. "You believe that a murder has been committed in Victoria Embankment Gardens, and you saw the body there, but you were in bed at the time?"

"Oh, no, no, you misunderstand me. The murder hasn't happened yet, thank God. If it had, you and I would not be having this conversation. You see—"

"How could you possibly see a dead body from a murder that hasn't happened yet?"

She took a deep breath and met his gaze across the desk. "I saw it in my mind."

He didn't need this. He didn't need one of the loony ones today. He was tired, he was hungry, and he was getting a headache. Rubbing his forehead with the tips of his fingers, he thought with wistful longing of his steak and chips. "It's lack of food," he muttered to himself. "I should've eaten that pasty."

"But you hate mutton, don't you?"

"What?" Mick lifted his head and stared at her, feeling again that little tingle along the back of his neck. What on earth had made her ask that? How could she know he hated mutton?

An explanation came to him at once. Billy and Rob. It had to be. His two best friends were behind this. They had hired this girl to come to him to report some incredible, silly, made-up crime. Another birthday joke.

Well, she was a damned fine actress. They'd probably found her in some run-down theater off Drury Lane. Now that he understood what his friends had done, Mick's good humor began to return, especially when he began plotting how to get them back. He leaned back in his chair and grinned at her. "How much?"

She stared at him. "I beg your pardon?"

"How much did they pay you?" When she didn't answer, he went on, "I'll tell Billy and Rob that this time they got me good and proper." His smile widened. "But I will get my revenge."

"I'm sorry," she said, shaking her head in confusion. "I have no idea who Billy and Rob are. Whoever they may be, they haven't 'gotten you yet,' as you put it. That's still to come, unless we can prevent it. You see—"

"Really?" he interrupted, laughing. "You mean there's more to their little joke?"

"Joke?" Her confused expression changed to one of consternation. "I should hope you don't find murder amusing. I don't, and I doubt you will either once I tell you about it."

"Right." Mick stood up. "I think I've heard enough already."

"No, wait." She rose as well, eyeing him in dismay. "I haven't finished."

"Don't worry. I'm seeing the lads in just a few minutes, and I'll be sure to tell them what a fine job you did." He pulled his jacket from the back of his chair. "Good-bye, Miss Haversham. If that's really your name."

He started for the door leading out to the courtyard, ignoring Fletcher's grin as he passed the constable's desk.

"Wait," the woman cried, jumping up to follow him. "Please, listen to me. I have to tell you the most important part." She caught up with him just before the door and grasped his sleeve, desperate to stop him. "I have to tell you who is going to die."

"Luv, I don't care if it's the prime minister." He shook off her restraining hand and walked across the huge foyer to the entrance doors of Scotland Yard.

The woman would not be deterred. She ran around in front of him and turned around, blocking his path out the door. "You *will* care, believe me."

She sounded so desperate that Mick gave in. Maybe she had to tell him the whole story or she wouldn't get paid. "All right, then," he said, laughing. "Who is going to be the victim of this murder in your mind that hasn't happened yet?"

She put a hand on his arm and stared at him with what seemed to be compassion. "You are."

Two

〜

He didn't believe her. Sophie could read Inspector Dunbar's mind well enough at this moment, and it didn't take any special talent to do so. He thought it was all a joke. He pushed his way past her without a word.

"Just don't go near Victoria Embankment Gardens!" she shouted after him as he walked away across the courtyard. "Especially at night."

His laughter echoed back to her, indicating just how seriously he viewed his imminent demise.

What else could she expect? Sophie berated herself bitterly, knowing she had bungled the whole thing, prattling on about Mr. Archer and street thieves. The fact that she had been badly shaken by seeing the very man she had dreamed about was no consolation. Now he would die, and it would be her fault.

She ran out to the street and looked up and down the sidewalk, but she did not see him. He had disappeared.

Sophie closed her eyes and tried to determine which way he had gone, but to no avail. She opened her eyes and cast an irritated glance heavenward, wondering why her psychic ability never came to her aid when a practical course of action was needed. But she could not summon psychic power on command.

There was nothing she could do but go home. Sophie walked to the corner and joined the queue waiting for an omnibus. She spent the journey home staring into space, feeling frustrated, discouraged, and afraid for Michael Dunbar.

All day, she had been debating with herself over what to do about last night's dream. She had never had a premonition of murder before, and her first thought had been to rush right down to Scotland Yard, but the dream had given her no specific facts to tell the police. Late this afternoon, in Piccadilly on an errand for her aunt, she had been overcome by a powerful feeling of dread, and she had almost fainted right there in Fortnum & Mason, not an uncommon occurrence if she had a premonition during her waking hours.

At that moment, she'd known she had to report what she knew, and she'd gone to Scotland Yard at once—only to be laughed at by the very man whose death she had dreamed of.

Until she had met him, he had been only the face of a stranger and a body covered in blood. Now, he was no longer a dream, no longer a stranger. He was real, he was going to die, and she had to find a way to prevent it.

The omnibus came to a stop at Berkeley Square. As Sophie left the bus and started walking home, an image of Inspector Dunbar flashed across her mind.

A handsome man, she supposed. His lean face, sky blue eyes, and thick black hair made him the matrimonial prayer of maidservants and shop girls, she had no doubt. Yes, he was handsome, and well-built, too. Taller than most, broad-shouldered and hard-muscled, he was the sort of man who seemed impervious to danger, the sort of man who could make a woman feel safe and protected. Sophie felt a pang of yearning. She couldn't remember the last time she'd felt safe and protected.

She shook off that sort of wishful thinking before it could take root. No man could take away the nightmares that made her afraid to go to sleep, that made her afraid of the dark. No man could prevent the premonitions that could flash through her mind at any time, anywhere. There wasn't a man alive who could make Sophie feel safe, not even Michael Dunbar.

She remembered the hard, uncompromising line of his mouth and the cool, assessing look in his eyes as he had watched her stumble through her story. His piercing, icy stare was probably very effective with criminals, who no doubt wilted immediately under such scrutiny and confessed all.

He was arrogant, too. She could pinpoint the exact moment when he had decided it was all a joke, the indolent way he had leaned back in his chair, the amused smile that had curved his lips. He was a man who believed only in cold, hard facts, a man who trusted only his own instincts and no one else's, a man who would never believe her.

The hardest thing about seeing the future was this sense of futility when she was not believed, this sick feeling in her stomach when she could see tragedy coming and there was no way to stop it. It was a burden she had carried for as long as she could remember, and it never got any easier to bear.

Only Aunt Violet understood her and accepted her just as she was. That was why Sophie now lived with Auntie. Violet didn't question how she knew things, how she could predict future events or why she could sometimes sense what people were thinking. Of course, Auntie was also a spiritualist who thought herself the reincarnation of Cleopatra and had an inconvenient love for other people's jewelry.

Sophie turned onto Mill Street, the quiet cluster of Georgian brick houses where she lived, large houses with beautiful gardens that had once been the height of luxury but were now somewhat the worse for wear.

Auntie had turned her home here into a lodging house. Though it was not an approved occupation for a woman of the upper classes, it had been Violet's only option after her husband's death. The house was now a dim version of the fashionable mansion it had once been. The cabbage-rose wallpaper was faded, the crystal chandeliers were dusty, and the stair carpets were worn nearly threadbare, but Mayfair was a fashionable address. With no money and too much pride to live on the charity of her relations, Violet had seen this house with its seven bedrooms as her only hope. She had invited Sophie to move down from Yorkshire to help her run the lodging house, and to Sophie, it had seemed the answer to a prayer.

Now, however, Sophie almost wished she was still in Yorkshire. As she opened the wrought iron gate in front of Auntie's house, she thought of last night's dream. She could see the inspector's once-white shirt saturated with blood. She remembered how he had looked only minutes ago sitting across that desk from her, no aura of light and life surrounding him.

Sophie slammed the gate behind her hard enough to rattle the iron railings and started up the walk to the house. The whole situation was ludicrous. He was a police inspector, for heaven's sake. If he couldn't protect himself from some knife-wielding lunatic, how could she be expected to do it for him?

When she entered the house, Grimstock was beside her at once to take her hat, gloves, and reticule. The job of butler suited him well—rather a surprise, considering the fact that in his younger days, Grimstock had been one of England's most successful confidence swindlers. Until he'd gone to prison, of course.

Sophie was the only person in the house who knew Grimstock's secret, but not because he had ever told her. She just knew, the same way she knew so many other little things. Of course, no respectable household would employ a former swindler as a butler. Their acquaintances would be shocked if they knew. Her mother and sister would be horrified. Sophie, however, had no intention of revealing Grimstock's secret to anyone. Though she had made it clear to him long ago that she knew of his past, he had proven time and again to be loyal, trustworthy, and discreet.

Sophie glanced at his face and sighed. Never was there a man more suited to his name than Grimstock. He was as gloomy as an undertaker. She suspected his countenance had been the main reason for his success in those funeral parlor swindles, but she didn't like to dwell on it.

"Smile, Grimmy," she ordered. "It won't crack your face."

"If you say so, Miss Sophie."

He made a valiant effort, she had to admit, but it made him look as if he had a toothache, and she deemed it hopeless. "Never mind."

"I might feel more like smiling, Miss Sophie," he murmured, "if it weren't for what I found today."

Sophie met the butler's steady gaze, and she understood at once. "What did you find?" she asked in a whisper. "And where?"

"In the dining room cupboard. I was dusting the Spode, and there it was in a trifle bowl."

Sophie pressed her fingers to her temples. "Is it valuable?"

"An emerald and diamond necklace. Quite valuable, I'd say, though jewels were never my specialty, Miss Sophie, as you know."

"But where could she have gotten it? She hasn't been to any jewelers of late, has she?"

The butler looked offended. "No, indeed. I promised you most faithfully that I would make certain that did not happen again. Not after that incident with the gold and lapis earrings."

"I'm sorry for doubting you, Grimmy. But where

did she get her hands on emeralds and diamonds? Who could they belong to?"

The butler gave a slight cough. "I believe your aunt paid a call on her cousin's wife, the Viscountess Fortescue, yesterday. She had me fetch a hansom and I heard her give the driver that address."

"Put the necklace in the usual place. If it does belong to Cousin Katherine, I'll return it when we go with them to Ascot."

"Ascot is two weeks from now, Miss Sophie. Surely your cousin will have discovered by then that the necklace is missing."

"What else can I do? She and Lord Fortescue left for Berkshire this morning. It isn't as if I can go to her house in London and slip upstairs sight unseen to return the thing."

"As to that, I know someone who could—" He broke off at the warning look she gave him. "Very well."

Grimstock started to turn away, then paused and said, "I know she can't help it, poor dear, and once she's taken something and hidden it somewhere, she forgets all about it. But one of these days she's going to get caught, and then there will be serious trouble, Miss Sophie. Mark my words."

She saw the concern in the butler's eyes, and she put a hand on his arm. "It's all right, Grimmy. I'll protect her."

"You can't protect her forever."

"Oh, yes, I can." Sophie turned away and walked into the drawing room, surprised to find Auntie and all the lodgers assembled there for tea.

Sophie glanced down to verify the time, but the watch she had pinned to her dress before leaving the house this afternoon was gone. She sighed. That made three watches lost this year, and they could hardly afford that expense. She was going to give up wearing watches altogether. "What time is it?"

Violet looked up from her book on Egyptology and glanced at her own watch. "Six o'clock. Did you lose another one, dear?"

"Yes, Auntie. Six o'clock is awfully late for tea."

Elderly Colonel Abercrombie, who was sitting in one corner of the room with the *Times,* frowned at her over the top of his newspaper. "Tea at six o'clock! Never had it that late in Poona. Those Indian fellows know how to run a proper household. Everything done on schedule."

Edward Dawes glanced up from his text on diseases of the throat, giving Violet a disapproving stare over the spectacles perched on his nose. "The problem is that no one in this house ever seems to know what time it is. It is very inconvenient to my university studies."

Aunt Violet did not seem offended by his criticism. "Time is infinite, Edward," she said and resumed reading her own book.

"We were waiting for Sophie, Mr. Dawes," explained Miss Peabody, turning to give the subject of her words a smile. She patted the cushion beside her on the settee.

"Some of us were, anyway," Miss Atwood put in from the other end of the room, where she was playing patience. She lifted her gaze from the cards on the table and looked at the crumbs scattered across Miss Peabody's ample bosom. "Others were not."

"It was only one seed cake, Josephine," Miss Peabody defended herself, brushing at her bodice.

"Two." Miss Atwood frowned down at the table, her lean profile rather reminiscent of a greyhound. "Now, I know I had another card to play, but I can't seem to see . . ."

"Red knave on black queen," Sophie told her abstractedly, accepting the invitation of the plump, amiable Miss Peabody to sit down. She was too sick with worry to eat anything. Inspector Dunbar could die at any moment.

Miss Atwood made a sound of satisfaction. "Thank you, dear," she said, taking it for granted that Sophie had been able to help her without even looking at the cards. "I do believe this patience is going to come out after all."

Miss Peabody leaned closer to Sophie. "Violet and I used the planchette today, and it told us the most interesting things."

"It was quite remarkable, my dear." Violet put aside her book and came to sit with them around the tea tray, eager to discuss the phenomenon. "A spirit named Abdul visited us. He spelled out his name for us quite clearly. I can't wait to tell the group about it at the meeting tonight."

Aunt Violet, Miss Peabody, and Miss Atwood all belonged to the London Society for the Investigation of Psychic Phenomena, a long name for a group that consisted of seven people, most of whom lived on their street. Violet had founded the group after the death of her husband, and they met twice a month, holding séances, having dessert, and gossiping about their neighbors.

"Abdul, indeed!" Mr. Dawes said with contempt as he turned a page of his book. "There is no scientific evidence that spirits communicate with us. And if they did, I cannot believe they would use a device as ridiculous and inconvenient as a piece of wood laid over a board painted with the alphabet."

"Oh no, I'm afraid I must disagree with you there," Violet said. "Many spirits have spoken to us through the planchette."

Dawes was clearly skeptical. "Such as?"

"Abdul, for one. Even some of our own departed loved ones have spoken to us, including my own dear Maxwell."

The pale, thin young man gave her a condescending smile. "I don't believe it for a moment."

"If you don't believe in spirits, Mr. Dawes, how do you account for Sophie's abilities?" Miss Atwood asked him without looking up from her cards.

"Miss Sophie's talents certainly seem remarkable," he admitted. "But she should put herself in the hands of scientists for further study under controlled conditions. Perhaps the British Society for Psychical Research."

Violet gave a disdainful sniff. "Psychical research, indeed. Skeptics and cynics, all of them. As for Sophie, she would never put herself in the hands of those frauds."

"What is the topic for tonight's meeting?" Miss Peabody asked Violet. "Perhaps Sophie would agree to tell everyone of her extraordinary dream last night."

Violet glanced at her niece doubtfully. "I don't think so, Hermione. You know how shy Sophie is about that sort of thing."

"I know, Violet, and I understand. It's such a shame, though. She could be so helpful to our research."

Sophie paid no heed to the conversation that discussed her as a possible conduit to the spirit world. The only spirit she was thinking about at this moment was Inspector Dunbar's. *Do something,* she told herself, but when it came to knowing just what she needed to do, she drew a blank.

"Sophie, darling, are you listening?"

"Hmm? What?" At the sound of her aunt's voice, Sophie came out of her reverie and looked about her. "I'm sorry. I was woolgathering, I'm afraid."

"Something is wrong," Miss Peabody said, frowning at her. "Sophie, you look quite ill."

"Dearest, are you all right?" Aunt Violet came to sit on Sophie's other side. "You must still be disturbed about your dream last night." She put an arm around her niece's shoulders.

"Of course she's upset." Miss Atwood slapped a card down on the table. "Dreams of blood and dead bodies would upset anyone."

"I went to the police," Sophie blurted out.

All three ladies looked at her in astonishment. Mr. Dawes peered at her over his spectacles as if she were an interesting species of bacteria. The colonel gave a disapproving humph and muttered, "A young lady getting herself involved with the police. It isn't done, I say. It simply isn't."

"Oh, but the man was dead, Colonel," Violet assured

him. "Sophie saw it. She had a duty to report it to the police."

"Yes, indeed," Miss Peabody agreed. "She couldn't just stand by and let the man be killed."

The colonel had no answer to that. He once again took refuge behind his newspaper, saying nothing more.

"What made you go to the police?" Violet asked Sophie. "I thought you had decided against it."

"I changed my mind." Feeling the need to talk about it, Sophie went on, "There I was in Fortnum & Mason, and all of a sudden, I knew I had to go to Scotland Yard at once. I'm sorry, Auntie. I was so distraught, I forgot all about your lemon curd."

Violet waved aside the lemon curd. "So you went to the police. Then what happened?"

"It was the most extraordinary thing. There I was, reporting the murder to some nice man in a blue uniform, when I looked up and saw *him*. The same man from my dream, the dead one. Only he wasn't dead, of course. He's a detective at Scotland Yard."

Violet gave a little gasp. "What did you do?"

"I told him, of course. I tried to warn him, but he didn't believe me." Sophie slumped forward in discouragement. "He seemed to think it was all some sort of prank. He practically tossed me out on my ear."

Miss Peabody made a sound of sympathy. "How horrible."

"What else can you expect from a policeman?" Miss Atwood put down the last card with a triumphant flourish and came to sit with them around the tea tray. "Not at all our sort."

Sophie refrained from pointing out that most people were not their sort. Most people did not believe themselves to be reincarnations of historical personages, or have dreams of the future that usually came true, or use a planchette to contact dead strangers named Abdul.

"We must make allowances for those who are skeptical of the spirit world," Violet said.

Mr. Dawes closed his book with a sigh of irritation and stood up. "It's impossible to study down here. How can I prepare for my examinations with all this chatter going on?"

The others paid little attention to that, and conversation about Sophie's experience resumed the moment Dawes departed.

"It must have been a most distressing experience for you, Sophie, darling." Violet patted her shoulder in a gesture of consolation. "But at least you tried. You did your best."

"Exactly," Miss Peabody concurred. "And there's nothing more you can do."

Sophie envisioned the inspector's face, so handsome and vibrant with life, and she sat up straight on the settee, her resolve renewed. "I am not giving up. Not by a long way."

Surprisingly, it was Colonel Abercrombie who endorsed her decision first. "Good girl," he said and tossed aside his newspaper. He came forward to help himself to a strawberry tart and cup of tea. "You shouldn't have gone to the police in the first place," he told her with a fatherly sort of frown. "But, once you've decided on your course, you'd best stick to it.

That has always been my way. I remember once in the Bengal—"

"Tell us, dear," Miss Atwood interrupted to prevent another of the colonel's long, rather tedious stories of his life in India, "what do you plan to do next?"

Sophie looked at the eager faces of the other four people assembled around the tea table, and she found herself at a loss. "I have no idea," she confessed. "But I'm going to think of something. I am not going to let him die."

The White Horse was not the pub of choice for most policemen around Whitehall. The Boar's Head, close to both New Scotland Yard and Cannon Row Police Station, usually held that honor. But thanks to Sir Roger Ellerton and his motorcar, the Boar's Head was closed for repairs, so the White Horse was crowded with off-duty bobbies, constables, and inspectors when Mick walked in.

Word of his part in Sir Roger's escapade had reached most of his comrades, and he bowed facetiously to the applause that greeted his arrival at the pub. His black eye was much admired, and his birthday provided the perfect excuse for another round.

Amid good-natured insults, slaps on the back, and birthday wishes, Mick accepted a complimentary pint of ale from the barkeep. He ordered a steak and chips from Annie, the prettiest barmaid at the White Horse, then he glanced around the crowded interior of the pub. He saw many men that he knew, including his friends Anthony Frye and Jack Hawthorne seated at a table nearby, but though he responded to their wave of greeting with a wave of his own, he did not cross the room to their table. Right now, the men he wanted to see were Billy and Rob. He spied them seated in a far corner of the pub, and he made his way through the labyrinth of people and the haze of cigar smoke to their table.

Billy Mackay and Rob Willis were veterans of the Metropolitan Police for two decades. Though only a few years older than Mick, they had no ambitions beyond their present jobs. Both of them enjoyed being bobbies on the beat. Though higher in rank, inspectors like Mick who dressed in plain clothes garnered even less trust and confidence from the populace than the uniformed officers did.

Billy and Rob took their work seriously, but that did not stop them from playing jokes on their fellow officers. They were, in fact, notorious for it. Mick had learned that his first day on the force. Barely eighteen, he'd been initiated into the ranks with a uniform they had rolled in poison ivy. In retaliation, Mick had dusted their uniforms with sneezing powder, and he'd been friends with the pair ever since.

"Well done, lad," Billy said as Mick sat down. "How many blots on your copybook do you get for arresting an earl's son?"

"Couldn't you have done something a bit more sensational for your birthday?" Rob asked. "Unmasking one of the Queen's nieces as a jewel thief would have been better, I think."

"Rather," Billy agreed. "Then you might have been in the penny papers."

"It'll be in the papers anyway," Mick assured them.

"When I passed the Boar's Head on my way here, I saw that artist for the *Daily Telegraph* sketching the scene." He took a hefty swallow of ale and licked the foam from his upper lip. "But enough of that. I want to know about the other."

"What other?" Rob grinned beneath his graying dark-brown mustache. "You mean you did something else today as stupid as arresting Sir Roger Ellerton?"

"It wasn't stupid," Mick defended himself.

"He's related to the Home Secretary," Billy told him.

"I know that now," Mick answered. "But I didn't know it at the time. Besides, I don't care who his relations are. He deserved to be arrested for striking a policeman." He took another swallow of ale, then set his glass down on the table. "Enough about that. I want to know about the woman."

"What woman?" both men asked at once.

They exchanged glances, then Billy leaned across the table. "You met a new woman? Congratulations!" He slapped Mick on the shoulder.

"God's balls, Billy!" Mick rubbed his aching shoulder. "Did you have to do that?"

"Shoulder hurts?" Rob looked at Billy. "He's getting old."

"Thirty-six is not old," Mick said and realized he was getting very tired of saying that. "It's the bullet I took in the Lambeth case, and you know it."

"Sorry, old chap." The words and the tone in which he said them made it clear Billy was unrepentant. "Tell us about the woman you met. Are you going to be in love with this one for more than a week?"

"What do you mean by that?" Mick asked, once again diverted from the subject of Miss Haversham.

"He means you fall in love all the time," Rob told him. "You just don't stay there very long."

"I don't know what you're blathering about."

"Yes, you do," Billy said with a laugh. "You go from woman to woman the way most men go from cigar to cigar. Every day a new one to enjoy. You're just not a one-woman sort of bloke."

"That's not true," Mick protested, stung. "I just haven't met the right one yet."

"That's a load of sheep dung, that is." Billy shook his head. "You meet women all the time. Women are always throwing themselves at you, and I'll tell you, it's been a rough go watching it over the years. I've been damned envious of you."

"What?" Mick stared at him. "Katie is a wonderful woman, and you're lucky to have her. If I had a wife like that—"

"Now that I have my Katie," Billy interrupted him, "it doesn't matter to me anymore, but before I was married, seeing the way women fall for you was bloody hard sometimes."

"But there were some benefits to it," Rob pointed out. "I spent one or two nights consoling his former sweethearts."

"True," Billy agreed. "You even married one of them."

"Count yourself lucky, Rob," Mick advised. "If I'd seen what a warm, loving woman Bridget was, I'd never have let her go."

"That's just it." Billy lifted his pint and took a sip.

Resting his elbows on the table, he looked at Mick over the rim of his glass, his expression suddenly serious. "You never see."

Mick sat back in his chair, too surprised by that statement to answer. But after a moment, he said, "Both of you found the right woman. Each of you knew the moment you met your wife that she was the one. I'm still waiting for that to happen to me."

"That just won't go down with us, Micky boy," Billy told him. "We've known you too long. Rob and I have met most of the women you've courted over the years, and all of them have been wonderful in their own way, but you don't see it. You find some unacceptable flaw with each and every one of them. The truth is that you don't like being tied down, you don't want our Saturday night poker game to be your only night out, and you certainly don't want to be faithful to one woman."

"You're raving," Mick told him. "I'd give anything to have the life you two have. A loving wife to come home to at the end of a hard day and a pack of children to take care of. I want to settle down." He frowned down into his ale, feeling even older than he was. "Honestly, I do."

"Sorry, Mick," Billy answered, shaking his head. "I don't believe it for a minute. You love your life just the way it is."

"I don't believe it either," Rob said. "You like your freedom too much to give it up."

Mick knew they didn't understand. "Be damned to you both. My private life isn't your business anyway."

"The lad's a bit hostile, isn't he?" Rob said.

"It's turning thirty-six that's got to him, that's what

it is," Billy answered. "Notice he shaved off his mustache?"

"I did notice that, I did indeed. It was going a bit gray, you know. That's probably why he shaved it off. He doesn't want the women thinking he's old."

Mick didn't need his two best friends rubbing salt in his wounds today. "Can we get back to one woman in particular, the one I met this afternoon?"

"Go on," Rob urged. "Tell us all about her. Is she pretty?"

"You should know. You two hired her."

They looked at him in a bewildered fashion, and Mick continued, "It was a good joke to play for my birthday, but what I want to know is, which of you thought of it?"

Both men continued to stare at him blankly.

"C'mon, lads. Which of you came up with the idea? And where did you find her? She was first rate."

Billy and Rob continued to stare at him, and Mick felt a sudden glimmer of doubt. It was clear they didn't know what he was on about. If they had done it, they'd have owned up to it by now. They couldn't have resisted the temptation to have a good laugh at his expense.

He straightened in his chair and looked from one man to the other. "You mean to tell me," he said slowly, "that the pair of you didn't send that woman over to the Yard this afternoon?"

Billy shook his head. "We didn't send anybody to see you."

Mick explained his encounter with Sophie Haversham, and though both men found the whole thing amusing, taking the prediction of Mick's impending death about as seriously as he did, they denied having anything to do with it.

"If you two weren't behind it, then what's it all about?" Mick asked them.

"Maybe she's just one of the crazy ones," Rob suggested. "It wouldn't be the first time."

It could be that. Crazy people that reported imaginary crimes to the police were common enough.

But you hate mutton, don't you?

Her artless remark came back to him, and Mick frowned, shaking his head. "She was an odd one, but I don't think she's mad. Lads, there were things she knew about me, things that she couldn't have known unless someone had told her."

Billy shrugged. "Maybe one of the fellows at the Yard is behind it. Thacker, perhaps."

It could have been Henry. He knew of Mick's aversion to mutton. Mick decided he'd have a talk with his sergeant first thing tomorrow morning.

Billy stood up, interrupting Mick's speculations. "I'd best be getting on home."

"I'm needing to be going as well." Rob also got to his feet.

Mick looked at both of them in surprise. "So soon?"

Billy gave him an apologetic shrug. "I'm sure Katie's got dinner near on the table by now. Expecting as she is, she gets upset over the smallest things, and she'll start crying if the food's cold when I get there. There's nothing worse than seeing her cry." He lifted his glass. "Happy birthday, old man," he told Mick and swallowed the last of his ale.

Mick scowled. "Good riddance to you, if you keep calling me old." He looked at the other man. "C'mon, Rob, stay a few minutes and have another pint."

Rob shook his head. "I'd like to, Mick, but I promised the boys I'd take them down to Lincoln's Inn Fields before dark and play a bit of football."

As Mick watched his two best friends depart, he couldn't help feeling a hint of envy. Each of those men had a beautiful, loving woman, children of his own, and a house that was truly a home. All Mick had waiting for him tonight was a one-room flat and an irate landlady.

He frowned, thinking of what his friends had laughingly said to him. They were dead wrong, of course. All his life he'd wanted a family of his own. He'd love to have sons he could take to Lincoln's Inn Fields for football, daughters he could spoil and protect. He'd love to come home to the scent of dinner cooking and one woman's welcoming arms. He'd love to be tied down and fenced in—to the right woman, his kind of woman.

She didn't have to be beautiful, but he had to feel something twist his guts when he looked at her, a feeling that made him want to ravish her even if they were in a room full of people. He wanted a woman who didn't nag if he forgot her birthday, didn't fuss if he had a pint or two with the lads, and didn't hate the smell of cigars. He wanted a woman who loved children and loved making them. He wanted a woman who was quiet, elegant, and self-contained, except in bed. Most important, he wanted a woman who didn't try to turn him inside out to find out everything he'd ever said or done or felt or thought. Even a wife didn't get that privilege.

Yes, Mick knew exactly what kind of woman was perfect for him. He just couldn't seem to find her.

Annie came up beside his chair, breaking into his thoughts as she set a plate in front of him that contained his steak and chips. Beside it, she set down a fresh pint of ale.

"Now that," he said, "is what I like."

"You might be liking this better." She slid onto his lap with a flirtatious smile. "Happy birthday, Mick."

She slid her arms around his neck and pulled him close, then gave him the longest, most passionate kiss the White Horse Pub had ever seen. At the touch of her lips, Mick forgot about what kind of wife he wanted, how quickly life was passing him by, and how lousy it felt to turn thirty-six.

Mick's flat was in Maiden Lane, an easy walk from the White Horse if he cut across Victoria Embankment. Sophie Haversham's warning notwithstanding, Mick had no intention of taking a longer route. He passed Cleopatra's Needle, made his way through a shrubbery, and started down the path through the moonlit gardens with a smile that widened as he approached the statue of Robert Burns. If thugs were going to jump out and murder him, they'd better do it soon.

He turned his head to give the poet a mock salute as he passed, and in that instant, he caught a glimpse of a small, dark figure stepping out from behind the statue. He saw the quicksilver flash of gunmetal in the moonlight.

Mick dove toward the ground just as the shot was fired, sending the gravel of the path spraying in all directions. He rolled into the herbaceous border that lined the walkway, flattening most of the flowers in the process, and ducked into a thicket of rhododendrons.

But his efforts to avoid getting shot at again proved unnecessary. He heard no more bullets fire. When he chanced a look between the shrubs, he saw no one. There was no dark, cloaked figure peeping at him from behind the statue waiting for another opportunity. His assailant had fled.

Mick's gaze scanned the gardens, but he had no indication of which direction the fellow had gone. Though the moon was bright enough that he might discern that information from footprints in the grass, he didn't want to give the man another opportunity to take a shot at him from the thick groves of trees and shrubs all around.

If it had been a man. Mick took several deep breaths, reliving the past few moments, focusing on the brief glimpse he'd had of his assailant. Small for a man, swathed in a long, hooded black cloak like some unearthly apparition from a Dickens story. It could have been a man or a woman. There was no way to know.

The gun had been a small-caliber weapon. Mick knew that from the sound of the shot, a popping sound like a champagne cork, the sound that came from the sort of gun a woman might use, one of those pretty little pearl-handled pistols jewelers sold to society women for twice the price of an ordinary gun. A gun that looked like a toy but was not a toy.

Mick combed his fingers through his hair, took another deep breath, and started home. One thing was certain. Sophie Haversham's visit to the Yard no longer seemed like a joke. She'd known about tonight's events. Perhaps she had overheard something, or perhaps she knew the killer. Despite her soft, dithery manner and big brown eyes, Sophie Haversham was not so innocent as she seemed.

He was going to find out what she knew, how she knew it, and why she had chosen to warn him. He was going to turn her inside out and find out everything about her. Including whether or not she owned a little pearl-handled pistol.

Three

❧

Sophie paid little attention to the conversation around her at dinner that evening. Unable to eat, she toyed with the food on her plate, her worry growing with every tick of the clock.

It wasn't as if she could go to Victoria Embankment Gardens now; a London park at night was too dangerous. The murder might not happen tonight, in any case. It might be tomorrow, or the day after or next week. There was no way to know, and she couldn't very well camp out in the Embankment like a gypsy.

He was a policeman, after all, she reminded herself. Big and strong and well able to protect himself, now that she had warned him. But his laughing face came before her eyes again, reminding her that her warning had done no good. He thought it a joke.

A joke. God in heaven.

Sophie tossed aside her dinner napkin and stood up. Her abrupt movement brought an immediate halt to the conversation, and the other five people at the table stared at her in surprise.

"Sophie?" Violet frowned with concern. "You're looking peaked again, as if you're going to faint. You always look that way when you're seeing things. Have you had another premonition about that policeman?"

"I can't stand it, Auntie. I must do something."

"But darling, you've warned the man. What else can you possibly do?"

An idea came to her in a flash of inspiration. "I think I'll pay a call on him, just to make certain that he got safely home."

"Now?" Miss Peabody glanced at the darkened window of the dining room. "Is that wise?"

"No, it is not," Miss Atwood answered for her. "Sophie, you don't even know where the man lives."

"I'll go to Scotland Yard and find out where he lives. I just need to satisfy myself that he's all right."

"Well, you can't go alone." Colonel Abercrombie stood up. "I'll go with you."

Sophie appreciated his gallantry, but she knew that wouldn't do. The colonel was seventy-six, and though he might have faced down wild tigers and rebel outbreaks in India many years ago, he wasn't up to adventures now. She smiled at him and shook her head. "And have you miss your game of dominoes with Mr. Shelton? It's Friday and you always go to Mr. Shelton's on Friday nights while the ladies have their meeting. I couldn't let you miss it."

Out of the corner of her eye, she saw Mr. Dawes

move to stand up. Unable to tolerate the thought of being trapped in a carriage with him and analyzed as if her psychic ability were some sort of fascinating disease, Sophie spoke quickly to forestall his impending offer to accompany her. "I'll take Grimstock."

She turned to the butler, who was standing by with a tray, ready to take away the dinner plates. "You'll come, won't you?"

The butler hesitated, and Sophie immediately understood the reason why. Though he no longer had anything to fear from the law, the mention of police was still enough to make him uneasy.

"Don't know why you're going to all this trouble for a copper," he mumbled. "They're ones can watch out for themselves."

Sophie didn't answer; she simply waited. Grimstock sighed and gave in to the inevitable. "Of course I'll go with you, Miss Sophie." He set the tray on the plum-colored mahogany sideboard. "You'll be wanting a hansom."

"Yes, we'll need a cab. And speak with Hannah, would you? Auntie's friends from the society are coming in half an hour for their meeting. Hannah will have to serve dessert on her own, since you're coming with me."

These necessities accomplished, Sophie and the butler set out. Their first call was at Scotland Yard. While Grimstock waited in the carriage outside, Sophie obtained Inspector Dunbar's address from a night constable, and soon they were at the detective's lodgings, a somewhat dingy house near Covent Garden.

She turned to the butler. "I'll just make certain he's

come in." She paused, giving him a dubious look. "I think perhaps it would be best if you waited here."

Grimstock was obviously relieved. "Thank you, Miss Sophie. I think so, too."

Sophie stepped down from the carriage and walked up to the house. Praying she would find the police inspector home safe and sound, she tapped the brass knocker. Inside the house a dog began to bark, and after several moments, the door was opened by a stout woman in black crepe who carried an oil lamp in her hand.

Peering at Sophie from behind the shelter of the woman's skirts was a Pekingese that now growled at her with a ferocity that was almost comical, given the animal's small size. It was not, Sophie knew, a nice dog. She suspected it had the tendency to bite any ankle within close proximity.

"Nanki Poo," the woman admonished in a cooing voice, bending to lift her pet with one hand. After tucking the Pekingese into the crook of her arm, she held the lamp higher and gazed at Sophie in some surprise. "Yes, miss? You be wanting a room?"

"No, thank you. I'm looking for someone." Sophie gave the woman her most charming smile. "Detective Inspector Dunbar."

The mention of his name caused the woman to scowl quite belligerently, and the dog gave another low growl.

"What you be wanting 'im for?" The woman looked her up and down with an appraising eye. " 'e's one for the gels, but you don't look 'is sort, dearie."

Realizing what she meant, what she must be thinking, Sophie was mortified. She hastily invented an explanation. "He promised a subscription for our dear missionaries in Africa. Half a crown, and I've come to see if I might collect it."

"Did 'e now? Fancy that. Willing to give to church charities, but not to find a poor, kidnaped dog for 'is own landlady. There I was, worrying all the day over Nanki Poo's disappearance, and 'e wouldn't do a thing to 'elp."

Sophie studied the Pekingese for a moment. She could have told the landlady her dog had not been kidnaped but had simply wanted to romp with the pretty little terrier around the corner, but she refrained. "How dreadful for you, but you must have felt so relieved when he was returned unharmed. You must tell me all about it." Before the woman could do that very thing, Sophie went on, "Could I possibly see Inspector Dunbar? I have so many houses left to visit, and it's getting quite late."

"Well, miss, 'e's not in yet. Off in some pub, I'm sure."

She might be sure, but Sophie wasn't. He could very well be dead. "Oh dear. I was hoping to find him in this evening. I—"

"Looks as if you'll be getting your wish, dearie," the landlady interrupted her. "That's 'im coming up the street."

Sophie turned, watching as a man came along the sidewalk toward them. The tall form of Inspector Dunbar was unmistakable, and Sophie grasped the doorjamb, weak with relief. He was alive, and he appeared to be unharmed. Furthermore, she could see the aura of soft golden light that surrounded him. Somehow, the danger had passed.

He caught sight of her standing on the front steps of his lodging house and paused for a moment beneath the streetlamp, looking at her. The lamplight caught on the glints of silver in his dark hair and showed the lines of anger in his lean face. Sophie felt the heat of that anger directed at her like the blast of a coal furnace, though she could not sense the reason for it.

Her relief that he was alive disintegrated, and she glanced at the hansom, but it was too late to make a hasty departure. He was already between her and the cab, and only a few more steps brought him to her side. "Just the woman I wish to see." He curled his hand beneath her elbow in a viselike grip, demonstrating to her quite clearly the strength he possessed. "Come with me."

He started pulling Sophie through the doorway, and out of the corner of her eye, she saw Grimstock jump out of the carriage with his fists clenched, ready to come to her aid.

"It's all right," she called to him as the detective pulled her through the doorway of the lodging house. The last thing she needed was for Grimstock to get arrested for assaulting a policeman. "Stay here," she ordered. "I'll be right back."

Inspector Dunbar dragged her through the doorway and kicked the door shut behind him. He gave his landlady a brief nod as he started for the stairs with Sophie in tow. "Mrs. Tribble, I see that Nanki Poo is home safe and sound."

"Aye, and no thanks to you," she called after him as

he pulled Sophie up the stairs. "And I run a respectable 'ouse, Mr. Dunbar. Missionaries, indeed!"

The meaning of the landlady's words was not lost on Sophie. She tried to jerk free of the inspector's hold, but it was useless. When he reached the top of the stairs, he pulled her down a dark hallway. Still keeping a firm grip on her, he stopped before a door about halfway down the passage and reached into his pocket for his latchkey. He unlocked the door, hauled her inside the room, and shut the door behind them. She heard the slide and click of a bolt locking into place. Only then did he let her go.

The room was utterly black, and Sophie had to fight back a wave of panic. God, how she hated the dark. Though she could see nothing, she knew he was standing right beside her. She could hear the measured rhythm of his breathing, she could feel the heat of his body and the full force of his anger. She tried to remember to breathe, but the darkness was all around her, and Sophie felt as if she were suffocating.

After several tense seconds, she was able to speak. "Could you—" Her voice failed her. She cleared her throat, then tried again. "It's so very dark in here. I know it probably seems silly to you, but I don't . . . I don't like the dark. I never have, not since I was a little girl. I have very frightening dreams sometimes, you see. Do you think you could light a lamp?"

He said nothing, but after a moment she heard the rasp of a match, and lamplight flooded the room.

Sophie took a glance around and saw that she was in the only room of a flat. It was sparsely furnished, scrupulously clean, and tidy. Between herself and the inspector was the lamp, resting on a small dining table. Nearby was a pair of overstuffed chintz chairs that had seen better days, and beyond them a bed stood in one corner, its sheets tucked in and its counterpane smoothly laid out. Against the wall to her right stood a tall bookcase, filled with books.

The sight of the books did rather surprise her. She wouldn't have thought a police inspector to be in any way intellectual. Still, she had no doubt the books were alphabetically laid out by author or grouped in some other logical manner. She knew Inspector Dunbar was a man who believed in keeping everything in his life well-ordered.

Beneath the window directly opposite to where she stood was a shelf containing a gas ring, a kettle, cups, and a bright red tin of tea. Other than the books and the tidiness, there was nothing about this room to show the personality of its tenant. There were no pictures on the walls, there were no photographs or daguerreotypes, no keepsakes, no objects of intimacy whatsoever.

She returned her gaze to him. The lamp illuminated his face, and she noticed he needed a shave. His clothing was rumpled, his tie was undone, and the bruise beneath his eye had darkened to deep purple. He looked more dangerous to Sophie's way of thinking than any member of the criminal classes could possibly be.

"Where is it?"

The question was so abrupt that it took Sophie a moment to assimilate it. When she had, she still didn't understand. "Where is what?"

"Where is the gun that fired the bullet that missed

my head by inches in Victoria Embankment Gardens less than an hour ago?"

"Oh, God." For a moment, Sophie was so relieved she could not reply to his question, but her relief was short-lived. When he circled the table and began walking toward her, his grim expression told her she had nothing to be relieved about. He looked as if he wanted to wring her neck.

Unnerved, she took a step back and hit the door behind her. With nowhere to run, she plunged into speech. "You don't appear to be wounded, so I take it the assassin missed, Inspector?"

He didn't answer but took another step toward her with ominous intent, and she rushed on, "Of course, at night, in the dark, I'm sure it's much harder to shoot someone than it would be in broad daylight. And I hadn't thought of a gun, in any case. I had thought a knife, what with all the blood. On the other hand, you don't look the sort of man to be easily overpowered—"

"Where is the pistol?"

She blinked, looking at him in bewilderment. "How on earth should I know?"

"You seem to know quite a lot."

"But not that. As I said, I hadn't even envisioned a weapon, though I had concluded that a knife must have been used. Because of the blood, you see."

He seized her wrists in one hand, raising her arms over her head and flattening her body against the door behind her. He was a head taller than she, and far stronger, and though Sophie reminded herself that he was a policeman, not a criminal, it did not stop the rapid pounding of her heart.

"If you still have it with you," he said, "by God, I'll have you in a cell before you have the chance to use it on me again."

"You think I shot at you? Why would I? I don't even know you!" She gasped, shocked, as he flattened his free hand against her hip. "What are you doing? Let go of me!"

He paid no heed. Sophie tried to lean away from his touch as he ran his palm down her leg, but it was useless. When he reached her ankle, his hand moved beneath her skirt and petticoats. He slid his palm back up her leg, the heat of his hand burning her through her stocking. When he reached the hem of her combination, Sophie couldn't help a cry of fright and humiliation. "I don't have any gun," she said, twisting against his touch like a leaf in the wind. "I don't have it."

Undeterred by her protestations, he continued his relentless search until he reached the top of her thigh, then he repeated the mortifying procedure with her other leg. He added insult to injury by running his hands all over her bodice, including the dip between her breasts, before he finally seemed satisfied that she had spoken the truth.

Mortified beyond description, Sophie felt her own anger flaring. "Now that you know I don't have this pistol you're looking for," she said through clenched teeth, "let go of me."

His grip on her wrists tightened. "Did you leave it in the cab? Or perhaps you dumped it in a rubbish heap on your way here?"

"I don't know what you're talking about. I—"

"Who's the man downstairs in the cab?"

"My butler."

"He's probably quite loyal to you, so maybe he did it on your behalf."

"What?" The idea was laughable, but just now she didn't find it amusing. "This may come as a shock to you, but I don't spend my evenings lurking in parks with my butler, waiting for detectives to walk by so I can shoot them! And if I did occupy myself with such a pastime, I wouldn't warn you in advance of my intent. That would be insane."

"Exactly."

After the accusations he had made and the indecent way he had run his hands over her, his implication that she was crazy was the last straw. Too angry to speak, she kicked him in the shin.

His grip on her wrists loosened, and she jerked free, kicking him in the other shin for good measure. "You swine," she said as she ducked past him. "You loathsome swine. I try to save your life," she continued, turning around to face him, "and in return, you manhandle me like some sort of criminal, accuse my butler and myself of heaven knows what, then you have the gall to imply I'm insane? *You're* the one who should be locked up."

"Save my life?" He leaned down to rub his sore shins. "Is that what you call taking shots at me in the park?"

"I didn't shoot at you. I don't even own a pistol, and I don't know anyone who does. Well, except the colonel. Since he was in the army, he might own a gun. Even if I did have such a weapon in my possession, I wouldn't have a clue how to use it."

"If you didn't shoot at me, who did?"

"I haven't the vaguest idea. As I tried to explain to you at Scotland Yard, I didn't see the murderer. If I had, I would have described him to you. All I saw was you covered in blood, lying in the grass beside a statue of Robert Burns, and you were dead."

"And you saw this in your mind?"

His contemptuous disbelief was plain. She thought she had long ago gotten used to skepticism, but from this man, at this moment, it was intolerable. "In a dream, actually. And," she added as he began to laugh, "there was nothing amusing about it. It scared me out of my wits."

"I'm not amused, I can assure you. You come to me, declaring that you had a dream I was lying dead and bloody in Victoria Embankment Gardens, then it very nearly happens. And when I reach home, I find you here, waiting for me. To my mind, all of that leads to one conclusion. You know all about it."

"It isn't knowledge, not in the sense you mean. It's just—" She broke off, reluctant to expose herself to additional contempt and ridicule. But he continued to study her with those cold blue eyes, and she knew he would never let her leave until she had at least tried to explain her role in tonight's events.

"Sometimes I can see the future. I often dream of things and then they happen exactly as I dreamed them. But sometimes it doesn't even happen in a dream. Sometimes, I see things when I'm awake. Of course, when that happens, I usually feel very faint and dizzy, which is inconvenient if I'm out at the shops or at the opera. Sometimes, I sense things about people. I'll see a woman standing next to me in a shop, for instance, a woman I've never seen before, and I'll know her brother just died. I just know things without being told."

He folded his arms across his broad chest, unimpressed. "Opening day at Epsom Downs is a week from now. If you can see the future, tell me which horse is going to win the first race, so I can put a quid down."

"It's not like electricity! I can't simply turn it on and off at will."

"How convenient for you."

The sarcasm in his voice told her any further attempts to explain were futile. She lifted her chin. "There's something else you need to know. Sometimes, I know what people are thinking. Right now, you are thinking things about me that nothing I could say would refute. This is hopeless, and I think I should leave."

He seized her arm as she started to walk past him. "So soon? I couldn't possibly allow that." He pulled her to one of the two chintz chairs, pushed her into it, then sat down in the opposite chair. He leaned back as if settling in for a long conversation.

"Let me see if I have this right. You had a dream I was going to be murdered, but you have no idea who the murderer might be." He studied her so closely that she had to fight back the impulse to squirm in her chair. "What was your reason for coming to see me? You decided to be a good citizen and warn me of my fate?"

"Actually, yes."

He made a sound of disbelief, and Sophie frowned

at him in vexation. "There's no point in trying to tell you anything. You aren't prepared to listen to a word I say."

His expression grew even more grim. "Tell me anyway."

"I didn't know the man in my dream was you until I saw you at Scotland Yard. All I knew was that a man was going to die unless I could prevent it, and my conscience dictated my actions. The only step I could think to take was going to the police, which is something I was loathe to do, believe me."

"Why? If you knew a murder was about to be committed, I should think you would be eager to inform the police about it." He straightened in his seat, and his gaze locked with hers. "Unless you were protecting the murderer."

That suggestion was as ludicrous as the other, and Sophie shook her head in disbelief. "You change theories so quickly, Inspector, you make my head spin."

He shrugged. "There are two possible solutions to this little puzzle. One is that you know who the potential assassin is, but having a conscience, you decided to warn me in advance. But you didn't want me to know the identity of this person, so you made up this rigmarole about a dream, and you came here tonight to find out if your visit to me this afternoon had worked. The only other theory is that you are the one who shot at me, and you came to warn me in advance because you are, shall we say, a bit touched in the head. Which scenario do you prefer?"

She jumped to her feet. "I think you are the one who is touched, Inspector." She folded her arms and glared down at him. "There is a third possibility, one which you have failed to consider. I might be telling the absolute truth."

"Right." He smiled. "I forgot about that one."

"It's a wonder Scotland Yard ever solves a crime. Are all police inspectors as rude and hardheaded as you?"

His smile vanished. "Forgive me, but getting shot at doesn't put me in a sociable mood."

"Well, I didn't shoot at you!"

"But I think you know who did." He stood up, his eyes narrowing as he stepped toward her, but when he spoke, his voice was deceptively soft. "I don't know what sort of game you're playing, but I don't find murder a game, especially when I am the possible corpse. If you know anything, this is not the time to be coy about it. You had best tell me everything you know. Right now."

"I've told you all I know."

"We can do this the easy way or the hard way. It's your choice."

He leaned closer to her, so close she could feel the warmth of his breath on her cheek. "The easy way," he murmured, "would be for you to tell me the truth."

"I already have."

"The hard way it is, then." He straightened away from her. "I don't know what your motives are in all this, but I will discover them, no matter how you try to hide them."

"I don't have any hidden motives. I told you—"

"Whoever has tried to kill me," he interrupted, "that person must be associated with you in some way.

To find out who that person is, I will turn your life inside out. I will uncover everything about you and every member of your family. I will interview every relative, servant, and acquaintance you have. You won't have any secrets left when I've finished with you. This will be unpleasant for you, but as I said, it's your choice."

Despite her resolve not to be intimidated, she suddenly felt afraid, but she refused to let him see it. "Do what you must, Inspector. I'm not afraid of you, and I don't have any secrets."

He stepped past her. "Everybody has secrets, luv. Everybody."

With that, he unlatched the door and opened it. Sophie ran out of the flat and down the stairs, sucking in great gulps of air as she stepped out into the warm spring night.

Catching sight of her, Grimstock jumped out of the cab, frowning with concern at the sight of her face in the moonlight. "Miss Sophie? What happened? Did that copper hurt you?"

She shook her head. "No, Grimmy, I'm perfectly well," she answered and stepped up into the hansom.

In reality, Sophie felt sick with dread. There was no doubt Dunbar meant what he said. He would find out things he had no business knowing, things that would expose her family and herself to scandal and ridicule. With a groan, Sophie leaned forward and lowered her face into her hands. Dear God, what had she done?

"What?" Chief Inspector DeWitt paused in the act of belting his smoking jacket over his pajamas and stared at Mick as if unable to believe what he had just heard. "Somebody did what?"

"Shot at me," Mick answered. "Around half past nine o'clock last night. Sorry to interrupt you at home, sir, but I thought I should tell you as soon as possible."

"I knew when you arrived at my door at this hour on a Saturday morning, it had to be a matter of vital importance." DeWitt ushered Mick into his study and closed the door behind them. "Could it have been some sort of accident?"

"No, sir. I saw the assailant just before the shot went off. He missed, but the gun was pointed at me."

"He?"

"Or she. It was dark, and from the size of the person, it could be either a man or a woman. But it was no accident."

DeWitt let out a low whistle and sat down at his desk. He gestured to the opposite chair for Mick to sit as well. "So you believe it was deliberate. For what reason?"

"I don't know yet." He gave his superior officer a smile. "I do have my very own spiritualist. Maybe she can help."

Despite the seriousness of the situation, Mick's smile widened at the dubious look DeWitt gave him. He handed his superintendent the case notes he'd written early this morning: a complete account of everything involving Miss Haversham, from her visit to the Yard yesterday afternoon to her departure from his flat last night. "This is what I know so far."

DeWitt read Mick's report without speaking. When he had finished, he set the notes aside and leaned back in his chair. "The girl probably did it. You agree?"

"I don't know. What I can't get at is the motive. The only motive I can see is someone from one of my past cases coming after me for revenge. Of course, we'll have to thoroughly investigate her background."

"Are you sure you don't know her?" DeWitt paused and slanted Mick a speculative look. "You have always been one for a bit of skirt, Mick."

Perhaps, but when he put his hands inside a woman's skirt, it usually wasn't to find a gun. Mick looked straight back at his superintendent. "I don't know this one, sir."

"There must be a connection somewhere."

"If there is, we'll find it. I've already sent Thacker out to learn more about her." Mick pulled his watch from his waistcoat. "That was two hours ago. I told him to meet me here. He should be arriving soon."

"What I don't understand is, why all the stuff and nonsense about dreams and seeing the future?"

"You didn't meet this woman," Mick answered, his voice wry. "She's . . ." His voice trailed off as he tried to find a way to sum up Sophie Haversham. "She's a bit odd, to say the least."

A knock on the study door interrupted their conversation, and a parlormaid opened the door. "Sorry, sir," she said with a bob to DeWitt, "but there be a Sergeant Thacker to see you."

"Send him in, Lizzie."

The girl departed, and Thacker entered the room. He closed the door behind him, tipped his cap to the chief inspector, and said, "I've got some information on Miss Haversham."

DeWitt motioned him forward, and Thacker moved to stand beside Mick's chair. Opening the small notebook in his hand, he began to read his report. "Sophie Marie Haversham, age twenty-four. Spinster. Born in Stoke-On-Trent, a small village in Yorkshire. Father was an attorney there, and he died twenty-one years ago. She has one sister, Charlotte Tamplin, who's married to an attorney and lives in Hampstead. The mother got married again about nine years ago, to the local vicar. She is the cousin of a viscount, by the way." He glanced at Mick. "Odd coincidence, that. The viscount is Lord Fortescue. If you remember, it was his wife what reported that stolen necklace yesterday."

"This could be a fine kettle of fish," DeWitt muttered. "Is her cousin relevant to any of this?"

"No way to tell at this point, sir." Thacker took a deep breath, licked his thumb, and turned to the second page of his notes. "Miss Haversham moved to London to live with her aunt, a Mrs. Violet Summerstreet, four years ago when the aunt's husband died. Mr. Maxwell Summerstreet left his wife badly off. Nice big house in Mayfair, but no money. She's turned it into a lodging house to make ends meet. Respectable people she's got living there. Miss Haversham moved here to assist her aunt with running the place. But there was also some talk about the young lady having been engaged to marry the Earl of Kenleigh, Charles Treaves. The wedding didn't come off. He jilted her at the altar, so they say. A few weeks later, she came to London."

"The aunt runs a lodging house," Mick said thoughtfully. "That has possibilities."

DeWitt gave him a sharp look. "You think it might be one of her lodgers who shot at you?"

"We can't speculate on that until we know whether or not they have alibis for half past nine last night."

"And if they do?" the chief inspector asked.

"Then I'll start studying her friends and acquaintances. The best way to do that, of course, would be to move in to that lodging house myself if I could."

"That's a dangerous game," DeWitt said. "I don't like it."

"If everyone in Miss Haversham's household can account for themselves at half past nine last night, the danger to me is no greater living there than in my own flat. Especially since whoever shot at me was willing to do so in a public place. Miss Haversham is connected to this, and the best way for me to find out how is to go right into the lion's den."

"I still don't like it," DeWitt grumbled. "The girl sounds off her chump to me."

"The aunt's a mad one, too," Thacker put in. "She's involved in that spiritualism business." He consulted his notes. "The London Society for Psychical Research, or something like that. Séances, planchettes, table turning, and the like. She thinks she's the reincarnation of Cleopatra."

Mick was not surprised. "Eccentricity runs in that family."

"Spiritualism is quite a fashion these days," DeWitt said, "and with people who ought to have more sense. My own wife—" He broke off and gave the sigh of a long-suffering husband. "That doesn't mean the aunt's mad."

Mick grinned. "With all due respect, sir, I doubt your wife thinks she's Cleopatra back from the dead."

"Thank God for that," DeWitt muttered with heartfelt relief. "But what about the girl? Is she crazy?"

"It's so easy to say she did it because she's crazy," Mick replied. "Too easy. I think we've got to go deeper than that."

DeWitt nodded. "Did you find any witnesses around the Embankment who might have seen something? Or heard something?"

"No, sir," Mick replied. "But it would surprise me if the bobbies who patrol that area heard anything. The gun was low caliber, and it didn't make much noise. Also, the assassin wore a long, dark cloak and wouldn't be easily spied at night."

DeWitt looked over at Thacker. "Anything else, Sergeant?"

"Not yet, sir. I'll keep digging." Thacker departed, closing the door behind him.

DeWitt leaned back. "Well, Mick, what do you want to do?"

Mick didn't hesitate. "I want to find out the truth. I don't much care for getting shot at. And I doubt that whoever did it will leave off just because the first attempt failed."

"What's your next step?"

"The girl is the key. If she did it, I need to know why. If she didn't do it, I need to find out how she learned this was going to happen and why she came to warn me. I'm going to see her now, and I'm going to find out what everyone in that household was up to at half past nine last night. If they all have valid alibis, I'll see if I can let a room in that lodging house."

"Keep me informed of your progress." DeWitt rose to his feet. "And for God's sake, be careful, Mick. I don't want to lose you. Keep your wits about you."

Mick also stood up. "I always do, sir," he answered and started for the door. "I always do."

Four

✑

Because of Michael Dunbar and his threats, Sophie had gotten very little sleep during the night, and she awoke feeling tired and cranky. After the way that wretched man had manhandled her and threatened her the night before, she was not at all surprised that someone wanted to kill him.

Something of what she felt must have shown in her face, for Violet commented on it as Sophie entered the dining room. "My dear, you still don't look well. The sooner this mystery about the murdered policeman is solved, the better."

"He hasn't been murdered yet," Sophie pointed out as she walked to the sideboard.

"Yes, I know. Grimstock told me last night."

Sophie ignored the hint of inquiry in her aunt's voice. She glanced around the dining room. Except for

Violet and herself, the room was empty. "Where is everyone? Am I so very late this morning?"

"It's nearly ten o'clock. Mr. Dawes has gone to cut up a cadaver at London University Hospital, and the colonel is out for his morning walk. Hermione and Josephine have gone to Harrods."

"Ten o'clock? Heavens, it is late." Sophie lifted lids from the warming dishes on the sideboard, noting the eggs and bacon with disinterest. She turned away from the food, poured herself a cup of tea from the silver teapot, and sat down in her usual place at the table, pushing aside the pile of letters waiting for her that had come in the morning post. She knew most of them were bills, and she also knew there wasn't enough money to pay them. "You didn't go to Harrods, too?"

"Of course not. I wanted to wait for you." Her aunt looked at her with gentle reproach. "You came in last night and didn't even tell me what had happened. I had to get the story from Grimstock. It's fortunate the police inspector is still alive."

Sophie knew her aunt wanted details of the night before, but she lowered her gaze to the teacup in her hand and changed the subject. "Auntie, I must speak with you about something else." She met her aunt's innocent blue gaze with a steady one of her own. "The emerald necklace you took from Cousin Katherine's house when you called on her the day before yesterday."

Violet looked at her in wide-eyed innocence. "What are you talking about, dear?"

"You took Cousin Katherine's necklace. Grimmy found it yesterday afternoon. You did take it, didn't you?"

Auntie's expression of innocence turned to one of shamefaced guilt. "I believe I did, now that you mention it."

Sophie lifted her hands in a gesture of despair. "Auntie, I've told you, you can't take things that don't belong to you just because you think they're pretty."

"I'm sorry, dear," Violet mumbled. "I don't know what comes over me. I see jewels, and I just can't resist. And then, of course, I forget all about it. I remember now, it was in her jewel case. You really should tell her to find a safer hiding place for her jewels," Violet added, shaking her head. "Why, a jewel case is the first place a thief would look."

"Well, that's true enough," Sophie responded with a sigh. "You did."

"What did you and Grimstock do with it?"

"I put it in a safe place," Sophie answered, thinking of the secret drawer in her secretaire, where she and Grimmy always put Auntie's little mistakes until they could be returned.

"Sophie, really! You didn't put it in the little hidden drawer of your desk, did you? Why, that's as bad as a jewel case. The best place to put jewelry is in your undergarments, rolled in a pair of knickers or a stocking. No one, not even a burglar, would think to go through a woman's unmentionables."

"Auntie, how did you know about the secret drawer?"

"Well, darling, it really is my desk, if you remember. I've known about it for many, many years. My mama showed it to me when I was a little girl."

Sophie was dismayed, thinking of all the stolen jewels she had placed in that drawer over the last four years. "If you think that's where I've been hiding the jewels you . . . umm . . . borrow, why haven't you taken them back again?"

Violet looked at her with gentle reproach. "Sophie, you keep your private correspondence in that desk, and I would never go through your things! Why, that would be quite improper." An almost wicked gleam came into her eye. "Besides, stealing things from you wouldn't be any fun. Too easy."

"Aren't you the least bit sorry for what you've done?"

"Of course I am, sweeting. I was only teasing you."

Sophie was doubtful on that point. She leaned forward in her chair and clasped her hands together, hoping that this time she could impress upon Violet just how serious her affliction was, and how dire the consequences if she were caught. "Auntie, you must stop this. Really you must. Think of the scandal if anyone found out. You could be arrested and sent to prison."

"What, an old woman like me? Whose cousin is a viscount? They wouldn't."

"The viscount is the one whose jewels you just stole. I hardly think Lord Fortescue would look kindly upon—"

"Victor and Katherine would never bring a charge of theft against me. They are quite fond of me. And they would hate a scandal. Besides, we're supposed to go to their house in Berkshire for Ascot Week when your mother comes, so I can return the necklace just as easily as I took it in the first place."

Sophie did not want to be reminded of her mother's impending visit from Yorkshire, nor did she wish to be diverted from the subject at hand. "That is not the point. Besides, I'm not letting you have those emeralds back for a moment."

"Then you can do it. I have every confidence that we'll manage to get the emeralds back to her somehow. We'll make her think she had them all along and it will all seem convincing."

"And in future? If you keep taking things, you will eventually be caught."

Violet smiled. "You worry too much about me, Sophie. The one to be concerned with is that poor police inspector. We really need to think about how to protect him from this assassin."

Sophie gave up. She didn't know why she'd even bothered to attempt a discussion with Auntie about the emeralds. On the other hand, she didn't want to talk about Inspector Dunbar, either.

"Grimstock said that the police inspector was alive," Violet went on, "but that was all he knew."

Sophie did not reply, but Violet continued to look at her across the table, waiting for details, and she capitulated. "He's fine. Someone shot at him with a gun, but missed."

"Thank heaven. Still, it must have been dreadful for the poor man."

Sophie thought of his threats of the night before and found it hard to feel much compassion for Inspector Dunbar just now.

"How fortunate that you warned him," Violet said. "But the assassin will surely try again."

"Auntie, he's fine. My dream did come true, but with a much better result than I had foreseen. Inspector Dunbar is alive, for the moment his life is not in danger, and he is no longer our responsibility."

"Sophie, I don't know how you can say that. Yesterday you were worried sick about him. Today, you seem quite callous."

Sophie stared down at her teacup and did not reply. Dunbar's words of last night echoed back to her.

I will uncover everything there is to know about you and every member of your family.

Dunbar would surely arrest Auntie if he caught her taking anything. Even if he wasn't that cruel, was he discreet? Auntie might not have money, but she had an impeccable reputation. Eccentricity was one thing, but kleptomania was something else. If people found out, Violet would be ruined.

Auntie wasn't the only one to consider. There was Grimstock. She knew Grimmy had reformed and was perfectly trustworthy, but she doubted family and friends would agree. And what lodgers wanted to stay in a house where there was a former criminal?

Then, of course, there was Harold. Sophie knew her sister's husband was taking money out of the trust funds of some of his clients. She wasn't much concerned for his well-being, but he and Charlotte had five children. What would happen to her sister and the children if Dunbar dragged Harold off to prison? More scandal, more humiliation for the family.

Everybody has secrets, luv. Everybody.

Sophie knew that better than anyone, and right

now, the burden of knowing other people's secrets weighed heavy. She rested her elbows on the table and rubbed her eyes with the tips of her fingers. Why, oh why, couldn't she just be an ordinary person with an ordinary life?

"Sophie, what is the matter?" Violet asked. "The police inspector is alive, yet you look as if the world is ending. Perhaps you should see Doctor Wayneflete about a tonic."

Sophie wished a tonic were the answer. "I'm just a bit tired this morning. That's all." She reached for the first letter on her pile of correspondence, opened it, and scanned the first few lines with growing dismay. She groaned aloud and met Violet's inquiring gaze. "Mama is matchmaking again."

Violet made a sound of sympathy. "She always does when she comes down to visit. You know that."

"Yes, but she writes that this time she wants to stay with us. You know how dreadful it was two years ago, when Charlotte's house was being painted and Mama had to stay here."

"I do remember." Violet nodded in agreement. Though she loved her sister, she had an opinion similar to Sophie's on the subject of Agatha's visits. "But Agatha always stays in Hampstead with Charlotte so she can see the grandchildren. Why, this time, does she want to stay with us?"

Sophie glanced through the letter again. "Mama writes that with each passing year, my spinsterhood becomes a more and more serious concern to her, and she is sure the reason for my affliction—" Sophie paused and winced. "She makes it sound as if

I have a disease. My affliction is due to a lack of social activity. Because of the Queen's Diamond Jubilee, she thinks this is the perfect time for her to supervise my social schedule. She is lengthening this visit to two months—what a dreadful prospect— and she has discussed her plans with Cousin Katherine already." Sophie paused again and looked at Auntie in horror. "They want to take me out everywhere and introduce me to proper young gentlemen during Jubilee. Oh, Auntie, this is more than dreadful. It's torture."

"Sophie, you have to expect your mother to do matchmaking on your behalf while she's here. And, you know, dear," she added gently, "you don't really make much of an effort to meet any young men. I have often worried about you on that score myself."

"You have?"

"Of course. But, unlike Agatha, I understand and appreciate your feelings in this matter. Charles meant a great deal to you, and his disgraceful and callous behavior—"

"It wasn't his fault," Sophie interrupted. "What shall we do about Mama? She can't stay with us. She'll put the servants in a dither again. If they discover that she's staying with us, they'll probably resign."

"There are my meetings with the London Society for the Investigation of Psychic Phenomena to consider, as well. Your mother hates spiritualism. She's so very High Church, you know, since she married Mr. Bedford, because he's a vicar. Why, we won't even be able to have a séance while she's here. Something must be done."

Sophie was in complete agreement. Her mother's personality was rather like a railway train, running over anything in her path. She strongly disapproved of Auntie's little society and would insist on an immediate halt to the séances, readings, and discussions that were Violet's greatest pleasure.

She would take every opportunity to change Sophie's state of spinsterhood to one of matrimonial bliss, smothering her with Jubilee cotillions, balls, and card parties. If Sophie failed to become engaged within the next two months to a gentleman her mother deemed suitable, Agatha would spend another year expressing her deep disappointment with her unsatisfactory younger daughter, and laud her elder daughters's matrimonial success to the skies.

There was also the matter of Inspector Dunbar to be considered. Agatha would be horrified to have the police nosing about. She would be sure to place the blame on poor Auntie, and might even be scandalized enough by the whole business to insist on Sophie's return to Yorkshire. That would be a fate worse than death.

"When does she arrive?" Violet asked, breaking into Sophie's thoughts.

"Tomorrow, at three o'clock. She says Charlotte has already planned a dinner party for that evening, so we will simply go on to their house from the train station and return here to Mayfair afterward. You see? She isn't even here yet, and she is trying to run my life."

"Tomorrow?" Violet cried. "Heavens, what can we do about this on such short notice?"

"I have the feeling Mother's short notice was deliberate." Sophie set the letter aside, thinking hard. If only there was a way to force her mother to stay with Charlotte. "Auntie, we have only one unused bedroom at present, is that right?"

"I don't know, dear. I rely on you to handle these things."

Sophie hadn't expected an answer; she was merely thinking out loud. "If that room were let immediately to a lodger, there would be nowhere for Mother to sleep. Then she would have to stay with Charlotte and Harold in Hampstead. We simply have to find a tenant to take that room before Mother arrives tomorrow."

"Excellent suggestion," her aunt said with approval. "I'm sure the spirits will guide us in finding someone suitable. I'll send a letter to Charlotte by runner to let her know the circumstances, which should make her happy. She probably wasn't pleased to learn Agatha was staying with us in any case."

"Charlotte is never happy," Sophie said dryly. Her elder sister had made her childhood a torture, calling her a freak and ridiculing her at every opportunity. Charlotte was now married, and Harold was a wealthy lawyer and eminently respectable, even if he was a criminal. Charlotte had children, possessed a lovely ten-bedroom house, and was the reigning queen of Hampstead's social circle, all of which gave her little time these days to torment her younger sister.

Sophie was quite glad for Charlotte's good fortune.

"Miss Sophie?"

Grimstock's voice interrupted, and both women

looked up to find the butler standing in the doorway.

"That police inspector is here," he said, his voice heavy with disapproval. Sophie opened her mouth to tell him to inform Inspector Dunbar that both she and her aunt were out, but Violet forestalled her.

"Oh, how lovely!" Violet exclaimed. "I will be able to meet him. Show him into the conservatory. It's such a lovely morning, and it will be delightful to receive him there."

"Auntie, why did you say we would see him?" Sophie asked after Grimstock left the dining room. "What possessed you?"

"Why shouldn't we see him?" Violet looked at her in bewilderment. "We have a humanitarian interest in his welfare."

Sophie said nothing.

"If you are not feeling up to callers today, I'll tell him you're indisposed," Violet said as she rose from the table. "I'll see him alone."

"No!" Sophie jumped to her feet, knowing she couldn't let her aunt visit with that man alone. God only knew what secrets he'd worm out of Violet if he had the chance. She followed her aunt down to the conservatory, where Dunbar was waiting for them.

He was studying a table of Sophie's prize orchids when they entered the conservatory. He heard their footsteps on the terrazzo floor and turned toward them, straightening to his full height as they approached. He was so tall that the ballerina-skirted fuchsias trailing down from the hanging baskets overhead touched his hair and caressed his broad shoulders, in sharp contrast to his dark hair and the gray morning suit, white shirt, and navy silk tie he wore.

He was such a large man and so powerfully built that he seemed to utterly dominate the feminine environment around him. Against the backdrop of soft pastoral frescoes and delicate ferns, surrounded by statues and flowers, he was such a stalwart presence of masculine strength and implacability that Sophie caught her breath. Her steps faltered, and she stumbled to a halt, staring at him.

Violet, however, seemed delighted to see the dreadful man, and she came forward to greet him with ease. "So, you are Sophie's dream man." She looked him over with approval and completely feminine appreciation for a moment, then ushered him to one of the cushioned wicker chairs that looked out over the rose garden. She seated herself on the wicker settee opposite and added, "She didn't tell me how handsome you were."

A modest man, a man of breeding, would have been embarrassed by such a compliment. Dunbar laughed, leaning back in his chair, looking completely at ease. "Thank you, ma'am."

Sophie sat down right beside her aunt. She didn't want to visit with him or watch him bask in Violet's admiration like a well-fed lion in the sun, but she had no choice. She must protect Auntie and make sure he didn't weasel any information out of her that was none of his business.

"Dunbar is a Scottish name," Violet commented in a conversational tone. "Is there by chance Irish in your ancestry?"

"I have no idea," he replied.

Sophie received a sudden flash of insight. "Mr. Dunbar is an orphan, Auntie."

Dunbar turned his head, giving Sophie a look of surprise. "I was orphaned as a boy," he admitted. "But how did you know that, Miss Haversham?"

Violet laughed. "Oh, Inspector, Sophie knows so many things about people, it's uncanny. You are already aware of how she warned you that your life was in danger, so you can see she has dreams about the future. She can even sense people's thoughts."

"Is that so, ma'am?" he asked politely and returned to their former subject. "To answer your question, I never knew my parents, and I don't know very much about my ancestry. But my Christian name is Michael, and my friends call me Mick, which is definitely Irish. Why do you ask if my ancestry is Irish?"

"You have Irish eyes. Blue, with those thick black lashes. Put in by an angel with a smutty finger. You know the saying, I'm sure."

"I have heard it before, ma'am." He turned his head and met Sophie's steady gaze with a smile. "I may not be able to read people's thoughts, but I can guess yours at this moment, Miss Haversham. I don't think you want to discuss my eyes."

"You are correct, sir."

He smiled at the primness in her voice. "We could discuss yours," he murmured. "Brown, like chocolate. I'm quite fond of chocolate."

There was something in the way he said the word *chocolate*—slowly, as if savoring the remembered taste of it—that was quite improper.

Her face grew hot.

"Tell me, Inspector," Violet said, not seeming to notice her niece's discomfiture, "have you any idea who is threatening your life?"

"He thinks I'm the one who shot at him, Auntie, or that I know who did. He thinks that I or someone I know goes around shooting innocent people in parks in the middle of the night for no apparent reason. He thinks there is no way I could have known an attempt would be made on his life unless I were involved."

Violet did not seem offended by that. She actually laughed and shook her head at Dunbar as if he were a naughty child. "You don't believe in psychic ability, Inspector?"

"I confess that when your niece first came to me yesterday, I was skeptical of her story. It did sound far-fetched."

"That's because you don't know Sophie," Violet answered. "If you did, you would know how accurate her predictions are, and would have believed her at once. Spirits work through her."

"It's no use, Auntie," Sophie said. "Inspector Dunbar is a nonbeliever. He thinks people like you and I are quite mad."

"Your niece misunderstands me," Dunbar protested, smiling in the face of Sophie's annoyance, which only annoyed her more. "I know that there are many baffling things in life," he went on, "things that cannot always be explained by conventional means."

Violet laughed. "That's a polite way of saying you are a nonbeliever, Mr. Dunbar."

"Perhaps," he admitted, laughing with her.

Sophie seemed to be the only one who didn't find it amusing.

"I understand you take in lodgers here, Mrs. Summerstreet," he said, changing the subject.

"That is so, yes. We have four lodgers at present. Two of them are spiritualists like myself. We hold meetings every other Friday night to discuss the phenomena in and around London. I believe you would find it quite fascinating, even though you are a nonbeliever. Last night we discussed the ghosts of Apsley House at great length."

"Really?" he said in a conversational tone. "How interesting. Are there ghosts in Apsley House?"

His pretended interest in the subject of spiritualism was galling enough, but as Auntie answered him, Sophie sensed his interest in the subject had a deeper purpose than simply making conversation. His next question proved it.

"Did all four of your lodgers attend this meeting?" he asked. "And how long did it last?"

He was trying to find out what everyone had been up to when the shot had been fired at him, and Sophie realized this might be her chance to be rid of him. Perhaps if he knew no one in her household could have done it, he'd go away and leave them alone.

"The colonel didn't attend, of course," Violet answered. "He plays dominoes with Mr. Shelton, the neighbor who lives behind us, on those nights. Mr. Dawes was out as well, at a coffeehouse in Chelsea with his friends, a place called Kelly's, if I remember what he said when he left last night. They were studying, I believe, since his examinations are in June. He's a medical student, you see."

She saw Violet smile at Dunbar, and she realized Auntie liked him, a fact that baffled her. "Like you," Violet continued, "Edward and the colonel are nonbelievers. But Miss Peabody, Miss Atwood, Mrs. Shelton, myself, and two of our other neighbors attended the meeting here. Sophie, of course, had gone to see you and make sure you were still alive. Our meeting lasted from half past eight to about eleven. When Sophie came home, we were just finishing our coffee."

Seeming to be satisfied by that explanation of everyone's whereabouts, Dunbar glanced at his surroundings, then returned his attention to Violet. "You have a beautiful home. It must be a very pleasant place for your lodgers to live."

Sophie stiffened, her suspicions about him sharpening again. Why was he buttering up Auntie? What did he want?

"Thank you," Violet replied, sounding pleased. "Sophie runs things, of course, but both of us think of the people who stay here as family, and we try to provide them with all the comforts of a home."

"Your lodgers are fortunate, ma'am. You seem to be concerned with their welfare. I wish my landlady had that same sense of consideration about her tenants. She doesn't much care about those of us who live in her lodging house, I'm sorry to say."

Somehow, Sophie felt a sudden empathy with Mrs. Tribble.

"Your lodgings are disagreeable to you?" Violet asked him.

"They are, ma'am, I must confess. But finding an affordable flat in London that is clean and respectable is a nearly impossible task. I make do."

Violet sighed. "It must be horrible to live in unpleasant surroundings."

Sophie heard the innocent tone of her aunt's voice, and she knew what was coming. "Oh, no!" she cried, horrified by what Violet was intending to do. "Auntie, no, he can't stay here!"

Dunbar was looking at Violet in surprise, but when he glanced at Sophie, she understood he'd had this in mind all along. "Are you offering me a room here, Mrs. Summerstreet?" he asked, returning his attention to Violet.

"No, she isn't." Sophie scowled at him. "She is most definitely not offering you a room."

"But, darling, it's perfect all round," Violet said. "So perfect, in fact, that I am certain the spirits have arranged it. I told you they would send us someone today."

"It's not perfect," Sophie said, panicking as she thought of Cousin Katherine's stolen necklace tucked in the secret drawer of her secretaire. "It's not perfect," she repeated with emphasis. "It's a disaster."

"But finding someone to take that last room before your mother arrives was your idea."

"Yes, Auntie, I know, but letting the room to Inspector Dunbar isn't what I had in mind.

"If Mr. Dunbar takes the last bedroom in the house," Violet went on as if her niece had not spoken, "dear Agatha will have to stay with Charlotte."

"I know, but—"

"We'll once again have the income from that room, which is always welcome, and we won't even have to pay for advertisements in the papers. I thought you'd welcome this, dear. You are always so concerned about our finances. And you won't have to deal with your mother's presence twenty-four hours a day."

"Yes, but—"

"Mr. Dunbar will have a decent place to live, and we will be able to watch over him so no one tries again to kill him."

"Yes, Auntie, but he thinks one of *us* is trying to kill him," she said, finally managing to make her point. She glared at the man across from her, who was sitting back in his chair listening to their discussion, silent and looking quite pleased with himself. "He thinks one of us is a murderer."

Her aunt looked at her with an indulgent smile. "Inspector Dunbar knows now that it was impossible for any of us to shoot at him. Besides, this is the perfect way for you to fulfill your responsibility to help him determine who is trying to kill him."

"Someone *is* trying to kill him!" she shot back. "That is the material point. It's not safe for us to have him here." Only she seemed to appreciate how true that was.

Violet studied her with a frown of concern. "Sophie, you're becoming overwrought. It's due to lack of sleep, I'm sure. Take some valerian tonight, dear, and you'll sleep better."

"Auntie, didn't you hear me? Having him here would be dangerous."

"If someone wants to kill him, I hardly think they will come breaking into our house to do so." She turned to Dunbar, who had not spoken during their discussion of him. "What is your opinion? If you were to take a room here, do you believe the villain trying to kill you would be any threat to us?"

"I doubt it," he answered. "Given your niece's dream, this person seems to have no connection with your household, and it would not serve him to inflict harm on any of you."

"Of course that's what you'd say," Sophie said through clenched teeth. "It's so self-serving."

"Sophie!" Violet turned her head to look at her niece. "What an extraordinary remark. What has gotten into you?"

Sophie bit her lip at the rebuke and fell silent.

"It is most likely," Dunbar went on, "that the assassin will come after me when I am alone, probably by another gunshot in the park or some other isolated area. Man, like all other animals, is not very original."

Violet nodded. "So you do believe he will try again?"

"Yes, ma'am. I think he will try again. And again, and again." He paused for what was clearly dramatic effect. "He will try until he succeeds."

"We must see that does not happen, Inspector, and that this fiend is caught and punished. If you are willing, I will have Hannah prepare a room for you, and you may stay with us as long as you wish. I hope three guineas a week is acceptable to you?"

Sophie looked at her aunt helplessly, knowing there was nothing she could say to prevent Auntie's awful idea from becoming reality. She glanced over at Michael Dunbar and found that he was watching her.

Beneath those thick black lashes, his eyes glimmered with amusement. He was laughing at her. It was galling. He looked like the cat who'd gotten into the cream pitcher. "My guardian angel," he said.

Sophie had a very unangelic impulse to throw the nearest pot of orchids at his head.

Five

～

Mick left Mrs. Summerstreet's house quite pleased. Things couldn't have worked out better for his plans. He returned to the Yard and requested that Thacker interview the serving girls at Kelly's Coffee House in Chelsea, and Violet's neighbors, the Sheltons. While these tasks were handled, Mick completed paperwork on two cases that needed to be closed out, then went upstairs to his newly painted office to make sure the walls weren't really chartreuse. He was glad to find them the same shade of eggshell white they had been before.

He then left the Yard and went in search of the hansom driver who had taken Sophie and her butler to his flat the night before. Since Mick had noted the cab's number the previous night, it didn't take him long to locate the driver. According to his account, he had dri-

ven Sophie and her butler from the Mayfair house to
Scotland Yard, then through the Embankment to
Mick's flat. The driver told him the cab had never
entered the Embankment Gardens. Other than when
Sophie had gone inside Scotland Yard to obtain Mick's
address, the driver swore that neither of his passengers
had left the carriage until it had stopped in front of
Mrs. Tribble's house.

That afternoon Mick met with Thacker, who confirmed that Violet, Josephine Atwood, and Hermione
Peabody had not been out of Mrs. Shelton's sight from
half past eight to eleven o'clock the night before. The
Colonel had been with Mr. Shelton. None of them could
have been in the Embankment at half past nine. The
same was true of Mr. Dawes. A young man working at
the coffeehouse the previous evening verified that
Dawes had been there from eight to well past midnight.

Mrs. Shelton had also confirmed the presence in the
house of the two female servants. Both the cook and
the maid had been seen many times during the evening
by those in the drawing room. Mick didn't see how
either of them could have slipped away long enough to
get to the Embankment, shoot at him, and return
home without her absence being noticed.

Mick went to his lodgings and packed a few of his
things. Not all of them, since he wasn't giving up his
flat. For now, however, Violet's house would give him
access to Sophie's acquaintances, and that was the only
way he was going to find out who had shot at him the
night before. He arrived on Mrs. Summerstreet's
doorstep just about teatime.

In his experience, no one was ever happy to see a

policeman, and Mick was accustomed to distress and resentment whenever he made inquiries into a crime. A detective moving into this house would be regarded as far worse, so when Violet's butler opened the front door to him for the second time that day, he expected an even colder reception from the fellow than he had received this morning. He was not disappointed.

Albert Grimstock had clearly been informed of the newest lodger, and he greeted Mick's arrival with all the frigidity of a Russian winter. He looked at Mick, then glanced down at the two worn leather valises by the door and raised one eyebrow in disapproval. "Wait here," he said and closed the door.

After a few minutes, the front door opened again, and Grimstock motioned Mick inside. "It is teatime, Inspector," the butler said coldly. "Would you prefer to be shown to your room or to take tea with the others?"

"I'll have tea," Mick replied.

The butler's expression became more pinched than before. He informed Mick that his things would be taken upstairs to his room in due course, accepted Mick's felt homburg hat, then led him to the drawing room, where six people were partaking of India tea, tomato sandwiches, and cream cakes.

Sophie was standing by the fireplace. She wore a white shirtwaist and pastel striped skirt. Her hair was swept up in a pile of curls and held in place atop her head by a pair of silver combs. She looked as sweet and delicious as a petit four, but the resentful look she gave him told Mick she wasn't all sweet over him. It also made him more convinced than ever that she was protecting someone from his investigations. But who was she protecting?

Everyone else stood up as he was announced, and Violet came forward to greet him, as pleasant and amiable as she had been that morning. She introduced him to the other lodgers and invited him to sit down beside her on the settee. As she poured him out a cup of tea, adding lemon and sugar at his request, Mick took the opportunity to study the others in the room.

Colonel Richard Abercrombie was a large, elderly man whose erect carriage, waxed mustache, and tanned, weathered face indicated him to be retired army, probably India. He gave Mick a hard stare as if thinking him an impudent young pup, then he sat back down in his chair and retreated behind the *Times*.

Miss Hermione Peabody was short and stout, with an amiable, sheeplike face, and Miss Josephine Atwood was tall and lean. Both were clearly proper spinsters whose slightly shabby clothes spoke of limited means.

Edward Dawes, he was told, studied medicine at London University Hospital, but the fellow looked more in need of medical attention than most patients did. He was thin to the point of emaciation, with a grayish complexion and a manner that was both nervous and supercilious, which wouldn't inspire the confidence of his patients when he became a practicing physician.

Though Violet's and Hermione's greetings had been warm and friendly, an awkward silence fell after his new landlady handed him his tea and passed him the sandwiches. Mick could feel the apprehension in the room, which he knew meant nothing at all. People were often nervous in the presence of police officers, and it seldom had anything to do with a crime.

"Grimstock will take your things upstairs, Inspector," Violet told him, breaking the silence. "After tea, one of us will show you your room."

The colonel made a huffing sound of disapproval from behind his paper. Violet ignored it. "I hope you will like your room," she continued. "If there is anything you need, please ask."

"Thank you, ma'am."

"Violet, dear, are you truly certain Agatha will agree to stay with Charlotte during her visit?" Miss Peabody asked.

"Of course she's certain," Miss Atwood answered in her deep bass voice before Violet could do so. "If Agatha stayed here, where would she sleep? The roof?"

Violet turned to Mick and explained, "My sister, Sophie's mother, is coming for a two-month visit, and she wanted to stay with us, but I'm afraid that's impossible because you are here, so she will be staying with her other daughter, Charlotte."

"Much to everyone's delight," Edward Dawes said, laughing.

"Really, Edward," Violet rebuked him with a frown. "You mustn't say such things."

"Why not?" the young man countered with a shrug. "It's true. None of us enjoy her company or want her here, not even you."

"Violet, dear," Miss Peabody spoke to cover Dawes's blunt statement, "what plans have you to entertain your sister?"

"There are dozens of things on for Jubilee," Violet replied, "so we've a great many choices, but I thought we would start by taking her to Ascot for the week of the races. Our cousin, Lord Fortescue, has a box there, as you know, and his estate is in Berkshire." She smiled at Mick. "Perhaps you would care to accompany us, Inspector?"

"I'm sure Ascot's much too pretentious for Mr. Dunbar," Sophie interjected before Mick could reply. "He prefers Epsom."

Mick had to admit that was true, but she only knew it because of his question to her the night before about the races at Epsom, not because she had some sort of psychic ability.

"Besides," Sophie went on, "any invitation to Lord Fortescue's Berkshire estate for Ascot Week should be made by him, Auntie, not by us."

"When did you become such a stickler for etiquette, dear?" Violet said with some surprise. "Victor won't mind."

"Katherine will."

"Probably," Violet was forced to concede with a sigh. "But, Sophie, really, how can you protect the inspector from the fiend who wishes to kill him if he is not nearby?"

Mick wanted to laugh at the notion of Sophie Haversham trying to protect him. He'd grown up in the toughest slums of London, and she lived amid the pampered of Mayfair. He was a policeman, she was a young lady. He was a man, she was a woman, he stood seven inches taller and about six stone heavier than she. Protect him? The idea was ludicrous.

Sophie was watching him. "Does something about the idea of my protection amuse you, Inspector?"

"Not at all," he said, turning his smile on her. "After all, you are my guardian angel."

Before she could reply, Mick turned to Violet. "I enjoy race-meetings very much, ma'am, and I would be happy to accept your invitation, but I do not wish to impose on your cousin."

"I'll write to Victor and get his permission for you to come for the week," Violet said and beamed at Sophie. "There, dear, another obstacle cleared away. It's quite obvious that the spirits want you to protect the inspector from harm."

Mick smiled in a joking fashion. "Do you think Miss Haversham could help us win a bit of sterling and tell us who the winner is before each race begins?"

"Sometimes she does try, Inspector," Violet assured him. "But only when no one places a bet."

"It seems the spirits don't wish me to profit from their guidance," Sophie told him. Her voice was bland, but there was defiance in the look she gave him, as if daring him to contradict the whole theory of spiritualism in front of the women present who firmly believed in it.

He had no intention of doing so. Instead, he turned her question back on her. "Do you believe the spirits guide you?"

"Of course."

Something told him she didn't believe in spirits any more than he did, a fact he found intriguing, but he was given no chance to pursue the subject.

"Violet told us she received you in the conservatory," Miss Peabody said. "What do you think of Sophie's tropical forest?"

"It's beautiful." He glanced at Sophie. "It must take a great deal of your time?"

She did not reply, so Violet spoke for her. "Gardening, both indoors and out, is my niece's favorite interest. She has quite a passion for flowers."

"Indeed?" Mick turned to Sophie with a smile. "I hope all your suitors are aware of this . . . umm . . . passion?"

She blushed a deep pink. "I don't have any suitors."

"Oh, Sophie, dear, of course you do!" Violet said, laughing. "There's Mr. Collier at the bank. Why, every time you go in there, he insists on being the one to wait on you. There's Mr. Shelton's son, Geoffrey, and Lord Heath's son, Robert."

Mick filed those names away in his memory to investigate those men later, as Violet went on, "All of them adore you, Sophie. Why, I'm sure if you let any one of them—"

"Since you seem so interested in flowers, Mr. Dunbar, perhaps you would like to see the garden?" Sophie interrupted, desperation in her voice. "I'll show it to you, if you like."

She wasn't asking him to the garden because she wanted the pleasure of his company, but that didn't bother him in the least. Perhaps he could goad her into accidentally letting some useful scrap of information slip out. He set down his teacup. "Any man would be happy to walk in the garden with you, Miss Haversham. I am honored by your charming invitation."

At his gallant words, Violet beamed with obvious

pleasure, Miss Peabody giggled, and even the sharp-faced Miss Atwood condescended to smile at him.

Sophie pressed her lips tight together, turned around, and started out the door without a word, beckoning him to follow her with an impatient wave of her hand.

"Sophie," Violet called after them as they left the drawing room, "if you are going out to the garden, would you do the flowers for dinner? I noticed the bourbon roses are in bloom. We might have some of those as a centerpiece."

"Of course, Auntie," Sophie called back as she stalked down the hallway, her heels churning up the muslin flounces of her lace-trimmed petticoat as she walked. Mick noticed that in the middle of the row of buttons down her back, one button had come undone, showing him a bit of the white lace corset underneath. He smiled, knowing she didn't have a clue she was giving him a peek at her undergarments.

He followed her to the kitchens at the back of the house, where she paused in the butler's pantry to don an apron, grab a basket, and put a pair of cutting shears in her apron pocket before she walked out the back door.

Mick continued to follow her, staring at her back and appreciating the artistic qualities of a woman's undone buttons as Sophie led him across a small expanse of lawn. They stepped onto a flagstone path that wove through the colorful landscape of a true English garden coming into bloom. The garden was surrounded on three sides by a high stone wall, which blocked out most of the urban noise of London and locked in the sweet, heavy fragrance of flowers.

He followed her down the path, but they had barely taken half a dozen steps before she turned around to face him. "My suitors are none of your business. Must you poke and pry into my private life?"

"You said you didn't have any suitors."

"The point I'm making is that I know what you are trying to do. You're asking questions in a way that sounds like casual conversation, but is really interrogation." Her eyes narrowed. "It's insulting, and it's futile. How could any suitors I have possibly concern you?"

"I judge what concerns me, Miss Haversham. If I think something might be relevant to my investigations, I will pursue it, and I really don't care if you find that uncomfortable."

Sophie placed her basket on the stone path, grabbed her shears out of her apron pocket, and began snipping half-opened roses from the closest bushes, dropping them into her basket as she worked. "You learned everyone's whereabouts when you were here this morning, and you must know now that we've all told you the truth. You finagled that invitation to move in here, but you wouldn't have acted on it if you still suspected one of us was trying to kill you."

"So?"

"So you are now going to try to find out all you can about my friends and acquaintances, and take guesses as to which of them might be your suspect. You want to know about my possible suitors because, if it's not one of us, you think it must be someone else I know. How accurate am I thus far?"

"You're very perceptive."

She shot him a wry look. "It's not perception. It's knowledge. There's a difference."

"What do you mean?"

"I told you, sometimes I can tell what people are thinking. I know what you are up to, and I brought you out here to tell you in private that I don't appreciate your motives."

"But why do you think it's futile? Do you really think no one you know is capable of murder? Are you that naive?"

"It's not about naivete. I know whoever tried to kill you has nothing to do with me. It has something to do with you."

"What evidence do you have?"

She didn't answer that. Instead, she picked up her basket and turned to continue along the path.

He watched her as she walked away. She still insisted she could see the future and read people's thoughts. He wondered if he'd been right in the first place. Maybe she really was off her onion.

She paused a dozen feet away and bent down to cut some sprays of bright yellow flowers, and when she straightened again, he grinned. Another of her buttons had come undone.

He wondered if he should offer to fasten them for her. The sway of her hips as she continued on down the path made that notion even more tempting. The bright sunlight backlit her body as she walked and gave him the shadowy outline of her legs through her skirts, legs that he remembered from his explorations the night before were long and shapely. Without that petticoat, though, he'd be seeing more than just a vague silhouette. "Damn," he murmured, "I wish women didn't wear so many clothes."

She stopped and turned around. "What are you doing way back there?" she called.

Mick tried to shove thoughts of her legs out of his mind as he walked to where she was standing. He reminded himself that she was a suspected conspirator in a plot to kill him, and that she was probably loony, but that didn't divert him from wanting to run his hands down those long legs of hers, to caress the sensitive skin at the backs of her knees. He took a deep breath. "How do you read people's minds?"

"I just do," she answered. "What someone else is thinking simply enters my head, as if that person were talking to me."

There was no way she was telling the truth. If she could read his mind right now, she'd slap his face.

"I really don't care whether you believe me or not," she went on. "What I do care about are your actions. Probing into our lives, asking questions about our friends, digging up rumor and innuendo, all for naught. Eventually you'll be forced to accept that no one we know had anything to do with the person who shot at you. Why don't you just go away?"

"Don't worry, Sophie. I might get killed before I find out any of your secrets."

"I don't want to see anyone die!" she cried. "That's why I went to Scotland Yard in the first place. I just don't understand why you feel the need to invade our privacy."

"Why does my presence worry you so much? Who are you trying to protect?" He took a step closer to her.

She moved as well, stepping off the curved stone path and straight back into an enormous brier of roses. She was trapped.

"C'mon, Sophie, tell me the truth." He reached out, pulling the basket from her hand before she realized his intent. He tossed the basket aside, ignoring her cry of indignation as flowers spilled across the ground.

He moved his body closer to her, and once again she stepped back, tangling herself more deeply in the brier. Pink petals fluttered down, and one caught on the silver hair comb by her ear.

He lifted his hand to her hair, and his fingertips brushed the velvety skin of her ear as he reached for the rose petal. She stiffened, her body going as rigid as one of those silly cupid statues in her conservatory. He could hear her rapid breathing and feel her desperation to escape, but amid the thorny branches, she dared not move. Slowly, he pulled the petal from her hair.

Mingling with the scent of roses was that elusive, erotic perfume she wore. What was it in that fragrance that aroused him so? Mick inhaled deeply and bent his head closer. "What's your secret, Sophie?" he murmured, brushing the rose petal beneath her chin. "A lover?"

"Don't—" She paused and turned her face away. She drew a deep, trembling breath. "Don't do that."

"You can tell me the truth," he whispered against her ear, and he felt her shiver. "Is it a lover you're protecting?"

"Stop it." There was panic in her voice as she flattened her hands against his chest and pushed at him.

Mick relented a bit, stepping back enough to give her a little breathing room.

She turned her face toward him, leaning her head back to look him in the eye. "You think this is about me, someone I know, but you're wrong. It has something to do with you."

"So you've said. Again, what's your evidence?"

"Do I need evidence? You are a policeman. You move within the lowest classes, dealing with fiends of the underworld all the time." She made a sound of contempt. "No doubt you've forgotten the manners of good society, because you treat everyone like a criminal. It's barbaric."

She spoke of him and his occupation with the contempt of a good housekeeper talking about black beetles in the larder. He couldn't help laughing. "You think I'm treating you like a criminal?"

"Aren't you?"

"No, luv. The way I deal with criminals is to torture them on the rack."

"That does not surprise me."

He put his hands on her waist and moved closer, catching that fragrance again. "You, I'd interrogate very differently."

"Let me go."

He knew he wasn't going to get any more information out of her just now, but he couldn't seem to move away. Beneath his hands, he could feel the whalebone pattern of her stays and the smooth coolness of her muslin apron, and he imagined her in his hands without all that fabric in the way. The thought made him burn, and he wondered if maybe he was the crazy one here.

He stepped back, letting his hands fall to his sides. Sophie started to move past him but had only taken one step before the sound of tearing fabric made her pause. Her skirt was caught on the thorns of the roses behind her.

Mick started to reach down to assist her, but she jerked her skirt free before he could do so, tearing the fabric even more. Free of the thorns, she stepped around him and walked to the basket he had tossed aside. She knelt beside it. "Do you manhandle all the women you meet?" she asked as she began putting the roses he had spilled back into the basket.

He started to deny it, but inconvenient memories of the night before flashed across his mind. He *had* manhandled her. Worse, he wanted to do it again. He thought again of those long, long legs. He imagined the taste of those lips. Sweet like cherries, he'd bet.

He caught himself up sharply at the dangerous direction his thoughts kept taking with this woman. He wasn't here to bed her, for God's sake. She knew who wanted him dead. She might even be behind the whole thing. If he let himself be persuaded of her innocence in all this, he could very well end up a corpse. No woman, no matter how luscious, was worth dying for.

"It isn't that I think of you as a criminal," he said. "But to me, your actions are suspicious. You are involved in all this somehow. That's a fact."

"Yes, I know that better than anyone," she said with a bitter edge to her voice. "I haven't had any more premonitions about your death. If I do, I'll be sure to tell you, despite your disbelief."

He knelt beside her. "I don't deal in premonitions. I deal in facts, in truth, in things that can be proved."

She gave a short, humorless laugh. "I've known that, sir, from the moment we met."

She reached for the last flower, dropped it in the basket, and started to stand, but something caught her attention, and she knelt down again. "Damnation!"

The unexpected curse from a woman who had just accused him of forgetting the manners of good society made him chuckle under his breath.

He watched as she leaned forward and began pulling at some sort of vine that was tangled around one of her roses. She yanked the roots of the plant out of the soft, damp earth, and dropped the tangle of vines, roots, and dirt into her basket.

"Part of dinner's centerpiece?" he asked.

"Bindweed," she answered with loathing. "It's irritating, persistent, and invasive." Looking over at him, she added, "A bit like you."

He grinned. "Thank you for the compliment. - You've just listed all the qualities needed for a good detective."

She did not reply. Instead, she continued to pull bindweed out of the ground and away from her flowers with such ruthlessness that Mick couldn't help wondering if she was taking out her frustration with him on helpless plants.

When the weed problem seemed to be solved, Sophie stood up and returned her attention to him. "I don't know anything more than I've told you." She rubbed her fingertips against her cheek in an absent-minded gesture that left a streak of mud on her face.

"I'm not trying to protect anyone, and I've answered every one of your questions truthfully. I can't help it if the truth sounds unbelievable to you."

She sounded so earnest, and she was so clearly unaware of the dirt on her face, that Mick couldn't help smiling.

She saw that smile and stiffened, misinterpreting it. "I see no humor, Inspector, in trying to do the right thing. In going to the police, my only motive was to prevent the murder I envisioned."

"Miss Haversham, I've seen so many fraudulent mediums and spiritualists take advantage of people and exploit their grief over dead loved ones, it's difficult not to be cynical on the subject."

"And you think I'm one of those?"

"I don't know, but I don't believe there are any legitimate fortune-tellers or psychics or mediums. I just don't believe it."

He could tell that his skepticism rankled her, but he couldn't help that. He didn't believe in magic, or wishing on stars, or blissful, everlasting love, either.

She folded her arms, oblivious to the mud she was smearing on her sleeves. "You want to see proof of my ability with your own eyes? Name whatever proof you want. What will convince you that I truly am psychic and that I can see future events, but that I have no idea whatsoever who is trying to kill you? What proof will make you go away for good?"

"I don't know. Perhaps if you stopped evading my questions it would help. If you're not protecting someone, and you're not afraid of what I'll find out, why are you so opposed to my presence here?"

"Because I don't like you."

Her swift, acerbic reply made him laugh. "Then things are going to be a bit difficult for you. After all, we have to see each other every day. And your aunt did invite me to Ascot."

"I don't know what Auntie was thinking." She straightened her arms, bent down, and grabbed her basket. "You at Ascot."

"Don't worry. Despite what you think, I have been known to behave like a gentleman on occasion."

"You'll need more than gentlemanly behavior." She studied him with a critical eye, her head tilted to one side. "You'll need a new suit."

"I might have been born within the sound of the Bow Bells, but even I can manage to find a suit for Ascot."

She bit her lip. "I didn't mean to be insulting. That was rude, and I apologize."

He suddenly wanted to reach out and brush away the streak of mud on her cheek, and he wondered what her reaction would be if he did. Shock, probably. She might be poorer than he, but men of Mick's class did not often get the chance to touch a woman like her. Maybe that was what made the temptation to do so almost irresistible. His mouth went dry, and he tried to remember all the things about her that he didn't like.

She was crazy. She said she could see the future and read people's minds. When she tried to explain things, it took her forever to get to the point. She always walked around with ribbons untied or buttons unfastened, looking as if she'd forgotten to finish getting dressed.

Oh, God.

A tiny frown knit her brows. "Why are you looking at me like that?" she asked, frowning at him.

He'd wager his last quid her cheek was as soft as the petals on those roses in her basket. He started to lift his hand to touch her face.

She knows who's trying to kill me.

Mick thrust his hands in his pockets. "Why don't you show me my room?"

"Very well." She stepped around him and started back up the path to the house without a word. She paused to wash her hands at the pump, then went inside the house. Mick followed her into the kitchen, where she set her basket down on a table. "Marjorie?" she called.

A rotund little woman stuck her head around the corner of the larder. "Aye, Miss Sophie?"

"Put the roses in a vase of water, please, and dispose of the bindweed. I'll arrange the flowers before dinner."

Marjorie nodded and cast an inquiring glance at Mick.

"This is our newest lodger, Detective Inspector Dunbar. Mr. Dunbar, our cook, Marjorie Willard."

Mick did not miss the look of disapproval from the stout little woman, but he had a thick skin.

Sophie led him out of the kitchen, across the foyer, and up the stairs. He followed her, trying not to look at the tantalizing gap of her undone buttons that showed her corset, or the tears in her skirt that revealed her petticoat, but he could not stop thinking about the curvaceous body beneath those lacy underclothes.

They reached the top of the stairs, and she led him to a door halfway down the hall. She opened it, and he followed her into a bedroom nearly the size of his entire flat at Mrs. Tribble's.

His valises had been placed beside the door. The room was done up in blue willow and white, with a plain iron bed, sturdy walnut furnishings, and only one fern. Mick breathed a heartfelt sigh of relief. Unlike the other rooms he had seen in Mrs. Summerstreet's house, this room had no crystal vases, no cabbage rose wallpaper, and no Mechlin lace. There were no pastoral murals, no cherubs, and no pink flowers. Thank God.

Sophie turned to him, and he thought he caught a hint of amusement in her eyes. "I took out the embroidered silk pillows, lace curtains, and beaded flowers," she said, almost as if she really had been able to tell what he was thinking.

"For an unmarried woman, you seem to have an unusual understanding of how men think."

With a little laugh, she said, "Perhaps that is one of the talents of a mind reader, but it hasn't helped me to matrimony, much to my mother's disappointment."

Her tone was light, but Mick could hear a hint of regret behind it. That wasn't surprising, since to most women and their mamas, getting married meant everything.

She cleared her throat and spoke again. "Hannah will bring you early tea every morning around seven if you wish it, and she'll bring you hot water and towels, too. Breakfast is usually between eight and nine o'clock. If you plan to be in for that meal, let Marjorie know the night before."

As she explained the rules of the house in a brisk and efficient way, one of the tiny silver combs fell from her hair. Mick picked it up from the floor and straightened. Reaching out, he grasped the tendril of her hair that had come loose. It felt like threads of silk in his fingers. She stopped talking and stood utterly still as he pinned her hair back in place.

It took everything he had to pull his hands away.

Clearing her throat, she went on, "Tea is usually about four, and dinner at eight. Sheets are changed each week. We will do your laundry for a charge of half a crown per week. The rent is due on the first day of each month, and you pay it to me. If you smoke, please do not do so inside the house. Fridays and Sunday afternoons are the days out for all the servants . . ."

Mick listened to her ramble on, and he couldn't stop thinking about those buttons. He told himself they offended his sense of neatness, but he knew it was a lie. He grasped her shoulders and turned her around, cutting off her talk in midsentence.

"What are you doing?" she gasped.

"You're coming undone." He buttoned her shirtwaist with his eyes closed, taking his time, stripping away the layers of her clothing in his mind and imagining the woman beneath. The smooth planes of her bare shoulders, the dent at the base of her spine, the curve of her buttocks.

He leaned closer to her, inhaling that delicate fragrance she wore, becoming addicted to it. He opened his eyes and let out his breath against her neck, making the short wisps of hair at her nape flutter. "I couldn't let you go back downstairs with your buttons undone. I wouldn't want anyone to think I had made improper advances toward you, or—"

"As I was saying," she interrupted desperately, pulling away the moment he was done buttoning her back up, "the servants' days out are Fridays and Sunday afternoons."

She turned around to face him but fixed her gaze on a point past his left shoulder, her cheeks even pinker than before, her voice even more brisk and efficient. "We fixed it that way because Marjorie and Hannah like to do things together. On Sundays, the servants attend early service, and the rest of us second service, Church of England, just around the corner."

He smiled. She'd told him herself that she rambled when she was nervous. It was true. "I'll try to remember all that," he said when she finally stopped talking.

"Then I'll leave you to unpack." Despite her words, she didn't move. He gave her a questioning look, and she said,

"About Ascot, I hope you aren't planning to interview everyone in Lord Fortescue's box, and ask them all sorts of embarrassing questions."

He would make no promises of that kind. "You're so unhappy about your aunt's invitation to me that perhaps you shouldn't go with us."

"And leave poor Auntie and the others to your questions and implications?" She shook her head and turned to leave. "Never."

He couldn't resist teasing her a bit. "It could be a problem for you, Sophie," he pointed out, following her to the door. "People might think you have a new suitor," he said, his hand curling over hers on the door handle as she tried to turn it. "What a scandal that would be. A merc policeman, a man orphaned as a boy, a man with no family and no connections. They'll be horrified." He leaned closer, his chest against her back, his lips only inches from the dab of mud on her cheek. "They'll talk about us."

She turned her head to meet his gaze, and there was a hard look in those chocolate brown eyes of hers. "I am not a snob, Inspector Dunbar. Despite what you may think, it isn't your station in life that I dislike. It's you."

Mick could resist temptation only so long. He lifted his hand and brushed away the bit of mud on her cheek with the tips of his fingers. Her face was just as soft as he had suspected. "What a pity."

Six

~

Throughout the evening, Inspector Dunbar was charming to Auntie and the other two elderly ladies, and his knowledge of the history of India impressed the colonel enough that the old gentleman actually challenged him to a game of dominoes. Dawes seemed uncomfortable with his presence and left just after dinner to meet with his study group.

Sophie wished she could escape as well, but she didn't dare. All evening, she felt tense and on guard. Until she could return the necklace, she had to find a safe place for it, and, as Auntie had pointed out, her desk was not a safe place. Dunbar was certain to search it, and a policeman must know all about secret drawers. On Monday she could take the necklace to the bank for safekeeping, but until then, she had to find a new place for it. She couldn't carry it about with her or she would surely lose it.

After dinner, while the men played dominoes and the ladies watched the game, Sophie settled herself in the library with a book, waiting until everyone retired for the night. She stared down at the book in her hands, but her mind was too preoccupied with thoughts of Mick Dunbar to read it.

He wanted her. Standing in his room with him earlier in the day, she had sensed his desire for her. She traced a line along her cheek with the tip of her finger, still able to feel the warmth of his touch on her skin. She couldn't stop thinking of how he had pinned up her hair and buttoned her shirtwaist.

Sophie stirred in her chair, recalling the brush of his knuckles against her spine as he had refastened her buttons. Her own shivers at his breath against her neck. The warmth that flowed through her limbs at the feel of his body behind her. So close.

She was still shocked by his bold behavior and even more shocked that it hadn't occurred to her to stop him from touching her. No gentleman would behave in such a way. Charles hadn't even touched her until they had become engaged.

Mick was as different from Charles as chalk from cheese, and he knew a great deal more about women than Charles ever had. In fact, when it came to women, she suspected Mick Dunbar could do just about anything he wanted. He knew it, too.

He had watched her throughout dinner that evening, smiling as if he were the one who could read other people's thoughts, as if he knew just how she felt, how flustered she had been by his touch. She vowed that if he ever tried to do anything like that again, she'd kick him again, and it wouldn't be in the shin.

One by one, the other members of the household went to bed, and through the open door of the library, she watched each of them go up the stairs. Mick went up as well, but Sophie didn't dare remove the necklace from its hiding place until she was sure everyone was asleep.

She waited until the gong of the grandfather clock in the foyer announced that a full two hours had gone by, then she put her book aside and walked over to her secretaire. Glancing up often enough to make sure no one was coming back down, Sophie removed the shallow center drawer from the desk and set it aside, then knelt and pushed a hairpin into the tiny wormhole at the back that triggered the mechanism and opened the secret compartment. She removed the necklace and put it in the pocket of her skirt, then she shut the tiny door of the space.

With a sigh of relief, she picked up the drawer of the desk, but her relief was short-lived. Through the open doorway, she saw Mick descending the stairs, and she barely had time to thrust the drawer into place and get to her feet before he turned and saw her standing there. She froze, and all thoughts of the necklace fled from her mind.

He wore no shirt, not even an undershirt. The only thing he had on was a pair of disheveled gray flannel trousers. Though she had seen statues of men in museums, she had never actually seen a real man's bare chest before. She didn't know men had hair on their chests. She was unable to look away from the swath of dark hair over his chest that tapered down into the waistband of his trousers. She was unable to move, fascinated by the muscles of his abdomen, shoulders, and arms. All of a sudden, the room felt much too warm.

He paused in the doorway, slanting her a knowing look from beneath those thick black lashes Violet had admired so much, and he smiled. Her breath caught in her throat. She'd been right. He knew a great deal about women.

He entered the room and walked toward her. She wanted to escape, but she couldn't seem to gather her wits. Didn't the man even wear pajamas or a nightshirt to bed?

"Still awake?" He came closer, walking around the secretaire toward her, and she couldn't help taking a step backward, then another. She hit the tall book-shelves behind her, and she could retreat no further.

She forced her gaze up to his face. "I don't sleep well."

He was standing right in front of her now, his wide chest like a wall, blocking out everything but him. She caught the scent of him, a masculine mixture of bay rum, castile soap, and a hint of tobacco. "I couldn't sleep either," he answered. "I came down for a book."

Sophie swallowed hard and struggled to think of something to say. "I didn't know you read."

His smile widened. He bent his head, bringing his face within inches of her own. "I do know how to read, luv."

Realizing the idiocy of her comment, she tried to gather her wits. But when she looked into his eyes, she felt a strange, melting sensation that pooled low in her abdomen, something she'd never felt before.

He reached up his hand, and she tensed, thinking he would touch her again, but he didn't. Instead, he lifted his hand above her head. "Pardon me," he said, his gaze still locked with hers as he pulled a book down from the shelf.

"I saw the books in your flat," she said, vacillating between hoping he would move away from her and hoping he wouldn't. "Of course you can read. I never meant to imply that you couldn't. I just meant that . . . that . . ." Her voice trailed off because even she didn't know what she'd meant.

Amusement crinkled the corners of his eyes, and she tried again. "I didn't have the chance to see what sort of books you had in your flat. Do you like classics, such as Shakespeare or Milton, or do you prefer modern novels? Detective stories, like Sherlock Holmes, perhaps? I like them all. I don't much care for parties, you see, and I hate dancing, so I read a lot. Auntie and Miss Peabody prefer books on Egyptology and spiritualism. The colonel reads the *Times* every day, and he loves Kipling. Mr. Dawes always reads medical texts, and Miss Atwood only reads *Punch,* though she plays patience, too. What do you like?"

He didn't answer. He simply continued to look into her eyes. But when she passed her tongue over her dry lips, the movement seemed to draw his attention. He lowered his gaze to her mouth.

He wanted to kiss her. He was thinking about it right now. Worse, she wanted him to.

"I like lots of things," he murmured, staring at her lips. "Cherries, especially."

She didn't know why he was bringing up food when she'd asked about books. Hadn't she asked him about books? Heavens, she couldn't think.

"Why do you hate dancing?"

That question brought her to her senses, because she had actually opened her mouth to answer it. She stiffened. What was wrong with her? She'd almost confessed her greatest social ineptitude to a man she barely knew, a man who was standing in front of her without most of his clothes. Sophie thrust her hands into the pockets of her dress, and the fingers of her right hand closed around the necklace. The jewels felt like ice in her hand.

"I think I'll go to bed. Good night." She ducked under his arm and practically ran for the door, fleeing the sight of his bare skin, the scent of bay rum, and probing questions she didn't want to answer. She raced up the stairs, grateful he did not try to stop her.

Once in her own room, she felt as if she could breathe again. She pulled the necklace out of her pocket, berating herself as a fool. What if he had kissed her? She touched her fingers to her lips. What if he had put his mouth on hers?

Sophie closed her eyes, and her fingertips brushed lightly across her lips. What if he had held her in his arms and pressed her body close to his own? What if he had explored her with his hands tonight as thoroughly as he had done in his flat?

He would have found the necklace.

Sophie jerked her hand away from her face and told herself firmly to stop being a silly schoolgirl. She must keep her wits about her. She must.

She stared down at the emeralds and diamonds that glittered in her hand for a moment, then looked up to stare straight at the drawers of her dresser. Auntie's advice about hiding places came back to her.

Sophie crossed the room and opened the bottom drawer. She pulled out a pair of her stockings, unrolled them, and dropped the necklace inside one of the stockings. She then rolled it back up and placed it in the bottom of her drawer, buried beneath other stockings, garters, and bows, and closed the drawer.

Auntie had said no man would think to look among a woman's most intimate garments, and when it came to searching through drawers, Auntie was an expert.

Though she had bemoaned the expense at the time, Sophie was now grateful that she'd had locks installed on all the bedroom doors three years ago when some lodgers had requested them. She now understood their concern for privacy. Though she never had before, she intended to start locking her door whenever she was not in her room.

Satisfied that she'd found the best possible hiding place and had done all she could to protect Auntie's secret from Inspector Dunbar, Sophie changed into her nightgown and crawled into bed. She closed her eyes, but it was a long time before she slept. She couldn't stop wondering why he had talked about cherries.

*　　　*　　　*

Victoria was the busiest train station in all of England, with countless passengers coming and going through its doors every day of the year, but now, with the Queen's Diamond Jubilee going on, the station was packed with people and porters. The hiss of steam engines, the clatter of luggage carts, and the noise of the crowds combined to form a roar that made ordinary conversation difficult.

"I'm sure Charlotte was pleased to receive my letter about Agatha staying with her instead of us," Violet shouted to Sophie over the din as they walked to the huge chalkboard showing information about arriving trains. "She prefers it that way."

"She might be pleased, but Mama won't," Sophie shouted back. "She'll be furious."

"Oh, no, she'll understand the circumstances. If she doesn't, dinner is going to be most uncomfortable."

"Isn't it always?"

Violet chose not to answer that. She glanced over the board and pointed to a line of writing nearly halfway down the board. "The Yorkshire Express is coming in on platform number twelve."

Sophie followed her aunt through the bustling crowds toward the platform for trains from the north. Charlotte and Harold were already there, and her sister watched their approach with her usual lack of warmth. Violet put an arm around Sophie's shoulders as they crossed the platform toward the other two. "Don't let her bother you, darling," she murmured.

"I don't, Auntie," she assured her. "I reconciled myself to Charlotte's contempt for me a long time ago."

"She's afraid of you, dear. That's what it is."

"I know."

They walked to where Charlotte and Harold were waiting for the train. Her sister's greeting was as pleasant as ever. "Late as usual, I see. You're quite lucky the train is late as well."

Sophie smiled at her sister so sweetly that it almost made her gag to do it. "Luck had nothing to do with it. I knew the train was going to be late."

Charlotte *hated* it when she referred to her psychic ability in any way, and her only reply was a humph of disbelief. Beside her, Harold shifted his weight from one foot to the other, ran a finger around the inside of his collar, and cleared his throat, looking uncomfortable.

Sophie knew the reason for that. Harold was afraid of her, too. He had good reason to be. He stepped closer to Violet and began chatting to her about the unseasonably hot spring they were having.

Harold Tamplin was a tall, plain man of high intelligence and low morals. He embezzled the trust funds of clients, he kept a blond mistress in a luxurious flat near his offices in the City, and he did not love his wife. Charlotte knew all that, but she didn't care. She had the life she had always wanted, and that was all that mattered to her. Sophie felt sorry for her sister, not because Charlotte received no love from her husband but because she was so incapable of giving love to anyone.

Her next words proved it. She leaned closer to Sophie, and murmured in a low voice, "I cannot believe what Mama is thinking, to have us bring you out into society again, as if it would do any good. I've just had a baby, and all these balls and such things are not good for my health."

"I'm so sad to hear you're feeling poorly, Charlotte," Sophie answered, knowing full well her sister would never miss a social engagement during Jubilee, baby or no. "Have you seen a doctor?"

"Don't play the game of sisterly consideration with me, Sophie," Charlotte whispered back. "Mama is determined to find a husband for you. As if that were possible! Besides, we both know you don't care at all about me or my health. You never have. You only care about yourself."

That was so unfair that Sophie had to bite her lip to keep back a sharp reply. Except when Mama came to visit, she never saw Charlotte and her husband, and at moments like this Sophie was most glad of it. She always ended up quarreling with her sister as if they were little girls again, fighting over things that were just as silly as who got the first ride on the new pony, or who got to stir the Christmas pudding first, or which of them the local squire's handsome son liked best. They were grown women now, and she would not trade insults with Charlotte. Fortunately the train pulled in at that moment, saving Sophie from further conversation with her sister, though she suspected there was worse to come. Her mother proved her right.

When Agatha stepped off the train, Charlotte's first words were more than a greeting. "Mama, it's wonderful to see you. I'm so glad you'll be staying with Harold and myself after all!"

Agatha frowned, her thin face forming lines of disapproval. She turned to Violet. "Didn't you receive my
letter?"

"I did, my dear sister," Violet said, not at all intimidated. She leaned forward to give Agatha a peck on
the cheek. "But it arrived only yesterday. We had no
time to write back to you and explain."

"Violet, what is there to explain? Jubilee is the perfect opportunity to bring Sophie out into society again.
How can she ever find a husband if all she does is root
about in her garden and her conservatory, never meeting any eligible young men? You have been most lax in
your efforts, Violet, and I have decided to do something about it."

"Of course," Violet answered. "I couldn't agree with
you more, but it's impossible to do that from the house
in Mill Street. We simply have no room. The only
empty bedroom we had left was let before we learned
of your plans to stay with us. We cannot throw the
poor man out. He is a very pleasant fellow."

Sophie could sense her mother's irritation growing
with every word, and she stepped in, hoping to smooth
things over with a compromise. "Mama, this won't
affect your plans in the least. It will be a bit more
inconvenient, perhaps, but I will attend whatever
functions you arrange." If she needed an excuse to get
out of any particularly awful occasion, she would
invent it later. "I leave that to you, Lady Fortescue, and
Charlotte."

Her ploy worked. Agatha nodded, accepting the
compromise, and kissed her on the cheek. "I'm glad to
see you are finally coming to your senses and have

stopped mooning about Lord Kenleigh." She paused, looking her over, and a look of such disappointment came over her face that Sophie wanted to take her conciliatory words back.

"But what is this thing you are wearing? Isn't this the same dress you wore last summer? And the summer before?" Agatha eyed her worn yellow silk dress and its many untied green bows with a tragic air. "Must you always look so down at heel, my darling?"

She tied up a few of the bows of Sophie's skirt, then gave that up and pushed Sophie's bonnet to a more fashionable angle, smoothed her sleeves, and fussed over her as if she were still a child of six. Finally satisfied that she'd done all she could, she stood back and eyed her younger daughter with a sigh.

"Charlotte, we simply must take Sophie to a decent dressmaker. This gown is three years out of fashion at least. Besides, your sister doesn't have your fashion sense, and she needs a bit of help to look presentable."

Sophie wanted to ask if Charlotte's help included the money to buy these fashionable new clothes, but as tempting as sarcasm might be, her mother would not understand. Her husband, the vicar, did not have a large income, but Mama still refused to accept the economic necessities of life, since Harold's money was always available to her when her own creditors became so unreasonable as to expect payment. Sophie, however, would join one of those American Wild West circus shows as a fortune-teller before she would ask Harold for tuppence.

Agatha turned to her own sister. "Violet, dear, it's wonderful to see you, but I hope you have at last abandoned that silly spiritualism business."

Sophie almost groaned. They weren't even out of the train station and she was starting on Auntie already. But Violet could hold her own against Agatha, and her next words proved it.

"On the contrary," she answered. "It is more fascinating than ever. Miss Peabody and I are now in communication with a spirit named Abdul. He was a copper merchant in Cairo two hundred years ago. He drowned in the Nile, he told us."

The tense silence was broken by Harold. "Awfully warm for spring, isn't it?" Without waiting for a reply, he went on, "Perhaps we should get your trunks, Agatha."

He took her claim ticket out of her hand and beckoned to the nearest porter. "My carriage is at the Wilton Road entrance," he told the man, handing over the ticket. "We'll await you there."

"Aye, sir." The porter tipped his hat to them and departed in search of Agatha's luggage.

Due to the noise, talking was impossible as the five of them left the platform and walked through the train station, but once they were seated in Harold's luxurious carriage, Agatha resumed discussion of her favorite topic.

"So, Violet, tell me of Sophie's circumstances at present. Does she have any suitors? Has she been out to any card parties, cotillions, or balls? Has she met any young men at all?"

"She has, actually. We have a very handsome man

staying with us at the moment. He's with Scotland Yard."

Sophie did not appreciate her aunt's impish streak just now. She nudged Violet with her foot.

"A policeman?" Agatha and Charlotte said in unison, staring at Sophie in horror from across the carriage as if she'd suddenly grown a second head.

"Not a mere policeman," Violet explained, oblivious to Sophie's elbow now jabbing her in the ribs. "A detective. He seems quite taken with our dear Sophie."

Sophie hastily spoke up. "He is not taken with me, Mama, nor I with him." She shot a warning glance at Violet and went on, "He is simply one of Auntie's lodgers, and I have nothing whatsoever to do with him."

"I should hope not," Agatha answered with a disdainful sniff. "A policeman is not the sort of man with whom a young lady should associate."

She looked at her sister. "Violet, while I am here, I will see that Sophie is introduced to unmarried men of Harold and Charlotte's acquaintance. She simply must associate with men of her own class if she is ever to find a suitable husband."

Sophie sent an anguished glance heavenward and wondered with wistful longing what it would have been like to have grown up an orphan like Mick Dunbar.

Looking through people's things without their knowledge or permission might have bothered some people. It didn't bother Mick at all.

Last night, he had planned to go through Sophie's

desk and make a search of the rest of the ground floor, but the fact that Sophie had still been awake when he'd come downstairs had forced him to postpone that plan.

Now it was Sunday afternoon, and no one was in the house but him. Sophie and her aunt had gone to church services, then continued on to Victoria Station, where they were meeting the train bringing Sophie's mother. They were planning to go on from there to a dinner party. The servants had gone to early service and were spending their afternoon out enjoying the festivities for Jubilee that were going on around the city. The other lodgers were out as well, no doubt also enjoying Jubilee.

Mick took full advantage of this opportunity to search the house. He started with Sophie's secretaire in the library.

In looking through her desk, he discovered that she was as haphazard about her papers as she was about her clothes. Most of the documents he found in her desk were bills, some marked paid, some not. There was also a bankbook for the household account which showed the meager balance of twelve pounds, nine shillings and sixpence, and that amount included Mick's first week's rent. Mixed in with the bills and bankbook were receipts, demands for payment, social invitations, unused bank drafts, letters, sealing wax, and other stationery supplies, all of it thrown together in a jumbled fashion.

Some of Sophie's letters were from female friends and acquaintances in Yorkshire and London, but most of her correspondence was from her mother, whose sole concerns appeared to be her daughter's lack of a husband and nonexistent efforts to find one. Mick scanned the letters, but he found nothing in any of them to show who might want to kill him. He did find a secret drawer, but it was empty.

Hampered by the furniture, bric-a-brac, and fancy, feminine whatnots that crowded the rooms, Mick had to make his search a cursory one. He decided to finish the ground-floor rooms another time, late at night when everyone was asleep. He went upstairs.

Miss Atwood was tidy, Miss Peabody was not. As Sophie had already told him, the colonel liked to read Kipling. He also smoked a pipe and enjoyed doing crosswords. In Dawes's room, Mick found medical texts, surgical instruments, hashish, and some very graphic pornography.

Mrs. Summerstreet's bedroom faced the back garden, had a balcony with a tiny wrought iron table and chair, and smelled of patchouli incense. There were a few imitation Egyptian artifacts on the mantel of her fireplace. Among her winter woolens, he found a few pieces of carnelian and lapis in the Egyptian style, but no gems of great value. Mick put the jewelry back where he had found it, smiling. Violet really did think she was Cleopatra.

He found Sophie's room locked, which instantly aroused his suspicions, but the lock was a simple one, and Mick easily got the door open with a hairpin from Violet's room.

Like her aunt, Sophie had a balcony overlooking the garden, but there the similarity ended. Mick was not surprised to find that Sophie's room was as flowery as her conservatory. There were flowers everywhere— cut roses in vases, a counterpane in a floral print, cabbage roses on the chintz-skirted dressing table. There were curtains of eyelet and lace, cut crystal lamps, and satin-covered pillows of pink and white stripe. It was the kind of room that made Mick long for a leather chair and a cigar.

The decor of her room might be that of an upperclass woman, but her wardrobe was not. It contained several shirtwaists and skirts, two dresses of striped cotton, one evening gown of wine red silk, three hats, and two pairs of shoes. Mick remembered what Thacker had said about the family having very little money, and it seemed to be the truth. From the balance of their bank account, the clothes in their bedrooms, and what he had observed with his own eyes, Sophie and her aunt lived in genteel poverty. After paying their servants and the expenses of running the lodging house, they probably had very little on which to live.

Unlike her aunt, Sophie had a jewel case, but the only items in it were a string of pearls and a set of small garnets. None of the pieces were worth much.

In the drawer of the table beside her bed were a quill pen, a bottle of ink, and a sheaf of notepaper. On the top sheet were scribbled notes in her handwriting, which he recognized from his search through her desk. Every note had a date beside it.

Mick sat down on the edge of her bed and studied the scribblings with great care, but they seemed to be just plain nonsense. There were sentence fragments such as "the Pekingese and the terrier," and "Black knave/red queen."

Was this some sort of code, and if so, what was it for?

Mick turned to the next page. The first words that caught his attention were "Scotland Yard," and he stiffened. Here was something at last. "Violent death," he read. "Dark blue suit, man, blood everywhere. Dark hair. Dead. Murdered. Knife?"

There was nothing written here she hadn't told him the day he'd met her, but Mick folded her notes and put them in the breast pocket of his jacket, then continued his search.

Sophie might write notes about blood and violent death, but as Mick began searching through her underclothes, he noticed that she also had a fondness for pretty things.

For Mick, who had spent much of his boyhood living among prostitutes in the East End, what women wore under their dresses had never been a mystery. But among the various lace-trimmed corsets, petticoats, chemises, combinations, and garters in the drawers of Sophie's dressing table, he found something that did surprise him. He lifted a piece of pink muslin out of the drawer, and the distinct shape of the garment made him grin. It was unmistakably a bust improver.

His fingers tightened around the fabric, and he closed his eyes. His grin faded as he held the garment in his hands, inhaled that special fragrance she wore, and remembered each and every luscious curve of her body. He'd explored those curves in his flat that night just long enough to fire his imagination, but he knew enough to say for certain that Sophie Haversham's shapely body didn't need any improvements.

Reluctantly, he returned the bust improver to the drawer, closed it, and opened the one below. The sight of her stockings immediately brought an image of her legs to his mind.

Bloody hell.

He shoved that delectable and dangerous vision out of his mind. He buried his hands in the untidy pile of filmy stockings that filled the drawer, and the delicate silk caught on the calluses of his hands as he searched.

When his fingers closed around something hard, he pulled it out of the drawer. It was a rather lumpy object rolled in a stocking. He unwrapped it, and what he saw caused him to give a low whistle.

"I'll be damned." He stared down at the diamonds and emeralds in his palm with surprise and appreciation, knowing full well he had in his hands the missing necklace of Sophie's cousin, Lady Fortescue. This piece matched the description he'd read in the police report in every detail, including the tiny lion's head clasp. What was it doing hidden among Sophie's stockings?

She was a cousin of Lord Fortescue, but if she had merely borrowed the necklace, the viscountess would not have reported it stolen. Mick had met plenty of thieves in his life, and he wouldn't have thought Sophie to be that type, although a woman who liked pretty underclothes might be tempted to steal pretty jewels, and a woman who was poor might steal them to sell. Either way, she was not so innocent as she pretended to be.

Mick stood up and slipped the emeralds into the pocket of his trousers. He intended to find out why the necklace was in Sophie's room, and he was also going to find out whom she was protecting. If he went about it the right way, he might be able to accomplish both goals at the same time.

Seven

❧

*A*ll Sophie wanted to do by the time she and Auntie reached home was fall into bed. Throughout the evening with her family, she had felt the powerful emotional undercurrents in the air, and they had exhausted her.

Nothing ever changes, she thought as she stood in the foyer removing her gloves. Her mother came to visit twice a year, and everything was the same each and every time. Mother still thought her an enormous disappointment, Charlotte still hated and feared her, and her brother-in-law was still a criminal whose oily politeness set her teeth on edge because she knew the character beneath. Still, what could she have expected? Did she really think that in the months that elapsed between her mother's visits some sort of magical transformation would take place within her family? She handed her gloves to Grimmy with a tired sigh.

Violet gave her a gentle pat on the arm. "I know these evenings can be quite tedious, even horrid," she said as they walked up the stairs together. "But despite all that, your mother does love you."

"I know, Auntie, but she'd love me more if I got married. And only to a gentleman she considers suitable. It's unfortunate for her that men are terrified of me."

"Not all men," Violet assured her. "You must not compare all other men to Charles. He was a kind man, as you know, but a weak one as well. He was not brave enough for marriage to you. It would not be easy to live with someone who has your special gifts."

"I won't pretend not to have them, Auntie. I tried that with Charles, but it didn't work."

"Oh, no, Sophie, I never meant to imply that you should," Violet assured her. "I am convinced there are men in the world braver than Charles, men who would not be intimidated by living with a woman who sees the future and can sometimes read their thoughts and sense their emotions."

"I've never met one."

"Don't be cynical, dear. Someday a truly wonderful man will come along, a man who won't be afraid of your abilities, a man who will appreciate you and love you just as you are."

To Sophie, that was impossible to believe. Auntie loved and accepted her just as she was, but most people, including the other members of her own family, were incapable of doing so. She thought she had come to accept that, but evenings such as this one served to remind her that it still hurt. "And if I don't meet this wonderful man?"

They paused outside Violet's bedroom door. "Then you and I will just muddle along until you're as gray as I am," her aunt said and wrapped her arms around her niece in a comforting hug. "Besides, despite what your mother says, and as wonderful as marriage can be, there is more to life." She pulled back and opened her bedroom door. "Good night, dear."

"Good night, Auntie."

Sophie walked several steps further down the hall and entered her own room. Hannah had evidently been there to light a lamp for her as usual. Sophie closed the door behind her and took two steps toward her wardrobe to undress, when she was overcome by the sense that she was not alone.

"Who's there?" She glanced toward the open French window and saw movement out on the balcony. She tensed, ready to turn and run, when the tall, powerful silhouette of Mick Dunbar appeared in the doorway.

She was caught between relief that thieves hadn't broken into the house, outrage that this man was in her room, and fear of what he might have found.

He wore no jacket or waistcoat, and his white shirt was a sharp contrast to the night shadows behind him. His face bore a dark shadow of beard stubble. He looked tired, and thoroughly displeased.

"What are you doing in my room?" she demanded.

Hands in the pockets of his dark gray trousers, he

stepped inside and kicked the French door shut behind him. "I've been waiting for you," he said, giving her the sort of look a tiger might give its prey just before the attack.

"Waiting for me? Why?"

"To ask you about this."

He pulled his hand out of his pocket, and Sophie stared at the glittering string of jewels that hung from the tips of his fingers.

She went cold with fear. Damn the man. Despite all her precautions, he'd found it.

He was looking at her, waiting for an explanation, and Sophie decided her best defense was to go on the offensive. "You searched my room?" she said, turning her fear into wrath. "You went through my things? My private things?"

"Indeed I did." He smiled. "Pretty falderals they were, too."

"I can't believe that you, even you, would go through my clothes, that you would see my—" She stopped. His actions were too appalling to say aloud. He'd seen her most intimate garments. Touched them.

"Don't worry, Sophie," he said. "You don't have anything I haven't seen before."

She made a grab for the necklace, but he was too quick for her, pulling the piece of jewelry out of her reach.

She glared at him. "When Auntie finds out what you've done, she'll throw you out."

He didn't seem worried. "Perhaps."

She narrowed her eyes, put her hands on her hips,

and took a step closer, trying to look really brave. "You've gone through my things without permission. Isn't that against the law?"

"What's against the law is stealing."

"I didn't steal that necklace."

"All right, then, where did it come from?" He held up his palm between them. "Wait. Don't tell me. Spirits brought it to you in the night, while you slept."

"Sarcasm is a most unattractive quality, Inspector. But then, it's coming from you, so that's not surprising, is it?"

"Thank you, Sophie. I'm fond of you, too." His expression hardened to that ruthless one she knew he reserved for the criminals. "I know this necklace belongs to your cousin."

She looked into his eyes, and she decided there was only one thing to do. Lie.

"The necklace isn't stolen. I . . . umm . . . I borrowed it from Katherine."

"Sophie, I have come across many liars in my life, and you are the lousiest one I've ever met."

He was right. She hated it when he was right, but she took a deep, steadying breath and tried again. "I borrowed it."

"That won't do. The viscountess reported it to Scotland Yard as stolen two days ago."

She was in the suds now. Sophie swallowed hard and closed her eyes for a moment, trying to invent a plausible story. But Mick didn't give her the time.

He stuffed the necklace back in his pocket, grabbed her by the shoulders, and turned her around. Before she could even try to get away, he had his hand wrapped around her wrists in a painful grip. "Sophie Marie Haversham, you are under arrest for possession of stolen property."

"You're arresting me?" she gasped, turning her head to look at him over one shoulder. "You are really arresting me?"

"Yes, ma'am."

"You . . . you . . ." She paused, striving to find an adjective to describe him, but she just couldn't think of one foul enough.

"Swine?" he suggested. "You called me that once before."

"That was before I really knew you," she shot back as he steered her toward the door. "Now I know your true nature. Calling you a swine would be an insult to pigs."

"How long are you going to keep her in there?"

Mick turned to Kyle Merrick, the newly promoted night-watch sergeant at CID. "I don't know," he replied with a shrug. "She's only been in there for half an hour. I'll give her a bit more time to think things over, then I'll go in and start asking questions."

Kyle nodded, glancing through the tiny peephole into the dimly lit room beyond. "She asked me to send for her butler when you first brought her in. You were off looking for an empty interrogation room."

"You didn't do it, did you?"

"Aye, I did."

Mick muttered an exasperated oath.

The young sergeant looked at him in surprise. "A young lady like that, with a butler—I assumed there wasn't any harm in it. I'm sorry, sir. You didn't tell me she couldn't have visitors."

Mick waved aside the apologies, reminding himself that it was only Merrick's second week as a sergeant. "It's all right. It's just that I wanted her to sit in that room with the peeling paint and the dirty floor a bit longer, just long enough for her to start wondering about what Newgate might be like before I start the interrogation."

"What's the charge?"

"Stealing a viscountess's emeralds."

Kyle raised an eyebrow. "A society woman from Mayfair stealing jewels from other society ladies sounds like quite a racket." He took another peek into the room beyond. "You wouldn't think it, would you?" he asked as he turned away. "A pretty young lady like that a thief. It's hard to believe."

Mick laughed. "No, it's not, Sergeant. You would be astounded at the number of beautiful women I've arrested over the years. When it comes to honesty, a pretty face means nothing." He pulled out his watch. "I'd better get in there before her champion arrives. When he does, come and tell me."

"Very good, sir." The sergeant tipped his cap and turned away. He walked down the hall and disappeared into the main room of CID. Mick returned his attention to his jewel thief.

Through the peephole, he could see her sitting at the table, facing him, her hands folded tightly together and her head bent as if in prayer. The two braids that had been wrapped in an intricate knot atop her head had come down. Now one fell over each of her shoulders, and she looked like a schoolgirl facing punishment by a harsh tutor—young, penitent, scared, and very vulnerable. But when she looked up and scowled fiercely in the direction of the peephole, Mick couldn't help a chuckle. Penitent like hell.

"I know you're out there, Michael Dunbar," she called. "I can feel your presence, and I know you're spying on me through that little hole in the wall. Are you planning to interrogate me now or just throw me into a cell? Whichever it is, I wish you'd get on with it."

He stepped to the door, opened it, and entered the interrogation room, watching as her scowl became even more fierce. There was no sign of a vulnerable schoolgirl about her now.

Mick pulled out a chair opposite her across the table and sat down, ready to be as tough on her as he needed to be in order to find out what he wanted to know. But before he could even open his mouth, she started talking.

"I'm not saying a word to you, not a word. I know you've been keeping me in here all this time just to make me more intimidated and afraid, but I'm not letting you bully me. I want a solicitor. Or do I mean a barrister?"

"Solicitor. Barristers are for when you go to trial in the high court."

She made a sound of disbelief at the mention of a trial, but Mick knew that despite her bravado, Sophie was nervous. She kept looking toward the door and twisting her hands together. Still, it was shrewd of her to realize why he'd waited so long to start questioning her. But then, he already knew she was a perceptive woman.

He pulled the notes he'd taken from her room out of his pocket. He unfolded them and shoved them across the table toward her. "Tell me about that."

"These are my notes. My dream notes." She looked up at him, and her eyes narrowed. "First you go through my unmentionables, then you read my private papers? Have you no morals at all?"

"None. What do you mean when you say these are your dream notes? Are we talking about this psychic nonsense again?"

She shoved the notes back at him. "I told you before, it won't work."

"What?"

"Blackmail. You arrested me so you'd have something to hold over my head, thinking that will force me to tell you who shot at you. What you can't seem to understand is that I don't know anything more than I've already told you. How many times do I have to explain?"

"As many times as it takes until I get the truth. Do you want me to walk you next door to Cannon Row Police Station now? If not, tell me who you're protecting."

She said nothing, and his voice became softer, more persuasive. "Sophie, think about this. If I bring charges of theft against you, you'll go before a judge, get your name in the newspapers, be ruined in society, and perhaps go to prison."

"Things will never get that far. When Cousin Katherine finds out it was I who took the necklace, she will recant any claim of a robbery. She would never allow the scandal."

That was probably true, but Mick wasn't finished yet. "We'll have to see. We'll call her down to Scotland Yard. In the meantime, you'll be spending your time in a cell next door."

She made a sound of exasperation. "This is such a waste of time. She will not prosecute."

"I think she will." He shoved back his chair. "Tomorrow, we'll find out which of us is right."

"Tomorrow?"

He pulled out his watch. "Sorry. I meant today. It's after midnight now." Tucking his watch back in his waistcoat pocket, he smiled at her. "Cheer up. You'll only be in a cell about fourteen more hours."

"You are going to keep me here that long? Even though you know the charges will be dropped? You can't be serious."

"I am completely serious, I assure you." He gave her a look of mock consolation. "Don't worry, Sophie. We don't have too many rats over at Cannon Row. And the prostitutes in the cell with you won't bother you much. They smell, of course, but we can't do much about that."

"Prostitutes?"

"You'll lose that cameo you're wearing, as well as most of the buttons and ribbons on your dress, but they always seem to be coming undone anyway—"

"They'll take them?" Her voice came out like a squeak, and she clutched at the cameo pinned to the high collar of her gown. "Really? The buttons and everything?"

He pretended to be surprised by her question. "Of course."

"All of them?" When he nodded, she shifted her position, wrapping her arms around herself. "But then my dress would come apart . . . I mean, I'd . . . I'd be . . . unclothed."

The last word came out in a whisper. She looked so appalled that Mick had to fight back a smile.

"I'm sure the day-watch sergeant over there would give you a cloak or something. His name is Anthony Frye. Nice fellow. I'm sure he'll pretend not to notice when he sees your corset."

Color flared in her cheeks, and he remembered how shocked she'd been to discover he'd been through her underclothes, that he'd touched her stockings and her knickers. Her body, too.

With that thought, he felt all his muscles tightening. He lowered his gaze to her crossed arms and the full breasts they shielded. He'd been right. She didn't need that bust improver.

He returned his gaze to her face. She was staring at him, her brown eyes wide, her lips slightly parted. She might be a little off her chump, but Sophie Haversham also had the most kissable mouth of any woman he'd ever seen.

Mick knew he was heading into dangerous territory again. She was probably a thief. Worse, she knew the identity of whoever had shot at him. Letting his body do the thinking could get him killed, but knowing that didn't stop him from wanting that hot, soft, cherry red mouth on his.

Suddenly, she stiffened and frowned at him, her expression of fear changing in less than a second to one of outrage. "You are such a cad. A low and despicable cad."

Mick sat back in his chair, startled by this lightning-quick change in her.

"You should be ashamed," she said. "Trying to frighten me about those prostitutes, when you know it's a lie."

If ever there was an example of women's intuition, Sophie was it, but Mick did not let his surprise show in his expression. "Good guess."

"This little trick you've played on me is cruel," she went on, "and most ungentlemanly. But then, I've known from the start you are no gentleman."

He smiled. "It must be that psychic ability of yours."

She refused to rise to the bait this time. "I want to send for a solicitor." With that, she folded her arms and pressed her lips together, making it quite clear she intended to say no more.

He considered what his next move should be, but before he could decide, there was a knock on the door, and Kyle entered the room. "Miss Haversham's butler is here. Her aunt is with him."

"Auntie's here?" Sophie cried. "I don't want her here! I don't!"

Mick glanced at her, noting her distress. She had quite a close relationship to her aunt and would probably be humiliated if her aunt knew she was a thief.

That just might do the trick. "Show both of them in," he ordered.

"No!" Sophie jumped to her feet and looked at Merrick. "I don't want my aunt in here."

The sergeant glanced at Mick. "Sir?"

Sophie turned to Mick as well. "Please, leave my aunt out of this. She has nothing to do with it."

"Who's trying to kill me?"

"I don't know. I don't know! I swear on my life."

Her hands were shaking. There was more to this than just humiliation or shame. Those eyes of hers were focused on him, those big, soft, dark brown eyes. A man could drown in melted chocolate eyes like that.

He didn't realize how hard he was gripping his pencil until it snapped in his hand.

The sound brought him to his senses. He couldn't let desire influence him. His policeman's instinct told him there was more going on here than Sophie stealing her cousin's emerald necklace, and he'd better stop thinking like a convict fresh out of prison and start thinking like the policeman that he was. He'd bloody well better remember his duty.

Still looking into her eyes, he said in a low, hard voice, "Show them both in."

Her eyes began to glisten.

Oh, Christ.

She was going to cry now. He hated it when suspects cried, especially the female ones.

But though there were tears in her eyes, she didn't let them fall. She bit down hard on her lower lip and sank back down in her chair, looking the picture of silent misery.

Mick wasn't going to feel sorry for her. He damn well wasn't.

Violet bustled into the room. That sour-faced butler followed her inside and closed the door behind them.

"Sophie, dear," Violet cried, "what is all this about?"

"Oh, Auntie!" Sophie said with a sob of dismay. "I told them to tell Grimmy not to bring you. I don't want you here. Go home."

"I will do no such thing!" Violet circled the table to her niece's side. Grimstock remained by the door. He was silent and even more somber than usual. Mick noticed that he also seemed to be very nervous.

Violet wrapped her arms around her niece. "Darling, what's this business of you being arrested for Katherine's necklace?"

She pulled back from Sophie and turned to Mick with a frown of such disapproval and disappointment that he almost felt like a recalcitrant boy sent down from school. "I thought better of you than this, Inspector. Sophie's no thief."

"Auntie, don't say any more!" Sophie put a hand on Violet's arm as if to both warn and reassure her. "It's all right."

"All right?" Violet's face creased with lines of worry. "This is all my fault, and I cannot let you—"

"Auntie, please be quiet. Don't say another word."

Mick heard the suddenly hard edge in Sophie's voice, and he knew she was afraid her aunt would blurt out something important.

Violet did not heed her niece's command. "No, no, Sophie, I won't let your reputation suffer because of me."

"Hang my reputation! I don't care."

"I do." Violet looked over at Mick with a resolute expression. She drew a deep breath and said, "My niece did not take Katherine's necklace, Inspector. I did."

"No, Auntie, no," Sophie moaned, lowering her head into her hands.

Mick stared at the older woman, nonplused. This was certainly an unexpected turn of events. The idea of Violet taking the emeralds had never occurred to him. He'd known all along Sophie was protecting someone, but he'd been thinking a murderer, not a thief. Not Violet.

"Why don't we all sit down?" he suggested, gesturing to the table. "I'll need a full statement."

"She's not going to make a statement." Sophie glared at him. "She's not saying another word. I took the necklace. Auntie had nothing to do with it."

Violet started to speak, but Sophie's voice rose over hers, loudly enough to drown her out. "Grimmy, I want you to send a runner to Harold at once. Tell him what's happened and bring him here as quickly as possible. Then later this morning I want you to go see the viscountess."

"No," Violet's voice cut in with an incisiveness surprising in an amiable, elderly lady. "Grimstock, you will do no such thing." She turned to her niece. "Sophie, enough of this. The inspector obviously doesn't believe you, and I don't blame him. You are such a dreadful liar. Dearest, you don't need to protect me anymore. I'm going to tell the inspector the truth."

Sophie started to speak, but Violet pressed a finger

to her niece's lips to silence her. "I may be a thief, but I will not let any other person take the blame. Especially not you, darling. I insist that you respect my wishes in this matter."

Mick saw the anguish in Sophie's face. She was beaten, and she knew it. With a resigned nod, she sank down in her chair.

Mick pulled a fresh pencil out of his jacket pocket and pulled his notepaper closer. He looked at Violet. "You admit that you stole your cousin's necklace?"

"I do." She raised her hands in a helpless gesture. "I take things. Jewelry, mostly. I am especially fond of lapis, having been an Egyptian queen in one of my past lives."

Mick paused in writing his notes. "Cleopatra. Yes, I know."

"Yes." She looked both surprised and pleased that he knew about that. "My dear Maxwell—that's my late husband, you know—he never believed he was Marc Antony, but I knew it for certain." A slight smile curved her lips. "He said Marc Antony made some very poor decisions at the battle of Actium, and he refused to believe he could be the reincarnation of someone that foolish."

Mick concluded that Maxwell Summerstreet had been a man of logic and good sense, but he didn't say so. "About the emeralds," he said, "where did you find them?"

"In Katherine's jewel case. Mrs. Peabody and I were having tea with her on the Thursday, and I just nipped upstairs to her room. I wanted to see the bath they just put in. It has one of those newfangled water closets—you know the ones I mean, where you pull the chain, and whoosh, the water goes down. Very sanitary, but make a horrendous amount of noise, I think."

Mick could see that Violet Summerstreet and Sophie Haversham were very much alike in some respects. "About the emeralds?"

"Yes, of course, let's keep to the subject at hand. Very sound, Inspector. You remind me of Maxwell, you know. Straightforward and to the point. Well, as I said, I went upstairs, intending to look over their new bath. I saw the door into Katherine's bedroom across the hall was open, and her jewel case was right there. Silly of her, really. Why, anyone could make away with it. I thought I'd have a peek."

She paused, gave a deep sigh, then went on, "Katherine's emeralds are very fine. They've been in the family for years. It was careless of her to leave them lying about, but then, Katherine is very absent-minded."

Mick glanced at Sophie, who was sitting slumped forward in her chair, with her fingertips pressed to her forehead as if she had a headache. With her aunt's confession, all the fight seemed to have gone out of her.

He returned his attention to Violet. "What happened then?"

"I'm afraid I don't know exactly." She frowned. "I must have tucked the necklace away in my pocket or something, then Mrs. Peabody and I came home, and I put the necklace—" She paused and turned to Sophie. "Where did I put it, dear?"

"In the Spode, Auntie," Sophie mumbled without lifting her head. "The trifle bowl. Grimstock decided to give all the china a dusting and found it."

"Yes, that's right. We almost never have trifle, so I must have thought that a very good hiding place."

Mick glanced over at the butler, who had not moved from his position by the door. "Is this true?"

"It is," Grimstock answered, turning to give him a resentful stare.

Satisfied by this corroboration, Mick turned to Sophie. "How did it get from the trifle bowl into your room?"

She looked up to meet his gaze across the table. "Grimmy told me he'd found the necklace, and he put it in my writing desk for safekeeping until I could return it. Then—"

"It *was* in the desk!" Violet cried. "Sophie, I told you, any thief might find things in that secret drawer."

"You also told me to put it in my stockings because that was the safest possible hiding place," Sophie answered. "I moved the necklace out of the desk and hid it in with my stockings. The inspector found it anyway. He searched our rooms and found it rolled up in one of my stockings." She cast a resentful glance in his direction. "We both thought a gentleman would never look through a woman's private things."

Mick's gaze locked with hers. "You were wrong."

"I said, 'a gentleman,' " she shot back. "I was not wrong."

"You went through my niece's stockings?" Violet looked at him with reproach. "That was most improper."

"I am a policeman, ma'am. I have my job to do, and I can't allow what's proper and what's not to interfere with my duty."

"That's true, of course. I hadn't thought of it quite that way. But what on earth were you looking for?"

"Proof," Sophie answered before he could do so. "Something that would indicate who tried to shoot him. He thinks I know who it is and that I'm trying to protect that person."

Violet waved one hand in the air in a gesture that dismissed that theory. "The only way you would know that is if you had another premonition. You haven't, have you, dear?"

"No. But it wouldn't matter if I had. Mr. Dunbar doesn't believe I have any psychic ability."

Violet ignored that. "If Sophie discerns the identity of this assassin, she'll tell you, Inspector. But I hope that from now on, if you need to search through my house, you will at least ask my permission first," she said sternly.

"I'll try to remember to do that, ma'am."

"What about Auntie?" Sophie asked and put an arm around the older woman's shoulders. "She's not really a thief. This is just a sort of compulsion she can't control. She didn't take it to sell or anything like that."

"Mrs. Summerstreet, what other jewels do you have in your possession that belong to other people?"

"None!" Sophie answered for her. "There aren't any hidden away anywhere, and if Grimmy or I discover any more jewels, we will do what we always do. We will find out who they belong to, and arrange for them to be returned at once. We always make certain that anything she takes is put back as soon as possible."

"I see. Is there anything else you want to tell me?"

"No. We've told you the whole sordid truth." She met his gaze steadily. "The real question is, what are you going to do about it?"

Eight

❧

Sophie's question hung in the air of the interrogation room at Scotland Yard as both she and Auntie waited for Mick's answer. Although Sophie often received very strong impressions of what other people were thinking and feeling, she had no idea what he intended to do. Auntie sat beside her, just as apprehensive as she was.

Mick looked from one woman to the other for a long time, as if trying to make up his mind. Finally, he looked at Violet. "Ma'am, why don't you take your butler and go out to the waiting room? Sergeant Merrick is out there, and he will be happy to make both of you a cup of tea, I'm sure."

It was not a request, and Auntie knew it. She stood up, nodding in acquiescence. "I know you'll do the right thing, Inspector," she said and walked out.

Grimmy followed her and closed the door after them.

Mick turned his attention to Sophie. "You still insist that you know nothing of the person who shot at me in the Embankment?"

If that was the stand he was going to take, Auntie was doomed. She was not too proud to beg for Auntie's sake. "Please don't do this," she pleaded. "I don't know who wants to kill you, and I've sworn it on my life. If you don't believe me, there's nothing more to say, but please don't arrest my aunt. She's elderly, she's frail, her reputation is at stake. If you need to blame someone, blame me."

"Even if I do what you ask, and even if your cousin doesn't prosecute, you have been arrested, and the newspapers will find the story irresistible. Your innocence won't save you from that. Are you certain you don't wish to change your story?"

She shook her head and met his gaze across the table. "Please, Mick. Please don't arrest my auntie."

"You care so much about your aunt's reputation that you're willing to sacrifice your own instead?"

The question astonished her. "Of course I would. She's my aunt. She's my family. I love her. There isn't anything I wouldn't do for her. That's what families do. At least," she amended, thinking of her sister, "that's what they're supposed to do."

Something in what she said caused him pain. She sensed it. Perhaps because he was an orphan who had no family. He wanted a family, though. A wife, children, but he didn't think he'd ever have them.

He shoved back his chair and startled her out of her thoughts about his life. She looked up at him. "Mick?"

"You're free to go, Sophie. I won't arrest a woman for a crime she did not commit."

Sophie's heart sank. It was all over then.

"Mrs. Summerstreet is a different matter," he went on, "and I honestly don't know what to do about that."

"You can't mean to keep her here?" Sophie looked at him in shock. "Oh, no, you can't! Please let me take her home."

He looked back at her for a long moment. Then he let out an exasperated sigh. "Take your aunt home. I'll let you know later today what I decide to do. As for the necklace, I'll be keeping it for the time being."

Sophie knew there was nothing to do now but wait. Pleading Auntie's case any further was futile. She stood up, and he opened the door to let her out.

She went to the main room of Criminal Investigations, where Auntie and Grimmy were waiting. "He'll let us know later what he's going to do."

During the carriage ride home, Sophie hoped her aunt might be worried enough to at least see the error of her ways, but she didn't seem at all concerned.

"Sophie, dear," she said, "the spirits led him to us. In fact, I'm certain that Maxwell is somehow behind all this. Michael Dunbar is very much like him, you know. I'm sure the dear boy isn't going to put me in prison."

Sophie, who did not think of Mick Dunbar as anything like a "dear boy" and who did not have much faith in the spirits of dead relatives, even that of Uncle Maxwell, was not reassured. "I'm not worried about prison, Auntie. Katherine would never bring charges against you, and he knows that. However, I'm terribly worried about gossip. If word of this gets to the newspapers, your reputation would be ruined."

Violet waved that aside. "Nonsense. How are the newspapers going to find out? As you pointed out, Katherine won't want scandal, so she won't say anything. You won't. I won't. And I'm sure Michael won't."

"The newspapers get word of any arrests, Auntie," she pointed out. "Inspector Dunbar told me that. The cousin of a viscount being arrested for jewel theft would be newsworthy."

"But Michael didn't actually arrest me."

"He did arrest me."

"Neither of us is going to end up in the newspapers. The spirits wouldn't send us someone to do us harm, darling."

Sophie let the subject drop, but she couldn't banish her worry, and even though it was nearly two o'clock in the morning, she couldn't sleep. After lying there for half an hour, worrying about what would happen to Violet and herself, she couldn't stand it. She got out of bed and did what she always did when she couldn't sleep. She went down to her conservatory.

After she had lit the gaslights, Sophie pushed her long, loose hair back over her shoulders, rolled up the sleeves of her nightgown, and decided to mix a batch of her new perfume. Making fragrances from her flowers was a special hobby, and she had recently invented a new scent. Katherine had loved the perfume the first time Sophie had worn it in her presence a few weeks previously and had requested some of the fragrance from her.

Distracted by recent events, Sophie had forgotten that request, and it was fortunate she remembered it now. They were going to Ascot in less than two weeks, and the recipe needed that long to distill so that the flower scents would blend together. Since she couldn't sleep, she might as well make some now to take with her to Berkshire.

Sophie went to her perfumery, one of several "rooms" she had created in the conservatory by using trees, vines, and other plants. From her shelf of tinctures, she selected the bottles she needed for her newest creation and took them to her worktable.

She loved being in here. There was something about this room that soothed her nerves and eased her mind, and making perfume from her own flowers was a hobby she thoroughly enjoyed.

Sophie had just gathered all the ingredients and tools she needed when she heard footsteps on the tile floor.

"Sophie?"

She stiffened. That was Mick's voice. Had he made a decision already? "I'm in my perfumery," she called back.

"Your what?"

She repeated her words, and the sound of her voice enabled him to find her amid all the exotic greenery. He walked in through the doorway she had made of two immense Grecian urns and looked around him. "A perfumery?" he said, glancing at the table and the array of bottles on it. "You make perfume?"

The hoarse tightness of his voice made her fear the worst.

"Do you wear the perfume you make?" he asked, his gaze moving slowly up her body to her face.

There was something in the way he was looking at her. It was the same way he had looked at her in the library. It was a look of desire, hot and fierce, scorching her.

She forced herself to say something. "I just invented a new recipe. It's my favorite. I wear it all the time. People seem to like it. My cousin wants some, and I'm going to make some for her. Lord Fortescue seemed to like the fragrance very much."

Mick jerked at his tie, loosening it. "I'll bet he did."

Her own mention of her cousin brought her back to the most important thing on her mind. "Did you make a decision about my aunt?"

"What?" He shook his head as if coming out of a reverie. "Yes," he finally answered. "I did."

"And?"

She bit her lip, gripping the edge of the table so tightly her hands began to ache. She held her breath, waiting.

"A reporter from one of the penny papers was at Scotland Yard," he went on. "Merrick had told him the cousin of a viscount had been arrested."

"Then Auntie's ruined," she murmured. She relaxed her grip and lowered her head, staring down at the vast array of bottles on the table before her. Four years of knowing Auntie's affliction and doing everything she could to protect her from scandal, and it had all been for naught.

"I wouldn't quite say ruined," he said.

Sophie looked up, still thinking the worst. "What does that mean?"

"I had a little talk with Sergeant Merrick, and I explained to him that those related to peers do not get arrested. It simply isn't done. He didn't understand that particular rule of the Metropolitan Police." He paused, then added obscurely, "He's not the only one."

"Does this mean you aren't going to arrest Auntie?"

"Yes, that's what it means."

Sophie choked back a sob.

"Don't cry," he said, "or I'll change my mind."

"I'm not going to cry," she assured him, so relieved she could hardly get the words out. "I'm just stunned. I never expected—"

"What?" he interrupted. "That I might have a heart?"

"Something like that," she admitted with a laugh. "I didn't think you believed me when I said I didn't know who shot at you, and that you were going to arrest Auntie to bring me to heel."

"I don't arrest elderly ladies who aren't harming anyone just because they technically break the law. There wouldn't have been evidence to hold her in any case, because like you, I cannot imagine Viscountess Fortescue pressing charges against Violet."

"I'm Katherine's cousin, too, and it didn't stop you from arresting me," she pointed out.

"You were never officially under arrest."

"I wasn't? It felt very official to me!"

"I didn't file an arrest report, or a police report, I

didn't take your fingerprints for the record, and I didn't put you in a cell."

"What about the newspaper journalist?"

"I told him that Sergeant Merrick was mistaken. You were only there to report a minor crime. Your aunt was with you, of course, as a proper chaperone, since no young lady would go to the police by herself."

Sophie studied him for a long moment, thinking for the first time that perhaps he was not so awful after all. "Thank you."

His lips tightened, and he looked away. "Forget about it. I have."

"What crime did I supposedly come to report?" she asked.

"A missing watch."

She burst out laughing, and he returned his gaze to her, his brows drawn together in puzzlement. "It was the best I could do on the spur of the moment," he said. "Why is it so amusing?"

"Because it's so appropriate," she explained, still laughing. "I am always losing watches. I've given up wearing them. I lose handkerchiefs, too."

His lashes lowered. "Buttons as well, it seems."

She glanced down, realizing that one of the buttons on her nightgown was indeed missing, revealing a bit of the bare skin between her breasts.

Sophie put her hand up to cover the gap in her gown, hotly embarrassed. "No one in this house likes to sew," she mumbled, knowing she was blushing. "Especially me."

He laughed low in his throat, and she fancied that it

sounded like the laugh a pirate might make, a touch of wickedness behind the amusement. He was staring at her, his gaze seeming to slice right through her hand to the gap in her gown and the skin beneath. Right to her heart.

She stood still, hand to her breast, paralyzed by that look. What was it about him that always seemed to catch her between the desire to move toward him and the desire to run away? It was like the fascination for a fire. One moved closer and closer, then got burned.

Sophie tore her gaze from his. His body blocked the only exit, and unless she wanted to crash through the camellias and fig trees surrounding her, there was no escape other than past him. She lifted her chin. "I think I'll go to bed," she said and circled the table, hoping he would move aside.

Of course, he didn't. In fact, he spread his arms, blocking her way completely. His hands touched the urns on either side, his arms placed low enough that she could not duck past him.

She looked at his hand, his strong, tanned fingers curled around the body of a Greek maiden carved in the white stone of the urn. Tongues of heat danced along her spine and down her legs, making her feel as if she were melting right there onto the terrazzo floor.

She cleared her throat. "Could you move out of my way?" she asked, trying to sound nonchalant and failing. "I'd really like to go to bed."

"So would I," he said with feeling, but he still didn't move. His lashes lowered, and he seemed to be staring at her mouth. "What's in that perfume of yours? An aphrodisiac?"

Before she could even think of a reply, he moved, wrapping an arm around her waist and pulling her close against his body. He lifted his free hand to her hair, wrapping the long strands in his fist, pulling her head back. Then he bent his head and kissed her.

Charles had kissed her once, in the garden of the vicarage at Stoke-On-Trent, right after she had accepted his proposal of marriage. He'd pressed his lips to hers in the quick and proper fashion of a gentleman. Mick's kiss, however, was anything but quick and proper. It was raw and powerful, his mouth opening over hers, his tongue brushing her lips until she parted them.

When she did, his tongue entered her mouth, tasting deeply of her. She'd never felt this quivering excitement, this hot neediness, the desperate longing for more.

His arm was a band of steel across her back, holding her so tight against him that she was standing on tiptoe. Through the thin fabric of her nightgown, she could feel the powerful strength of his body, the pressing of him, hard and aroused, against her. She knew what that meant, too.

This wasn't about love, only desire. But even as she told herself that, Sophie wrapped her arms around his neck, hanging on to him, the only solid thing when everything else seemed to be spinning. She deepened the kiss even more, meeting his tongue with her own.

He tore his lips from hers with a groan. "Good God," he muttered. "What am I doing?"

She felt him beginning to pull away from her, and she didn't want him to pull away. She tightened her arms around his neck. "Mick," she gasped, pressing her body closer to his, moving her body against his, guided by instinct and a hot desperation she didn't understand.

"This has got to stop," he said, but instead of pushing her away, he kept his arms tight around her and buried his face against the side of her neck, his breathing quick and hot on her skin. "God, woman, what's in that stuff?" he mumbled. "Spanish fly?"

"Jasmine," she gasped, shivering as he tasted her skin with his tongue. "Lemon."

"That's not what I meant." He trailed kisses up the side of her neck to her ear. "No, I mean the secret ingredient."

"What secret ingredient?"

"The one that makes me insane, that makes me do things that are stupid." He pulled her earlobe between his lips, sucking it like a piece of candy, teasing, tasting. She began to shiver.

"Mick."

Her whisper of his name seemed to trigger something in him, and he tore himself away from her with such suddenness that she swayed on her feet, disoriented for a moment without his arms around her. She blinked, trying to get her bearings as he backed away from her, and she was bewildered by his abrupt withdrawal.

"Stupid," he muttered, shaking his head, staring at her as if he couldn't believe what had just happened. "I must be the stupidest bastard in the entire country."

She didn't know what he meant. She couldn't sense his thoughts or feelings. In fact, she couldn't seem to think at all.

"Don't wear that perfume around me anymore," he said curtly, turned, and was gone. Sophie stared at the opening between the urns, the tips of her fingers pressed to her mouth, as his footsteps on the tile faded away and she was alone.

Now she understood what it meant to want a man, to want his kiss, his touch. To need that heat and feel that desperation. Mick had shown her all that, ignited something in her that had not been there before, and she knew she would never be able to hate him again.

Nine

❧

During the two weeks that followed, Sophie saw little of Mick, and she didn't know whether to be glad of it or not.

She knew he wanted her, but men wanted women all the time. That meant nothing. It was her own behavior that night in the conservatory that shocked her. The way she had responded to him, the way she had clung to him, with some undefinable, aching need for his touch was nothing short of wanton. She hardly knew him, she wasn't sure she even liked him, yet she had returned his kiss with a passion she had never felt before.

Violet asked her how on earth they were supposed to watch over Mick and protect him if he was never there, and in response, Sophie reassured her aunt that if Inspector Dunbar was in imminent danger, she would know.

That wasn't a lie. The few times she had seen him during the past two weeks, she had also been able to see his aura. If it disappeared again, she would know to take action to protect him, but until then, she knew he was safe.

Her worry that he would browbeat and interrogate all her friends and acquaintances proved to be somewhat exaggerated. He did ask people she knew about her, but never by revealing that he was a detective making inquiries. He seemed to be giving people the impression that he was interested in Sophie in a romantic way, which shocked those of her acquaintance who were snobs, and intrigued those who were not. Sophie was not flattered. He might desire her, but he still suspected her to be involved with a criminal. She also sensed that Mick was a man for whom women were like dessert, a delicious treat to be enjoyed and soon forgotten.

Fortunately, she had little time to dwell on it. The campaign to find Sophie a suitable husband had begun the day after Agatha's arrival with a trip to dressmakers in Regent Street for a new wardrobe. Though Sophie fought to prevent it, she was fitted for an entirely new wardrobe, bought for her with Harold's money, a fact Charlotte would bring up for the rest of their lives. Once Sophie had suitable clothes, the social whirl began. Sophie was dragged to card parties, teas, cotillions, balls, and so many other events that she lost count.

Balls were the worst, since she was so bad at dancing. All the lessons in the world couldn't stop her from feeling like a stiff and awkward mannequin every time she walked onto a ballroom floor. She made excuses to refuse at every opportunity, and a fight with her mother always ensued afterward. She knew the only way to defeat Mama was outright defiance, but Agatha was a difficult person to defy.

By the time they joined Victor and Katherine in Berkshire for Ascot week, Sophie was exhausted from the struggle.

Ascot was always a grand occasion, even more so this year because of the Queen's Diamond Jubilee. The gentlemen were on their best behavior, and careful not to become too intoxicated. Ladies wore their most fashionable new hats and gowns. Sophie was now as suitably attired as the rest, but she had never paid much attention to fashion and really didn't care.

Mick was waiting for them by the Grand Stand when they arrived at the racecourse for the opening day.

Even Charlotte could not have found fault with the way he looked. He was impeccably dressed for Ascot in a pearl gray suit, white shirt and white waistcoat, and gray felt homburg hat.

Violet greeted him warmly and introduced him to the other members of the family. With the exception of Lord Fortescue, there was no mistaking the coolness of their greeting. Victor was the only one besides Auntie who didn't seem to hate the idea of having him there.

Violet, however, did not seem to sense the tension in the air. She talked with Mick as if it were nothing out of the ordinary to bring a policeman along to Ascot, but Sophie knew differently. The other women were horrified. Harold was afraid.

She remained a few feet away from the group, watching. Mick didn't seem to mind their antagonism, and received their frigidly polite greetings with the ease of any gentleman.

After the introductions, he turned to Victor. "My lord, thank you for the invitation to join you here. Which do you favor as the winner of the Ascot Stakes today? I predict Masque II."

There was nothing of the snob about Victor. The viscount beamed on the younger man as if he'd just found a kindred spirit. "Masque II is my choice, as well. Clearly has the best chance all around." He put a hand on Mick's shoulder. "Glad to have a man along who knows racing. Did you arrive this morning?"

"I did. I forwarded my things on to your estate as your cousin, Mrs. Summerstreet, instructed." He turned to Katherine. "Viscountess Fortescue, I believe you and I have a connection, of sorts."

Katherine did not seem impressed. "Indeed? What connection is that?"

Sophie watched Mick reach into his pocket with his free hand, and she tensed as he pulled out Katherine's emerald necklace. He picked up the viscountess's hand and placed the string of jewels in her palm. "This, I believe, belongs to you."

"Indeed, yes, it does!" She took it, and some of her coldness faded away. "Look, Fortescue," she cried in amazement. "My emeralds have been recovered."

Victor glanced at them, then at Mick, and Sophie

sensed his favorable impression growing. "I never thought the police would recover them."

"Why, it's unaccountable," the viscountess added. "However did you find them, Inspector?"

"In a most unexpected way." As he spoke with Katherine, Sophie noticed he continued to hold the viscountess's hand in his. Katherine was even allowing it.

"What is all this about your necklace?" Agatha demanded. "Katherine, you went to the police?"

The viscountess managed to tear her gaze from Mick's, and she withdrew her hand from his. "I did, Agatha. I discovered my favorite necklace was missing, and I contacted Scotland Yard at once."

Agatha gave a disapproving sniff, but Katherine was delighted by the results of what some, including Sophie's mother, would consider to be an inappropriate action. She returned her attention to Mick and actually began a conversation with him. "Have you been to Ascot before, Inspector?"

"Yes, indeed, my lady, many times. When I worked at Special Branch, I was twice assigned to stand with other officers as guard during the royal procession, and I have also come solely for the pleasure of the races."

"You must tell me how you recovered my emeralds," Katherine said, and it was clear her frigid demeanor toward Mick had thawed completely. "Tell us all."

The entire party turned their attention to him, and Sophie's stomach twisted into knots as she watched him, wondering what he would say.

"I'm afraid neither I nor Scotland Yard can claim credit here, my lady. They were anonymously sent to the Lost Property Department."

Sophie laughed under her breath. What a perfect story. No long explanations, no inconvenient questions. "What a fortunate circumstance," she murmured, causing Mick to glance in her direction. He turned that smile of his on her, and Sophie couldn't help thinking of what had happened that night in the conservatory a fortnight ago. Mick was thinking of it, too. She looked into his face, and she knew. She forced her gaze away.

"It's extraordinary," Katherine was saying. "I wonder who sent them to Scotland Yard. This shows there are some honest people in the world."

"I'm happy the emeralds are recovered, of course," Agatha put in, "but going to the police is going rather too far, don't you think?"

"Victor didn't mind."

"Going to the police is the only thing to do," Lord Fortescue put in. "What are they there for, in heaven's name?"

"Still," Charlotte put in, "it must have been a difficult dilemma for you, my dear cousin."

"Not at all." Katherine shrugged her slim shoulders. "If I hadn't gone to the police, I might never have recovered them. The men at Scotland Yard wouldn't have known where to return them."

Agatha dismissed the whole matter with a wave of her hand, and conversation turned to the day's races. Mick moved to Sophie's side.

"Thank you for what you just did," she murmured.

"For your tact and for your discretion. I can't tell you how grateful I am."

He edged closer to her. "Prove it."

Sophie looked at him, and something in those two words sent an inexplicable thrill through her, a shot of pleasure and trepidation. The pirate's thrill. "How—" She stopped, words suddenly caught in her throat. He had the bluest eyes she'd ever seen, lighter around the pupils, like the sky, then darkening to thin rings of deep lapis around his irises. She swallowed, tried again. "Prove it how?"

"Answer the question I asked you in the garden."

She felt the remembered brush of rose petals beneath her chin.

Is it a lover you're protecting?

"I don't have a lover," she whispered and felt herself leaning closer to him. Her hand fluttered in the air. She wanted so badly to touch him, to feel the hard wall of his chest beneath her fingers.

"Michael?"

Violet's voice broke in, and Sophie straightened away from him with a jerking motion. Lord, she was surrounded by a crowd of people, and she'd almost put her hands on him. Sophie took a step back and bit her lip, her heart beating like the wings of a hummingbird.

Mick turned his attention to Violet, who had now joined them. "Yes, ma'am?"

"Dear boy, I must speak with you." Violet put a hand on his arm, and Sophie felt a flash of envy. She clasped her hands behind her back. "I must thank you for your kindness to me."

His expression became stern, but Sophie thought there was a hint of humor in his eyes. "I'm going to tell you again, Violet, no more jewel thefts," he murmured, his voice low. "Detectives receive rewards for arrests, and there are other members of the Metropolitan Police who wouldn't have any compunction about sending you off to prison for a pound or two of reward money. And if you steal something from someone who is willing to prosecute, you'll be in serious trouble."

"Mick is right, Auntie," Sophie whispered. "You were very fortunate this time. In future, you must try to control yourself."

"I'll try, my dear," Violet pledged, crossing her heart, "Honestly."

Sophie looked into her dear aunt's face and could detect little sign of penitence. She sighed. Mick chuckled. "Violet, I believe you are the most adorable criminal I've ever met."

"Why, thank you, Michael. I will take that as a compliment."

"What are the three of you whispering about over there?" Agatha called out to them in a tone that demanded an answer.

Violet turned in her sister's direction. "Dear Michael was telling us some fascinating stories."

"About crime and vice, no doubt," Agatha said with a shudder.

Violet moved to rejoin her sister and the others. "Actually, no, dear," she told Agatha, "Michael was telling us about some of the important and fascinating people he's met over the years. Do you know, he actually knows the Duke of Ethridge?" She turned to Victor. "Cousin, tell us what is happening in Parliament."

Victor, a vehement Whig, began a heated dissertation on the most recent antics of the Tories, which were ridiculous, and the campaign of the Labor Party, which was impossible to take seriously. Harold joined in the discussion, and the ladies listened politely, pretending to be interested.

Sophie returned her attention to Mick. "How does she know that you know the Duke of Ethridge?"

"I haven't a clue. I've never met the man in my life."

She laughed. "Dear Auntie. She likes you, you see, so she is trying to impress the others with your connections, even if she has to make them up."

"I arrested Sir Roger Ellerton, son of Lord Chadwick, not long ago. Does that count?"

"I don't think so. Why on earth did you arrest Sir Roger?"

"For drunkenness, being a public nuisance, and striking a police officer."

"Ah, the black eye. I was right, then."

"Yes, you were. Good guess."

"It wasn't a guess," Sophie assured him. "I knew it because I saw it happen."

"I didn't know you were in the Cannon Row Police Station when Sir Roger hit me."

"I saw it in my mind. You know perfectly well what I meant."

Agatha's voice interrupted before Mick could reply. "Sophie, dear, come over here. I have some exciting news."

"Yes, Mother?" She moved to join the others, and

Mick followed her. "What exciting news?" she asked.

"Lord Heath is in residence at Crossroads, and they have invited us to a card party after the races today."

"Breathtaking news, indeed." Sophie fanned herself with her hands. "I am all astonishment."

"Sophie, dear, don't be tiresome. Lord Heath's youngest son Robert is not yet married. I believe the two of you might suit. He has always been quite fond of you."

That her mother was talking about her marital prospects in front of her cousins was bad enough, but in front of Mick, it was humiliating. Something inside her snapped. "Robert is not fond of me at all," Sophie answered tartly. "He prefers the servant girls, especially the kitchen maid."

Without waiting for a reply to her scandalous words, Sophie turned on her heel and walked away, seething. She marched down the steps of the Grand Stand and across the manicured lawns, so furious and mortified that she paid no heed to where she was going. She did not stop until she hit the white rail of the paddocks that housed the horses.

Breathing hard, she curled her fingers around the fence rail and rested her forehead between her hands. She was an oddity, a freak. She "saw" things. To marry any man, she would have to pretend. She would have to lie, and she was a very bad liar. She'd tried to deceive Charles, but it had not worked. She would never pretend again.

"Why are you so opposed to your mother's efforts to marry you off?"

Sophie stiffened at the sound of Mick's voice as she felt him stop beside her. She turned her head to look at him. "You're a detective. Draw your own conclusions."

"All right." He folded his arms across his chest and leaned his hip against the fence post. "Perhaps it's because your mother keeps shoving it at you, and no one wants anything that is pushed at them over and over again."

She turned and looked out at the horses in the paddock. She did not reply.

"Or," he went on in a musing, gentle voice, "perhaps it's because you don't think any man would want to marry you, and you don't want to get hurt."

Sophie let out an exasperated breath. "No one understands!" she cried, turning toward him. "It's much more than that. I won't pretend anymore. I spent my entire childhood trying to be a good girl, an ordinary girl, the kind of daughter any mother would be proud of. The more my sister ridiculed me, the more my mother silenced me, the harder I tried to be what they wanted. But I couldn't stop these . . . these things that would pop into my head. I would try to deny them, but I couldn't. I'd have visions, images that would flash through my mind and make my head hurt. They'd overwhelm me, and I'd faint. I was always fainting." She began to laugh. "My mother told people I was delicate."

Mick said nothing. He just watched her, his head tilted slightly to one side.

"I would have these dreams all the time. I would wake up sobbing, because I had dreamed that old Mr. Carr at the smithy was going to die the next day, or because I knew that Freddie Lowe was torturing cats again because he liked to do it."

"Dreams can be very frightening. I have nightmares about criminals I've met. Cases I've worked on."

"It isn't the same. You have dreams about things that have already happened, or things that aren't ever going to happen. What I dream comes true. The things I see actually occur."

The breeze whipped a loose tendril of hair across her cheek, and before she could push it back, he did it for her, tucking it behind her ear. She pushed his hand away. "I used to pretend that I didn't see things, that I didn't dream the future. I'd pretend I was normal. It didn't work. I won't pretend any more, and people think I'm a freak."

"I don't think you're a freak." A tiny smile tipped the corners of his mouth. "A little odd, perhaps. A bit disconcerting when you blurt out secrets, like Lord Heath's son and the kitchen maid. A bit dithery." His lashes swept down as his gaze lowered. "Always coming undone."

Sophie looked down and saw that the enormous bow of the sash at her waist had loosened to a half-knot. With a cry of dismay, she retied the bow. "I don't know why I can't keep my clothes in place."

He gave a shout of laughter, and she looked up again, glaring at him. "That's not what I meant."

He smothered his amusement. "I know what you meant. Your finch is falling over."

Her hands lifted to her hat, and she adjusted the bird ornament that trimmed it back to the proper angle. "Is that better?"

"Much better. I don't suppose I should tell you about your missing earring?" He reached into his pocket and pulled out the pearl droplet. "It came off on the path down here."

He took her hand and dropped the piece of jewelry into her palm. "Thank you." Her gloved fingers closed around the earring and she looked up at him. "Why are you suddenly being so nice?"

"Maybe I'm just a nice bloke," he murmured.

Sophie shook her head but began to laugh. "No, that's not it."

"You think not?" He gave her a look of mock pity. "If you were truly psychic, you would know that I am in truth a nice, decent, hardworking, fair-minded fellow, responsible and trustworthy. You would be able to appreciate all my fine qualities."

Ignoring her sound of disbelief, he gestured to the horses in the paddock. "You want me to believe you have psychic ability. If you could tell me who's going to win the first race, I might become convinced."

"It won't do. This sort of thing never works for me. I never have premonitions about horse races or sweeps numbers or shares on the exchange, or anything that involves money. Sometimes I can see what cards will come up if Miss Atwood is playing patience. But not on command, and certainly not if there is money involved."

"It's worth a try, isn't it?"

She studied him, and her eyes narrowed. "If I can convince you I'm psychic, do you agree to stop prying into my life and that of my friends and family?"

"Why should it bother you?" he countered. "Now

that I've discovered the skeleton in your family closet, what do you care?" Suddenly his gaze hardened. "Or perhaps there are more skeletons I haven't uncovered?"

If Violet being a kleptomaniac wasn't scandal enough to ruin the family, Harold going to prison for fraud and embezzlement certainly would be. And she doubted Mick would be quite as nice about her brother-in-law as he'd been about Auntie. After all, Auntie was an elderly lady who couldn't help herself. Harold, on the other hand, was an out-and-out criminal. Mick wouldn't hesitate to send him to prison, but the scandal would be just as humiliating.

"Don't be ridiculous."

"Don't be defensive."

"Defensive with you, you mean. And that's easily explained now that you know about Auntie."

"There's more here than just your aunt."

"Of course there is. People don't like being asked all sorts of questions and being under suspicion for things they didn't do."

"My life is at stake here," he reminded her. "Forgive me for not putting your sensibilities first."

"I appreciate the dangers you face. I truly do. It is always very frightening to me when I predict someone's death. Why can't you believe me?"

She looked at him, and she knew her earnest attempt to convince him of the truth had failed. "I don't know why I am always so disheartened and frustrated by skepticism," she murmured. "I should be used to it by now."

He pulled off his hat and raked a hand through his

hair. The sun shimmered off a few silver-gray strands amid the black ones, and the breeze danced in the longer tendrils at his collar. "Sophie, you can't expect me to just take your word for it," he said, looking down at the hat in his hands. "I never take anyone's word for anything."

"You needn't take my word alone. Ask Auntie or Miss Peabody or Miss Atwood. They can give you many examples of predictions I've had that have come true."

"All of them are spiritualists," he pointed out and lifted his head to look at her. "They would see a connection between one of your predictions and any vaguely similar incident."

"Grimstock, then. He knows."

"He's very loyal to you and your aunt. He would say whatever you wanted him to say."

"You see," she said bitterly. "You will try to explain away anything I tried to tell you as something other than the psychic power that it is. And you still believe I'm involved with whoever shot at you."

"Sophie, I am fully prepared to acknowledge that you are a very perceptive woman and you possess strong intuition, but I cannot believe what you say about yourself without solid proof. I need evidence. I've spent seventeen years as a policeman, and I can't set that aside to believe in some sort of spiritualistic theory that can't be proved. Until then, I must regard you as a suspect. You want me to believe you can read my mind and see the future. I just can't swallow it."

"Fine." She turned toward the horses. "I'll see if I can change your mind."

There were eight geldings, two gray, two chestnut, three black, and one dun yellow. She closed her eyes, but she could sense nothing from these racehorses to indicate which might win. Nothing at all.

"Well?" Mick asked beside her. "Which are the winners?"

"I don't know." She shook her head, unable to help feeling discouraged despite her knowledge all along that it wouldn't work. "I have no idea."

"Perhaps you will for the next race."

Sophie took the very blandness of those words as a challenge. With every race that day, she studied the horses with great attention, but not once did she get a premonition of a winner. Not even a glimmer of insight. It was very disheartening.

The day was not made any better by her mother and sister. Though Mick's manners were impeccable, neither her mother nor her sister said a word to him through the entire afternoon, nor did they once acknowledge his presence.

They spent their time in an open discussion of various possibilities for Sophie's matrimonial future. Sophie tried to ignore their conversation, but she did notice that Charlotte's suggestions always had a sting: men who were old enough to be her grandfather, or notorious for drunkenness, or inveterate gamblers. The two women deigned to ask Sophie's opinion once, and when she tartly replied that she wanted to marry the costermonger at the end of her street, they gave up and did not ask her again. Sophie was glad when the last race had been run.

Her mother had said they were supposed to go on to

supper and cards afterward at Crossroads, but the last thing Sophie wanted was to be thrust at Lord Heath's son as if she were meat on display in a butcher's window. She longed for a cup of tea and a quiet, peaceful evening. She wished she could think of an excuse to go back to Victor's estate.

It was starting to rain a bit as they left Ascot. The entire party paused outside the gates of the racecourse to coordinate the carriage ride to Crossroads.

Victor offered Mick a ride in his carriage, but Mick refused. "I hired a carriage of my own at the station, my lord, and—"

"Victor," Harold interrupted, "Mr. Dunbar was not invited to the party, and we can hardly bring him along uninvited."

"Nonsense!" Victor said. "No one cares about that sort of thing these days."

"With all due respect, I must agree with my husband," Charlotte interjected, making no effort to hide her eagerness to be rid of Mick. "Lady Heath would care. You know what a stickler she is for proprieties. She would be shocked. And a policeman, no less."

As Charlotte spoke, an idea began to form in Sophie's mind, and she hoped Auntie would understand and help her along.

She made a moan loud enough to get everyone's attention, pressed a hand to her forehead, and tried to look as pathetic as possible. "Oh, dear," she said and moaned again. "I feel quite dizzy all of a sudden, and I have such a headache. I think I'm going to—"

Everyone watched as Sophie suddenly went limp. Her knees buckled beneath her, and her eyes closed. She set her jaw, bracing herself for what she knew was going to be a hard landing on the gravel, then collapsed as if she had fainted dead away. She hoped it was a convincing performance.

Ten

❧

She never even hit the ground. Mick, standing close by, caught her as she fell, curving one arm behind her back and the other beneath her knees. He lifted her into his arms as if she weighed nothing, his action so quick and effortless that Sophie wondered if detectives were trained to rescue fainting ladies.

Her family was quite alarmed. With her eyes closed she could not see their faces, but she could hear their voices and sense their concern. Agatha asked for smelling salts. Katherine suggested that someone find a doctor. Charlotte said they should get her out of the rain. Victor and Harold agreed how astonishing it was that women were such fragile creatures.

"Perhaps she's had a vision," Violet said. "She faints whenever she has a vision."

"Don't be ridiculous," Agatha snapped. "She's probably just laced too tight."

"Do we have to stand out in the rain?" Charlotte wailed.

Mick's voice, deep and decisive, cut through all the others. "We need to get her home."

Sophie was starting to like him.

She had never been held in a man's arms this way before, and it was rather wonderful. The perfect fit of her cheek against the curve in his shoulder, the strength of his arms as he held her without moving, the warmth of his body, made her feel protected and safe. She yearned to curl her arms around his neck, savor the scent of bay rum that clung to his skin, but she couldn't. She was supposed to be unconscious, after all.

Mick's suggestion to get her home was agreed upon by all the family, but Sophie had no chance to feel relieved.

"I'll go with her," Agatha declared.

That would never do. Sophie had been counting on Auntie to volunteer to go home with her. Alone with Agatha, she'd never have a quiet, peaceful evening. She could hear the lectures starting already.

If you'd try a bit harder, dear, and not be so outspoken, you could have any gentleman in the country. And your figure is excellent, if you'd dress properly and make the most of it.

Sophie decided she'd better wake up at once.

With another moan, she lifted her head from Mick's shoulder and opened her eyes, blinking at everyone in sleepy surprise. "Oh, dear. What happened?"

"You fainted," Mick told her gravely, but when she looked up at him, she thought she detected a suspicious curve to one corner of his mouth.

Sophie ignored it. "I did?" She looked about in pretended astonishment, then frowned. "My head aches."

"We must get you home, dear." Agatha looked at Mick. "Put her down at once."

"With all due respect, ma'am, I don't think that's wise," Mick answered, and Sophie felt his arms tighten around her. "She might faint again, you know."

"Very well, then, let's at least get her into the carriage and out of this rain."

"Mother, I'm all right," Sophie said, desperate to divert her mother from the intention of accompanying her. "I just need to go home and go straight to bed. You needn't come along. I wouldn't dream of ruining your evening."

"Nonsense. Of course I'm going with you. We'll get you home and send for a doctor."

"It's probably a bilious attack," Charlotte said, disinterested.

"It's her head that hurts, Charlotte, not her tummy," Violet pointed out. "It's just a sick headache, isn't it, dear? You didn't have a vision?"

Sophie shook her head, and Auntie patted her cheek with a smile of affection. "You'll be fine after a good night's rest. There's no reason for any of us to go along." She looked up at Mick. "Please escort her home safely, Michael, in your carriage. I'll ride to Crossroads with Victor and Katherine."

Sophie was so astonished that she couldn't help blurting out, "Auntie, you're not coming?"

"Darling, there's no need. Michael will escort you home, you'll take a spoonful of my tonic—the one in the brown bottle, not the blue—and go to bed. Come along, Agatha."

"Violet, we can't go to the party!" Agatha cried. "We need to go home with Sophie."

"Nonsense. What good would we be? She has a headache, and she's going straight to bed. Michael will escort her there, and see that she arrives home safely, won't you, dear boy?"

"Of course," Mick answered. "We'll go straightaway."

"What?" Agatha's voice boomed out in horror. "He can't take her home alone. Him? Without a chaperone?"

"He *is* a policeman," Violet pointed out. "How could she possibly be any safer than that?"

Agatha started to protest again, but Violet interrupted. "My dear sister, Sophie hasn't been sleeping well of late, and she's just tired. She needs peace, quiet, and a decent night's rest. There is no need for us to go. Besides, you never get to see Lord and Lady Heath, since you're usually only a short while in London each year. Sophie will be perfectly safe in Inspector Dunbar's company, and he will escort her home. She'll get a good sleep and by tomorrow she'll be right as rain. Come along, dear."

"Sophie will be fine, Mother," Charlotte said with an impatient tug on Agatha's sleeve. "For heaven's sake, let's be on our way before we get soaked out here. It's starting to pour."

The rain was indeed coming down harder now, and

Sophie watched as her mother reluctantly allowed herself to be led toward Harold's carriage. Mick turned in the opposite direction and carried Sophie to another hansom.

The driver had put the top of the carriage up before the rain started, and the interior was dry. Mick instructed the driver to take them to Lord Fortescue's estate, then he lifted her into the carriage and laid her across the seat. He followed her in and took the opposite seat as the driver shut the door.

The carriage jerked into motion, then moved along the graveled drive that led to the main road, only one of many vehicles leaving the racecourse. Sophie sat up, pressing her fingers to her temples with what she hoped was a pain-filled whimper.

Mick burst out laughing.

She looked at him, pretending wide-eyed surprise. "What is so amusing?"

"Excellent acting, Sophie," he said as he leaned back against the dark red leather of the seat. Still laughing, he pulled off his hat and tossed it aside. "You almost had me convinced."

"I don't know what you mean."

"Damn me if you don't. You pretended to faint so you wouldn't have to go to the party and have your mother push Lord Heath's son at you as a potential husband. Clear as daylight."

"I didn't pretend anything."

"Uh-huh. That's why you were snuggling into my shoulder like a happy kitten. Because you were unconscious."

"I did no such thing!"

"Liar. You were practically purring."

"I was not." She glared at him. "Besides, no well-bred gentleman would ever accuse a lady of lying."

"You already know I'm not a gentleman, and I'm not well bred. I grew up in the East End, and the only family I ever had was an old prostitute named Flossie Mulvaney who let me live in her flat for the price of six handkerchiefs a week."

"Handkerchiefs?" she asked, temporarily diverted from arguing with him. "What do they have to do with paying rent?"

"Handkerchiefs bring a ha'penny apiece from any receiver."

Sophie was puzzled. "But what is a receiver?"

"A receiver pays thieves for stolen goods, then sells them secondhand to the public."

"Stolen handkerchiefs?" She stared at him in disbelief. "You? But you're a policeman!"

"I wasn't a policeman when I was ten."

"No, you were a pickpocket."

"I was born in an orphanage. My mother had died there having me. When I was six, they sent me to the workhouse, and I ran away from there when I was ten. After that, I had to survive on the street. I became a pickpocket." He grinned at her. "Just like the Dickens story, don't you think? I'm still waiting for the rich man to adopt me."

She didn't know whether to feel sorry for him or laugh at the irony. She decided to laugh. "The policeman who used to be a pickpocket."

"It's an asset to me now. Having been a thief myself, having been around the gangs and prostitutes who work the streets, I understand the criminal mind pretty well. It helps me immensely in my work, and that's why I've risen to my present rank so quickly. Most men my age are still detective sergeants, or possibly divisional detective inspectors."

"But you're a detective inspector, too."

"I work out of Scotland Yard itself, not a specific division. I am one of only a few detectives who have roving commissions. I have authority to work any case in any division."

She slid back, settling herself more comfortably on the seat of the carriage. "What on earth made you decide to become a policeman in the first place?"

"It's a good job for a man with no formal education. But I really wanted to be a private detective."

She smiled. "Like Sherlock Holmes?"

"Just like Sherlock Holmes. When I read the first story in *The Strand Magazine,* I thought that was the most interesting profession a man could have, but I went into the police force because I needed food to eat and a place to live, and I didn't want to be a petty thief for the rest of my life. Nor did I want to settle for work in a factory or on the docks."

"How did you learn to read?"

"I taught myself when I was fifteen. Flossie and I moved around too much for me to go to a national school."

Sophie was astonished. Though she had very little money, there were things she had always taken for granted. A governess had taught her to read, and she'd always had food to eat and a warm, comfortable place to live. Though her family had their flaws, at least they were there, and even Charlotte could be counted on for help if she ever got into real trouble, even if it was only to avoid a scandal. "I can't imagine anyone teaching himself to read," she said with admiration. "How did you do it?"

"The truth?" When she nodded, he said, "I dug old newspapers out of rubbish heaps, and I'd stand on street corners, newspaper in hand, and ask people to read me the headlines as they passed by. When they told me what a headline said, I memorized what the words looked like."

Sophie tilted her head to one side, studying him. The corner of his mouth curved in a hint of a smile and his gaze seemed focused on the far distance, as if he were remembering himself standing on that street corner, asking people to read him the headlines. "You must have been quite determined to learn," she murmured, bringing his gaze back to her.

"I knew the only way to get out of the gutter was to learn to read, so I did it. I also taught myself French and German, by correspondence course when I was a constable. It helps an officer get promoted if he knows more than one language. I also took diction classes for several years to rid myself of the worst of my dialect."

The more he talked about his upbringing, the more she wanted to know. "Why did you move around so much?"

"It doesn't take the local constables long to identify thieves and keep close watch on them. Because of that, I've been in just about every street, alley, mews, crescent, or lane from Kensington to East Ham. I know this city and its environs like the back of my hand."

"How did you meet this Flossie?"

"I hooked up with her one night in an alley off Bishopsgate. I saw her with some bloke who—" He broke off and looked out the window. "We're coming up to the main road. We should be at Lord Fortescue's in half an hour or so."

He clearly didn't want to tell her any more. "You saw her with some man. Then what?"

After a moment of silence, he finally looked at her and said, "She didn't fancy this bloke, and he didn't take it very well. I hit him over the head with an empty gin bottle."

"You came to her rescue like that, and you were only ten years old?"

He gave a cough of embarrassment at her choice of words and went on, "Don't start thinking I was being heroic or anything like that. Between us, Flossie and I took two quid and six from his pockets."

"In my opinion, he deserved it."

"I thought so. Flossie taught me how to be a pick-pocket. She let me live in her flat and got me food, even meat when she could afford it."

She watched his mouth turn down in an expression of distaste, and she knew why. "That's why you hate mutton. Because it's a cheaper cut of meat, and it was the only meat you got as a boy." She gave him a defiant glance. "There now, go ahead and tell me I just made a lucky guess."

Mick held up his hands, palms facing her in a gesture of peace. "I am enjoying this truce we have at the moment. Let's not ruin it by quarreling. Agreed?"

He smiled at her, and she found herself smiling back. She didn't want to quarrel with him. "Agreed."

"Good. Now, since we've called a truce, be honest. Admit I was right, and fainting was all an act to get out of spending the evening with your mother. Wasn't it?"

Sophie raised her brows at him, as if surprised he could ask such a question. "You met my mother," she pointed out. "Would you enjoy spending the entire day and evening with her?"

"Honestly?"

"Honestly."

He drew a deep breath, then let it out. "No," he admitted. "But what I think doesn't matter. She is your mother, she lives a long distance away, and I would guess you don't see her often. You should spend as much time with her as possible."

"You're not serious!" She stared at him in astonishment, but he just looked right back at her, unblinking, and she finally said with a sigh, "I suppose you're right, but it's easy for you to say. She's not your mother."

"True." He glanced out the window of the carriage and added as if to himself, "I've never had any family."

"Do you want mine?" Sophie countered in mock desperation. "Except for Auntie, of course."

Mick chuckled. "They weren't too bad. Conventional enough that they didn't think much of a policeman in their midst."

"Didn't it bother you?" Sophie asked, surprised that he didn't seem to mind the rude way he had been treated by her mother, her sister, and her brother-in-law.

"I'm used to it," he said with a shrug. "Besides, a beautiful young lady told me only a short while ago that people don't like being asked all sorts of inconvenient questions, or being under suspicion for something they didn't do."

She frowned, uncertain whether to believe him or not. "You're flirting with me."

"Wrong." He leaned back and folded his arms across his wide chest. "And you say you can read people's thoughts? If you could really do that, you would know that I meant exactly what I said. You are a beautiful woman."

She ducked her head. His words sent a rush of pleasure through her. She knew she wasn't one to need a hat that hid most of her face, but she'd never been called beautiful before. By anybody. To hear him say it, knowing he wasn't being cheeky and flirting with her, made Sophie feel as if she'd taken a second glass of wine with dinner, giddy and warm and wanting to laugh.

He leaned forward, his hands reaching toward her face. He tipped her chin up. "But you really need to learn to tie your ribbons tighter."

She caught her breath, unable to move as he began tying a ribbon at her throat that had come undone.

As he formed the ribbon into a bow, his knuckles lightly brushed against the skin beneath her jaw, sending an involuntary shiver through her.

He felt it. He looked at her, and this time he wasn't

smiling. "There's something I want to know," he said in a low, tight voice. He let go of the ribbon and moved to sit beside her. "You've been telling me you can see the future, is that right?"

"Yes."

He pulled the curtains closed at the carriage window, and her heart began to pound hard against her breast. What was he doing? she thought wildly, sensing the change in him, a tenseness, a waiting.

He moved even closer. His hip touched hers, and she jumped, quivering inside, as if her body were full of butterflies. She started to move away, but his arm came up around her shoulders to prevent it. He leaned closer, then closer still, until his lips brushed her ear. "You still insist you can read people's thoughts?"

"Sometimes," she whispered. "I said sometimes."

"So you did." He turned her toward him and tilted her head back. "Can you read my thoughts right now?" he murmured, his lips lightly brushing against hers as he spoke.

"No."

"Thank God," he muttered and kissed her.

Sophie was lost in the sensation of his mouth on hers. She felt herself sliding off the edge of the earth and grasped the lapels of his jacket. She knew she should stop him, but her lips parted beneath his without any resistance at all, and any thought of stopping him went right out of her head. Never before had she been kissed the way Mick kissed her, a way that was so blatantly sensual, so powerful that it heated her blood and made her ache.

His arm around her, he leaned back, pulling her with him until he was lying on the seat with her on top of him, and she could feel the strength in his lean, powerful body stretched out beneath her.

The movement broke the kiss, and he trailed soft, wet kisses up to her ear. He began to nibble on her earlobe, and she shivered again, gasping at the pleasure of it.

He shifted his body beneath her, and she felt his knee touch her between her thighs. The scorching intimacy of it made her feel as if her whole body was on fire. "Mick, oh, Mick," she moaned, unable to stop herself from calling his name.

He slid his hands to her hips and straightened his leg, aligning her body with his. Even through her skirts, she could feel him, hard and aroused against the apex of her thighs. He lifted his hips, rocking back and forth against her, and the delicious sensations came again, this time in waves, shooting through her like bolts of electricity, tearing tiny moans from her throat.

Afraid of what she was feeling, she flattened her palms against his chest, starting to push herself away from him.

"Don't move," he groaned, wrapping his arms around her to keep her body pressed to his. "Stay right there."

"This must stop." She tried to gather her wits, but she could not seem to manage it.

"I know. I'll stop. I promise I will," he muttered. His breath came fast and uneven as his hands moved up her hips, along her back to the high collar of her dress. "But not yet. God, Sophie, not yet."

He pulled one end of the ribbon at her throat, undoing the bow he had tied only moments before, then he moved his hands down her back, undoing buttons as he nuzzled her neck. He pulled back her collar and kissed the pulse at the base of her throat.

"I told you not to wear that perfume around me anymore," he murmured against her skin. "It makes me insane." He grasped the edges of her dress and pulled it apart until he could get it over her shoulders. Then he reached under the silk to undo the front buttons of her corset cover.

She should stop him. She really should.

He slid his hands inside her corset cover and cupped her breasts in his palms. She could feel the warmth of his hands on her even through her corset and chemise. He seemed to be doing magical things to her with his mouth and his hands and his body that she couldn't stop. She turned her head and captured his lips with her own, kissing him with a sudden frantic urgency. With that kiss came her complete capitulation, and she knew she was lost.

Mick knew it, too. His hands caressed her breasts, his thumbs brushing bare skin above the lace of her corset. "Sophie," he groaned against her mouth. "Sophie, you are so soft. So beautiful."

He slid the tips of his fingers beneath the edge of her undergarments, touching as much of her bare skin as he could, given the restrictive corset. His touch felt so good that Sophie arched her back, pressing her hips against his groin. She began to move her body against his, the way he had done to her moments before, wanting more.

"Christ Almighty," he swore under his breath.

Suddenly, she was sitting up and so was he. She opened her eyes, disoriented and confused. She looked into his face, and the harshness of his expression did nothing to banish her bewilderment.

His mouth was set in a grim, tight line, and his lashes were lowered, preventing her from looking into his eyes. There was nothing in his face that showed a hint of what they had just shared, but his groans of pleasure still echoed in her mind, and she knew she had not been the only one to feel the exquisite pleasure only a few moments before.

She could feel him pulling her dress, jerking the edges back over her shoulders and into place. "Mick?"

He didn't respond. Instead, he simply grabbed her by the shoulders and turned her around. He began fastening buttons without a word.

"What are you doing?" she asked over one shoulder, feeling abandoned and bereft by his sudden withdrawal. "Why did you stop?"

She heard him let out his breath in a rush, and his hands stilled. "Because I told you I would," he answered and resumed buttoning her dress. "I don't break promises, especially that one."

Sophie knew what he meant, and what the consequences would have been had he broken his word. She also knew she would not have had the resolve to stop him. Never had she felt the pleasure he had aroused in her, nor could she have predicted the passion of her own willing response. If Mick had broken his promise, a promise given in the heat of the moment, the consequences could have been dire indeed.

"I take back what I said when we first met," she whispered over her shoulder. "You are a gentleman."

He fastened the last button, then kissed the base of her neck just above her collar. "Don't bet on it."

Eleven

∼

He was trying to keep his promise. He really was. But Sophie, sitting across from him in the carriage, with her hair about to come tumbling down and her lips swollen with his kisses, was a sight that wasn't helping his resolve.

He was rock hard and softheaded about a woman who was somehow involved in a plot to kill him. He was an idiot.

What had he been thinking? Even as he asked the question, he wanted to laugh. Thinking had nothing to do with what had just happened. Thinking had nothing to do with the ache in his body or her soft cries of pleasure that still echoed through his mind.

He knew he hadn't satisfied her, and he was angry with himself because he wanted to. Even now, even as he reminded himself how stupid it was to get involved with a suspect, he wanted to feel her body against his again. He had to clench his hands into fists to stop himself from reaching for her.

He looked out the window at the rain-washed Berkshire countryside, because looking at her only made him want her more. yet he couldn't ignore the scent of her perfume which clung to his clothes. He couldn't ignore the sound of rustling silk as she crossed her legs, a sound that drove him wild because he wanted those legs wrapped around him.

The carriage turned off the main road, and Mick hoped they would soon be at Lord Fortescue's estate. When the limestone walls of Parkfair came into view, Mick let out a long, low sigh of relief, but he knew he had several more days of this ahead.

When the carriage came to a halt in the drive before the house, Mick exited first, then held out his hand to Sophie. But she had barely stepped down from the carriage when she jerked her hand out of his with a suddenness that startled him. She dropped her reticule, and it fell to the graveled drive as she pressed her hands to her head with a moan of agony. Another moan followed, and she began rocking back and forth on her feet as if she was in intense pain. This was nothing like her pretense at Ascot. This was real.

"Sophie?" Alarmed, Mick grasped her shoulders, watching as her eyes closed and all the color drained from her face. Several servants began running toward the carriage from the house, and the driver stepped down from his seat, but Mick waved them back as Sophie let out another moan of pain. "Sophie, what's wrong?"

She didn't answer him. Instead, she shook her head, her hands still pressed to her temples. "Oh, God, not another one," she whispered. "He's dead."

Sophie collapsed, and for the second time that day, Mick lifted her into his arms. She felt like dead weight, and he knew she was unconscious. He swept past the servants gathered in the drive and carried her up the front steps into the house. He found the drawing room and laid her on a sofa there. He gave a terse command to the housekeeper for smelling salts, then sat down on the edge of the sofa beside her, rubbing her wrists and commanding her to wake up, but she did not open her eyes.

It seemed like hours before the housekeeper returned. Mick grabbed the tiny bottle from the woman's fingers, and as she watched, Mick held the vial of ammonium carbonate under Sophie's nose.

She came awake, gasping, as if waking from a terrible nightmare. She pushed aside his hand and sat up, her breathing hard and fast as if she'd been running. Her face was white, and her brown eyes looked straight through him as if with some unidentifiable horror. It was the look in her eyes more than anything else that alarmed Mick. She looked as if she were in shock.

Before he could even ask what had come over her, she grasped his arm and said in a shaking voice, "Mick, we have to go to London at once. There may still be time."

That threw him completely off his trolley. "Time for what?"

"It's so horrible." She seemed on the verge of tears.

"We have to do something. We can't let it happen."

Mick glanced up at the housekeeper, who was hovering anxiously nearby. "Tea," he ordered. "With lots of sugar."

"Yes, sir. Tea is good for ladies after a fainting spell, and sugar is important when you've had a shock." The housekeeper departed.

Mick returned his attention to Sophie. He didn't think she was truly in shock, but she did seem close to hysteria, and for no reason he could fathom. "Sophie," he said, tucking a loose tendril of her hair behind her ear. "Try to calm down. You fainted, and now you're—"

"Yes, yes, I know what happened, but despite what you're thinking, I'm not hysterical," she said, her voice rising with each word. "And I'm not in shock. I'm frightened. It's happening again, and we have to go to London."

"Now?"

"Yes, right now." She started to stand up, but he pushed her back onto the sofa.

"Sophie, you are not going anywhere."

"But—"

"You just fainted, you are overwrought, and you are not going anywhere." She started to rise again, but again he pushed her back down. "If you don't stay put, by God, I'll handcuff you to this sofa."

"We don't have time to argue about this." Her voice quivered with desperation. "We have to go now. This time, I know when, I know where, and I'm going to do something about it."

"What do you mean?" Mick felt his guts tighten, and

he had a feeling he knew what was coming. His concern for her faded as his hardened detective instincts took control. "Sophie, just what are you trying to tell me?"

She grasped his sleeve in her fingers. "Mick, he's all bloody, and I know he's dead. We have to prevent it. We have to go and stop it."

"What are you saying? There's going to be a murder?"

"Yes."

Mick studied Sophie's pale face, wide eyes, and trembling lips. She looked scared to death, but in his entire career as a police officer and detective, he'd seen many fine actresses. Earlier today, he'd known at once her fainting spell was pretense, but this time, he'd have sworn it was real.

He could not detect any duplicity in her, but after what had happened in the carriage only a short while ago, he knew his own judgment could not be trusted just now. "I suppose this is another one of your predictions?"

She nodded, not seeming to notice the sudden cynicism in his voice. "Yes. It's going to happen tonight, after dark. We have to do something about it. When I tried to warn you about what was going to happen to you, I made such a bungle of things that you didn't believe me, and you almost died. I won't make the same mistake again."

She wasn't the only one who didn't intend to make a second mistake. Mick was on his feet in an instant. He grabbed her by the arm and began propelling her toward the door. There wasn't time for an interrogation now. He could ask her any questions he needed to once they were on the train. "Come on."

In the doorway, they almost collided with the parlormaid, who was bringing a tray laden with a silver tea service, cups, sugar, lemon, milk, and a plate of sweet biscuits.

The maid looked at them in confusion. "Mrs. Price told me to bring the tea, miss," she said, looking at Sophie. "But—"

"It's all right, Dorcas," Sophie said as Mick pulled her past the girl. "We won't be needing any tea after all."

They had reached the entrance hall when Sophie jerked free of his hold. "Wait! I have to leave a note for Auntie."

"You can telephone from the Yard."

"Lord Fortescue doesn't have a telephone here. This won't take long." Before he could stop her, she ran for the stairs.

"It's already half past six," he shouted to her, "and we have to make the train. If we don't, there isn't another one until morning."

"We won't miss the train," she called back to him as she ran up the curving staircase at the far end of the hall. "Get a carriage. I'll be right back."

Mick turned to the parlormaid, who was staring at him in bewilderment. "Get a carriage," he told her. "At once."

The girl departed immediately to follow his orders. Mick remained in the entrance hall, pacing, impatient, trying to sort this out. If Sophie had found out about a second murder and had decided to tell him about it, why would she do so in such an extraordinary way? He could not understand any of this.

When Sophie came back down, he had the door open before she even reached it. She followed him through the front door and out to the carriage waiting in the drive. "I told Auntie I had a vision of another murder," she told him as they climbed into the waiting carriage. "I'm sure I don't know what Mama will think."

"Probably that you've eloped with that appalling policeman."

Sophie looked at him in horror as the carriage began to move. "That's exactly what she'll think. Oh, dear. I hope Auntie makes up a convincing story. If she thinks we've eloped, I'll never live it down."

"I'm flattered."

"I didn't mean it that way. It's just—"

"Don't worry," he broke in, "I'll tell her that I, in my duty as a detective of Scotland Yard, made you go back to London as a material witness to a crime."

Sophie groaned. "Lovely. That will make her feel so much better about the whole thing. Still, it can't be helped."

"Look at it this way," he said, settling back in his seat. "If you're wrong about this murder, I'll be in serious trouble with my superintendent."

"I'm not wrong."

"You may be sure of that," he muttered as the carriage pulled onto the main road, "but I'm not."

The carriage ride from Parkfair to the train station at Windsor was about twenty minutes. Mick did not ask Sophie any questions. She knew he was waiting for her to tell him what she knew, but she wanted to wait until they were on the train. Then there would be plenty of time to tell him everything.

Because of the number of Ascot attendees who had only come for opening day, the line for tickets to London was long and the process wretchedly slow. They barely made the train, jumping on board just seconds before the final whistle blew and the train pulled out of the station.

Mick led her through the crowded train coach, making for a pair of seats near the back. When he moved aside, Sophie slid over to the inside seat. "What time is it?" she asked, glancing up at him.

He pulled out his watch. "Four minutes past seven," he told her, and put the timepiece back in his pocket.

"Your watch must gain a bit." Without thinking, she added, "Probably because it belonged to your father, and it's so old."

That stopped him cold. He stood there in the aisle, staring at her in astonishment.

"How do you know about my watch?"

"I just know."

An elderly woman came up behind Mick, nudging him with her cane to move out of the aisle, and he sat down beside Sophie, still looking a bit stunned. "You can't possibly know it belonged to my father." He turned in his seat to face her. "No one knows that for certain, not even me."

"I do. I know it. Your mother had it when she died, didn't she?"

She watched a shadow cross his face, a shadow of anger. "All right, Sophie, I've had enough rigmarole about psychics and spiritualists and all that rot. You've obviously investigated my background, got someone at the orphanage to tell you about the watch, thinking that will make me believe in these powers of yours. It won't work."

Sophie stared at him, and she wanted to scream with frustration. "You still think I'm involved in some plot to kill you? You are the most stubborn man I've ever known in my life." She was becoming angry herself. "Once you get an idea in your head, you just can't rid yourself of it. That particular character flaw would seem to me to be a great handicap to a detective."

He ignored the jibe. "Did you really think pulling this little trick about my watch would convince me of anything?"

"I doubt anything would convince you," she shot back. "I could predict an earthquake for tomorrow and you'd twist everything around and find some ridiculous, convoluted explanation. You just refuse to face facts."

"The fact that you are psychic, you mean?"

She ignored the sarcastic tone of his voice. "The idea that I have that kind of power scares you. You are a man who loathes even the idea of being frightened of something, so you deny its existence."

"You say I twist things around?" he countered, also raising his voice. "Woman, when it comes to that, you are far better than I. And so far, I haven't been all that impressed with these so-called powers of yours. They seem very convenient to me."

"Well, they're damned inconvenient to me!"

Sophie turned away from him and found every person in the train car staring back at them over the tops of their seats. Some were laughing, some were frowning at such a public display of emotion, and some were looking at them with rather dubious curiosity as if wondering whether the pair had escaped from the nearest asylum. Sophie bit her lip and sank down in her seat.

She knew how hard these things were for most people to understand. Even she did not always understand the images that came to her or the things she just knew. She also knew she and Mick had to work together. She just wished he would stop regarding her as a suspect and start regarding her as an ally.

"So, are you going to tell me about this murder?"

Mick's voice broke into her thoughts, and she opened her eyes. "Yes, but the more accusatory and suspicious you are, the less likely it is that I'll remember details. So be nice."

He muttered an oath under his breath, then held up his hands, palms outward in a gesture of truce. "Fine. Just tell me anything you can."

She closed her eyes, trying to relax and concentrate at the same time. "I see a man. He's lying on some cobblestones, on his side with his back to me."

"What's he wearing?"

"A dark suit. He's a policeman like you."

"How do you know? Is he wearing a uniform?"

"No, but I'm sure he's a police officer. His hat is lying nearby, and it looks crushed, as if someone stepped on it." She paused, trying to hone in on the image that was fading in and out of her mind. "He's dead, but—" She opened her eyes to look at Mick. "How much blood is there when someone gets shot?"

"It depends."

"Depends on what?"

"Where on the body that person's been shot and with what sort of weapon."

"He has been shot. I know that for certain. But there's so much blood. It's just like what I saw with you." She shuddered, cold all of a sudden.

"Why is it like what you saw with me?" he asked. "How is it the same?"

"In the dream I had about you, I hadn't realized you'd been shot. All the blood made me think of a knife, but I didn't actually see a knife. Of course, I don't always see everything. It isn't like one clear photograph, it's more like a series of photographs flashed before my eyes, none there long enough for me to get all the details at once. But then, I have very few visions of violent death. Usually it's just someone old dying peacefully in bed. Or something trivial, like knowing the boy who delivers the fish is in love with our maid, Hannah. She thinks of him as a friend, but—" She broke off. "Sorry, I'm rambling. I do that sometimes."

"Yes, I know."

She leaned back and closed her eyes again. "I see blood all over the ground by his body, but I don't know what wound it's coming from." She stopped, unable to go on. What she had just seen was too horrific to describe. Her stomach twisted.

"What is it?" Mick leaned closer to her, brushing loose tendrils of hair back from her cheek to better see her profile. "You're white as chalk. What is it?"

"Dear God," she whispered, pressing her hand to her mouth, afraid she was going to be sick. She opened her eyes and turned to look at Mick. "He has no heart," she choked from behind her hand.

"What?"

"He has no heart."

"What do you mean?" he demanded. "Are you speaking poetically or—"

"No, no, no. I mean exactly what I'm saying. His heart is gone. It's been . . . cut out with a knife." She wrapped her arms around herself and doubled over in her seat. "Why?" she moaned. "Why do these things happen? Why do I have to see them?"

Mick looked at her hunched over in her seat and felt a glimmer of doubt. Even as he tried to tell himself she was playing some sort of game, he wanted to comfort her, soothe her. He wanted to tell her not to say any more, to tell her everything was going to be all right. He moved his arm as if to wrap it around her, as if to carry out that impulse to hold her until her nightmarish visions had stopped, then he jerked back.

What was it about this woman that made him lose his head? Now he was starting to believe in spiritualists. He leaned back against his seat and combed his hands through his hair, trying to think like the detective he was. What else did she know?

He turned his head to look at her again. She was still doubled over in her seat, shaking. He put a hand on her shoulder. "Sophie?"

The moment she sat up, he pulled his hand back. Touching her did not help him think. It only made him want to comfort her, and a detective damn well didn't comfort a material witness in a murder case.

She was crying, and being Sophie, she'd probably lost her handkerchief. He pulled out a square of neatly folded linen. "Here," he said, holding it out to her.

"Thank you." She accepted the handkerchief and began dabbing at her face, then put the piece of linen in her pocket. "Maybe you should just ask me questions, and I'll try to answer them."

"Do you have any idea where the murder is going to happen?"

He didn't expect an answer to that question, but to his surprise, she nodded in the affirmative. "Oh, yes. It's somewhere near the Covent Garden Market. I saw the flower girls."

He knew immediately what she meant. Flower girls went there in the evenings to buy the last of the day's flowers, getting them at a cheap price because they weren't as fresh by the end of the day. They made bouquets and posies tied up with ribbon to sell in front of the Royal Opera House and the theaters and music halls of Drury Lane during the evening. "So it's near the market. That's still very vague. Do you know the exact location?"

"I'm afraid not. I didn't see a street sign or anything. In fact, that in itself is odd. Quite often, there's something to go by, a landmark, if you will." She stiffened. "Horses."

"Horses? What do horses have to do with it?"

"I don't know, but I keep getting a strong impression of horses. Not real horses, if you understand me. They represent something. Three horses. I keep sensing three horses."

Mick frowned. "There's a pub near Covent Garden Market called the Three Horses. Do you mean that?"

"It could be that. But the body isn't in a pub. It's in an alley."

"What else do you—" He cleared his throat. "What else do you see?"

"There's hate. Lots and lots of hate. It's like black dust in the air."

He made a sound of disbelief. "You mean London coal soot."

She shook her head and turned toward him, trying to explain. "No, no. You don't understand. The image of black is an aura. Auras are visual symbols of very strong emotions or energy. When I first met you, you had no aura at all, which meant you were going to die very soon, unless I stopped it. When I see an aura of black, that is always a feeling of hate. Evil, too, sometimes."

She rubbed her arms as if she were cold. "I don't remember any more."

He knew he couldn't push her any further. He sat back in his seat and went over what she had told him.

Sometimes I can read minds.

He just couldn't swallow it. No one could read someone else's thoughts. She claimed to be psychic, and she was very convincing. There were times when she did seem to sense the future or read his mind.

But wasn't that what phony psychics always seemed able to do? Weren't all of them good at sizing people up and determining, as if by spirit guidance, what another person was like? They took your measure, determined your character, then said things that made you feel as if they understood you, felt your pain, read your mind.

On the other hand, there were things here he just couldn't explain. His theory all along had been that she was protecting the identity of someone she knew who had murderous intentions. But he couldn't find any connection between anyone she knew and himself. Even more important, he was coming to know Sophie and understand her character, and he just couldn't see her trying to protect someone who would do anything as horrible as what she had just described.

Nothing seemed to make sense now, but Mick knew one thing for certain. If he didn't figure out the truth, someone was going to die. It might even be him.

Twelve

~

The journey from Windsor to Paddington Station usually took a little over an hour, but when they were about halfway to London, the train slowed for no apparent reason and came to a stop. The conductor came through, explaining that during the rainstorm that afternoon, powerful winds had felled several ancient walnut trees across the tracks. They would have to be removed, and several pieces of badly mangled track would need to be replaced before they could continue. He explained there would be about an hour's delay, though they would try to make up a bit of the time during the remainder of the trip.

"Oh, no." Sophie, dismayed, looked at Mick. "We could be too late."

"You said the murder was going to happen after dark, and it doesn't get dark until nearly ten o'clock at this time of year. We'll be at Covent Garden by about half past nine. That gives us plenty of time."

"I hope you're right," Sophie murmured, but she still had grave misgivings, especially when the hour wait turned into two. With the vision of the murdered man still in her mind, every minute seemed an eternity, and by the time the train once again got underway, she was as taut as a bowstring. She said nothing, but she was very much afraid their efforts would be for naught.

Mick was as silent as she, frowning and abstracted, and she left him to his thoughts during the remaining train ride to London.

By the time they got to Paddington Station, it was half past ten and darkness had fallen. The theaters had let out, and hansoms were in short supply. They finally hailed one and reached Covent Garden by quarter past eleven. Just as they turned onto Bow Street, Sophie was overcome by a feeling of complete emptiness, and she knew they were too late. She grabbed Mick's hand in hers, entwining their fingers tightly together.

"What is it?" he asked, looking at her in surprise.

"He's dead, Mick. He's already dead. We're too late."

He didn't answer, but she felt his hand tighten around hers. When the cab turned onto Tavistock Street, where the Three Horses Pub was located, they found the street completely blocked off by the wooden barricades of the Metropolitan Police.

"Bloody hell," Mick muttered. The carriage had barely come to a stop before he jumped down. Tossing a sixpence to the driver, he ran to the pair of bobbies stationed at the barricade, and Sophie followed him.

"Rob, Archie," Mick greeted them, nodding to each one as he said their names. "What's happened?"

The one called Rob glanced at Sophie, then returned his attention to Mick. "Murder back there," he said, jerking his thumb to the street behind him, which was crowded with policemen, reporters, and spectators who lived along that street and couldn't be required to stay back.

"Who is it?" Mick asked. Though his voice was steady as he asked the question, Sophie knew he was dreading the answer.

Rob put a hand on Mick's shoulder. "Mate, it's Jack."

"What? Jack Hawthorne?"

It was clear to Sophie that Mick knew the dead man. Of course, many policemen probably knew each other, but she sensed that this Jack Hawthorne had been a friend.

"I'm going back there," Mick said and shouldered past the pair of bobbies. They did not stop him, but when Sophie tried to follow him past the barricade, the one named Archie put a hand on her shoulder. "Sorry, miss. No one's allowed back there."

Mick turned around. "She comes with me."

Archie shook his head. "Sir, it's DeWitt's orders. If we let the lookers in, our lads won't be able to move back there."

"I know the rule, Constable. She's a material witness in this case. Is DeWitt here?"

"Not yet."

"When he gets here, I'll clear it with him."

"It's a gruesome sight, sir. I'm not sure a woman should—" Archie broke off at the look Mick gave him, then he shrugged and let Sophie through. "As you please, sir."

Mick reached behind him for her hand, and she took it, following him toward the entrance to the Three Horses. His tall frame and broad shoulders made it easy to cut a path through the crowd. Still holding his hand, Sophie followed him inside the pub, straight through, and out the back door, where another crowd of police officers were gathered. Some of them closest to the center of the circle were holding lanterns high above their heads. Spectators leaned out the windows of the building across the alley, watching the scene. There were some spectators actually taking notes.

Mick paused outside the pub's back door. "Wait here," he told her and walked toward the group of officers in the alley. Sophie watched as he entered the circle. Because he was several inches taller than the other men, she could see his expression as he looked down at the body on the cobblestones, but she hadn't needed to. She felt his pain. She walked toward him.

Mick saw her coming. He met her halfway, grabbed her by the shoulders, and turned her around, keeping her away.

"Mick, I need to see it."

"No."

"I've already seen it, in a way," she told him. "But I want to see it for real. This is important, Mick."

His hands tightened on her shoulders for a moment,

then he let her go. "All right, but if you get sick, it's your own fault."

"I won't be sick. He was your friend wasn't he? Will you . . . will you be all right?"

"I'm fine."

She knew he was lying.

He led her to the body. The other officers at the scene began to notice her presence, and they looked at her curiously.

"Who's this woman?" one mumbled to another. "DeWitt will have Mick's head for showing the body to some woman."

She could feel their curious gazes fixed on her, but she ignored them. She focused on the dead man. The lanterns were still held high by several officers, and when Sophie reached the body, she saw a photographer setting up his camera to take pictures.

Sophie lowered her gaze from the photographer to the bloody mess that had once been a police detective named Jack Hawthorne. It was so much more vivid in reality. She felt the back of her throat tighten, and she almost did exactly what Mick had predicted. She almost threw up.

She turned her face away and found Mick right there, so solid and strong, like a rock to cling to. She grabbed his lapels and buried her face against his shirt front.

He stood there, holding her, with his friend on the ground and a group of fellow officers staring at him as if he'd lost his mind.

"I'm all right now," Sophie said and straightened away from him. He let her go.

"Do you sense anything?" he asked.

"You'll have to give me a few minutes. Go and do whatever you need to do. I'll just step back out of the way and see if anything comes to me."

He walked her back to the doorway of the pub, and she stood there watching as he returned to the body. He bent down on one knee and lowered his head, paying his final respects to a friend. Opposite Mick, there was another man on his knees over the body, a man wearing a bloodstained apron, and Sophie realized he was a doctor.

When a third man approached the body, Mick stood up to speak with him. Though she could not hear their conversation, she could tell that they began to argue almost immediately.

Sophie peeked between the people who moved past her to watch them. They were arguing about her. She saw the shorter man point in her direction, and she knew he was enraged by her presence. The doctor remained on his knees, ignoring the heated discussion going on above him. But a fourth man moved quite close to the pair, and began taking notes at a furious pace. He was not wearing a uniform, and Sophie wondered who he was.

The argument was brief, lasting only a minute or two. Then the short, angry man walked away, the man taking notes began to talk with the doctor, and Mick returned to her side.

"What is it?" Sophie asked. "That man seemed quite upset about me."

"Well, he's my superintendent. He felt that a young lady such as yourself has no place at a crime scene."

There was more to it than that. Sophie opened her mouth, but before she could ask the real reason they'd been arguing, Mick spoke again.

"You were right. Jack was shot in the head. Looks like a small-caliber weapon, just like the one that was fired at me."

She nodded. "When I saw it in my mind, I saw that his hat had a hole in it. That's how I knew."

"You were right about something else." Mick took a deep breath and looked into her eyes. "His heart was cut out and taken away."

She reached up and touched his cheek, sensing his pain, but he turned his face away.

"It was quite well done, too," he went on, and she let her hand fall away. "Neat and quick, like a surgeon might do. It was done after he was dead. But why remove it? What for?"

Sophie knew the reason. "It's a message."

"What sort of message?"

"The heart is symbolic of love, of kindness and tenderness. The killer took it to convey the message that the man he killed had no heart. No compassion. No mercy." She cleared her throat. "Mick, there's something else."

"What?"

"The killer isn't finished."

"I was afraid you were going to say that."

By the time Sophie returned to the house in Mill Street, it was nearly one o'clock in the morning. She said good night to the young constable who had escorted her home in a cab on Mick's orders. She entered the house and found it dark and silent. It was clear that all the lodgers and servants had gone to bed long ago.

She fumbled for the lamp that Grimstock always left by the door for Sophie and her aunt when they went out in the evening, but it wasn't there. Of course, Grimstock wasn't expecting their return for several days yet. Sophie bit her lip, hovering near the front door. Thinking about what had happened tonight, what she had seen, only made her more afraid of the dark. She wished Mick were here. If he were here, she'd feel safe.

Being afraid of the dark was silly, she told herself. She took a deep breath, then held it as she ran up the stairs to her own room. Her bedroom wasn't lit, but there were always a lamp and matches by her bed. It was only after the lamp was lit that Sophie was able to breathe again, taking in deep gulps of air until her heart resumed a normal rhythm and she felt calmer. But even after she had undressed, put on a nightgown, and climbed into bed, she still felt cold and afraid.

She wrapped her arms around her pillow and hugged it tight, wanting Mick there to hold her, but Mick wasn't there. She was sick at heart and wanted to cry, but she couldn't cry. She was exhausted and wanted to sleep, but she couldn't sleep. All she could do was lie there and wonder why such horrible things happened in the world.

After about half an hour of lying there, she still couldn't relax enough to go to sleep. She was unable to think of anything but that poor man Jack Hawthorne and the wife and children she knew he'd left behind.

She got out of bed and put on a pair of slippers, then

carried the lamp downstairs. She went to the place that had comforted her on many sleepless nights, that had soothed many of her nightmares away, that took her mind off the troubling things she often saw. She went into the conservatory.

She lit all the gaslights and took a look around, seeking something to do. Grimstock had watered everything while she was away, but she'd been quite neglectful of her gardens, both indoors and out, during the past few weeks.

She decided repotting some of the palms was the most important of the many tasks she could choose from. Sophie rolled up the sleeves of her nightgown, donned an apron, and set to work.

Though the house belonged to Auntie, the conservatory was Sophie's. She'd earned that right by restoring the room to its former glory, one plant at a time.

She loved the outdoor gardens, too, but it was this room to which she fled when she was troubled. As she worked amid the delicate plants and flowers, listening to the soothing sound of the fountain, the shock of what had happened and what she had seen began to fade.

"Sophie?"

At the sound of Mick's voice, she peered around the tall palm on the worktable, but the trees and shrubs of the conservatory blocked her view. "I'm back here," she called, and a few moments later, Mick found her.

"Is there any news?" she asked as he stepped between a pair of marble columns entwined with trumpet vines.

"No."

He looked so tired. His new suit was rumpled, his tie was undone, the top buttons of his shirt were unfastened. It was so unlike him to be so disheveled that anyone who knew him could tell something terrible had happened. There were harsh lines of grief and anger in his face, showing the grim reality of what they had both seen, and she sensed that the pain he felt at the brutal murder of a man who had been his close friend had only worsened during the last few hours. "When did you come in?" she asked.

"Only a few minutes ago. I went upstairs and saw that your door was open and your bed was turned down, as if you'd tried to sleep and couldn't. I guessed I'd find you here. Since I am in no frame of mind to sleep myself, I thought I'd join you." He leaned back against the column behind him. "What is it you're doing?"

With her trowel, she waved to the wheelbarrow full of soil and compost beside her and the cluster of palms nearby. "I'm repotting palms."

"That sounds fascinating."

She smiled at that. "It's not the most glamorous thing one could do, I suppose."

His gaze lowered along her body and back again. "I don't know about that," he answered. "An apron over a nightgown seems quite posh to me."

She looked down and saw the dirt that stained her apron and dusted the sleeves of her white lawn nightgown. Laughing, she answered, "If Mama saw me now, I'd be whisked away to the dressmaker at once."

"I didn't know dressmakers were open at two o'clock in the morning."

"My mother would find one."

"She does seem quite determined in her quest to marry you off."

"She has always considered the successful marriages of her daughters to be her life's work," Sophie answered as she scooped dirt into the terra-cotta pot before her, placing it around the root ball of the palm. "With Charlotte, she succeeded." Sophie paused, her head tilted to one side. "If one considers Harold a success."

Mick did not reply. Sophie looked over at him and found that he was leaning against the column behind him, his eyes closed, almost as if asleep on his feet. "Mick?"

He opened his eyes. "Hmm?"

"I'm so sorry about your friend."

He closed his eyes again and was silent for a long time. "Jack saved my life once," he finally said, not opening his eyes. "We were working a case in Lambeth. Some very nasty characters that we suspected of running a burglary ring out of Limehouse were hiding in a warehouse there, and we went in after them. Jack saw one of them pull out a pistol and aim it at me. He hurled himself at me as if we were playing rugby and slammed me down behind some crates stuffed with burlap bags of tobacco. I took a bullet in the shoulder as we went down, but if it hadn't been for Jack, I'd have taken that bullet in the head, and I'd have died."

He straightened away from the column and rubbed a hand over his eyes. "He saved my life. Damn it all to hell, I wish I could have saved his."

"I wish I could have seen this sooner, but I can never predict—"

He looked at her. "Don't," he ordered, his voice harsh. "Don't."

"I have to say this. Mick, if I knew who had done this terrible thing, I would have told you. There is no one among my acquaintance that I would protect from a brutal crime such as this, even if I knew who that person was. Even if that person were someone I loved, I would not save them from the punishment they rightly deserved had they committed this crime. And I would never be able to live with myself if I kept silent, knowing I caused someone's death."

"I know that. I realized it today, when I saw you looking down at Jack's body. But Sophie, if you're not protecting someone, then——" He stopped, not saying what he'd intended to say.

"There are some things, Mick, that can't be proven. Some things just don't have facts and evidence to back them up. Some things have to be taken on faith."

They looked at each other for a long moment. Finally, slowly, he shook his head. "Sophie, I can't," he murmured, sounding almost as if he wished he could. "You're asking me to believe in something that is unbelievable. I can't."

Desolation came over her, dark and cold like a thick winter fog. She wanted Mick to believe in her, to accept her the way she truly was. "I understand," she said in a tiny voice, and lowered her gaze to her hands. She was holding the trowel so tightly that her knuckles were white. She forced herself to relax her grip and told herself it didn't matter what he thought, but that was a lie. It did matter.

She felt his gaze on her as she resumed her task, but

she didn't look at him. She tamped down the dirt she had placed in the pot, then picked up her watering can and gave the palm a good soaking. She moved to lift it off the table, but Mick's voice stopped her. "Don't do that. It's too heavy. Let me do it."

"I've done it before," she said as he moved to her side.

"I don't care." Mick lifted the huge pot easily from the table. "Where do you want it?"

"I'll show you," she said, and led him to the front of the conservatory. She pointed to a spot just behind one of the wicker chairs where they'd had tea only a week ago, and he placed it there.

"Thank you," she said as he straightened and brushed the dirt from his hands. "I think I'll make myself a cup of tea." She hesitated, then asked, "Would you like one?"

"I would."

She crossed the room, weaving her way amid the greenery, and Mick followed. "Where are you taking me?" he asked when she did not head toward the door. "The forests of the Argentine?"

"It does seem like that, doesn't it?" she said, laughing as she ducked beneath one of the huge leaves of a fiddle-leaf fig and entered a clearing, where a gas ring, kettle, and other tea things stood on a papier-mâché tea table.

"We keep a gas ring and tea things in here," she told him. "I often work in here, and I usually like a cup of tea while I'm working."

There was an old-fashioned water pump set into the terrazzo floor nearby, and after washing the dirt from her hands, she used the pump to fill the teakettle.

"This conservatory is a beautiful place."

She lit the gas ring and put the kettle on to boil. "You should have seen it before."

"Before?"

"Before I came to live with Auntie. The first time I walked in here, I thought I *was* in the Argentine, it was such a jungle. Auntie had hired a young boy to come every day and water the plants, but she couldn't afford a gardener, and she knows nothing of plants herself. Everything was overgrown, the vines were running wild. All it needed then was a monkey."

Mick grinned at that. "I'm sure your mother would love to have a monkey climb all over her when she comes to visit."

"What a wonderful idea," she said as she began placing cups, spoons, and other tea things on a tray. Looking up, she paused in her task and asked him, "Where does one get a monkey?"

A warning glint came into his deep blue eyes. "I was only joking."

"I wasn't."

That made him smile. "Yes, you were. Besides, you wouldn't want a monkey. I've known a few organ grinders. Monkeys make quite a mess."

"You're saying that because you're obsessed with neatness."

"I'm not obsessed. I just don't like things in disarray."

She shrugged. "Define it any way you want to."

When the kettle whistled, she finished making their tea, but when she picked up the tray, Mick stepped forward. "Let me carry it," he said, taking the tray from her hands. "You lead the way."

This time she did not argue. They walked back to the furniture near the front of the room, where Mick set the tray on the wicker tea table. Sophie sank down on the cushioned settee. It wasn't until she sat down that she realized how exhausted she was. She leaned forward, rubbing her eyes with her hands.

Mick sat down on the settee beside her. "Are you all right?"

"I'm fine," she answered and straightened in her chair. She poured out their tea. "I'm just tired."

"If you're fine and you're tired, then why don't you go to bed?"

"For the same reason as you. I couldn't possibly sleep just now. I don't sleep well, even at the best of times." She stirred sugar into his tea and handed the cup to him.

"Because you have dreams about murder?"

There was no hint of skepticism or disbelief in his voice, and Sophie didn't know what to think. He had just told her moments ago that he couldn't believe she was psychic, and yet, he no longer seemed absolutely sure she wasn't.

"I don't usually dream about murder," she answered, "though I do dream about death. And sometimes other tragedies."

"And you keep quill and paper by your bed to take notes of what you dream. I remember when I found them in your room, I couldn't understand what they meant."

"Yes, I often write down my dreams. It helps. I also have a tendency to speak my predictions aloud at the moment I have them." She gave him a rueful smile. "That gets me in real trouble sometimes, especially with my mother."

"What are you going to tell your family about tonight?"

"I don't know, but I'll have to think of something. I imagine they will take the first train they can get, which is about six hours from now, and the moment they arrive, my mother will be demanding explanations."

"True, but you did leave a note."

"My mother will still think it quite the scandal." She looked at him with sympathy. "Be prepared for some harsh words."

He didn't seem to mind. "I was just doing my duty. I consider you to be a material witness to a crime, and as such, I brought you back to London."

Horrified, Sophie stared at him. "We can't tell them that!"

"Why not? It's the truth."

"You don't understand."

"On the contrary, I understand perfectly. People like your mother and your sister consider themselves above the law. They feel that their place in society, in and of itself, proves their innocence. They feel that it is an appalling presumption on my part to even question them about a crime. Though some at Scotland Yard might agree with that, I don't. Your family's position doesn't impress me in the slightest."

"You make them sound like such snobs."

"So they are."

"I am gratified to note that you did not put my aunt or myself in that category."

"Your aunt is adorable. A very charming lady."

"And what am I?"

He met her gaze straight on. "I haven't figured you out yet. I'm working on it."

"I see." She leaned back in her chair and closed her eyes.

"You need to sleep," he said.

Sophie kept her eyes closed. She couldn't look at him, she couldn't confess that she was a coward. It was his life that was in danger, yet he didn't seem afraid. She was the one who was afraid. It was pure fear that prevented her from going back to bed. She didn't want to sleep because she didn't want to dream. She didn't want to see blood and death, she didn't want to feel the black evil of someone's twisted mind. "I don't want to go to sleep. I just want to sit here quietly."

"Do you want me to leave?" He stood up.

"No!" she cried, gripped by a sudden panic as powerful as any vision she'd ever had. Turning toward him, she reached for his hand. "I didn't mean I wanted you to go. Please, don't leave. Don't leave me alone. I—" She broke off, realizing how hysterical she sounded. Taking a deep breath, she let go of his hand and wrapped her arms around herself. "Sorry, I don't know what came over me. That was rude. I don't want to keep you from your rest. You're exhausted. I mean, after everything you've been through, losing your friend, your own life at risk—"

"Would you like me to stay?"

"Yes."

"Then I'll stay." He sat back down beside her. He slid his hand beneath her jaw, turning her face toward him. "You've had a rough day," he said, his voice gentler than she'd ever heard it before. He rubbed the pad of his thumb back and forth across her cheek. "You're still in shock."

Sophie looked at him and shook her head. "I'm not in shock. I'm scared."

"This madman isn't after you."

"No," she whispered. "He's after you."

"Well, I'm a tough bloke. He won't get me. He's not intelligent enough."

She tried to smile at that, but she couldn't. She felt so cold. She hugged herself tighter. "But he's evil, and he's obsessed with one idea. Killing."

"You're trembling." He slid one arm down behind her back, and the other beneath her knees. Before she could even realize his intention, she found herself sitting on his lap.

"You have no excuses now." He settled back against the settee and pulled her close. Against her hair, he murmured, "You're safe. Go to sleep."

Sleep? She stared at him, wondering how she could possibly sleep like this. She was sitting on his lap, for heaven's sake.

Sophie pushed at his chest, but she might just as well have pushed at a brick wall. His arms were wrapped tight around her, and she was forced to remain where she was.

She rested her cheek against his shoulder with an

exasperated sigh. After everything that had happened, after the horrifying events of the evening, he expected her to fall asleep. Here? On his lap? There was no way, she thought, yawning, that she was going to fall asleep now.

No way at all.

Thirteen

❧

"**W**here is she? I demand to be taken to her at once!"

The loud voice penetrated Sophie's consciousness as if it were a cannon going off far in the distance. With the vague, hazy logic of a person still half asleep, she assumed she was dreaming. Ignoring the sound, she snuggled deeper against the pillow beneath her cheek.

"What do you mean she's not in her room?"

The voice was louder now. Sophie frowned and opened her eyes, blinking at the bright sunlight pouring in from all the windows of the conservatory. She lifted her head and realized she was still sitting on Mick's lap. She had fallen asleep in his arms, with her head resting not on a pillow but in the comfortable dent of his shoulder.

"Where is she?"

The voice was getting closer, louder. It was her mother. God in heaven. Mick's body stirred beneath her, and she was off his lap in an instant.

Another voice was heard. "Ma'am, she's about the house, I'm sure," Hannah said. "Her bed's been slept in. Maybe she's in the conservatory."

Sophie pushed her hair out of her face and rubbed the sleep from her eyes, then turned toward the door and tried to brace herself for the coming confrontation.

She heard Mick stand up behind her and felt his hands on her waist. Startled by the intimate contact, she jumped. "What do we do?" she whispered. "We left in such a rush yesterday, and now we're here alone together. Oh, God, I'm still in my nightgown. You and I both know that she'll think the worst."

Mick's hands left her waist, and he moved away. She glanced over her shoulder to see him grab his empty teacup and saucer.

"Let's get out of here." He tucked one piece in each pocket of his jacket and grabbed Sophie's hand. She had no choice but to follow him out the French doors that led into the garden. Mick closed the doors, and they raced around the corner of the house and out of sight. When the others entered the conservatory, they would find no one there.

Mick and Sophie halted by the side of the house, breathing hard. "What do we do now?" she asked in a low voice. "We can't hide out here all day."

Mick glanced around and pointed to a door nearby that led back into the house. "You go back in, sneak upstairs, get dressed, then come back down, acting as if you've just gotten up," he said, pulling the cup and saucer from his pockets and handing them to her. "Hide these somewhere until you can put them back. I'll wait a few minutes, then come in as if I've just arrived after being out all night. Take your time getting back downstairs. I don't want you facing your mother all alone."

That sounded like a very good plan, but Sophie had one other question. "What are we going to tell them about yesterday?"

"The truth." She started to protest, but Mick interrupted her. "We have no choice. This case is going to be in all the newspapers."

Only minutes later, Sophie discovered just how true Mick's words would prove to be. She had managed to get back upstairs without being seen, and once safely in her room, she had followed Mick's instructions to take her time.

Hannah had already put fresh water in the pitcher on her washstand, and a cup of morning tea was on her dressing table. It was cold, but Sophie drank it anyway. She washed her face, used her toothbrush and toothpowder, and combed out her hair, pinning it up into a twist at the back of her head. As she dressed in a striped skirt and shirtwaist, Sophie decided her excuse for being missing was that she'd been out in the garden. What she didn't know was how Mick was going to explain the truth to her mother in a palatable way. It would not be easy.

By the time she went downstairs, knowing Mick would be with her, Sophie felt much more prepared to face the onslaught of questions she was sure to get from her mother. When she entered the drawing room, she saw that not only were Agatha and Violet there but so were her sister, Charlotte, and Auntie's lodgers.

She realized in dismay that Mick had not yet arrived.

Before she could even open her mouth to greet anyone, her mother was standing in front of her, holding a copy of a newspaper out to her. It was folded back to a particular article with a prominent headline.

Scotland Yard Using Psychics Now? What Are We Coming To?

Sophie took the paper and stared at the words, assimilating their meaning with growing dismay. And that wasn't all. There was a sketch of a man and a woman standing beside the dead body of Jack Hawthorne, and though hastily drawn, the couple bore an unmistakable resemblance to Mick and herself.

"Heavens above, Sophie Marie, where have you been? We've turned this house upside down looking for you all morning. As for last night—"

"I was in the garden, taking a walk," Sophie interrupted, giving her prepared lie automatically, still staring at the newspaper in her hands.

"Well?" Her mother tapped the paper with one gloved finger. "What have you to say for yourself? Do you realize the ramifications of this? You are ruined. Absolutely ruined."

Sophie looked from the newspaper to Agatha's furious face. "Mama—"

"People thinking you're psychic now, and you racing about London in the middle of the night, working with the police on these horrible things that no proper young lady should even read about much less participate in. Where is Mr. Dunbar? I want to know what he has to say about this. Where is he?"

"I have no idea."

"I knew he was the lowest class of person the moment I met him. How he could allow this is beyond my comprehension. He is a cur of the lowest description."

She jumped to Mick's defense. "Mama, really! That is so unfair. You don't understand the circumstances—"

"Quite right. I don't understand any circumstances that could justify this. Sophie Marie Haversham, I don't know what has come over you. I might expect such uncivil behavior from a policeman. They are so common. But you? What on earth were you thinking?"

"She didn't think at all," another voice piped up, and Sophie turned to see her sister glaring at her. Sophie sensed not only outrage at how Sophie's actions might affect the reputation of herself and her husband but also a certain pleasure that Sophie was in trouble with their mother. Again. "She's ruined all of us. Harold and I will suffer by association. How will I bear the shame?"

Aunt Violet's voice entered the conversation. "Charlotte, these theatrics are hardly helpful. I'm sure Sophie had no intention of causing anyone any shame. She was only trying to help the police in any way she could."

"Quite so," put in Miss Atwood.

"Perhaps. Perhaps," the colonel said, "but going to the police just isn't done."

"To say the least." Agatha nodded, the feather on her hat bouncing with each emphatic movement. "Sophie, I am so appalled, I don't know how to begin. What has gotten into you?"

"She's always been this way," Charlotte said. "With her talk about seeing things, and all her ghoulish, made-up stories."

Those words snapped Sophie out of her numbed state. "I didn't invent the murder of that policeman!" she shouted as she slapped the newspaper she held across the palm of her other hand. "Can't you think of anyone but yourself, Charlotte? A man is dead, for heaven's sake. And he had a wife and children."

"Well, it's my own husband and children I'm thinking of just now. We will all share in your disgrace!"

"Not only murdered, Miss Haversham," Mr. Dawes spoke up with macabre enjoyment. "His heart was cut out with surgical precision, so the papers say."

"Must we discuss such gory details?" roared Agatha.

"Can't we all calm down?" wailed Miss Peabody. "I'm getting a headache."

She wasn't the only one. Sophie felt herself getting one as well. But despite Miss Peabody's plea, no one seemed willing to calm down. Everyone began talking at once. Sophie sank down into the nearest chair. Dropping the newspaper to the floor, she pressed her fingertips to her throbbing temples and prayed that Mick could rescue her from this mess.

"That will be enough."

Mick's voice cut through all the others like the firing of a gun, and Sophie closed her eyes in gratitude that her prayer had been answered. A silence fell over the group, and all of them turned toward the doorway as Mick entered the drawing room. After a quick glance around, he turned to where Miss Peabody and Miss Atwood stood beside the fireplace.

"Ladies," he said with a bow, "I believe we are about to enter into some long and tedious discussions, which I'm sure you will find quite dull." He looked at Charlotte, who was standing quite close to him. He smiled at her. "Mrs. Tamplin, I'm sure you and the other ladies would enjoy a walk through the gardens. It's quite fine out, and the gardens here are lovely, as you know."

"Of course," the two older ladies murmured in unison and started edging toward the door. Charlotte, however, glared at Mick as if he were a piece of meat gone bad, folded her arms, and did not move. "Wild horses couldn't drag me out of this room."

Mick's smile widened. He bent his head and whispered something in Charlotte's ear.

She leaned back, looking up into his face, an expression of horror on her own. Clamping her lips together, she whirled around, slamming her reticule against the doorjamb in a fit of temper as she walked out of the room.

"Colonel," Mick said, "would you and Mr. Dawes mind escorting the ladies around the garden?"

"Of course not," Colonel Abercrombie said, and it was plain that he was relieved to escape the emotional furor in the room. He turned to Mr. Dawes, who had remained seated in his chair, and hauled the young man to his feet. "Come along. We can't leave the ladies to take their stroll alone. Just isn't done, you know."

Dragging the reluctant Dawes with him, the colonel ushered Miss Atwood and Miss Peabody out of the room. Mick closed the doors behind them, then returned his attention to Sophie's mother and aunt. "I suggest, ladies, that we sit down."

His words did not have the tone of a suggestion. Even Agatha sank into a chair, her face still creased with anger.

Mick picked up the newspaper from the floor, glanced at the story, then sat down almost directly opposite Sophie and set the *Daily Bugle* on the table beside his chair as if it were of no consequence. She gave him a look of gratitude, glad not to be facing her mother's wrath on her own.

Mick turned to Agatha. "Ma'am, I am going to tell you what has happened during the last twelve hours. I know you will have many questions, but I also know that you won't interrupt my narrative. A lady such as yourself, who knows decorum and proper behavior, would never do anything as rude as that."

Sophie sat back, listening as Mick outlined the events of the night before. He gave her mother the bare facts. He made no embellishments, he made no excuses, and he told the absolute truth. Except that when he was done, the impression left on her mother and aunt was that somehow a telephone in Windsor, not Sophie's psychic ability, had been the source of information about the murder; he had forced Sophie to come back with him on the ten o'clock train, not the seven o'clock; that she had been the victim of his zeal as a police officer; and that she had been given no choice in the matter. He took full responsibility for Sophie's involvement.

"We can discuss your appalling conduct at a later date," Agatha told him when he had finished. "But what about this?" She snatched the newspaper from the table between their chairs and held it up. "Do you know what people will think?"

He shrugged. "They'll think what everyone thinks about everything that appears in the *Daily Bugle*. They'll think it's the trash that it is, and ignore it."

"Quite right," Violet put in. "This will all blow over and be forgotten in less than a week."

Sophie knew her mother was going to disagree, and she spoke before Mother could dispute Auntie's words. "Mr. Dunbar is right. No one believes what appears in the *Daily Bugle* anyway."

"Well, we'll find out, won't we?" Agatha opened her reticule and pulled out a sheet of folded pale pink paper. "Katherine managed to gain us an invitation to Lady Dalrymple's ball a week from now. If you are well received there, you'll be proved right. If you are given the cut, we'll know where we stand, and you will return with me to Yorkshire so that the scandal may die down."

Sophie had no intention of returning to Yorkshire, regardless of the circumstances, and she looked at the invitation her mother was holding without enthusiasm. Still, she supposed going to another ball was a small price to pay if it meant her mother would let this whole issue drop.

The door opened, and Grimstock stepped through the doorway. "Pardon me, madam," he said to Agatha, "but Mr. Tamplin has arrived in a hansom. He has left the cab waiting outside, and has asked me to convey to you that it is now half past twelve. He suggests luncheon at Claridge's."

"Oh, Agatha, you must go!" Violet cried, jumping to her feet. "You know how Harold hates to pay the fare of a waiting cab, and you must not miss luncheon. I managed to have some breakfast this morning before we left, but you've had nothing to eat. For the sake of your health, you should not go so long without food. Luncheon at Claridge's is excellent, you know."

Reluctantly, Agatha got to her feet. Sophie gave her mother a peck on the cheek in farewell, but Agatha gave her a sharp look in return. "We'll see what sort of damage this does to your reputation, young lady. The Dalrymple Ball will tell us if we can still hold up our heads in society."

She turned to Mick. "I don't expect my daughter's name to appear in any newspapers again, and I will not have her associating in any way with the police. If you do not respect my wishes in this, I will have my cousin, Lord Fortescue, take this matter to the Home Secretary himself."

With that, she marched out.

"Whew!" Violet said as the three of them sat down. "It's a good thing Harold arrived when he did. By the time you see your mother again, Sophie, she'll be calmer and more reasonable."

"I'm not so sure." Sophie turned to Mick. "Thank you."

Mick shrugged. "I told the truth."

"And told it in a most clever way, too," Violet said,

smiling. "You are now the most vile man of Agatha's acquaintance, but Sophie seems to have escaped unscathed, at least for now."

"I hope so, ma'am." He rose to his feet. "I need to get to Scotland Yard. I've a great deal of work to do."

"Wait." Sophie grasped his sleeve. "There's one thing I have to know. What was it you whispered in Charlotte's ear that got her to leave?"

He slanted Sophie a wicked look. "I said, 'Charlotte, if you don't leave right now, I will drag you out by your hair.'"

"You didn't!"

"I did."

Sophie and Violet both laughed as Mick bowed to them and turned to leave.

"You know, Sophie," Violet murmured as they watched Mick walk out the doors, "I think your mother and sister have met their match in that man. I have come to admire him a great deal."

"So have I, Auntie," she replied, astonished by the realization. "So have I."

When Mick arrived at the Yard, he found that Sophie's mother was not the only person upset by the article in the *Daily Bugle*. Only a few moments after he went upstairs and entered his office, Sergeant Thacker brought him a crate of case files and a note from DeWitt. The note demanded to see Mick at once.

After reading the terse demand, he looked up at Thacker, who stood beside his chair. "Is he upset?"

Thacker's wooden countenance softened with a rueful smile. "You might say that, sir. I believe that throwing a newspaper across the room and cursing you for idiocy qualifies as upset."

Mick grimaced. "I think I'll wait until he calms down before I go up to his office. What are these files you've brought me?"

"I remembered the theory we discussed after you were shot, that perhaps it was vengeance for a previous case you'd solved." He placed the crate of files on Mick's desk. "With Jack's death, I decided to pull all the cases the two of you have worked on together. I did that this morning."

Mick eyed the crate. "My God, how many are there?"

"Twenty-seven."

"I hadn't realized Jack and I worked so many cases together."

"There may be more. If so, it will take time to find them. You know how difficult it is to find records in this building."

"That's because there's nowhere to put them. There are always boxes of files and reports stacked in the hallways, piled on the stairs. We've only been in this building seven years, and we've already outgrown it."

"As you say, sir. It makes things a bit difficult, but if there are any more, I'll find them."

Mick loosened his tie and rolled up his sleeves. "Thank you, Henry."

"There is one other thing I wanted to tell you. Miss Haversham's brother-in-law is being investigated by CID. Detective Hull was just put in charge of the case."

"Investigated for what?"

"Fraud involving the trust funds of some of his clients. He's an attorney."

"Jack wasn't involved in the investigation, was he?"

"No, sir. Still, I thought you should know."

"Thank you, Henry."

Thacker started to leave, but he paused at the door. "Sir?"

"Yes?"

"What about Miss Haversham?"

"What about her?"

The sergeant didn't answer at once. He hesitated a moment. Finally, he said, "Well, sir, there's been quite a bit of talk this morning about her being at the scene of Jack's murder. It's a bit of a fag, I know, but you know how gossip gets around."

Mick frowned. "What do you mean?"

"With the article in the *Daily Bugle* and all, some of the lads are thinking you're giving credence to what this girl says."

"And that bothers them?"

"It does, sir. There's been some laughing about her, but what's really on their minds is that one of our own was murdered, and you're listening to this bird babbling her psychic nonsense instead of investigating her for what she really knows about it all. That's just some of the talk, sir," he added. "Not all the lads think you're believing her nonsense, but some of them do."

"What about you?" Mick looked at the sergeant with curiosity. Thacker was so impassive that it was hard to tell what he thought of anything. He did his job, obeyed orders, and kept his mouth shut. He was an exemplary officer. "Do you think I'm starting to believe in psychics?"

"If you are, I'm not sure you're wrong, sir." His face flushed brick red. "I mean, there might be something to it. My mother and I went to one of these spiritualists once after my father died. She missed him something fierce, and she wanted to talk to him, you see, so she went to this medium, and I went with her to make sure she didn't get taken by some swindle. But that woman told us things that she couldn't have known beforehand. It's eerie, the things she knew, specific things."

Mick nodded. "I know what you mean. Miss Haversham seems to know things others don't, seems to have an ability to see future events. I've seen evidence of it myself. Still . . ."

"As you say," Thacker said with a nod, "she could be a fraud. The theory that she's protecting someone could be right."

"We'll know soon enough," Mick assured him. "We are going to solve this murder, and find out what the truth really is."

"Yes, sir. And thank you again, about recommending me for detective." Thacker departed, closing the door behind him. Mick looked down on his desk at the note from DeWitt and shoved himself to his feet with a sigh. He buttoned his cuffs, straightened his tie, and went up to DeWitt's office. He knew he was about to get a damn good thrashing.

When Mick entered the chief inspector's office and sat down, DeWitt opened the conversation simply by tossing the *Daily Bugle* into his lap. Mick looked up. "I've seen it, sir."

"Have you read it?"

"Not yet, sir."

"I suggest you do!" DeWitt shouted. "Blasted journalists! Make us look like a pack of idiot dogs who couldn't hunt down a baby rabbit." He scowled as he looked across the desk. "As for you, I still don't understand what the bloody hell you were thinking to bring that woman to the crime scene."

Mick rubbed a hand across his forehead. "Didn't we already have this argument last night?"

"We did. And the entire Metropolitan Police Force looks like a group of complete fools, thanks to you."

Mick knew he had to tread carefully. After a moment, he said, "I have been investigating this woman and her acquaintances for several weeks now."

"Yes, yes, because of that shot taken at you in the Embankment. I remember. But what does she—" DeWitt paused, ran a hand over his bald head, loosened his tie, and said, "You think the two events are connected?"

"I do."

"Why? Because both of you were shot at?"

"Yes, sir. And we're both police officers. I think it ties up with some past case Jack and I worked on together."

DeWitt tugged at his mustache. "That's pretty thin, lad. Pretty thin. What else do you know?"

Mick was not going to get into Sophie's psychic abilities, especially not in light of the *Daily Bugle* story. He merely said, "The surgeon told me at the scene last night that the gun used to kill Jack was a .41 caliber, probably a Colt No. 3 Derringer. That's a pocket pistol, intended to be used at close range. Whoever shot at me was only about a dozen feet away. We are both police officers, and I think the killer's intent was to shoot me down, then cut my heart out, just like Jack."

"Yes, it's clear the heart was some kind of sick, symbolic gesture." He rubbed his hands across his balding head. "I hope we don't have another Ripper on our hands, one who's killing policemen instead of prostitutes. Anything else?"

"Gut instinct."

"What about the girl? What were you thinking?"

Mick drew a deep breath. He'd hoped not to go down this road. "She didn't do it, if that's what you mean. She was with me all day, up until we saw Jack's body. She couldn't have done it."

"But your theory has been that she knows who did."

Mick shook his head. "That was my theory, yes, but I'm beginning to think it's not that simple. I thought that she was involved, and that she came to warn me in advance because she wants to prevent murder while protecting the person responsible. But Jack's death negates that theory. She didn't try to warn Jack in advance. Why warn me of my impending death, but not Jack?"

"Plenty of reasons." DeWitt began counting them off on his fingers. "Maybe she didn't know about this one. Or, if she was with you all day, perhaps she just didn't have the opportunity to warn Hawthorne. Or she might have wanted him to die and not you, for reasons we know nothing about. Or maybe she's what Thacker says she is. Crazy in the head."

"I've been with her quite a bit the past several weeks, sir, and I don't think she's crazy at all. Again, that's my instinct as an officer."

DeWitt gave Mick a long, hard stare. "Or maybe," he said, "she's a very pretty girl that you've spent far too much time with, and you're letting your instincts as a man interfere with your instincts as a police detective."

With those words, a memory of yesterday afternoon in that carriage with Sophie hit all his senses at once. He could see the dark red highlights in the strands of her chestnut brown hair. He could still smell the scent of her, taste the sweetness of her mouth, feel the silken texture of her skin.

His hands clenched into fists. Was that it? Was he getting so soft about her that he was losing his perspective? Mick knew that right now he couldn't make sense out of anything involving Sophie Haversham, and that was dangerous.

DeWitt spoke again. "I don't have to tell you that there's plenty of outrage about this within the Metropolitan Police. You know how we are when one of our own is killed. The brutality of it will inflame the public. God help us if another officer dies, because then we will have another Ripper, and you've already been targeted. This tripe in the *Daily Bugle* doesn't help. I know the girl says she's psychic, but we both know you don't believe such tripe. Why did you bring her to the scene?"

"I wanted to see her reactions to the sight of the murder. That perhaps she would give me some useful information as a result."

"Lad, the result of it is that the newspapers now believe we are using psychics to solve our crimes. Psychics, indeed!"

He grabbed the newspaper off his desk and tossed it into the wastepaper basket. Then he stood up, indicating that their meeting was over. "Continue to investigate the girl if you feel it's warranted, but I damn well better not see another story in the papers about how we're using her so-called impressions at the scene. And I'd better not find out there's anything romantic going on between the two of you. She's a suspect."

Mick met DeWitt's concerned gaze with a determined one of his own as he rose to his feet. "Sir, no woman is going to interfere with my job. I don't give a damn how pretty she is."

DeWitt continued to study him for several moments more. Then he slowly nodded his head. "Very well. I'll let you go on with this. Put a team together to work on it, and I'll meet with the lot of you in a few days to see how you're getting on. And everything thus far indicates you've been targeted by this maniac, so watch your step. I'd like to play this close to the vest, so no press interviews. Your answer to any journalist's question is, 'No comment.' If, God forbid, we have another officer killed, it's going to be chaos."

Mick, who felt that journalists were only slightly above leeches in the natural scheme of things, was in complete agreement with his superintendent. "Yes, sir," he replied and started to leave, but DeWitt's voice stopped him at the door.

"Mick, I have one more thing to say. If I see that this girl is interfering with your judgment in any way that affects your job, I'll pull you off this case in a heartbeat. Is that clear?"

"Perfectly clear, sir."

Mick walked out of DeWitt's office. Closing the door behind him, he leaned back against it and drew a deep, steadying breath. He had to stay objective. He was not going to let lust for a woman get in the way of solving this case. Her long legs, ripe-cherry lips, and the erotic scent of her skin be damned.

Fourteen

❧

During the fortnight that followed, Sophie saw so little of Mick that he might have been a ghost rather than a real person. He left before she woke in the morning and returned long after she went to bed at night. There were many times, Hannah told her, he didn't come in at all. She knew he was working hard on the Jack Hawthorne case. He interviewed her twice about the murder, attempting to glean any details she might have missed or forgotten, but Sophie didn't know why he bothered. It wasn't as if he believed in her. Whatever his reasons, she did her best to help, but she could not remember anything more, and in the days after the murder, she had nothing new to tell him. She could sense that he was still safe, but she also knew that the situation could change in an instant.

She missed him terribly. Over and over in her mind,

she remembered things. The carriage ride, his finger-tips caressing her throat.

Can you read my thoughts right now?

His hands on her, undoing her buttons this time instead of fastening them, touching her bare skin, his lips against the swell of her breasts above her corset, making her shiver and burn all at once. The feel of his body beneath her, his knee between her thighs, and the explosive sparks inside herself she'd never imagined anyone could feel. She closed her eyes, remembering him, remembering *that,* at least twenty times a day.

She kept remembering that night in the conservatory, too. Sitting on his lap, curled within the protection of his strength, feeling truly safe for the first time in her life. Without him, she felt desolate, incomplete.

Though she saw little of him, she had some idea of what he was doing. His name was in the newspapers every day. Not that there was much to say. No one at Scotland Yard was talking, a fact that caused more than one frustrated journalist to insult the capability of the Metropolitan Police.

Sophie had her own problems with the press. Reporters lined up outside her front door every day. She was followed wherever she went, and every move she made seemed to be news. They even lined up out-side Madame Giraud's dressmaking salon when she went there to be fitted for yet another ball gown, and the next morning it was reported that to the Dalrymple Ball, Miss Sophie Haversham would wear a gown of pink-tinged magnolia damask with the new off-shoul-der neckline and trimmed in deep rose satin.

Why journalists reported what she wore or where

she went was incomprehensible to Sophie, but she seemed to be a cause celebre.

She wasn't the only one harassed by the press. They swarmed like bees around any member of the household who dared to step outside, and that took a toll on everyone. Grimstock was exhausted from answering the constant rings of the doorbell and stating that the ladies were not receiving visitors that day. Questions were fired at Hannah over the garden wall every time she went out to pick vegetables or herbs for a meal. The colonel buried himself deeper in the *Times* and dominoes, and Dawes, who had failed his June examinations, was forced to study for the autumn tests at coffeehouses and libraries. Even sweet Miss Peabody began to complain about the situation.

Journalists weren't the only difficulty. The article in the *Daily Bugle* brought ordinary people to Auntie's doorstep. People with problems, people with missing loved ones, people with dead relatives they wanted to talk to all began crowding around outside Auntie's house wanting to talk to Sophie the Psychic.

Dear Aunt Violet made the tentative suggestion to Sophie that perhaps she should try to help some of those grieving, unfortunate people lined up outside, but Sophie quashed the notion at once. Her aunt's response to that—a tear-filled and somewhat accusing gaze—was hard enough, but the sensory onslaught of so many desperate, grieving people asking for her help whenever she walked out the door was more than Sophie could bear. It was like an enormous tide washing over her. If she let it take over, that tide would never ebb, and their pain and suffering would overwhelm her.

Despite that, there were times during her infrequent trips out of the house that her psychic senses would not be suppressed. During those times, she would stop only long enough to murmur something in a person's ear before dashing for a waiting hansom cab. To a tearful new bride, Sophie made a suggestion of what to do about her mother-in-law. She gave the much-needed assurance to a grieving mother that her dear son was just fine on the other side. To a jealous husband, the emphatic reply that his wife was not having an affair.

Without any cooperation from Scotland Yard or the psychic, frustrated journalists made do with whatever they could find. They speculated on motives, guessed at the significance of the removed heart, and did a complete biography of Jack Hawthorne.

They investigated Sophie's family, tried to interview her mother, her sister, Harold, Victor, Katherine, and anyone else within Sophie's circle of acquaintances, most of whom remained blessedly silent. Her broken engagement to Charles, Lord Kenleigh, was given great attention. Charles refused to grant any interviews on the matter, but that did not stop the journalists from making all sorts of sordid speculations.

The irony of the situation did not escape Sophie. She'd been so afraid of Mick prying into her life and finding out things, but now it was the journalists who were doing that, and Mick came in for his share of scrutiny and gossip.

Inquiries into Mick's childhood brought the reporters little information, but all were forced to admit that with the exception of an unfortunate incident involving Sir

Roger Ellerton, Mick's record as a police officer and detective had been exemplary, and in some cases, heroic. Of course, the newspapers made much of the fact that Mick lived in Auntie's lodging house. Some even gave sordid hints of what really went on behind the closed doors of 18 Mill Street.

The reaction of Sophie's family was no less violent than she expected. All things considered, she was able to cope with that rather well, since the crowds outside the house were enough to keep her mother and sister from calling to express their opinions. They did write to her, but their letters were lost in the deluge of correspondence Sophie was receiving every day. Letters from complete strangers, some as far away as Holland and Germany, were beside her plate every morning at breakfast and every evening at dinner.

She didn't even open most of them, knowing the people who had written them were motivated by the same desires and emotions as those of the visitors outside her door. But one morning, about two weeks after the tragedy, Sophie received a letter that was different from all the others.

She pulled it out of the pile without even thinking and the veneer of calm resignation she had wrapped around herself during the last two weeks shattered. She felt waves of such venomous fury emanate from the letter that she almost blacked out.

Sophie dropped the letter with a cry of agony and clamped her hands to her head, overcome by the intensity of the impression.

Everyone looked up from their breakfast, startled by Sophie's cry. Violet took one look at her, jumped out of her chair, and ran down to Sophie's end of the table. "My dear, what on earth is the matter?" she cried, wrapping her arms around her niece. "You're shivering. You feel so cold. Oh, you've seen something. I know you have."

As if from a great distance, she could hear her aunt and the concerned voices of the lodgers, and she focused on that. After a few moments, the rush of hatred and violence she was sensing from the letter began to fade away, and things gradually shifted back to a more normal perspective.

"Darling, darling, it's all right," she heard Violet say. "Grimstock, get a doctor."

"No, no." Sophie shook her head and straightened in her chair, back in control of herself now that the blackness was passing. "No, I don't need a doctor. The feeling has passed. Grimmy, what I do need is a cab."

"A cab?" Violet grasped Sophie's chin, turning her niece's face up so that she could look into her eyes. "Why on earth do you need a cab?"

Sophie patted Auntie's hand, then gently pulled it away from her face. She then shoved back her chair and stood up. "The obvious reason. I'm going somewhere."

"Oh no you're not!" Violet cried. "In this state? You're not going anywhere."

"Auntie, I'm all right now. I have to go see Mick." She pointed to the letter on the floor. "I have to take that to him."

"Then I'm going with you."

"No, Auntie, you can't. If the reporters find out, they

will start speculating that you're assisting Scotland Yard too, and that you might be a psychic, a killer, or heaven knows what. There'll be no end of a fuss. Mama has enough to worry her with my reputation. She doesn't need to be fretting about yours."

She turned to Grimstock, who was hovering in the doorway, clearly uncertain whether to get a doctor, a cab, both, or neither. "Grimmy, you're coming with me." She pointed to the letter on the floor, and she couldn't help shuddering at the horrific feelings it had evoked in her. She didn't dare touch it again. "I want you to bring that letter, but don't touch it. The police may want to check fingerprints or some such thing. Get a pair of tongs, put the letter in another, larger envelope, then put it in your pocket and get me that cab. We're going to Scotland Yard."

Mick had six detectives and three sergeants helping him with the Hawthorne case, yet after two weeks of investigation, they had turned up very little additional information. Mick was frustrated by their lack of progress, and DeWitt was not happy with it either.

"What am I going to tell the press?" the chief inspector demanded, glancing from one face to another in the group of detectives gathered around a long table in one of the meeting rooms at the Yard. "They've been breathing down my neck for two bloody weeks, and I've been promising them a report on our investigation to pacify them. I can't put them off forever. They are wondering if we are even bothering to investigate the murder of one of our own, and they want to know just what we've been doing. The public is terrified we've got another Jack the Ripper on our hands. And the only thing I can tell them is that we don't know who killed Hawthorne, we don't know why, and we don't know who might be next. That will go down very well with the people of this city, I'm sure. What have the lot of you been doing?"

"The public can be assured that only police officers seem to be targeted," Thacker suggested from where he stood by the door.

"Lovely." DeWitt tossed down his pencil. "That will make them feel so much safer. Thank you."

Mick cleared his throat. "Sir, if you'll allow me to go through what we do know, it might help you to understand what we're doing, and you'll be able to judge what is appropriate to tell the press and what is not."

DeWitt turned in his chair to the man seated beside him. "I'm listening."

"The autopsy shows that Jack was killed shortly before he was found. The body was still warm, and rigor mortis had not yet set in. He must have been killed around half past ten. The pub had closed for the evening, but the pattern of blood indicates that Jack was killed and his body desecrated inside the Three Horses. He was dragged into the alley afterward."

"With the fireworks going off for Jubilee, I can believe no one heard the shot. Are there any witnesses?"

"We haven't found anybody who saw Jack's body dragged into the alley," Mick replied. "The owner of the pub doesn't seem to be involved, but we're still looking into that."

Sergeant MacNeil, another officer assigned to the case, spoke up. "The Three Horses is only a block from Jack's flat. He often cut through that alley on his way home. The pub was already closed for the night, but the back door had been broken into. Jack probably saw that, and he stopped to have a look."

DeWitt stared at him in disbelief. "Are you telling me this is a case of a burglar being caught breaking into a pub? Bosh!"

"No, sir," Mick answered for MacNeil and gestured to the other men gathered around the table. "We all agree that Jack and I were both intended targets of this killer."

"But didn't somebody see something?" DeWitt shouted in frustration.

"The killer's timing was impeccable. All the public houses were closed, but most of the people around Covent Garden were on Bow Street in front of the Royal Opera House, wanting to see the Prince and Princess of Wales who had just come out. We had dozens of constables in the area, but they also stayed close to the royal family. We've asked the newspapers to tell people who might have seen something to come forward. But so far, we haven't had anyone come forward other than the usual crowd. You know, people who want to confess to the crime, or people who want to feel important and come forward claiming they've seen something."

"Aye," Sergeant MacNeil spoke again, "like that loony Haversham bird."

An unreasoning anger flared inside Mick at those words. He opened his mouth to defend her, but he caught DeWitt giving him a hard stare, and he forced himself to be silent.

He remembered his own attitude toward Sophie, how he had laughed at her, too. Mick had plenty of common sense, and he believed in his instincts. His instincts told him that Sophie was telling him the truth, that she had some sort of power he couldn't explain away as lucky guesses or perception or women's intuition. Common sense told him power like that was impossible.

There are some things, Mick, that can't be proven. Some things just don't have facts and evidence to back them up. Some things have to be taken on faith.

"Mick?"

DeWitt's voice broke into his thoughts. He glanced up and found everyone looking at him, including his superintendent. "Sorry," he said, straightening in his chair. "I was thinking. What was the question, sir?"

"What is your next step?"

"To find a witness. Somebody must have seen something. We've questioned quite a few people, but we still have many other leads to check."

"Do you still believe revenge for a past case is the motive?"

"Yes, sir." Mick pulled out his notes. "Sergeant Thacker gathered information on all the cases Jack and I have worked on together, but in every one of those cases, all the criminals we helped to convict are still in prison, dead, or have alibis for that night. We're investigating any connection between those cases and Miss Haversham, but we haven't found any. There are quite a few cases to go through, especially from my days at Bow Street Station, when Jack was my sergeant ten years ago. There are many leads yet to pursue, and you know how time-consuming it is. We need more time."

There were murmurs of agreement from the other officers present, but before DeWitt could comment on that, there was a knock on the closed door of the meeting room. The door opened and a young clerk stepped inside, an envelope in his hands. "Pardon me, sir," he said to DeWitt, "but a young lady is here to see Detective Inspector Dunbar."

"We're having a meeting, Mr. Stover," DeWitt pointed out with a frown that would have sent most young clerks scurrying for their desks. This clerk did not move from his place by the door.

"Yes, sir, but this young lady was the one what was at the crime scene, and she says she's got some more information about Jack's murder." He held up the envelope in his hands in verification of his statement. "She said she needs to see Inspector Dunbar at once. Quite adamant about it, she was."

There were chuckles, questions, and sarcastic comments from the group of men around the table.

"What, did she have another vision?"

"Maybe she brought her crystal ball."

"She's obviously batty, but she knows something. What's her connection?"

"Spirit guidance."

At that last comment, laughter broke out around the room, and Mick shoved back his chair. He stood up, knowing he had to get out of here. Losing his temper would not help him solve this case.

"I'll talk to her." As he followed Stover out the door, he said over one shoulder, "Thacker, continue where I left off. I'll be right back."

"C'mon, Mick, you're not really going to talk to her, are you?" someone called after him as he walked out the door. "We're not that desperate, are we?"

Mick set his jaw and shut the door, silencing the laughter that emanated from the meeting room.

"Where is she?" he asked the clerk.

"I put her in your office, sir. Her butler came with her, and he is waiting for her in the CID main room."

Mick pulled the envelope out of Stover's hands and strode down the stairs to the floor below. The clerk followed him all the way to his office.

Sophie turned her head as he walked in, and the moment he saw her face, he knew something was very wrong. He turned to the clerk, who was hovering just outside his office. "You may return to your duties, Mr. Stover," he said and shut the door.

The moment the door closed and Mick turned toward her, Sophie let out a sob and ran to him. "I'm so glad to see you," she choked, throwing her arms around his neck. "I was so afraid they wouldn't let me."

She was trembling. Mick closed his eyes and stood perfectly still, wanting to hold her now more than he'd ever wanted anything in his life, but he knew he couldn't give in to that temptation. Not here. Not now.

He glanced at the glass windows set into the wall and door that separated his office from the hallway outside. Thank God he didn't see Stover peeking in. Mick grasped Sophie's arms and pushed her away. "Sophie, it's not private here," he reminded her.

"Of course," she murmured and bit her lip at the curtness of his voice. "I'm sorry."

He looked away and gestured to the chair opposite his desk. "Sit down and tell me what's happened."

She obeyed. With a glance around, she said, "This wasn't your office the first time I was here."

"That office was temporary," he explained and moved to sit behind his desk. "Mine was being painted." He held up the envelope in his hands. "What's this?"

"A letter from the killer. I got it in the post this morning." She saw him turn it over in his hands and frown at the fact that there was no address or postmark on it, and she went on, "The letter itself is inside. We put it in there so we wouldn't muddle it up with our fingerprints. I didn't know if that was right or not, but I assumed it was better to be safe than sorry . . ."

Her rambling faded away into silence as Mick opened the outer envelope and found a smaller one inside. Without touching it, he dumped it out onto the table. He could see Sophie's name and address written on it in printed characters. Using a pencil, he turned it over, then looked at Sophie sharply. "How do you know it's from the killer? You haven't opened it."

She shook her head. Her face pale, she said, "I couldn't. It was . . . it was too much. When I touched it, I almost blacked out."

Mick noticed that as she spoke, her hands began to shake. He could hear the fear in her voice. Whether her statement was true or not, she clearly believed it. He reached into his desk and pulled out a pair of gloves. After putting them on, he carefully slit the envelope with his letter opener, pulled a letter from inside, and unfolded it.

Mick had seen many sick things in his career, but this had to be one of the sickest. He read the letter through twice. As the killer outlined in lurid detail what he was going to do to Sophie if she continued to interfere with his plans, Mick's rage against this lunatic became a hot, hard knot of fire in his belly. No matter what he had to do, he was going to get this sick bastard.

"What does it say?"

Mick didn't answer her question. Instead, he asked one of his own. "Did you get any impressions from it?"

She lifted her hands in a gesture of bewilderment. "Hate. Evil. Danger."

"Nothing specific?"

"I think . . ." She frowned, staring at the letter. "I don't think this is some prankster who's been reading the papers. The author of this letter is the same person who tried to kill you and who did kill Jack Hawthorne. I'm certain of it."

"Anything else?"

"I sense one other thing." She looked up to meet his gaze. "This person is a man."

That much was evident from the sick things in the letter, but he didn't say so. She hadn't read the letter, and it wasn't necessary that she should.

"Yes. A man somehow connected with you. A friend or—"

"What?" He looked at her across the desk, shaking his head. "That's not possible."

"I'm certain of it."

"I don't believe it. All my friends are police officers." Mick shook his head, refusing to accept that. "An officer doing a brutal murder like that to a fellow officer? No." He held up the letter in his gloved hand. "An officer writing sick garbage such as this? No. You're wrong."

She looked at him unhappily. "I didn't say it was an officer, but it is someone connected with you. What does the letter say?"

Mick looked at her. The hand she held out to take the letter from him was shaking, her dark eyes were filled with fear. There was no way he was going to let her read what this madman planned to do to her after he finished cutting up the next policeman. "It doesn't say anything important," he answered as he put the letter back in its envelope. "It's just vile trash. He's just using you to taunt Scotland Yard."

"You're lying to me."

He looked across the desk at her. Meeting her gaze straight on, he said, "No, I'm not."

"Then let me read it." She watched him shake his head, and she made a sound of frustration. "Mick, I have a right to read it. It was addressed to me."

"I don't give a damn what your rights are," he shot back. "You're not a police officer, this is evidence, and even touching it scares the hell out of you! You're not reading it!"

Sophie leaned back in her chair. "It's bad, isn't it?" She pressed her gloved fingers to her lips. Behind her hand, she whispered, "Oh, God, I knew it."

Mick stood up. "I'm sending a pair of constables home with you. They are going to keep watch over you day and night until this is resolved."

"Why?" Sophie also stood up. Studying his face, she said, "Why do I need somebody watching me? He's threatening to kill me, too. Isn't he?"

Mick didn't answer, and she slammed a fist on the desk between them in her own burst of temper. "If this involves having guards on me, I have a right to know what I'm being threatened with! What does the letter say?"

He circled his desk without answering, walked past her, and opened the door. "Stover!" he shouted down the hall. "Get in here!"

When the clerk came scurrying around the corner, Mick said, "Get a constable to take Miss Haversham home. Tell him to stay with her every single minute until I can get there. Then send for a fingerprint man to go up to the meeting room. And send the CID surgeon, too. Go!"

"Yes, sir." Stover raced away to obey Mick's orders, and Mick returned his attention to Sophie. "That Dalrymple affair is tonight, isn't it?"

"Yes. Why?"

"You're not going."

"What? I have to go. If I try to get out of it, Mother will drag me there, and your constables won't be able to stop her, believe me."

"Even if you're in danger?"

"Am I?" she countered. "How are you going to convince her of that without showing her the letter?"

Mick had no intention of debating the issue. "You're not going."

"Mick, I would love to get out of this ball, believe me. But Mama will make my life a misery if I don't at least put in an appearance. And I hardly think some crazed maniac is going to shoot me and cut my heart out in the midst of a ball, do you?"

"Christ, Sophie, don't say things like that!" he said savagely, thinking of the letter. "Don't."

"You really do believe something could happen to me?"

"Nothing is going to happen to you. If you insist on going to that ball, I'm going with you."

She groaned. "That's even worse. My mother's purpose is to find me a suitable husband, and your presence is going to make her very unhappy. I hate it when my mother is unhappy."

"Too bad."

Unexpectedly, she smiled. It was a rueful one. "I think things have turned around."

"What do you mean?"

"Now, it seems, you're *my* guardian angel."

Fifteen

~

Sophie decided not to tell her mother anything about the letter, though she did tell Aunt Violet that evening as they were getting ready for the ball. She immediately wondered if she'd made a mistake in doing so.

"Oh, dear." Violet pressed a hand to her heart and leaned back against the vanity table in her room. "Oh, heavens! Your life in danger? What are we going to do?"

Sophie patted her aunt's arm and put on a brave face. "There's not much we can do but carry on as usual."

Violet ignored that. "Perhaps we should leave London. Brighton, perhaps. Or the country house of some acquaintance, although—"

"Auntie, I'm not leaving London. Mick needs my help to find the killer. I'm going to help him."

"Did he ask for your help?"

Sophie didn't reply to that question. Instead, she patted her aunt's arm and said, "We'd best be getting downstairs. We're already quite late as it is."

Violet did not move. "Did Michael ask for your help?"

"No," she admitted, "he didn't. But he's going to need it."

"Sophie, my dear, this is not the same as knowing the old coster on the corner is going to die of heart failure tomorrow! If this fiend has threatened you, we must leave London at once."

"Auntie, please don't fret. Mick is not going to let anything happen to me." She paused and closed her eyes for a brief instant, remembering the strength and reassurance of his arms around her earlier today. "He's going to watch over me as much as he can, and there's some sort of bodyguard watching the house."

"Bodyguard?" Violet's voice rose on a frantic note. "Is it as bad as that?"

There was no point in sugarcoating things, since two constables were patrolling the house at this moment, and Mick was waiting downstairs to escort them to the Dalrymple Ball. "Yes, Auntie, it's as bad as that."

Violet sank down on the padded bench in front of her vanity table. "And to think it was I who encouraged you to take your premonition to the police in the first place. I am the one that encouraged you to watch over Michael. If anything happens to you, I will never forgive myself."

Sophie looked at her aunt, and Violet's expression of misery and concern was hard to bear. "Oh, Auntie, please don't!" she cried, wrapping an arm around the older woman's shoulders. "Everything is going to be all right. You'll see."

Violet reached up to her shoulder and grasped Sophie's hand tight in her own. "Of course it's going to be all right, darling," she murmured, but her words sounded dismal and unconvincing. Sophie decided the best thing was a distraction.

"Auntie, you have to help me. Mick is going to the ball with us, and—"

"You mean he's watching over you?"

"Yes, but Mick isn't my main concern just now. Auntie, what am I going to tell Mother? She's going to see Mick the minute we arrive, and I have to think up a plausible story."

"Sophie, your mother has the right to know the truth."

"She'll insist I go home with her to Yorkshire. You know she will. I'll refuse, and there will be a big row about it."

"Yorkshire doesn't sound like a bad idea just now."

"Auntie, you know I can't leave. I have a duty to do what I can to help the police."

"Yes, dear, I understand your sense of responsibility. But don't you think this might be carrying your sense of obligation too far?"

"No, Auntie, I don't. Please don't try to change my mind."

"Very well." Violet stood up, facing her niece with a resolute air. "But I insist you tell your mother the truth."

Sophie knew her aunt was right. Mother deserved

to know what was happening. "Very well," she agreed. "When we arrive at the ball, I'll take her aside and tell her everything."

Violet smiled and hooked her arm through Sophie's. "If Michael is waiting for us, we'd best get downstairs. I'm sure he's pacing by now, wondering why on earth it takes women so long to get dressed."

Sophie laughed as they left Violet's bedroom and started down the stairs. "Well, at least Mick can't get so impatient that he leaves without us. Uncle Maxwell would have done so by now."

"Dear Maxwell never did understand the concept of being fashionably late."

They entered the drawing room and found that Mick was indeed waiting for them, but he wasn't pacing. In fact, he was playing dominoes with the colonel. Occupied with tallying the last score, he did not notice they had come in, but Miss Peabody did.

"At last!" she cried, clapping her hands together with delight, making the two men look up from their game. "Sophie, dear, how lovely you look! Doesn't she look lovely, Josephine?"

Sophie didn't hear Miss Atwood's opinion. She was staring at Mick. In his black evening suit, white shirt, and white silk waistcoat, he was more handsome than ever. Looking at him did funny things to her insides, and she couldn't seem to catch her breath. He was looking straight back at her, his blue gaze like liquid fire as it flowed over her, starting at the white gardenia in her hair, pausing briefly at the low neckline of her gown, and continuing down over her hips and legs to her pink satin shoes. In that moment, something inside her opened and bloomed like a flower, something that bloomed for him, and no one else.

Miss Peabody spoke again, but it took Sophie a moment to realize it. She blinked, turning toward the older woman, and tried to regain her composure. "Hmm? What?"

Miss Peabody laughed. "You're not nervous, are you, dear? I know how you hate dancing. I just wanted you to take a turn so we can see your dress."

She made a spinning motion with her fingers, and Sophie did a slow turn.

"Your gown is beautiful, Sophie, dear," Miss Atwood said and smiled.

Sophie patted the appliqué of rose pink beaded flowers along one side of the skirt, feeling quite self-conscious. "It isn't too ornate, is it?"

Miss Atwood and Miss Peabody both hastened to reassure her on that point, but it was to Mick she looked, hoping he would say something. He did, but given the way he was looking at her, it was not what she expected.

"I think it's time for you to tell me why you hate dancing."

"Because I'm hopeless at it." She laughed to cover the painful admission that she could not do something most young ladies did quite easily, and she regretted for the first time in her life that she'd never practiced enough to dance well.

He shook his head. "I don't believe you. No woman is hopeless at dancing. If she is, then her partner is to blame."

"Remind yourself of that when I tread on your feet."

He laughed. "If you do, I'll simply lift you off the ground and carry you around the ballroom floor."

The image those outrageous words evoked gave her a heady feeling, as if she'd been drinking champagne, and Sophie suddenly wished for the first time in many years that she was a different person. That wish startled her.

She thought she had come to terms with being considered an oddity or a freak. She'd thought she had become resigned to her fate of spinsterhood, she thought she had accepted the fact that she would never find a man who loved her as she was.

Now, looking at Mick, she knew she hadn't accepted the truth about herself at all. Because what she really wanted was just to be a woman, an ordinary woman, loved by a man. And though Sophie could often see the future, she knew there was no hope for a future like that.

The ball was held by Lord and Lady Dalrymple at their country estate in Chiswick, just outside London. It was in honor of the Queen's Diamond Jubilee, though the Queen herself was too infirm to attend. Rumor had it, however, that the Prince and Princess of Wales would be there, which made this ball one of the most sought-after invitations in society.

A maid stopped before Mick with a silver tray filled with champagne glasses. He took one, wishing it were a pint of ale, and glanced around. Violet was talking with Lord and Lady Fortescue and Harold Tamplin. Sophie was standing about two dozen feet from him, deep in conversation with her mother and sister. Mick knew his presence here was the subject being discussed, and he could tell from Sophie's face that it wasn't going well.

He decided to take a stroll in that direction. It seemed to be two against one, and he figured she needed reinforcements. As he approached, Sophie, who was facing his way, saw him and waved him over with obvious relief.

"Inspector Dunbar," she said, so sweetly that Mick knew she was furious, "would you explain to my mother just what it is that makes it necessary for you to be here? She feels that your presence at this ball is hampering her attempts to marry me off."

"Sophie Marie Haversham, I don't need your impertinence," Agatha said with heavy disapproval. "I am looking out for your future, since you seem oblivious to it." She turned to Mick. "I'm sure you understand, Mr. Dunbar, that my daughter is very important to me, and—"

"Indeed, I do, ma'am," he interrupted, "and that's why I am here. Sophie received a letter from the madman who recently murdered a policeman, and in that letter he threatened to kill her, too. I am here to make certain she is safe."

"Yes, yes, Sophie told us," Charlotte said, "after we dragged it out of her. But really, Inspector, it is ridiculous to think anyone here would wish my sister ill."

"He doesn't just wish her ill, Mrs. Tamplin. He wants to kill her."

Charlotte gasped at his deliberate brutality. She was silent for a moment, then she recovered her poise and said, "I'm sure we know no one who would want to kill anyone. We don't mingle with the criminal classes."

"For heaven's sake!" Sophie snapped her fan closed. "Don't you understand anything Mick said? The killer has threatened my life. You may take the notion of my death lightly, but I don't!"

She turned and stalked away as Agatha called after her, "That is utterly untrue, and unworthy of you, Sophie." But her daughter did not hear or chose to ignore her words, and Agatha sighed as she watched Sophie walk away. "I'm only trying to do my duty as her mother," she said.

Mick knew she was talking to herself, not to Charlotte, and not to him. Nonetheless, he said, "Sophie knows that."

Agatha turned on him. "You had best watch your step, Inspector. I am acquainted with the Home Secretary, and I will not hesitate to use my cousin's influence with him to keep you away from my daughter."

"Ma'am, the Home Secretary himself knows of this case, and endorses having police officers watch over your daughter. Complaining to him will serve no purpose. I must reiterate that your daughter's life has been threatened, and we take such threats seriously at Scotland Yard."

She sniffed, unimpressed, and walked away.

"I realize you feel the need to do your job, Inspector," Charlotte said, "however ridiculous it may be, but you are not the only one conducting investigations. My husband and I have been conducting one of our own."

He was trying hard to remain polite, but Charlotte Tamplin was really more than any man should have to bear. He felt an enormous pity for Harold. Even if the man was a criminal, he didn't deserve this. "Indeed?" he murmured, keeping an eye on Sophie, who was now standing along the far wall of the ballroom, her reflection against the windows behind her as she talked with a stout woman in purple satin. Mick noted she was at the opposite end of the room from her mother.

"I've been reading about you in the newspapers," Charlotte went on, "and I know that you have no family and no connections. My sister is quite above you in station. So if you have any marital aspirations regarding my sister, you will be disappointed."

Mick turned to Charlotte and smiled. "I assure you, Mrs. Tamplin, you may rest easy on that score," he said in as pleasant a voice as he could manage. "I have no desire to marry into your family. I would hate to have to arrest my own brother-in-law for fraud."

Her face went pale. "What do you mean?"

"Ask Harold about the trust accounts of his clients he's been stealing from. He's being investigated by Scotland Yard, so he'd better put the money back soon, because we are tightening our net around him." He bowed. "If you will pardon me?"

He turned and walked away, knowing he might have just ended any chance of the Yard catching Tamplin in his crooked schemes, but for Sophie's sake, he had no regrets. As for Charlotte, well, living with her was Harold's true punishment. "What a poisonous woman," Mick muttered under his breath.

He headed toward where Sophie was standing, but after taking only a few steps in that direction, he realized she was no longer there.

Mick strode across the crowded ballroom as quickly as he could, his gaze scanning the crowd in search of her, feeling a sudden twist of fear in his guts as he reached the spot where he had last seen her and found that she was nowhere nearby. He saw a pair of French doors that led out to the gardens. Mick strode outside, hoping to hell she'd only gone out into the gardens for some air.

Sure enough, he found her seated on one of three curved stone benches that encircled a fountain, surrounded by a large expanse of lawn.

In the moonlight, her creamy satin dress gleamed, and the beads that decorated it sparkled like diamonds. She was moving her fan back and forth so rapidly that Mick knew she was seething. He didn't blame her.

Sophie sensed his approach and turned toward him. "What a lovely time I'm having," she said through clenched teeth. "How about you?"

"Never had more fun in my life."

She gave a humorless laugh as he sat down beside her. The fan she waved brought the delicate fragrance of her to his nose, along with the sharper scent of the freshly cut grass.

"I give it up," she said. "How can any rational person deal with my mother?"

"Look at it this way. You only see her twice a year."

"That's two times too many by my reckoning." Sophie slumped. "She's so exhausting. And let's not even talk about my sister."

"I agree. Let's not."

She pressed her fingers to her temples. "May I go home?"

"No. You have to dance with me first."

"I told you, I don't dance."

Mick opened his mouth to reply, but a female voice interrupted. "What a lovely prospect from the terrace!"

A man's voice responded, a voice Sophie knew very well. "I told you Lord Dalrymple's Chiswick estate is one of the finest properties I know."

Sophie looked up and moaned under her breath. She could not mistake the male figure standing on the terrace a dozen yards away. "This evening is going from bad to worse," she groaned.

Mick stepped a respectable distance away from where she sat as the man and woman came down the terrace steps and onto the lawn. At the sight of Sophie and her companion, they halted.

Sophie stared in dismay at the boyish, handsome face of Charles Treaves, the Earl of Kenleigh, the man she had once loved.

Too many things happening in too short a time. Her name in the papers, crowds outside her door, threats on her life, and now Charles. Sophie felt a numbness come over her as she watched them approach her. She lifted her chin, bracing herself for the encounter as she pasted on a smile and stood up. "Why, Charles! What a surprise."

Her voice sounded brittle to her own ears.

Charles shook his head. "Of all the people to run into," he said. "I thought you hated events of this kind."

"I do, but my mother feels I don't mix enough in society."

"She's right. Whenever we attend social gatherings in London, we never see you." He smiled. "I saw Agatha earlier. She seems just the same."

The woman on Charles's arm gave a slight cough, and Charles looked at her, smiling. "I'm sorry, my dear," he said to her. "Allow me to introduce you. This is Miss Sophie Haversham. Sophie, my wife."

"How do you do, Lady Kenleigh?" Sophie murmured. She gestured to where Mick stood a few paces away. "Michael Dunbar, Lord and Lady Kenleigh."

"Dunbar?" Charles looked at him with interest. "You are the Scotland Yard man the papers are talking about."

"I am." Mick bent his head slightly, but other than that slight acknowledgment, he stood like a statue, unmoving, hands behind his back, his face expressionless.

"Your men have already interviewed me, Mr. Dunbar," Charles went on, "and I want you to know I am perfectly willing to cooperate with them in any way I can."

"Thank you, my lord." The words were clipped, dismissive, and Mick made no further attempt at conversation.

There was an awkward silence, then Charles and his wife looked at each other, and Charles said, "Well, we should be moving along. It was good to see you again, Sophie."

The couple continued on their moonlight stroll and soon vanished around the corner of the house, leaving Sophie and Mick alone again.

"Heavens, this has been quite the day." Sophie tried to laugh as she sank down onto the bench, still feeling an odd sense of numbness.

Mick stepped in front of her and held out his hand. "Dance with me."

She looked up at him in astonishment. "What, now? Here?"

"Why not? The ballroom is lit, and we're outside in the dark. No one will see you step on my feet out here."

"Are you trying to distract me?"

His hand remained outstretched. "I gave up my Saturday night poker game with the lads for this ball. Make it worth my while."

She smiled. "You didn't really."

"I did."

"I've always wanted to learn to play poker."

"Aye, I'll bet you have, since you can tell if people are bluffing." He gestured impatiently with his hand. "Come and dance. Stop stalling."

Sophie stood up. Mick put one hand on her waist and grasped her other hand in his. He pulled her close to his body. Through her gloved hand, she could feel the warmth of his palm as he entwined their fingers.

"Ready?" he asked.

She took a deep breath. "No."

"You have to trust me."

She looked straight into his eyes. "I trust you," she said, and meant it. "I'm just awful at dancing."

She proved her words when he began to lead her in the steps. She immediately stumbled, tripping over her own feet and stepping on his. "Sorry," she told him. "I warned you."

"Just relax," he said. "Relax and let me do the work."

That was easier said than done. He was so close, and the touch of his hand on her waist did crazy things to her insides. She couldn't help remembering the carriage ride, when his body had been beneath hers and how she had felt beautiful and desired when he'd touched her, when he'd looked at her.

She looked up at him and caught her breath. He was looking at her like that now. The man who had just left the garden had never looked at her the way this man did.

She stepped on his foot again and came to a stop, pulling her hands away. "See, I told you I was hopeless at this. Let's just forget it."

Mick didn't answer. He didn't move. He just stood there looking at her, and she knew what he was thinking.

"He jilted me at the altar," she whispered.

"I know."

She tried to laugh. "Of course. Everybody knows, don't they? It's been in all the newspapers this week."

"Did he give you a reason for breaking your engagement?"

"He did." She took a deep breath. "He said he couldn't live with a woman who could read his thoughts or see into his mind. It was like being raped, he said."

Mick stiffened, and she sensed he understood exactly what Charles had meant. She'd been right. He wouldn't want to marry her either. No man would. And she could not change. She would not pretend.

"I can't change what I am," she said. "Charles understood that better than I. That was why he couldn't marry me."

She turned away, looking out over the lawn. For five years, she had dreaded the idea of meeting Charles again, of seeing him again, but now that the worst had happened, she was astonished to realize that thinking of Charles didn't hurt anymore. Somehow, time had healed that wound without her even realizing it.

She felt Mick's fingertips brush the back of her neck. "Are you all right?"

"Actually, I'm fine now," she said and turned to face him. "It was just the momentary shock of seeing him again. The truth is, I got over Charles long ago, and I just didn't know it."

"Good." He lifted her hand in his and put his hand on her waist as if to resume their dance.

"I don't want to do this," she protested.

"You'll be fine. You just need a bit of help."

Before she knew what was happening, his arm was wrapped around her waist, and she was being lifted from the ground. With a shriek of laughter, she tried to protest, but his arm was tight around her, and her feet dangled several inches off the lawn. She flung her arm around his neck to hang on as he began to move across the lawn in the swaying steps of a waltz, holding her body pressed hard against his to keep her from falling.

"See how easy it is," he murmured. "Anyone can do it."

Sophie felt as if she were floating on air as he waltzed her around the lawn. She hardly noticed when the music ended. Mick came to a halt, but he didn't put her down.

Sophie felt his desire for her, and all the memories with which she had been torturing herself came back to haunt her now. "Mick," she whispered and touched her lips to his.

"DeWitt will take a strip out of me for getting involved with you," he murmured against her mouth. "I could lose my job."

Before she could reply, his mouth opened over hers in a hard, hot kiss. He lifted her up until his forearm was beneath her bottom, and his other arm was around her back like a steel band, holding her in place as his tongue entered her mouth.

Sophie wrapped her arms around his neck and clung to him. She curled her leg around him, wrapping his hip in the heavy damask of her ball gown.

He opened her lips with his, his tongue caressed hers, and he groaned into her mouth, giving voice to the same pleasure she was feeling. Sophie could not stop herself from moving against his body just as she had in the carriage. She wanted those sensations she'd felt before.

The sound of a woman's tinkling laugh was like a shower of ice water over both of them. Sophie felt herself sliding to the ground. Mick stepped back several feet, and Sophie tried to regain her equilibrium.

The woman's laughter came again, and Sophie and Mick looked over to where a very drunken pair of couples stumbled around the corner of the house toward them, carrying glasses of champagne and spilling most of it as they walked.

Sophie looked down and noticed that the hem of her skirt was turned up six inches, revealing the lacy trim of her petticoat. She hastily bent down and turned the hem back down as the couples came closer. They passed by as Sophie and Mick stared at one another, breathing hard and trying not to.

"We should go back," he said.

"Yes, of course," she whispered, her heart thudding like the rhythm of a runaway train.

Neither of them moved.

She watched Mick's mouth tighten. "If we don't go in," he said, "your mother will be the next one to walk by, and then I'll be in serious trouble."

He did not offer her his arm, and they walked back to the ballroom without touching. Sophie struggled to regain her composure as they entered the ballroom, but she felt as if every eye must be on them, including her mother's, and she snapped open her fan to shield her face, which she felt must be scarlet with embarrassment.

She and Mick took a place along one wall, and she fanned her face, pretending to watch the dancers, but all she could think of was how her body seemed to be on fire everywhere Mick had touched her. She dared not look at him.

"Miss Haversham!" a loud, insistent voice called. "Just the person I've been looking for!"

Sophie turned and saw the stout, unmistakable figure of her hostess bearing down on her. She hoped she now looked more serene than she felt.

"How wonderful to see you!" Lady Dalrymple exclaimed, clasping Sophie's hand. "I'm so glad you came to my little party."

"I'm delighted you invited me," Sophie said politely.

"This is such perfect timing, Sophie. I've just been telling the ladies all about your extraordinary talents." She turned to the group of women with her. "Ladies, this is Sophie Haversham. You know, the psychic and spiritualist the newspapers have been talking about. She's so accurate that it's uncanny."

Sophie groaned under her breath. This was adding insult to injury. "Good Lord," she whispered to Mick behind her fan as Lady Dalrymple sang her praises, "I didn't know I was that astounding."

Lady Dalrymple turned back around, and Sophie pasted a smile on her face. "You say such kind things, Countess," she said, "but please believe me when I say the newspapers have exaggerated my abilities."

Lady Dalrymple ignored that. "I have an idea!" she exclaimed. "You can tell fortunes tonight."

"What?" Sophie choked. "You're joking."

"Not at all. It's such wonderful entertainment to have a skilled psychic read the cards. I have a tarot deck you may use."

Sophie listened with growing dismay as the countess decided that the card room would be just the right place for Sophie to tell fortunes. "It will be grand," she said and turned to her friends again. "So entertaining, don't you think so? Why, it's just the perfect thing all around. And Miss Haversham is very talented. It's amazing what tricks she can do."

Mick leaned close to her. "And your sister thinks it's only us poor blokes in the working class who have bad manners."

"She's talking about me as if I'm a trained seal,"

Sophie whispered back. She listened to Lady Dalrymple ramble on happily to the others, and more than ever she wanted to leave. What was she then, a circus performer?

Feeling smothered, Sophie turned to Mick. "Please, please get me out of here."

Sixteen

❧

Sophie looked at the sign over the door of a small, inconspicuous building on Bow Street. "A police station?" She glanced at Mick doubtfully.

"How much safer can we be than at a police station?" he countered and opened the door.

"When I asked to leave the ball, this wasn't what I had in mind."

Sophie followed Mick through the front room of the station, greeting the men on duty as he passed and seeming to ignore their stares of curiosity.

Mick led her into a room at the back of the station, and when she walked in, she saw a group of three constables gathered around a table in one corner of the room, playing cards. They looked up as she and Mick entered the room.

"Hell's bells," one of the men said, looking Mick up and down. "Where's the funeral?"

Sophie laughed, and the man turned his head toward her, skimming her with a speculative glance. "Well now, a woman with a fine sense of humor." He took her hand in his. "Who might you be? And what on earth is a beautiful woman like you doing with our Mick? I'm sure he'll be dead of the shock by morning. He's not used to beautiful women."

"Lads, this is Miss Sophie Haversham. Sophie, this is Billy Mackay," Mick said, pulling her hand away from the other man's grasp. "He was, until a moment ago, a friend of mine."

She was introduced to the other two men at the table, Rob Willis and Anthony Frye. The one named Rob she remembered from the night Jack Hawthorne was killed, and he gave her a nod of recognition when they were introduced. She sensed a bit of surprise from all three men at her presence with Mick, but given the incredible stories in the papers, she could understand why. She was Sophie the Psychic, after all.

Billy glanced at the two men on the other side of the poker table. "Cleans up rather good, our Mick, doesn't he?"

"He does," Rob agreed. "For a moment, I didn't recognize him in that monkey suit."

Mick adjusted his tie. "Unlike the lot of you, I get enough invitations to actually own an evening suit."

"Ouch, that hurt." Billy looked both of them up and down. "So, what are you two all dressed up for?"

"We were at a ball," Sophie explained, "but I didn't want to stay. It's hard to like balls when you can't dance."

"You can't dance? I thought all society girls knew how to dance."

She shook her head, and several of her hairpins came tumbling down. Billy bent and picked them up. He handed them to her, grinning.

"Thank you," she said and started pinning up her hair again. "Why are you smiling at me like that, Mr. Mackay?"

The grin was gone in an instant. "No reason," he said. "You are just not . . ." He didn't finish the sentence, but in that moment, she read his mind just like a book.

Not the sort of woman Mick usually likes.

She wanted to ask what sort of woman he preferred, but it didn't matter. Mick wasn't a marrying, settling down sort of man. She knew that much.

"Micky boy," Anthony put it, "you brought her here from a ball? Here?" He shook his head, looking at Mick sadly. "This is your way of showing a woman a bit of fun?"

"Of course," Mick answered, "but I didn't know you were going to be here or I'd have known better."

Sophie listened to the men trade good natured insults almost as if she were listening to a foreign language. She'd never been around a group composed entirely of men before, and she liked their easygoing manner.

She glanced at the table and noticed the cards and the pile of brightly colored disks in the center, and she turned to Mick, laughing, remembering their conversation earlier. "This is your Saturday night poker game. That's why you brought me here! You're going to teach me how to play poker."

"If the lads don't mind, I thought I would." He turned to the other men. "Sophie has always wanted to play poker, but among the high-society circle she moves in, ladies are only allowed to play proper games like whist. She finds it dull."

"Whist?" Billy grinned. "Who wouldn't?"

"I don't know," Rob said, shaking his head as he looked at Sophie. "Aren't you the one all the papers claim is a psychic? Are you going to know when I'm bluffing?"

She saw the amusement in his eyes, and she knew he didn't really believe she was psychic. But that was all right. "It depends," she answered. "Is there money involved?"

"Of course. What would be the point otherwise?"

"Then you're safe. I don't get psychic impressions from cards if there's money involved. Mick tried to get me to help him win at Ascot, but I just couldn't do it."

"Ascot?" Anthony looked at Mick. "You went to Ascot? Isn't it a bit highbrow for you, Micky boy?"

"I've been before," Mick said with a shrug. "So, lads, is she in?"

"I don't know." Billy studied her for a moment. "You're sure, being psychic and that, you can't cheat?"

"I'm sure." Sophie sighed. "My auntie thinks it's because the spirits don't want me to profit from my psychic ability."

"The spirits, eh?" Billy grinned again and glanced at Mick. Somehow, Sophie knew Billy wasn't laughing at her, but she couldn't quite pinpoint the source of his amusement. Something to do with Mick. "Are you a medium?"

"Oh, no. I can't communicate with spirits, although Auntie's spiritualism society wishes I could. They have to use a planchette instead."

"A planchette?" Rob made a choking sound. "I see."

"What is this spiritualism society, Sophie?"

"Oh, it's just my aunt and a few of her friends." Sophie waved her hand in an airy gesture, and her garnet bracelet came undone, falling to the floor. "They talk about ghosts and spirits and reincarnation."

Mick bent and picked up her bracelet. He handed it to her, and she refastened it around her wrist as she went on, "Auntie thinks she's the reincarnation of Cleopatra. Of course, I don't try to argue with her about it."

All three men at the table glanced at Mick, but he didn't seem to notice. "Give us some chips," he said and handed Billy a pound note. "We'll see how she does, eh, lads?"

The men at the table made room, chairs were pulled up for them, and Mick explained the fundamentals of the game to her. He did not play. Instead, he sat behind Sophie's chair to guide her play if she needed it.

She tried to keep her mind on the play, but when Mick would bring his arm around her to point at her cards and whisper suggestions in her ear, she couldn't concentrate on anything. An hour and a half later, she was out of money.

"See?" she told Rob with a sigh, plunking one elbow down on the table and resting her chin in her hand. "I never see anything when there's money involved. I never win the sweeps, or wager on the winning horses, or anything like that."

"Tell me something, Sophie," Billy said as he shuffled the cards. "The *Daily Bugle* insisted that you foresaw Jack's death. Is that true?"

Given how sensitive the case was, and how silent Scotland Yard had been about Sophie's involvement, she didn't know whether or not to answer that question. She straightened and glanced at Mick, then she said, "It is true. For once, the *Daily Bugle* actually printed something accurate."

No one spoke. Mick's three friends stared at her without attempting to hide their skepticism. Sophie was not surprised. "I know you don't believe me, gentlemen," she said quietly. "Many people don't. But I can't help that."

It was Mick who broke the silence. "I believe you."

All of them, including Sophie, stared at him in astonishment.

"I didn't at first," he continued, meeting her gaze straight on. "But some things just have to be taken on faith."

She could feel the incredulity of Mick's friends, and she knew what it had cost him to admit this in front of men whose opinion mattered to him. For this, he would be ridiculed, yet he had gone out of his way to show her that his opinion of her had changed. He was doing what even most of her family had been unable to do. He was accepting her for exactly what she was.

It was at that moment that Sophie fell in love with him.

"We'd better go," he said and stood up. "Lads, I'll see you for next week's game."

Sophie stood up, waving good night to the men around the table as she followed Mick out of the police station.

She paused beside him on the sidewalk, still reeling from what had just happened. He believed in her. It was a wondrous feeling.

He hailed a cab. "Eighteen Mill Street," he told the driver, and those words snapped her out of her reverie. "Oh, no!" she cried. "It's not even midnight yet! Must we go home already?"

"Where do you want to go?" he asked.

"I'd love a cup of tea and something to eat. I'm starving. We left before the supper."

"The tea shops are closed by now." He tilted his head to one side, watching her. "What is your mother going to think of you being out alone with me?"

"She won't know. The ball won't be over for hours yet, three or four o'clock, at least. Besides, only Auntie will come back to Mill Street, and she won't mind as long as I'm with you. She has a very high opinion of you, you know."

"Not very wise of her." He turned away. He was silent a moment, then he said, "Take us to number 5, Maiden Lane."

"Aye, guv'nor." The driver climbed up onto the seat as Sophie and Mick got into the carriage.

"That's your old flat!" she said as they settled themselves inside. "Why are we going there?"

"I didn't move out," he said, looking out the window. "I've got some tea things there."

"You didn't give up your flat? I don't understand. Why not?"

He met her questioning glance. "Because when this case is over, I'll be going back."

"Oh." She hadn't thought about what would happen when this case was over. "Auntie's lodging house is better than your flat. You wouldn't . . . stay on?"

"I don't think that would be a good idea."

"No, I suppose not." She was ashamed that she couldn't keep the disappointment out of her voice. He believed in her, but he was leaving. Going back to his old life. Of course he would. She should have known that all along. She loved him. He didn't love her. She knew that, too.

Mick gave a heavy sigh and leaned forward in his seat. "Sophie, look. I come and go at all hours. It's an inconvenience to your servants, never knowing when I'll be in for a meal. Your house is all the way across London from my office."

"I understand." Her words were the truth. She did understand, more than he knew. She understood that the reasons he'd just given her were excuses. The truth was that he didn't want to get entangled with her. How ironic. When he came to believe in her, she fell in love with him, but it was his belief in her that was driving him away now. Just like Charles. Oh, yes, she understood. She understood perfectly.

Mick knew the fact he'd kept his own flat had disappointed her somehow, but God, what did she expect?

Neither of them spoke as he unlocked the door of his flat, and they went inside. He lit a lamp, then grabbed the teakettle. "I'll be right back," he said and left the flat.

He lit a second lamp to light his way and went downstairs to fill the kettle from the pump in Mrs. Tribble's kitchen. In the doorway leading to the kitchen, he could see a brownish gray ball of fur lift its head and growl at him.

"Make another sound, and I'll turn you into a real dust mop," he told the Pekingese dog. He stepped over the animal and into the kitchen.

As he filled the teakettle from the pump, he realized he was asking for trouble, bringing Sophie here. But, God, he wanted another taste of what he'd had at Ascot. Just a taste.

When he once again entered the flat, he didn't see her anywhere in the room. "Sophie?"

"I'm out here."

He then realized she was standing out on the fire escape. He lit the gas ring, put the kettle on for tea, then moved to join her outside, but he paused for a moment in the doorway.

The moonlight shone off the white flower in her hair and the satiny sheen of her gown. The pearl buttons down her back gleamed. All of them were fastened, and he rather thought that a shame.

He came up behind her and put his hands on her shoulders. Her skin was soft and warm beneath his fingers.

"Why are you out here?" he asked, breathing in deeply of the scent of gardenia.

"Why not? It's a lovely night."

That was true. The sky was so clear that even above the coal soot and gaslights, the stars were plainly visible. He slid his arms around her waist, content to just stand here and hold her. Just realizing that made him want to laugh at himself. This beautiful woman in a candy confection of a dress, smelling like flowers and feeling like heaven in his hands, and holding her was enough?

Maybe he was actually starting to like crystal chandeliers, cabbage rose wallpaper, and the color pink.

Both of them stood looking at the stars, silent for a long time. Then she spoke.

"Mick?" She turned her head and looked at him over her shoulder. "Do you think Charles was right? Do you think that having someone see your thoughts is an invasion? Like . . . like rape."

"Rape?" He shook his head. "That's going a bit far."

"But you do think that my ability to read people's thoughts is an invasion?"

He wasn't going to lie to her. His arms slid away. "Yes, Sophie. I do."

She didn't try to argue the point. She nodded. "I see."

The kettle whistled, and they went back inside. Mick poured out their tea and handed her a cup. He put a tin of sweet biscuits and an orange on the table. "I'm afraid that's all I've got in the flat to eat."

He sliced the orange into sections, placing them on two plates along with some biscuits, and they sat down at the table. Sophie stared down at her plate, but she made no move to eat.

"I thought you were hungry," he said.

She looked up. "It's fear, isn't it?"

"Fear?" Mick repeated, not knowing what she was on about.

She nodded, and he saw pain in her eyes. "I frightened Charles. I frighten most men. In fact—" She paused and gave him a tiny smile. "This is an odd thing to say to a man like you, but the truth is that even you are afraid of me."

His first impulse was to deny it, assure her he wasn't afraid of anything, especially a woman, but somehow the words wouldn't come because she was right. Mick lowered his gaze to the cup in his hands.

Sophie did scare him. She got into his mind and could know what he was thinking. She could get into his heart and feel what he was feeling. She could see into the future, and he just didn't want to know what was down the road. Every man had his weaknesses, and what man wanted a woman to discover those?

Mick finally broke the long silence that had fallen between them. "You're right. I hate to admit it, but you're right. I am afraid of you. I'm afraid of what you can do because I don't understand it, and I don't like what I don't understand."

"I know. Believe me, I know."

Her gaze remained on his face, but he knew she wasn't really looking at him. "Once Charles realized the truth, realized what I was and what I could do, he couldn't marry me. It was my fault he didn't know until the day before the wedding. I deceived him."

The corners of her mouth tilted up a bit. "I'd known all along that if I let him see the truth, he wouldn't marry me. And I loved him so much that I couldn't bear the idea of losing him. So I tried to hide my abilities from him. I pretended to be something I was not. I suppressed the psychic impressions that flashed into my head, I kept my mouth closed, and I pretended. But, of course, it didn't work. You can't keep up that sort of deception. When Charles realized and accepted the truth, he broke our engagement. And I knew that it would be the same with any man who showed an interest in me. Once a man knew what I was, he wouldn't want me. So I stopped pretending, and I am a spinster."

She laughed, a hollow, humorless sound. "My mother has not given up, however. As you have seen, hope springs eternal in her breast that I will marry, and she keeps trying to force the issue, thinking that my psychic ability is merely a character flaw, like bad manners or a quick temper, and if I only tried harder, I could control it. When I was a little girl and I first started to have these premonitions, I would say them at once and my mother would tell me to stop making up stories. She was afraid of me, too, thinking she'd borne a child who was mad."

"Yes, but you're talking about something that would be very hard for a parent to accept."

"Yes, I know. I felt her disapproval, her fear, and for years, I tried to suppress my feelings, my impressions, my knowledge, to please my mother. I tried so hard."

The pain in her voice sliced through him like a sword, and in that moment, he suddenly saw the world through her eyes, saw what a burden her unique talent could be. "Sophie, I've met your mother. No one could please her. It's impossible."

"You're wrong," Sophie told him and picked up an orange slice. After eating the fruit and setting the rind on the table, she added, "My mother thinks my sister is perfect."

"Your sister is a bitch."

This time her laughter was genuine, ringing through the small flat. "And I've always thought I was the only one who thought so. But then, I'm not objective on the matter. My sister despises me, and it's hard to love someone who hates you."

"I may not be psychic, but even I can read your sister's feelings. What I don't understand is why. Why does she despise you so much?"

The laughter faded from her face, and she became serious once again. "It's fear again. Her fear of me makes her hate me. When we were children, she and her friends tormented me cruelly. I was crazy, they said. I was a freak, they said." She shrugged. "I've learned to accept myself. She hasn't."

"What about your father?"

"I don't remember much about Papa. He died when I was three years old, and my psychic abilities had barely started to manifest themselves, so I'm not sure he knew anything about it. But I do remember that he was a very kind, gentle man."

Mick rested his elbows on the table, his fingers curled around the teacup in his hands, studying her over the rim. "What about people other than your parents? Your ability doesn't seem to bother your aunt or the other people living in the house."

She smiled. "Dear Auntie. She accepts me for exactly what I am, and that's one of the reasons I love her so much. Of course, it helps that I indulge her belief that she was Cleopatra in a previous life, and I never say a skeptical word about her little group of spiritualists."

He laughed. "Don't you believe in ghosts?"

"Yes, but not in the sense that Auntie does."

Mick's laughter faded, and he gave Sophie a skeptical glance over the rim of his cup. "You really believe in ghosts?"

"Of course. Because of my psychic sense, I've seen quite a few. But ghosts are not what most people think they are. They are not the walking spirits of the dead."

"What are they, then?"

"They are echoes of the past, emotions imprinted on the air, almost like photographic impressions are printed on paper."

"Ghosts?" He shook his head. "I'm not sure I can swallow that."

"Why not?" she countered. "You believe in photography, don't you? Ghosts are the same. Auntie doesn't think so, but I don't dispute her belief. If she wants to believe that Maxwell's spirit is always nearby or that she can talk to her children whenever she likes, it helps her feel better and not miss them so much."

"I didn't know your aunt had any children."

"She did. Three sons. All of them died. One in childbirth, and the other two, twins, died during a cholera epidemic when they were eight. It broke Auntie's heart when that happened, but Maxwell's death was the most devastating blow of all. She discovered séances and spiritualism, and it helps her to know she can talk to her loved ones whenever she likes. That's why Auntie and I get along so well. We each accept the eccentricities of the other, and love each other anyway. As for the others, well, Miss Atwood and Miss Peabody are spiritualists, too, so they think I'm a medium. The colonel doesn't know what to make of me. As for Mr. Dawes, he's so preoccupied with himself that he doesn't bother with anyone else."

Mick hesitated, wondering if he should tell her what he had found in Dawes's room. Given the current situation, he decided it would be best if he did. "Sophie, did you know that Edward Dawes keeps pictures in his room? Pictures of women."

To his astonishment, she didn't seem bothered by that. "Oh, yes, naked ones. I know all about that." She sent Mick a reproving glance across the table. "And not because I searched his room, like some people."

"I refuse to feel guilty about that. I was doing my duty."

"I suppose I have to agree with you, but you don't know how scared I was that you would find out about Auntie!"

"I knew you were afraid I'd find out something, but I completely misinterpreted it. Does your aunt know about Dawes?"

"No, and I'm not going to tell her. I do try to protect the privacy of people whose secrets I know. But once people find out that I know things, they pull away from me. That's why I have so few friends. I make people uncomfortable. Even those who know me think I'm an oddity. Some people don't believe me and think I'm crazy. Either way, it doesn't allow anyone to get close to me."

Sophie paused and took a sip of tea. Putting the cup

down, she went on, "Do you know what it's like when people think you are crazy? You begin to wonder yourself. It's so hard to keep your balance. To see things and not have the power to stop them or change them. To be standing in the queue, waiting for an omnibus, and know that the person in front of you is going to die in a carriage accident. What do you do? Do you tell them? Try to warn them? I've tried. Oh, so many times, I've tried. But they never believe you. You didn't."

Mick's hand tightened around his cup. Her words cut him to the core, but she was speaking the truth, and there was nothing he could say.

"And now," she went on, "there's some villain out there who blames me for interfering in his plans, and wants to kill me." She looked at Mick across the table. "I'm right, aren't I?"

He wanted to tell her she was wrong. He wanted to get up, go around the table, and hold her in his arms. He wanted to tell her she was safe and that he wouldn't let anything happen to her. He wanted to kiss her and hold her and make love to her until her fears disappeared. He didn't move.

"It's an odd thing to know what people are thinking, to sense their feelings. I'm sorry if you think this is an invasion of your privacy, but I know what you're thinking right now." Her voice was shaking, but she looked at him steadily.

His throat went dry. "What am I thinking?"

Sophie stood up and walked slowly around to his side of the table. "You're thinking about me, about us, about . . ." In the lamplight, her face took on a blush of pink, and she drew a deep breath. "You want me. I can feel it."

"God, woman, you do speak your mind," Mick said with a half-laugh, leaning back to look at the woman beside his chair.

"I'm right, though, aren't I?"

He moved, turning the chair so he could face her directly. He let his gaze move down the length of her, savoring every curve of her body, imagining her naked in front of him.

"Yes," he admitted it freely. "I do want you. I've wanted you from the moment I first saw you. You were telling me all about some murder that hadn't happened yet, and I thought you were crazy, but I wanted you. The last time you were here in my flat, and I had my hands on you, while I was thinking you had just shot a pistol at me, I wanted you. Even when I searched through your room, found that necklace, and thought you were a thief, I wanted you. I had your stockings in my hands, and I couldn't think about anything but what it would be like to have you. That night in the conservatory, I wanted to just unbutton that nightgown, touch you, feel your naked body move under mine. That afternoon in the carriage, I almost lost my head and did exactly that."

"What stopped you?"

"Christ, Sophie, what do you think I am? I may be from the streets of Spitalfields, but I'm not about to take a girl's innocence, especially on the seat of a carriage during a half hour ride."

"I'm not a girl." She moved, her body edging between his knees, threatening to decimate whatever self-control he had left. She cupped his face in her hands. "I'm a woman, and this isn't a carriage, and we have more than half an hour."

Mick closed his eyes, and he almost groaned aloud under the feel of her hands on his skin. "You don't know what you're saying. If you keep touching me like that, I'm going to take you right here, right now."

"Go ahead," she whispered. "What are you waiting for?"

Seventeen

❧

Mick inhaled the scent of her skin as she bent closer to him. Above the low neckline of her gown, he could see the generous swell of her breasts. He closed his eyes against the tantalizing sight, trying to remind himself of his duty as an officer and his honor as a man. "God, Sophie, you don't know what you're saying."

"Perhaps, but I know what I want," she murmured, running a hand through his hair. "I want you."

She tilted her head to one side and moved to kiss him, but he grasped her chin in his fingers to stop her. "Sophie, you have no idea what you're asking for."

"Oh, yes, I do." Her brown eyes looked straight into his without embarrassment. "Just because I've never been with a man doesn't mean that I don't know what happens." She smiled faintly and grasped his wrist, pulling his hand down to her breast. "I am psychic, you know."

Mick opened his hand, savoring the full, round shape of her breast even through layers of fabric. The contact sent shudders of pleasure through him, but when she slid her arms around his neck and pressed closer to him, he knew he had to end this while he still could. Seizing her wrists, he pulled her arms down, then shoved back his chair and rose to his feet. Knowing the possible consequences of what she was asking for, Mick forced himself to be blunt. "Sophie, my friends always say I'm not a marrying man. I keep denying it, but deep down, I know they're right."

"I know it, too." She stood on her tiptoes, bringing her lips closer to his. "But it doesn't matter, because I will never marry. That's why I want this night. Just once in my life, Mick, I want to know how it feels. I want to feel you touch me. I want to feel your hands on me."

She stood on her tiptoes, and he bent his head to meet her kiss before he could stop himself. She touched her lips to his. Against his mouth, she murmured, "Make love to me, Mick," and he knew he was lost.

Her mouth opened under his, soft and warm, tasting faintly of oranges, and when she touched his tongue with her own, the tentative contact sent shudders of pleasure through his body. The other times he had kissed her, he'd taken the lead, knowing her inexperience, but right now she was in charge, and Mick found the combination of her innocence and seduction incredibly erotic. He wondered how far she would go on her own.

Sophie grabbed the silk facings of his jacket and pulled them back, sliding the jacket off his shoulders. She tossed it aside, then unbuttoned his waistcoat and undid his tie, and those garments soon joined his jacket on the floor.

Sophie lifted her hands to the collar of his shirt. He stood still, rigid as a sword, as she unfastened the buttons. She pulled his shirttails out of his trousers, but when she tried to remove his shirt, she faced an obstacle she clearly hadn't expected. She was unable to free his arms from the sleeves.

Mick couldn't help smiling. "I'm wearing cuff links," he pointed out.

"Oh, of course." She laughed, but Mick heard the nervousness behind it. She fumbled with the gold stud at his wrist, and he decided to help her a bit.

"Let me do it," he said. Within seconds, his cuff links were in the pocket of his shirt, and his shirt was on the floor. He faced her and waited for her to make her next move, but she didn't seem to know what that move should be. She hesitated, biting her lip as if suddenly uncertain. She looked up at his face with a questioning glance. He grabbed her wrists and pulled her hands to his chest.

"Touch me, Sophie," he said hoarsely. "Touch me."

He let go of her wrists, and she pressed her palms flat against his chest. Mick closed his eyes as she ran her hands up to his shoulders, down his arms and back up again, then down his ribs and lower still. He sucked in his breath, the pleasure of her touch washing over him in waves, but when she began unbuttoning his trousers, he knew he'd let her take the lead long enough. If he let her go on this way, the two of them were going to end up on the floor, her skirts would be up around her waist, and her first experience with lovemaking would not be what she was hoping for. He was not going to let that happen.

"Enough," he said with a half-laugh as he grasped her wrists and pulled her hands away.

"What do you mean?" She looked up at him again, a puzzled frown drawing her brows together. "Didn't you like it?"

"I liked it a little too much." Bending his head, he pressed a kiss to the side of her neck. "You asked me to make love to you, not the other way around, remember?"

"Oh."

She stood perfectly still and closed her eyes as he began unfastening the hooks of her dress. As the dress came apart Mick trailed kisses from her neck to her shoulder. Sophie shivered as he tasted her skin with his tongue. He pulled the brocade ball gown down her arms, and it fell in a puff of satin and lace to her feet.

Sophie knew this was the only time in her life that she would have this experience, and she savored every move he made as he undressed her. Her corset, petticoats, slippers, garters, stockings—one by one, he removed them from her body.

The sureness of his movements told her he must have undressed many women before, but she knew that tonight she was the only woman in the world he wanted. Tonight would have to be enough to last her a lifetime. When he grasped the hem of her chemise, she instinctively lifted her arms above her head, and he pulled the garment off, baring her breasts to his gaze.

"Oh, God," he whispered, letting her chemise fall from his fingers. "Sophie."

He slid his hands along her ribs to cup her breasts, and his thumbs brushed back and forth across her erect nipples. She moaned, lost in a sensuous haze at the exquisite pleasure of his touch.

He opened his mouth over her breast, suckling her, teasing and toying with her nipple, sending jolts of sensation through her entire body. Startled, she cried out, and her knees buckled beneath her. She wrapped her arms around his neck, holding on tightly and shuddering with the mindless pleasure of it.

When he sank to his knees in front of her, she put her arms around his head, cradling him, pulling him closer, exhilarated by the brush of his hair against her bare skin, the glide of his fingertips across her ribs, the warmth of his breath as he kissed her navel.

He untied the ribbon that held up her drawers, and soon they had joined the other clothes at her feet. But then he stopped, and she opened her eyes, suddenly aware that he was no longer touching her. "Mick?"

He didn't seem to hear. He was sitting back on his heels, staring at her, his gaze running up and down her body. Sophie suddenly realized she was standing in front of him as naked as the day she was born. She moved, thinking to cover herself, but he grasped her hips in his hands, stopping her.

"Don't," he murmured. "Sophie, you are so beautiful, you take my breath away. I—"

He stopped and drew a deep breath, then let his hands fall away. He looked up, and his gaze locked with hers. "Take your hair down."

Sophie reached up and began pulling pins from her hair as he resumed his slow and deliberate perusal of her body. She realized he had imagined this moment a dozen times, and that knowledge banished any shyness she felt. She dropped the pins and shook her head to loosen her hair. She relaxed and let him look his fill, exhilarated by the knowledge that he meant what he said. He thought she was beautiful.

Then he leaned forward and wrapped one arm around her hips. He pressed slow, hot kisses to her stomach as his free hand slid between her legs. He began to caress her in a way that made her feel as if she were melting. She cried out and grasped his shoulders to keep herself from falling, moving with his hand, unable to stop herself, unable to stop the moans that he was tearing from her throat with each stroke of his fingers. Exquisite pleasure washed over her in waves, higher and higher, until suddenly everything seemed to explode inside her.

"Mick, Mick," she cried as she felt herself collapsing, but he did not let her fall. He held her hips in his hands to keep her on her feet, his breath hot and quick against her.

After a few moments, Mick stood up. He took her hand in his and led her across the room to the bed. Flinging back the counterpane and top sheet, he gave her an inquiring glance. Sophie knew he was giving her one last chance to change her mind, but she didn't want to change her mind. The sheet felt cool and smooth against her skin as she lay down on her back, still looking at him.

Slowly, his eyes never leaving hers, he took off his shoes, then began to unbutton his trousers.

The mattress dipped with his weight as he stretched out naked beside her on the bed. He turned on his side, facing her, and his hand spread over her stomach, then moved lower, sliding again between her thighs. She stiffened as she felt his finger push against her, into her, a stretching sensation that was quite strange, but not unpleasant.

His finger moved, stroking her inside as his thumb brushed her curls in a tiny circle that teased and toyed with her. "Mick," she gasped, shivering as if she had a fever. "Oh, oh, Mick, please."

He withdrew his hand and rolled on top of her, his weight pressing her into the mattress. He held himself suspended above her, his weight on his arms, his mouth a harsh line in the dim light, his hips moving slowly against hers. She could feel the hard and aroused part of him rubbing against her where his fingers had touched her moments before, and the pleasure washed over her again at the extraordinary caress. She gasped and shivered as the feeling rose within her, growing stronger, hotter, until she was arching against him, straining, feeling that wild euphoria, that flooding sensation that made her shudder with exquisite pleasure. She cried out at the peak, her hands convulsively kneading the powerful muscles of his back.

He slid his arms beneath her back, lowering himself onto her. He kissed her hair, her throat, her cheek, his breath quick and hot against her skin.

"Sophie, it's time," he said in a hoarse whisper. "I can't hold back any longer."

Instinct guiding her, she parted her legs, and the movement seemed to ignite something inside him. He made a rough sound deep in his throat as he turned his head to capture her mouth with his. He kissed her hard, and without warning, he gave a powerful thrust of his hips against hers that brought him fully inside her.

Startled by the stinging pain, she cried out against his mouth, and she broke the kiss, turning her face away. She thought she'd known what to expect, but she hadn't expected it to hurt.

He stilled on top of her, rigid, unmoving. He nuzzled her neck, tasting her skin. He kissed her ear, her hair, her temple, her cheeks. He touched her, caressing her anywhere he could reach. "Sophie, Sophie, it'll be all right."

The pain was already receding, and she heard the regret in his voice. She didn't want him to regret anything. She moved beneath him, trying to accustom herself to the feel of him inside her. The sharp pain was gone, and all she felt was a slight soreness deep inside. She wrapped her arms around him and moved again.

"Sophie, don't," he said through clenched teeth. "Luv, be still. I'm trying to wait."

He held himself so rigid above her, as unyielding as stone, and she could feel the tension within him. The realization that he was striving to hold back for her sake, to let her get used to this, made her love him all the more, but she did not want him to wait. Guided by instinct, she rocked her hips in a way she hoped would push him over the edge.

"Oh, God," he groaned. "Sophie, wait, wait."

With a sudden knowledge of her own power, she arched upward against him, bringing him fully inside her again. He gave a harsh cry, and then suddenly he was thrusting into her, again and again, his weight pressing her into the mattress.

She adapted to the pace he set, moving with him. It hurt a bit still, but she knew he was holding back nothing with her now, he was losing himself in her with passionate abandon, and she was glad.

She wrapped her legs around his hips, loving the feel of what was no longer pain but pleasure. The pleasure of giving.

Suddenly he clutched her tighter, she felt him shudder, and she knew she was giving him the same moment of intense, exquisite pleasure that he had given her moments before. His whole body went rigid for an instant, then he fell against her, breathing hard, his face buried against her hair.

After a few moments, he lifted his head and pulled back enough to look into her face. "Sophie," he whispered, lifting one hand to caress her cheek. "I don't ever want you to regret this night."

"I won't."

"Neither will I."

For a long time, she lay beneath him, content to simply savor the feel of his body, heavy and solid and reassuring, as she caressed his back and felt his breath against her ear.

After a few moments, he stirred. "I must be getting heavy."

He pressed a kiss to her ear and rolled away from her. Then he rose from the bed.

With that movement, Sophie felt suddenly bereft. Without the heat of his body, she felt cold. "Where are you going?"

He laughed. "Miss me already?"

"As a matter of fact, yes." Sophie lifted herself on one elbow, watching him as he crossed the room. There was grace in the contours of his body, power in the knotted muscles of his back and arms, strength in his broad shoulders. It had never occurred to her before that a man's body was beautiful, but Mick's body was exactly that, more beautiful than any sculpture any artist could create. She smiled, enjoying the pleasure of simply watching him.

But when she saw him move as if to turn out the lamp, her smile vanished and she sat up in the bed, panicking. "Mick, don't!" she cried. "Leave it on. I can't sleep without a light."

He met her gaze over the top of the lamp. "Sophie, the dark is harmless," he said quietly, studying her face. "There's nothing to be afraid of."

Oh, yes, there was. She knew there was plenty to be afraid of. Biting her lip, she turned her head away. She didn't want him to think she was a coward. But when the light went out, she began to shake. She curled into a ball, wrapping her arms around her bent knees, her fear smothering her.

She heard his footsteps as he came back toward the bed, but in the pitch blackness, she couldn't see him.

When the sound of his footsteps stopped, she reached for him blindly. "Mick?"

He knelt on the bed, and his arms came up around her. "Sophie, it's all right."

Within the shelter of his arms, her fear gradually subsided. The feel of his body was like a protective wall between her and her dreams. "I don't like the dark. I know it's stupid to be afraid," she whispered, "but I can't help it."

"It isn't stupid. It's understandable. If I had dreams about death and violence and could see the future, I'd be scared of the dark, too."

"I can't imagine you afraid of anything."

"But I am."

She turned her head and buried her face against his chest. "What are you afraid of?"

"Heaps of things," he said carelessly.

"Such as?"

"Spiders."

She couldn't help it. She burst out laughing.

"That's the last time I confess my secret fears to you," he said with mock severity, moving to lie on his back.

She stretched out beside him, resting her weight on her elbow and her cheek in her hand. "I'm sorry," she choked, trying to smother her laughter. "Really."

He folded his arms over his chest. "Don't apologize now. The damage is done."

Smiling, Sophie reached out to touch him, spreading her fingers across his stomach. "What else are you afraid of?"

There was a long pause. Then he said, "Getting old."

She caressed his hard stomach with her fingertips. "I wouldn't worry about that," she murmured. "It seems to me you're in your prime."

"Just don't say I'm seasoned. That's the worst." Mick sat up and reached for the counterpane tangled around their feet. He pulled it over them both, then he slid one arm beneath her head to act as her pillow and wrapped his other arm around her waist. "You're safe, Sophie," he murmured, pulling her close against his body. "With me, you are safe."

Within moments, she felt his body relax into lethargy, and she knew from the even cadence of his breathing that he had fallen asleep.

She lay awake for a long time within the circle of his arms, her cheek against his shoulder, savoring a serenity she had never known before.

She loved this man. With him, she was safe. In his arms, she had peace. Even in the dark, she was not afraid. With him beside her, there was nothing to fear tonight. As for tomorrow, she'd worry about that when it came.

A loud pounding on his door woke Mick from a sound sleep. "What the hell?" he muttered, sitting up in bed as a man's voice began calling his name.

"Mick! Mick! God, I hope you're here!"

He was not awake enough to recognize the voice, but beside him Sophie whispered, "It's a policeman." She fumbled in the dark and grabbed his hand in hers. "Mick, I know something terrible has happened."

Mick hoped that just this once, Sophie's psychic senses weren't working. "I'm here," he called back in answer to the knocks on his door as he got out of bed. To Sophie, he whispered, "For the sake of your reputation, I don't want him to see you. Slide back against the wall and pile the covers over your head."

It was still pitch black, so Mick lit a lamp. He pulled on a pair of trousers, then opened the door.

Sophie was right. Standing outside his flat, his fist raised to knock again, was Constable Fletcher, one of the young officers on duty last night at Sophie's house. "Thank God you're here," the young constable said at the sight of him. "When they couldn't find you at Mill Street, they had me searching everywhere for you."

"Why? What's going on?"

"There's been another murder, sir."

Mick felt sick. "Another policeman?"

"Yes, sir, and killed the same way as Jack Hawthorne. River Police officer named Richard Munro."

"Richard? River Police?" At the constable's confirming nod, Mick felt a vague stirring of memory. He'd seen Richard not long ago, but he couldn't remember the circumstances. "Where?"

"His body was found at Bull Wharf Lane, just west of the Southwark Bridge."

"I know where it is. I'll go at once. Fletcher, I suggest you return to your post."

"Yes, sir." The young man started to turn away, but Mick stopped him. "Fletcher?"

"Yes, sir?" The young constable looked at him inquiringly.

Mick hesitated, not certain how to phrase the question. "Does anyone at Mill Street know about this?"

"No, sir. Sergeant Thacker came in search of you,

but I was on guard out front and he asked me if you were there. I said no, you had not come in all night. He sent me in search of you and returned to the crime scene. I decided to try your flat."

Mick nodded. "Very good. You may go."

The constable departed. As soon as Mick shut the door, Sophie emerged from beneath the covers. Her face was pale, her eyes wide. "Heaven help us," she murmured. "I was right."

Mick raked a hand through his hair. "I wish you were wrong."

Eighteen

~

*H*eartsick and exhausted, Sophie sank down in the chair across from Mick's desk and leaned forward, covering her face with her shaking hands. The picture of the bloody body in Bull Wharf Lane was still vivid in her mind two hours after viewing the scene with Mick. "Just like Jack Hawthorne," she moaned softly. "Why? Why is he doing this?"

"I wish you'd tell me."

At the sound of Mick's voice, she sat up and turned her head to see him standing in the doorway of his office holding a cup of tea.

"Do you have any idea what's going on in this bloke's head?" Mick asked as he handed her the cup.

"No. He's mad. He's evil. But why?" She shook her head. "I don't know." She lifted the teacup but did not take a sip of the amber-colored liquid. "This isn't tea. It's brandy."

"I thought that would do you a bit more good than tea," he said and circled his desk to sit down.

"I suppose so." She took a swallow of brandy, then set the cup on the desk and leaned back in her chair with a sigh. "So often, I wish I could just sense things on command. But it doesn't work that way."

"I know." He studied her for a moment, then stood up. "I'm going to have an officer take you home. There's nothing more you can do here. It's nearly dawn, and you need to get some sleep."

She didn't want to go home. She wanted to help. "Mick—"

"Don't argue with me." He walked to her chair and pulled her to her feet. "Look at it this way. You'll be of more use to me once you've had some sleep. You certainly haven't had much of that during this past night."

This was the first time either of them had mentioned the pleasure they had shared. After all that had happened since, their lovemaking almost seemed like a dream to Sophie. A wonderful dream, followed by a horrible nightmare. Suddenly, she started to sob.

"Steady on," he said, and his arms came up around her. "It's all right," he murmured against her hair. "You've had a shock, that's all."

She buried her face against his broad chest, grasping the folds of his shirt in her hands. "I should have seen this before it happened," she cried. "I should have known. Why didn't I see it? I might have prevented it, Mick. I might have prevented it."

"Ssh," he murmured, stroking her back in a soothing motion. "There's nothing you could have done. As you said, you don't have impressions on command."

"Yes, but—"

"Hush, now. Don't do this to yourself." He pulled back and grasped her shoulders. "You are not to blame. The one to blame is the monster that killed these men. And we're going to find that monster." He gave her a little shake, and his voice rose. "It's not your fault. Do you hear me?"

She took a deep breath, striving for control. "Yes," she said with a shaky laugh. "I think half the people on this floor heard you."

"To hell with them." He reached for the cup on his desk and pressed it to her lips. "Here, finish your brandy."

She took the cup and swallowed the remainder of the liquor. Coughing, she handed the cup back to him. "Any more of this," she gasped, "and I'll be drunk."

He pressed a quick kiss to her mouth. "Go home and rest. If I hear any news, I'll let you know."

"All right. But if I sense anything, I'm coming straight back, and don't you argue with me."

He leaned closer to her. "One night in my bed, and you're already giving me orders?"

She knew he was teasing, being deliberately provoking in order to distract her. But nothing could prevent her from going home with a heavy heart. Nothing could prevent her from feeling that somehow she should have been able to prevent the death of Richard Munro.

It was nearly half past nine in the morning when the carriage with the Scotland Yard insignia pulled to a stop in front of Sophie's house. A huge crowd of reporters was gathered on the front walk. Dismayed, she realized that word of the new murder and her presence at that crime scene had spread to all the newspaper reporters in London by now.

The constable who'd accompanied Sophie got out of the carriage first, and she was relieved to see young Fletcher step forward out of the crowd to join his fellow officer. Fletcher led her up the walk to the door, using his truncheon to keep the reporters at bay, and the other constable walked behind her to protect her back, but the two men couldn't stop the questions the journalists fired at her.

"Miss Haversham, are you using psychic powers to assist the police with this new murder?"

"Who killed Detective Munro?"

"Why is this fiend murdering policemen?"

"What does the killer mean by removing their hearts?"

"Who will be next?"

Sophie walked with one constable in front of her and one behind, her lips pressed tight together, saying nothing. As they reached the front door it was flung open by Auntie, and the moment Sophie was safely inside and the door was closed, Violet's arms wrapped around her.

"Sophie, oh heavens!" she cried. "At last you're home. We have been worried to death!"

The hug felt so warm and comforting that Sophie nearly burst into tears again. She pulled back, trying to keep her tears at bay. "Auntie, I'm sorry, but I've had no chance to get word to you about what's happened."

"We've been quite alarmed, Miss Sophie."

She turned at the sound of Grimstock's voice, and noticed that he, Hannah, Marjorie, and all the lodgers were gathered at one end of the foyer.

"I'm sorry I've worried all of you so much, but honestly, I am just f-fine." Her voice broke, and she had to pause a moment. She was not going to break down, not in front of everyone, not in front of Auntie.

She turned to the servants. "Marjorie, I haven't eaten all night. Do you think you could fix me a bit of breakfast and some tea? Hannah, please get hot water going for a bath for me. Grimmy, you may take these. If any of you need me, I'll be in the conservatory." She handed her pink silk shawl, fan, and evening bag to the butler, then she turned to her aunt.

"You want to know the whole story, of course," she said, wondering how she was going to explain the hours between her departure from the ball and the murder. She hated lying, especially to Auntie, but she had no choice.

"Of course I do!" Violet cried, her voice quivering with the aftereffects of a night of worry. "Where have you been all night?"

"Come with me, and I'll tell you about it." Sophie hooked her arm through her aunt's, and they walked down the hall.

The sun shone brightly through the windows of the conservatory when they entered that room. To Sophie, it seemed somehow inappropriate that it was such a beautiful day.

She sank down onto the wicker settee. "Oh, Auntie, I don't know how to begin."

"The ball would be a good place to start," Violet said as she sat down on a chair. "You disappeared before supper was served, and we couldn't find you or Michael. I told your mother that you had tired of the ball and Michael had taken you home. Your mother was quite displeased about that, and she's becoming very worried that you are falling in love with a policeman. Are you?"

"Auntie, not now," Sophie cried, not wanting to talk about Mick. "What else did Mother say?"

"She said she'd have a long talk with you about it today. When I arrived home last night, you weren't in your bed, and I have not slept a moment, waiting for you to come home. And then, about an hour ago, all these reporters started arriving and asking about the second murder." She frowned into her niece's face. "Darling, what has happened? Grimstock saw the journalists outside at dawn, and when the papers came, he told me there had been another policeman murdered, but he threw the papers on the fire before I could see them. Has another policeman been murdered?"

"Yes, Auntie, I'm afraid so." Sophie told Auntie about seeing Charles, and Mrs. Dalrymple's behavior that had prompted her to leave the ball. Mick, of course, wouldn't let her go alone. She told of the poker game they had attended, implying that it was at that card game that they had learned of the second murder. They had gone to Southwark, and from there on to Scotland Yard.

"Oh, Auntie!" she burst out at the end of her narrative. "Another police officer is dead, and Mick could very well be next. I am so frightened."

"Darling, of course you're frightened!" Violet moved to sit beside her on the settee. "So am I. You are in danger, too."

"Miss Sophie?"

She and Violet both looked up to find Hannah in the doorway. "Your breakfast is ready."

Violet took her hand and pulled her to her feet. "You must eat," her aunt said. "You must keep up your strength."

She followed Auntie to the dining room, not feeling as if she could eat a thing, but when she smelled the scent of bacon, she was amazed to discover she was famished. She consumed a full plate of bacon, eggs, and toast before she finally pushed back her plate.

She glanced with disinterest at the pile of letters neatly stacked on her right, but the moment she did so, she felt again that sick blackness and nausea, and she jumped up from the table.

Not again.

"Sophie?" Violet looked up from her own correspondence, caught her niece's expression, and immediately jumped out of her chair to run to Sophie's side.

"He's written me another letter," Sophie whispered and reached toward the stack of mail.

"No, Sophie, don't!" Violet cried out. "Don't touch it. I'll fetch the constables in and send Grimstock to find Mick at once. Let the police deal with it."

She moved as if to act on her words, but Sophie stopped her. "No, don't get the constables yet. I want to read the letter first."

"No, no," Violet protested. "Remember the last time, you nearly fainted dead away. Don't do it."

Sophie looked up at the woman who stood beside her chair. "Auntie, I'm all right," she said with a calm she did not feel. "This time I know what to expect. Please, sit down."

Reluctantly, Violet returned to her seat, but Sophie could feel her aunt's concerned gaze on her as she began sorting through the correspondence, searching for the one letter she knew was in the pile. When she found it, Sophie slowly picked it up by the edge, fighting not to black out as a now-familiar sensation of revulsion and fear swept over her. This time, she was going to read the words of this madman for herself.

Sophie used a napkin to hold the letter as she slit it open with her silver letter opener, then used the sugar tongs to pull the sheet of paper from its envelope and unfold it on the table. Fighting against nausea, she read the letter.

Sophie, Sophie, you just didn't listen to me the last time, did you? I told you what I would do to you if you continued to interfere with my lifelong dream, and you ignored me. I don't like being ignored.

I saw you there on the wharf, looking at Richard's body. Didn't I make a wonderful job of cutting his heart out? No surgeon could have done better. I would send it to you as a souvenir of our little adventure, but that is not possible, since I ate it for breakfast this morning. I wonder how your heart will taste. Sweet, I am sure. Yours in death. Heart-Eater.

PS—What do you think of my new name? I think the press will adore it. What a sensation it will make.

As she read the words, Sophie's revulsion and nausea dissipated. Her fear remained, since she knew this was a dangerous killer, but she also saw what else he was—a petty, vengeful boy in a man's body. Somehow that made him less frightening and infinitely more pathetic.

"What does it say?" Violet demanded. "Is he threatening you again? What about Michael?"

Sophie did not reply to any of her aunt's concerned questions. She stood up.

"Auntie, I'm going to go upstairs to take a bath and change. Then I'm taking this letter to Mick. Would you tell Fletcher what has happened and have him fetch a hansom?"

"Of course, but Sophie, aren't you going to tell me what it says?"

Sophie walked out of the dining room. "Believe me, he didn't say anything worth repeating."

Ninety minutes later, Sophie was sitting in a meeting room at Scotland Yard with a bevy of CID detectives, sergeants, and constables, trying to explain what she knew of the killer. Mick was sitting at the opposite end of the long conference table from her, and she knew he was the only one who was taking her seriously. Mick had called the meeting and insisted the other officers associated with the case listen to her, but she could tell they didn't want to hear what she had to say.

"He's a child," she told them. "I mean, he's a man, but emotionally he's a little boy who has some sort of petty grievance against the police, a grievance that he has carried with him for much of his life. He hates the police force. For now, he is directing his rage against the specific officers he feels are to blame for whatever his grievance is. I don't know how he thinks these police officers have wronged him, but whatever it is, he has blown it all out of proportion. He hates Mick—Inspector Dunbar—most of all, and I believe his original intention was to kill Mick first, but when his attempt failed, he changed his mind."

She felt smothered by impatience, skepticism, and even hostility from all the men in the room, but Mick's belief in her gave her the courage to go on. "The killer changed his mind because to him, this has become a game, and he's saving Inspector Dunbar for last, like dessert. Again, his behavior is like that of a small boy. He reminds me of—"

She caught sight of Mick pressing his finger to his lips, and she knew that meant she was starting to ramble. She took a deep breath, reminding herself to stick to the main issues. "Anyway, I don't know how many more police officers he intends to kill. He wants Inspector Dunbar to be the last one, but the more people he kills, the easier it becomes to kill the next one, and murder will become a habit with this man. The name he has given himself is another example of a boy playing a game. Also, he's cutting out their hearts as a metaphor that policemen have no hearts. You're dealing with a man who is petty, immature, filled with hatred for the police, and has a willingness to take risks to achieve his aims."

The silence in the room was deafening. The hostility of the officers was now so palpable that Sophie could hardly breathe.

After several seconds of silence, questions started flying at her like bullets from all around the table.

"How do you know this is a man?"

"What do you mean, he's a little boy? This isn't a game."

"What makes you such an authority? Your psychic power?"

"You seem pretty sure of your facts, miss. How involved are you with this man?"

Mick shoved back his chair and stood up. Using his thumb and forefinger, he let out a painfully loud, shrill whistle that silenced the questions as quickly as they had begun. "That's enough, gentlemen. I wanted all of you to know the most recent developments in this case, and I don't have to remind you that Miss Haversham has also been targeted by this madman and subjected to his vile threats, something no woman should have to experience. It's our job to see that she, our fellow officers, and the people of this city are safe. All of you know what your job is here, so get to work. I want a fingerprint analysis, an autopsy report, and every witness statement you can get for Richard's murder on my desk by the end of the day so I can report to DeWitt. As usual, we make statement to the press. That's all, gentlemen."

The men filed out of the room, casting resentful and contemptuous glances at Sophie as they departed.

When they were gone, Mick closed the door and came to sit beside her. "I'm sorry about that," he said quietly. "They just don't understand."

She almost wanted to laugh. "Do you really think I don't know that? I've been dealing with people like your officers my entire life."

She started to rise from her chair, but Mick put a hand on her shoulder to keep her from getting up. "You shouldn't have read that letter, Sophie. You should have given it to Fletcher at once."

Sophie shook her head. "I had to read that letter. I knew it would give me some very valuable insights into this man's mind. And it did."

"Well and good, but I'll be damned if I'm going to let valuable insights scare you out of your wits. I want you to stay out of this as much as possible. The more of a threat he perceives you to be, the greater the danger to you." He leaned closer to her and cupped her cheek in his hand. "I promised you I'd keep you safe, remember?"

His touch was so protective and reassuring, and she never wanted him to pull away. Those stolen hours of last night seemed ages ago, and yet she could recall every detail of every moment of them. "Yes," she whispered, "I remember."

"Then don't make it a difficult promise to keep."

"Return the favor. Don't get killed."

Mick shook his head and gave her a careless grin that didn't fool her for a second. "He's not going to kill me. I'm too tough to die."

She turned her head and pressed a kiss into his palm. "No one's that tough, Mick. Not even you."

* * *

Mick got what he demanded. By the end of the day, he had a stack of reports on his desk a foot high. By the time he finished sorting through them all, it was nearly eleven o'clock, he was hungry, he was tired, and more than anything else, he needed a pint.

The Boar's Head was full, as usual. Billy and Rob were sitting at their usual corner table, and, after getting a pint of ale from the barkeep, Mick walked across the room to join them.

As he sat down, he noticed that his two best friends were looking at him rather oddly. Maybe Sophie's psychic power was contagious, because Mick had a feeling he knew what the other two were thinking.

"No," he said before either of them could speak. "I haven't lost my mind, and no, I don't really care if people think I have, and yes, I do think Sophie Haversham is truly a psychic. There," he added defiantly and leaned back in his chair, "make the most of that, lads."

But to his astonishment, neither man proceeded to remind him of all the phony psychic confidence swindlers Mick had arrested in his career. They didn't accuse him of losing his mind or his judgment. They didn't suggest he take a long holiday at Brighton.

Instead, they looked at each other and lifted their beer glasses in a toast. Billy said, "How the mighty are fallen."

They each took a swallow of ale and set their glasses down, grinning at his belligerent look.

"What are the two of you on about?" Mick demanded, though he understood just what they meant.

"Do you think it's real this time?" Rob asked Billy. "I mean, he keeps saying he wants the right woman, doesn't he? Do you think the right woman might be a brown-haired, brown-eyed society beauty with gorgeous lips who thinks she's psychic but can't play poker worth a damn?"

Mick made a sound of contempt but did not reply.

Billy chuckled. "What a good joke. Our Mick, the man obsessed with neatness, who has no social connections and heaps of good sense, the man in search of the perfect woman, falls in love with a dithery fortune-telling society girl who sees the future."

"And," Rob added, "whose aunt thinks she's Cleopatra reincarnated."

Billy raised his glass again. "To Mick, the man who wanted the perfect family."

Both men started laughing.

"Enough!" Mick scowled at the pair of them. "I don't need this from you. Besides, the way you're talking, I'm thinking you don't like her." He glared at Billy. "You seemed to like her a great deal last night."

"Like her?" Billy stared at him in amazement. "She's a charming girl. With her hairpins falling out, and her bracelets falling off, talking nineteen to the dozen when she's got no cards and she's trying to bluff. She's adorable." Billy started laughing again. "You've fallen for a girl who's everything that drives you to your wits' end. That's what's so funny. But how long will it last?"

"Sod off," Mick said.

"What's that cologne she wears?" Rob asked. "I

could've sat next to her all night. Lor', she smelled good."

"I know," Billy agreed. "If I weren't married—"

Something inside Mick exploded at the thought of any other man wanting Sophie. He slammed his glass down. "Bugger off, mate," he said in a low, hard voice to one of his best friends.

"Hey, Mick," a voice interrupted from another table, and Mick turned to see Sergeant Lloyd MacNeil, one of the men from that morning's meeting. "When is that Haversham woman going to look into her crystal ball and tell us who killed Jack and Richard?"

"Forget about that," said the other sergeant seated at MacNeil's table. "Why didn't she get out her tarot cards? She could have told our fortunes today."

"I'd rather have her hold my hand and read my palm," MacNeil said, laughing. "She's a pretty, long-legged bit of skirt, I'll say that."

Mick was on his feet in an instant, but he barely took one step toward the other table before Billy and Rob grabbed him by the arms to hold him back.

"Hey, now, ease off, lad," Billy muttered close to his ear. "They're only having you on."

"Don't do anything stupid, Micky boy," Rob said. "Let it go."

Mick knew his friends were right. He took a deep breath and nodded, forcing his rage down. When Billy and Rob relaxed their grip, he jerked free and grabbed his jacket off the back of the chair. "I'm leaving," he said and picked up his pint.

"Aye," Billy and Rob said at the same time, "Sophie's the one."

Mick didn't bother to reply. He turned away and headed for the door, passing the table of Sergeant MacNeil and the other man who'd been ridiculing Sophie. As much as he wanted to, he didn't take a swing at either of them. But he did take a great deal of satisfaction in dumping his ale over MacNeil's head as he walked by.

Nineteen

◈

Sophie woke from a deep sleep, gasping for breath as she sat up. Beside her, the lamp was burning, and she could feel the coolness of a breeze through the doors opening onto her balcony. It was a dream. Mick was not dead. Yet.

She hugged her pillow tight, shivering as if she were cold. She began taking slow, deep breaths, pushing her dream of Mick's funeral away, trying not to think of it as a premonition, trying to force aside the fear that he was lying dead somewhere, trying to overcome the panic that made her chest ache as if she'd been running. Mick was not going to die, she told herself over and over.

Yet she couldn't stop shivering. Sophie got out of bed, picked up the lamp from her bedside, and left her bedroom. She walked several steps down the hall to

Mick's door, and, as quietly as possible, she opened it. He was in bed, sound asleep.

Sophie closed the door and drew a deep, steadying breath. She stood there for a long moment, waiting for the horror of her dream to fade away, telling herself Mick was alive, he was safe.

She returned to her room and did what she always did after a dream. She sat down with quill, ink, and paper, and she wrote down as much as she could remember.

It had never been this hard to do. The first time she had dreamed of Mick's death, she hadn't been in love with him, she hadn't even known him. Now, she could barely bring herself to write down anything about her dream, but she knew she had to do it.

After she had written down every detail she could recall, Sophie set her quill back down on the bedside table and recapped the bottle of ink. She knew any attempt to go back to sleep now was futile, and she put on her carpet slippers, picked up her lamp, and left her room again.

She went downstairs, but as she turned to walk down the hall toward her conservatory, she saw Mick standing in the doorway of that room, and she stopped walking. He had his back to her, he held a lamp in his hand, and he was wearing nothing but that pair of worn gray flannel trousers.

Noticing the light of her lamp, he turned around and saw her standing there. He smiled, and she almost ran straight into his arms, but something held her back, a feeling she couldn't quite define, a feeling that made her walk slowly down the hall to where he stood at the door.

"Hullo," he greeted her in a low voice. "Wandering around in the middle of the night again, are you?"

"What are you doing down here?" she whispered back. "You were in bed, fast asleep."

"I was, until a beautiful ghost in a long white night-gown appeared at my door and shone a lamp in my face."

"Sorry. I just—"

She stopped, lowering her gaze to the wall of his bare chest, wanting more than anything she'd ever wanted in her life to lean against the hard strength of his body, to feel safe in his arms. She wanted him to kiss her, and make love to her, and drive the demons away. She looked up into his face. "I had a dream about your funeral," she whispered.

She saw his mouth tighten, and he lifted his hand to touch her cheek. "Sophie, my luv, I'm not going to have a funeral until I'm at least eighty-seven."

His love.

She wasn't. She knew that.

Pulling back from his touch, she stepped around him and entered the conservatory. He followed her as she wove through the trees and rare plants to the tea table. Setting down the lamp, she reached for the teakettle, then looked at him. "Would you like a cup?"

"No."

There was something in his eyes that she knew and understood, because it was what she wanted. Just the thought of lovemaking with him made her body feel warm and soft, pliant and willing. He set his lamp on the floor, then took a step toward her.

She was a woman he desired, the way he had desired many women before. Though she had finally convinced him of her psychic ability, she knew he couldn't accept it enough to live with it. Like Charles, like most people, Mick wanted his private thoughts to remain private. He could not love a woman who was so odd, so different, so invasive. *Like rape.*

She took a step back, shaking her head. "No," she said. "No."

He didn't reply. He just took another step forward, bringing him to within a hand's breadth of her. She took another step back, and her hips hit the oak table behind her. Mick reached around her and removed her lamp from the table. He walked away to set her lamp on the floor beside his own, and she drew a sigh of relief at the space he had put between them.

But her relief was short-lived. He returned to stand in front of her, and his eyes still had that look of desire. He bent his head to kiss her.

"I don't think this is a good idea," she said, turning away to avoid his kiss as she flattened her palms against his chest. His skin was warm beneath her hands.

"Probably not," he agreed and pressed his lips to one corner of hers. He slid one hand into her hair to turn her face toward him. Tilting his head, he kissed the opposite corner of her mouth. "But let's do it anyway."

"Stop it," she whispered. "What if someone comes in?"

"At one o'clock in the morning?" His lips brushed over hers. "I doubt it."

"I can't," she said, frantic now, stiffening in his hold, resisting him with everything she had. "Not here. We're in the conservatory of my aunt's house, for heaven's sake."

Undeterred, he continued to kiss her, his mouth coaxing her to respond. But she brought her arms up protectively between them and remained stiff and unyielding. "Sophie," he murmured, and began to brush his tongue back and forth across the plump curve of her lower lip as he slid one arm around her waist. He ran his fingers lazily up and down her spine and nibbled on her lip until slowly, very slowly, some of the rigidity left her body and her lips parted beneath his persuasion.

"Sophie, Sophie," he coaxed against her mouth, "kiss me back."

She couldn't withstand this tender persuasion any longer. With a moan, she slid her arms around his neck and pressed closer to him instead of pulling away, her body molding to his as she surrendered. His hungry body responded instantly to the move, and he deepened the kiss, slanting his mouth over hers and sliding his tongue between her teeth to taste her.

She met him halfway, her tongue touched his, and lust surged through his bloodstream like wildfire. His hand left her hair and slid between them. He began unfastening her nightgown, his knuckles brushing against her breasts as he slipped the pearl buttons out of their holes. He stopped at her waist and pulled the edges of the gown apart to kiss her exposed throat, tasting her scented skin. "You want this as much as I do. I can feel it."

He was right. She did want this, but she also knew she wanted more than this, and he couldn't give her more. She broke the kiss and turned her face away. "We can't do this."

Undeterred, he pressed tiny kisses along the column of her throat to her collarbone. "Aye, we can. No one has to know."

"Mick, listen to me." She pushed at him, but it was a halfhearted effort, and he ignored it.

"I don't want to listen to you," he countered, his lips warm against her skin. "Because you'll try to talk both of us out of it."

She began to quiver in his hold, and she could feel her resistance slipping away. He seemed to feel it, too. He moved his hands to her waist, grasped the edges of her nightgown in his fists, and pulled the soft lawn fabric apart. The pearl buttons from her waist to her feet easily slipped free of their holes. Before she could assimilate what was happening, his hands spanned her waist, and she felt herself lifted up onto the table.

He wants me now, she thought, closing her eyes and desperately trying to hang on to her resolve and her pride as he slid his hands up her torso to caress her breasts. *He doesn't want me forever.*

She opened her mouth to tell him again to stop, but instead, she heard herself making small gasping sounds that didn't sound anything like a refusal. She couldn't seem to stop herself from tilting her head back in a yielding arch.

He pressed his advantage, lowering his head to her breast, licking her. She shivered as his tongue circled her nipple again and again, as he brought his hand up to cup her other breast. She couldn't seem to stop her own arms from coming up to cradle his head as he teased and toyed with her breasts.

Slowly, he kissed his way up her body, his hands still caressing her breasts. "Sophie," he murmured against her ear as he brushed his thumbs back and forth across her nipples. "Unbutton my trousers."

"I won't," she gasped in one last valiant attempt to fight what they both wanted.

"Then I will." He continued to caress the taut tip of one breast as he undid his trousers with his free hand. She heard the rustle of fabric as his trousers slid down his hips. She felt herself being pushed backward until her shoulder blades met the hard surface of the table. She felt the heaviness of his body as he moved on top of her, and she no longer had the will to fight him. She couldn't. She did want him. She loved him. She parted her legs, willing now, eager to have him inside her.

But he didn't enter her. He remained still, poised above her, hard against her, waiting. "Open your eyes and look at me," he said.

She did, and his face seemed to fill the whole world.

"If you really want me to stop," he said unsteadily, "then say it. Now. Look me in the eye and tell me to stop."

She couldn't, and he knew it. She knew it, too.

Sophie wrapped her arms around his neck and pulled his face down to hers for a long, hungry kiss.

Her capitulation seemed to ignite something inside

him. He slid his hands beneath her buttocks and lifted her as she wrapped her legs around his waist. He entered her, one hard push bringing him fully inside her. She buried her face against his shoulder as he thrust into her again and again, and she savored the feel of him as the muscles deep within her own body tightened around him in quick pulsations that brought her to that dizzying peak of sensation. She cried out, her senses exploding in a white-hot flash that sent waves of almost unbearable pleasure through her body as he surged into her one last time and was still.

Sophie kept her eyes closed. She could not look at him. Not now, not at this moment. If she did, she'd come apart. She had to harden herself against him. Now. If she didn't, he'd tear her heart apart when he left.

Mick frowned, feeling her body stiffen beneath him when only moments before she had been soft and yielding. Now, she kept her eyes tightly shut, and she was biting her lip as if she were in pain.

"Sophie?"

The sound of her name seemed to spark something inside her, but it wasn't the sort of spark a man wanted. She pushed at his chest. "Mick, let me up."

The table was wide enough for him to roll to his side, and she was off the table the moment he did so. Turning her back to him, she began to refasten the buttons of her nightgown.

He watched her for a moment, completely at sea. First she didn't want him, then she did, then she didn't.

He eased off the table, pulled up his trousers, and buttoned them, still watching her. Five minutes ago, she had burned like fire in his hands, now she was a glacier. She had enjoyed their lovemaking as much as he had. Why the coldness now?

This reading his thoughts and sensing his feelings was more than invasive. It was damned frustrating. It gave her a power and control over every situation that he could not match, it enabled her to always have an advantage over him. He enjoyed a woman who was strong-minded and strong-willed, but if an argument was in the works, he sure as hell wanted an even playing field on which to have it. With Sophie, that was impossible.

It wasn't until she had finished buttoning her nightgown that she finally turned around and faced him. "I'd like to be alone."

"Too bad." He leaned one shoulder against the column beside him and folded his arms. "What is this?" he asked. "This is not the same woman I held in my arms five minutes ago. That woman was soft and tender. The woman I'm looking at now is anything but."

"I'm sorry if my mood displeases you," she said smoothly and turned away to pick up the teakettle. "All the more reason for you to go back to bed, I think."

Her peremptory dismissal sparked a flare of anger inside him. "What the bloody hell is going on?" he demanded. "One minute I'm with a loving, passionate woman, and the next I'm with a peevish shrew. Is this what making love with me is going to do to you?"

"Love?" She whirled around to face him again. "What does love have to do with anything?" Her face twisted with pain and anger, and as if she could no longer remain so cooly self-possessed, she turned away and threw the teakettle. It hit a weeping fig tree and fell, clanging as it bounced across the tile floor. She pressed her fingers to her lips as if shocked by her own burst of anger. She turned again to face him. "There!" she cried. "Now you've made me lose my temper. I hope you may be satisfied!"

"Satisfied? No." He straightened away from the column and walked over to her. He put his hands on her waist. "A few minutes ago, I was very satisfied," he said softly. "But—"

She pulled herself out of his grasp. "Don't you dare be glib about our lovemaking!" she cried, choking back a sob as she walked backward away from him. "It's been the most wonderful experience of my life!"

He was becoming more confused by the second. "Wonderful? From the way you're acting, I wouldn't know."

"How do you want me to act, Mick? Like a starry-eyed lover in a passionate affair? There's no future in this, and we both know that. I went into this with my eyes wide open, and I will never regret what happened between us. But I know how you feel about marriage, and I know how you feel about me. You said you're not a marrying man, and you said you think my ability is an invasion. I know you were telling me the plain and honest truth, and I accept it. But where does that leave us, Mick? There's nowhere for us to go from here. Don't you see?"

He tilted his head to one side, studying her for a moment, weighing his words before he spoke. "What I see," he finally said, "is what an advantage you have over other people."

"What are you talking about?"

"You can sense what people are feeling, sometimes know what they are thinking, know their secrets, understand their motivations and desires. That gives you a very high amount of control over every situation."

"You think I enjoy this?" She was pale, staring at him in disbelief. "You think I like having these things thrust on me?"

"Like it or not, you seem willing to use them when it suits you."

"That's not fair."

"Isn't it?" Mick stepped closer to her. "You seem willing to bring the truth about me, about my insecurities and feelings out in the open. Let's bring out the truth about you. Maybe I'm not psychic, but I have damned good instincts, and I have concluded a few things." He took a deep breath. "You are accustomed to knowing things about people, and that's a very safe place to be. But you are so afraid of being ridiculed for what you are that you never let anyone get close to you. You are terrified that every man who takes an interest is bound to feel as Charles did."

"You feel that way."

"I do. Any man would."

"Thank you for proving my point."

He shook his head. "No, the point is that you never give any man a chance to get used to it."

"Really?" she countered, placing her hands on her hips and glaring at him. "Would you get used to it? Do you want to take that time and spend it with me? Do you want to court me, fall in love with me, marry me?"

He opened his mouth as if to answer, but he did not

know what to say. He was forced to admit to himself with brutal honesty that the idea of marrying her had never entered his mind.

"You see?" she said in the wake of his silence. "We both know you don't want that at all. What you want is an illicit affair."

There was enough truth in her words that they stung. "I told you I was not a marrying man," he shot back in sheer defense.

"What you want," she continued as if he had not spoken, "is to be my lover until one or the other of us tires of the situation and ends it." She picked up the kettle and put it over the gas ring. Meeting his gaze again, she added, "After all, isn't that what you want from every woman you meet?"

"Damn it, stop reading my mind! I hate it when you do that!"

But she turned her back on him and did not reply. He watched her for several moments more, and he knew with a bitterness he'd never felt in his life before that her psychic senses were working perfectly. He turned away and strode out of the conservatory, feeling like an absolute bastard.

Sophie knew she had done the right thing, but instead of easing with his departure, the ache in her heart only seemed to worsen. "I did the right thing," she whispered, but there was no one there to agree.

She turned away from the windows, grabbed her shears, and walked over to a tall iron pillar covered with masses of bougainvillea vines that badly needed cutting back.

With each vine she ruthlessly pruned away, she reminded herself that there was no future for her with Mick.

I invade his private thoughts, and just like any man would, he hates that.

Snip.

I knew how he felt. I knew and I did it anyway.

Snip.

But I don't want an affair. I couldn't bear that.

Snip.

What if there's a child? He doesn't want to marry me.

Snip.

He doesn't really want to marry any woman.

Snip.

He's looking for the perfect woman, a woman who doesn't exist, a woman who will make no demands on him, a woman who is always beautiful, never difficult, always amiable and willing to please, never frustrating, always passionate, always desirable.

"Good luck," she muttered.

Snip.

He isn't in love with me.

There it was. The truth. She'd finally said it. Sophie looked down at the huge pile of cut vines she had just removed from the plant, vines covered with masses of bright pink leaves that lay in a tangle at her feet. Then she looked up at the nearly naked pillar in front of her and burst into tears.

The next day at Scotland Yard, most of the men who worked in CID thought Mick was ill. Any police officer on the force who had ever worked with him knew that he never let anything in his private life affect his work, so they all assumed his lack of concentration, his inattention to conversation, and a tendency to lose his temper over trivialities were due to some physical ailment. It would never have occurred to most of them that Mick might be having woman troubles, especially not with Sophie Haversham.

Most of the men he worked with in CID had been astonished, frustrated, and angry when he'd brought Miss Haversham into the Yard for such a ridiculous meeting, but they had also recognized the importance of the letter she had been sent through the post. Many of his colleagues were sure Mick had far too much sense to be romantically involved with a woman who was a witness in an ongoing investigation and who also happened to be as nutty as a Christmas fruitcake, but there were those who thought otherwise.

All of this was conveyed to Mick by Henry Thacker at about eleven o'clock that evening, because the sergeant had brought him a cup of tea for about the tenth time that day, and Mick had finally snapped at him, "Henry, why in Hades do you keep bringing me tea?"

The sergeant had responded that tea was good for someone who was ill and went on to explain that Mick's volatile behavior over the course of the day had prompted a concern for his health. Thacker added that there were a few officers who believed Mick was having a love affair with Miss Haversham.

After the accusation Sophie had hurled at him the night before, Thacker's words flicked him on the raw. "I'm not having an affair with Sophie Haversham!" he shouted. "Am I the only one who understands that she is our best connection to the killer?"

Thacker looked at him with patient gravity. "Sir, some of the men believe she is the killer and wrote those letters herself."

That idea was impossible as well as ludicrous, but Mick wasn't going to argue about it. He leaned back in his chair and rubbed his fingertips over his tired eyes.

"Why don't we call it a day, sir?" Thacker suggested. "It's quite late. Everyone else on this floor left hours ago, and with you being ill, I'm concerned."

Mick knew he wasn't ill. He was coming apart.

He shoved back his chair and stood up. "You're right, Henry. It's time to quit for the day."

The two men left Mick's office and went downstairs together. Outside the gates, Mick hailed a cab. He asked if Henry needed to be driven home, but the sergeant shook his head. "No, sir, my flat is only a short walk away."

Mick gave the driver the address of his own flat in Maiden Lane.

That seemed to surprise the sergeant. "You're not staying at Mill Street?"

"Not for the time being."

"If you've moved back into your flat, you should have told me, sir," Henry said severely. "With your life in danger, we need constables to watch your flat if you're staying there."

He knew Henry was right, but the idea of spending the night at his own flat had only just occurred to him. He couldn't go back to Sophie's just yet. Not after last night. "I did keep my flat for when the case was over.

When I'm working very late, my flat is closer to the Yard and more convenient than Mayfair."

"Still," the sergeant said, "you should have told me. I'll telephone Bow Street and have them send a constable to your address. He'll be there by the time the hansom reaches your flat."

"Thank you, Sergeant. I appreciate your concern."

"We don't need you to die too, sir." Thacker turned to retrace his steps back to the Yard to use the telephone, and Mick went home.

When the cab stopped in front of Mick's flat, the coster's cart nearby was still open and he bought a beef and potato Cornish pasty and a bottle of lemonade. Inside his flat, he sat down at the table, but he didn't eat his late supper. He stared at the empty chair across from him and remembered how he and Sophie had sat here, eating biscuits and drinking tea. He remembered how desperately he had wanted her, and how she had looked at him with a Mona Lisa smile, knowing it all the time.

Mick leaned back in his chair and closed his eyes. In his mind, he recalled every curve of her body, every sound she'd made, every word she'd said. He recalled the silken feel of her hair, the scent of her skin, the beauty of her face when he had made love to her.

He remembered how she'd felt beneath him last night, too. On a table, for God's sake, in her aunt's conservatory. He sat there for a long time, torturing himself with the memory of a woman he couldn't marry, a woman he had never even considered as the right woman for him.

An illicit affair . . . isn't that what you want from every woman you meet?

Sophie had made it quite clear that a love affair was out of the question, and he couldn't blame her. Most women, regardless of their rank or circumstances, wanted to be married, and though Sophie might have resigned herself to spinsterhood, she was no different from any other woman in that respect.

Mick remembered how his friends had ragged him in the pub the night of his birthday about how he just wasn't a marrying man. He'd said he was waiting for the right woman to come along, and they'd told him that was bunkum. They had said he didn't want to settle down with one woman.

Now he knew they'd been wrong, and so had he. All this time, he'd been holding back, waiting, not to find the perfect woman, or even the right woman. All this time, he'd been waiting to fall in love. Now he had. He was in love with Sophie.

He loved her, yes. He wanted her, yes, more than he had ever wanted any woman in his life—but how could he live with having his mind probed on a daily basis?

He understood how the Earl of Kenleigh had felt, loving a woman who at any moment would tell you what you were thinking. Who would know what you felt before you did, who knew your secrets before you had the chance or the choice to tell her. It wasn't that a man wanted to keep secrets from his wife, but he wanted to have the choice of how and when to tell them to her.

Sophie, of course, had already known that, had appreciated the impossibility of their situation long before he had. But Mick was sure that long after this case was solved, he would be tortured with wanting her, wanting to hold her, kiss her, make love to her, and not be able to have her. He knew it was a torture he deserved. When the case was over, walking away from Sophie was going to be the hardest thing he would ever do in his life.

If both of them lived that long.

A knock on the door startled him, and he opened his eyes. Through the door, he heard Sergeant Thacker say his name. He walked to the door and opened it to find the sergeant standing there, a case file in his hands. "Henry? What are you doing here?"

"I'm glad to see you're not in bed yet, sir." The sergeant held out the file to Mick.

"Why are you bringing me this?" Mick asked as he took the file. "Has something happened?"

"Well, yes and no."

"What does that mean?" He opened the door wider for the sergeant to enter the flat. "When I left you, you were going back inside to use the telephone."

"Yes, sir." Thacker stepped inside and closed the door behind him. "I went back in to telephone for a constable," he explained, "and as I was waiting for the call to go through, I was thinking about the cases we've pulled that you, Jack, and Richard worked on together. You know how long those exchange operators can take to put a call through."

"Forever, sometimes."

"Yes, sir. Anyway, while I was waiting, I got an idea that maybe this was the case that held the key to the whole mystery, so after I telephoned Bow Street, I decided to go back upstairs and pull out that file. When I read it, I brought it to you at once."

Mick opened the file and began to read it as he crossed the room to the table. "This is the Clapham case from '85."

"Exactly." Henry followed Mick to the table, and as Mick pulled out a chair and sat down, Henry moved to stand beside him. "Remember that suicide case Munro brought you? Jane Anne Clapham, the woman who jumped off Tower Bridge? Her husband was Henry Clapham."

"Yes, yes, I remember. Richard reminded me of that case when we were in the morgue with Mrs. Clapham's body."

"But do you remember this case?"

"I don't. It was ages ago." He glanced up at the man beside his chair. "What makes you think that the Henry Clapham case is pertinent to the murders of Jack and Richard?"

"It involves all three of you, and the motive of vengeance makes sense. Read the notes on that case."

Mick scanned the file, reading aloud some of the notes he had written twelve years ago, as Thacker leaned over his shoulder to read along with him. "Clapham ran an opium smuggling operation out of a group of storage warehouses in Isle of Dogs. He was a ruthless man, and anyone who betrayed his trust was killed by his command. The Yard knew of at least seven men who had been murdered on his orders. Jack and I were assigned to work with Richard and the other River Police on solving the murders of those he killed and destroying his operation."

Mick stopped reading the file. The case was coming back to him as he spoke, and he began remembering the details. "Jack, Richard, and I got involved in his operation, pretending to be opium dealers, and over the next six months, we got a great deal of information about how he smuggled the opium into the country. When we had the evidence we needed to make arrests, we raided the warehouses, and during that raid, the three of us found Clapham himself hiding in one of the buildings. We were able to finally overpower him. He was arrested, tried, and convicted. He was hanged."

"I've been doing some investigating of my own about this Clapham fellow's wife and family. Read my notes."

"You really do want to make detective, don't you, Henry?" Mick scanned the report the sergeant had written on the background of Jane Anne Clapham, who had drowned herself in the Thames not long ago. "Jane Anne and Henry Clapham had a luxurious house in Crooms Hill, and a plentiful income from his ill-gotten opium. She lost all that when her husband was hanged. They had one son . . ."

Mick's voice trailed off as he read the next paragraph of Thacker's report, a short biography of Henry Clapham, the second, who had gone into the navy and had supposedly drowned at sea, but whose body had never been found.

He's connected with you.

Sophie had told him that, and he had refused to believe it.

Mick slowly put down the file as he realized the truth. It all came together in his mind like the pieces of a jigsaw puzzle, but before he could even move, Mick felt the cold muzzle of a gun pressed against the base of his skull, and he heard the hammer being pulled back.

"You see, don't you?" Thacker asked eagerly. "I had to lead you by the hand the whole way, but at last you see the truth."

"I see perfectly," Mick murmured, wondering how the hell to knock the pistol out of Thacker's hand without getting his head blown off. "You changed your surname when you left the Royal Navy. You lied on your application to join the Metropolitan Police. You requested a transfer from division to be a CID sergeant at the Yard to get closer to Jack and me. You murdered Jack and Richard."

"Exactly so. And now I'm going to kill you, Micky boy. I never forget a betrayal. Like father, like son, you know."

Twenty

~

Sophie came to her senses to find she was lying on the carpeted floor of her room. She was in her nightgown, and she'd clearly been getting ready for bed. She knew she had blacked out, but she had no idea how long ago that had been.

Her head ached terribly, but she could recall the vision she'd had in vivid detail, as if it were a photograph burned onto her mind. She was standing in the doorway of Mick's flat. She could see Mick sitting at the table and another officer standing behind him. Both men were in profile to her, and Sophie could see a gun at the base of Mick's skull. She could also see, for the first time, the killer's face. She didn't know him, she had never seen him before, but she knew he was about to kill Mick.

"Oh, my God." She threw back the covers and

jumped out of bed, tugging off her nightgown as she crossed to her armoire. She yanked on a shirtwaist and skirt, then grabbed a pair of evening slippers. She wasn't going to waste any time with high-button shoes and button hooks now. She grabbed a shilling from her jewelry box for cab fare and dropped it into her pocket, then raced out of her room, down the stairs, and out the front door. She was halfway down the walk before she felt a hand grab her by the arm, yanking her back. She turned, and in the moonlight, she saw the young and serious face of Constable Fletcher.

"Steady on, miss," he said, relaxing his grip once he realized it was her. "Now where do you think you're going in the middle of the night?"

"Constable, I've never been so happy to see anybody in my life." In her panic, she had forgotten she had Scotland Yard right at her door. This time, it was her turn to grab his arm. "Come with me at once. We have to go to Mick's flat."

"What, now?" The young man, who was much stronger than Sophie, did not move, no matter how hard she pulled at him. "Miss, it's the middle of the night."

"I know, but we have to go at once. Mick is there, and he's in danger."

Fletcher frowned at her, unmoving.

They were wasting precious time talking about this, but Sophie also knew he wasn't going to let her go alone. She struggled for patience. "Constable, please listen to me. I know Mick is in danger, and we have to go to his flat now. Right now."

"I'm ordered not to leave my post, Miss Haversham."

"Yes, but your purpose is to guard me, is it not? If you're with me, you're guarding me."

"I also have a responsibility to guard the others in the house."

Sophie drew a deep breath, trying not to lose her temper. "There are two of you here. The other constable guards the house, too, so you come with me. Let's go."

She turned and started down the walk again, but she wasn't even able to take a step before the constable once again seized her by the arm. "For heaven's sake!" she cried, jerking free. "We don't have time to argue about this. Mick could be killed at any moment. I know it, I feel it. We have to go now!"

The moment the words were out of her mouth, she knew they were the wrong thing to say. Fletcher's grip on her arm tightened, and the derisive skepticism in his expression was plain. "What is this?" he demanded. "Did you have a vision?" Without waiting for an answer, he began pulling her back toward the house. "Come along, miss. Go on back to bed. Go on, now."

She wanted to shout that she could leave her own house if she wanted to, and that she wasn't some recalcitrant child throwing a tantrum, nor was she some insane woman who needed to be locked up in an asylum, but Sophie went back inside the house, pretending meekness and obedience. The second the front door closed behind her, she was running through the pitch black house toward the conservatory.

Once inside, she went to the French doors that led outside, slipped into the garden, and closed the doors quietly behind her. She ducked down behind some tall rhododendrons as Harper, the second constable watching the house, passed by, and the moment he was around the corner on the side of the house, she ran for the fruit trees at the back corner of the garden.

She climbed up into the low, sturdy branches of a plum tree at the very back. She was over the stone wall into the Sheltons' back garden in an instant, and five minutes later she was on Brooks Street a few blocks away, flagging down one of the hansom cabs that circled Claridge's Hotel at all hours of the night.

When the cab reached its destination in Maiden Lane, Sophie was out of the carriage in an instant. She tossed the driver the shilling in her pocket and raced for the front doors of Mrs. Tribble's lodging house. To her surprise, the landlady had not yet locked her doors for the night, and Sophie was able to slip inside the dark foyer without being seen.

She started up the stairs as quietly as possible, her sense of foreboding increasing with each step. He was here, with Mick. She could feel it. She could feel his hate in the air, his hate and his rage. See it, smell it, taste it. She closed her eyes for a moment, fighting not to black out again, gripping the stair rail as she continued up to the first floor.

At Mick's door, she paused. From inside, she heard a man's voice say, "Like father, like son, you know."

She did not recognize the voice, but she knew the man had killed Jack Hawthorne and Richard Munro and now he had a gun pointed at the back of Mick's head. What should she do?

Even as she asked herself that question, a strange and unexpected sense of calm came over her. Any feeling of faintness vanished, and though she was frightened out of her wits, her hand did not shake as she reached for the doorknob. She knew just how to help Mick. For the first time in her life, Sophie was truly grateful for the gift she had been given.

She turned the knob slowly, then she eased the door open without making a sound, thankful that Mick's methodical personality had impelled him to keep the hinges of his door well oiled. She pushed the door wide.

The scene before her was the same as her vision, an exact duplicate in every detail. Both men in profile to her at the table across the room, Mick seated, with the other man standing behind him, holding a gun to Mick's head. Strangely, Sophie's sense of calm did not dissipate at the sight.

"Hullo."

The sound of her voice caught both men off guard, but it was Mick who reacted first. He turned around in his chair and hit the other man's wrist, trying to dislodge the gun. Though Mick's assailant managed to hang on to the weapon, it went off, making a popping sound like a bottle of champagne being opened, as the bullet sank into the wooden floor.

Mick was on his feet in an instant, and the two men faced each other with about eight feet between them. The killer cocked the gun again, pointing it at Mick's chest.

Sophie glanced at the papers on the table, and she knew everything she needed to know. "Henry, Henry," she said in a chiding voice that sounded unfamiliar to her own ears, "you mustn't be so impatient. You know how I hate it when you get impatient."

Henry looked at her, then back at Mick. She could see the sweat break out on his face, and she knew her ploy was working. She had to keep talking.

"Remember what I always said, Henry. Keep that hate inside. Hide it from everybody, then when the time is right, you can use it. The time isn't right yet. Not yet."

"Stop it!" Henry screamed, but he did not look at her. "You're not my mother. She died. She jumped off Tower Bridge and killed herself because of her grief." He lifted the gun a bit higher. "And it's all his fault. Him and Hawthorne and Munro. They killed her, and they killed my father."

Mick stood perfectly still and said nothing.

"Henry," she went on, "I am your mother. I'm talking to you through this woman. She's a medium; it's the only way I can talk to you now. I know I always told you those policemen killed your father. They hanged him. As you were growing up, I put all my hate into you, knowing you would get revenge on the men who killed your father. But I shouldn't have done that. It was wrong."

"It wasn't wrong!" The hand that held the gun began to shake. "They deserve to die, all of them. They killed Papa, and they killed you."

"No, Henry. I killed myself because I knew what you were planning to do, and I blamed myself. I raised you wrong. I raised you to hate, and that's not right."

Sophie took a deep breath, knowing now was the

moment for the biggest risk of all. "I'm in heaven, Henry. With your father. The Lord has forgiven us both, and we know he will forgive you, but only if you stop killing people."

"Stop it!" Henry turned on her, pointing the gun straight at her heart. "You're not my mother. She's dead. Stop playing these parlor tricks!"

Mick jumped forward, tackling Henry to the floor. The gun went off again, but Mick had deflected the other man's arm, and the bullet sank into the wall at least six feet from where Sophie stood.

Henry, a small man, was no match for Mick, who easily overpowered him and took his gun. He cuffed Henry's hands behind his back and sat astride him, with the weapon now at the back of Henry's head. "Sophie," he said without taking his eyes from his captive, "are you all right?"

"Yes."

"Good. I'm not taking any chances with this weasel, so there's something I need you to do. You remember where Bow Street Police Station is?"

"Yes, about three blocks from here."

"I want you to run over there and tell the sergeant on night watch that I've caught the man who killed Jack and Richard, and I'm requesting reinforcements. Go. And when you've done that, I want you to go home."

"But I don't want to leave you—"

"Don't argue with me. Go."

She turned away and raced down the stairs, passing the landlady, who stood at the foot of the stairs, holding her growling Pekingese dog in the crook of her arm. "What is going on up there, miss, if I may ask?" she demanded as Sophie ran past her. "I run a respectable 'ouse, I do. What's the world coming to?"

"Mick's just caught the Heart-Eater, right here in your house," she called over her shoulder. "Just think what the reporters will pay you for your story. Don't take less than a hundred pounds."

Sophie ran out the front door, and the last thing she heard the landlady say was, "A hundred pounds! Lord have mercy, I'll be rich!"

Within minutes, eight constables had reached Bow Street station and were dispatched to Mick's flat. Sophie sat down in a chair at the front of the station, ignoring Mick's order that she go home. She wasn't going anywhere.

As she waited, Sophie berated herself for the argument they'd had in the conservatory. Was it only one night ago? It seemed years. In the silence of the nearly empty police station, she couldn't help remembering every moment of their lovemaking, and regretting every word of the argument that had followed.

She told herself she'd been right to end things. She didn't want a love affair with Mick, because she was in love with him and an affair wasn't enough. She wanted to be married to him, share his life, have children with him, grow old with him. But he didn't want that life, not with her, and there was nothing she could do about the reason why.

Her dismal thoughts were interrupted by the arrival of the constables with the man known to his fellow officers as Henry Thacker. Handcuffed, struggling, and still screaming that he was going to kill them all, he was dragged past her through the station. Mick started to follow them, but he caught sight of her and stopped. "I told you to go home."

She stood up. "I wanted to be sure you were all right."

"I'm fine. Sophie," he said and shoved his hands in his pockets, "I want you to go home. There's nothing you can do here right now."

Sophie met his gaze, but there was nothing there she could read. This was one of those times when she could not sense anything of what he thought or felt, except that he meant what he said. He wanted her to leave.

She nodded, a feeling of dread coming over her. "All right. I'll go."

"Good. I'll get a constable to escort you home." Mick turned away and strode toward the back of the station before she could reply.

"Good-bye, Mick," she whispered, watching as he walked through the doorway where the constables had taken Henry, and she knew their time together was at an end. She turned away and left the station, not waiting for the escort Mick had promised. When she cried, she liked to be alone.

By the following afternoon, the newspapers were filled with accounts of the story, though her part in the events was not mentioned. Sophie knew from their articles that Mick was completely occupied with gathering as much evidence as possible against Henry Clapham for the inquest. She read all the papers hungrily, eager to torture herself with seeing his name in print and reading about what he was doing, hoping that he hadn't come to her because he was busy with police business, and that when things calmed down in a day or so, he would come to her.

He didn't.

She did receive a visit from the police, but it wasn't Mick. Two days after Clapham's arrest, a constable brought her a letter from the chief superintendent of CID, requesting her testimony at the inquest three days hence. That same afternoon, a barrister for the Crown arrived and asked her a series of questions in preparation for that testimony.

By the third day after Clapham had been arrested, Sophie had still not seen Mick, nor had she received any word from him. Unable to bear it alone, she poured out her feelings to Violet, confessing that she loved him but he didn't want to marry her. Auntie, after she got over her astonishment that Sophie was in love with Mick, refused to believe her assertion that Mick didn't love her in return. "He's not Charles, darling. Have a little faith."

Sophie couldn't manage it. If he wasn't breaking it off with her, why didn't he come to see her? Auntie said it was probably that he was too busy.

"Is he too busy to send me a note?" Sophie countered, and Auntie couldn't come up with an answer to that.

There were other people, however, who were very eager to see her. Her mother and sister came. Agatha demanded to know what had made her leave the ball in such an extraordinary way the other night, and how she despaired of her younger daughter ever finding a husband, she really did. Charlotte simply gloated that her sister was in trouble again. In no mood for either of them, Sophie left the drawing room, locked herself in her bedroom, and refused to come out until they had gone.

Once they had left, Sophie took refuge in her conservatory. Yet even her favorite place was no comfort to her heart. As she wandered aimlessly amid the trees, vines, and flowers, she seemed to see Mick everywhere. By the tea table, in her perfumery, sitting across from her in a wicker chair, making love to her on a worktable.

I'm not a marrying man.

She stared at the wicker settee, remembering the first time she'd slept in his arms, the first time she'd felt safe enough to fall into a dreamless sleep. Sophie lowered her face into her hands, vowing that she wasn't going to cry again. She'd already shed too many tears over him, over the things about herself she could not change, over the impossibility of Mick ever falling in love with her.

"If you're crying, I'm leaving."

Sophie stiffened at the sound of Mick's voice, and she thought for a moment she'd imagined it.

"I'm not going to cry," she said with a sniff. She didn't turn around.

He's come for his things, she told herself. *Of course.*

"Good, because I'm sure you don't have a handkerchief, and since you took my last one, neither do I. I'll bet my last quid you don't have a watch, either."

She shook her head. "I don't own a watch anymore."

"Aye, I know."

Her heart felt as if it were tearing in half. She turned around and looked at him, drinking in the sight of his lean, handsome face and deep blue eyes as if he'd been gone for years, not days. It took her several moments to notice the small, white paper box in his hand.

He held it out to her. "I remember you told me you don't own a watch. That's why I bought you a new one."

She didn't understand. "Mick, I always lose watches."

"I know." He continued to hold the box out to her. "But you're not going to lose this one."

Sophie took a step toward him, then another, then another, until she was standing in front of him. Numbly, she took the box from his hand and pulled off the lid.

It was a watch, indeed, but it wasn't like any watch she'd ever seen before. A wide band of silver filigree, it was like a lacy bracelet. Set in it was an oval timepiece. The clasp was like a tiny lock, and attached with a thin, pink ribbon was a key.

"It works a bit like the lock on handcuffs," he explained, pulling the watch out of the box. He put it on her wrist and closed the clasp with a snap. "This watch isn't going to come off of your wrist unless you unlock it with the key. The best part is, Violet can't steal it."

Sophie caught back a sob at those words. "Mick, I'll lose the key."

"I know."

She looked up at him, bewildered, and found him smiling at her with infinite tenderness. He pulled out his own watch from his waistcoat pocket and pointed to something attached to the fob. "That's why I have a duplicate key."

Sophie bit her lip, afraid, so afraid. It took her a long time to say, "Does that mean you're going to keep living here?"

He tilted his head to one side and seemed to consider that question. "I don't know," he finally said. "It's a bit crowded. Where would the children sleep?"

"Children?" she choked.

Mick rubbed a hand over his jaw. "Of course, lack of room means your mother can't visit. That's a good thing."

She couldn't move. She couldn't speak. He didn't mean it. He couldn't mean it. She drew a deep, steadying breath. "Mick, what are you talking about?"

He looked at her in surprise. "Where we're going to live after we get married, of course. Couldn't you tell what I was talking about? I thought you could read my mind."

"Not this time." She lowered her gaze to his shirt-front. "But I can sometimes. I thought you couldn't live with that."

"I didn't think I could, either." He cupped her cheeks in his hands and lifted her face. "What you said was right. I didn't want a woman who could tell what I was thinking, even if it was only sometimes. You were right that it frightened me. It still does. But when Henry pointed that gun at you, I got my own vision of the future. It was a future without you, and I knew I couldn't let that happen."

He paused for breath, then went on before she could reply, as if he was afraid she would make some sort of objection. "But I was thinking that if we got married, my being a policeman wouldn't do. I work at all hours, I get in danger, and you'd have visions of me getting killed and all sorts of things like that, so I thought I'd do something else with my life. I'd open up that private detective agency I was talking about. It wouldn't be a large income at first, but I've got savings, and I'd support you all right. I'd keep you safe, and you wouldn't have to sleep with a light on anymore, and—" He broke off. "Why are you smiling?"

"You ramble when you're nervous. Did you know that?"

"Of course I'm bloody well nervous. I'm standing here with my heart laid out in front of a woman for the first time in my life. Do you think you could give me an answer?"

She wanted to, more than anything. "Did you ask me a question?"

He took a deep breath. "Will you marry me?"

"You're not a marrying man."

"That was true until I met the right woman. I love you, and that makes you the right woman for me."

Sophie threw her arms around Mick's neck, buried her face against his shirtfront, and mumbled, "I was so afraid when you sent me home the other night, then didn't come and didn't come, and I thought you were ending things with me, that you didn't want me anymore."

He lifted her chin and kissed her forehead. "I had something important to do," he said and pressed a light kiss to her mouth.

She nodded. "The case."

"Wrong, mind reader," he said, smiling. "It took me three days to get the watch made."

Sophie made a sound that was half-laugh, half-sob. "I love you."

"So, does that mean you're going to marry me?"

"Yes, yes, yes," she answered, kissing him between each word. "Did you really mean it about leaving the Yard and becoming a private detective, like Sherlock Holmes?"

His fingertips brushed her cheek. "I meant it, Watson."

She pulled back, staring at him in shock. "You want me to help you with it?"

He laughed. "Do you think I could stop you? Besides, I think it would be very valuable for a private detective to have a psychic assistant."

She lifted her face, expecting him to kiss her, but he didn't. Instead, he put his hands on her arms and pushed her back a bit. "Now, I'm going to ask you a second question."

"What question?"

"What's in that damned perfume of yours?"

"Why do you want to know?" she whispered, pressing her body against his.

"You know why." He reached behind him and closed the door. She heard the key turn in the lock.

"Tell me anyway. Why do you want to know?"

"Tell me the recipe first," he murmured, bent his head, and kissed her ear.

"Jasmine, lemon, alcohol, rose water." She gasped as he blew soft breath in her ear. "Lavender," she went on, barely able to get the words out as he began to nibble on her earlobe, "neroli, cinnamon, bergamot, cloves, and one very special final ingredient."

"What ingredient?"

She turned her face and kissed him. As she did so, she grasped the lapels of his jacket and began walking backward, pulling him with her toward the worktable in the back. "I'll tell you later," she murmured against his mouth. "Much later."